THE AVENUE, CLAYTON CITY

C. ERIC LINCOLN

BALLANTINE BOOKS • NEW YORK

Library of Congress Catalog Card Number: 87-23581

ISBN 0-345-36034-6

This edition published by arrangement with William Morrow & Company, Inc.

Manufactured in the United States of America

First Ballantine Books Edition: February 1989

Walker Evans, title Street Scene, Vicsburg Mississippi March 1936, collection Library of Congress.

To Alex Haley
A Late Installment
on an Old Promise

CONTENTS

Under the Streetlight

*G*UTS *GALLIMORE* turned out the light in the Blue Flame and stepped out onto the concrete apron that marked the entrance to his establishment. The night was warm and humid, and he sighed resignedly at the thought that though the day was finally over, tomorrow was still to come. Tomorrow would be another hot day, and a long day just like today, and the day after tomorrow. And all the other days were long and hot. Hot and long. He sighed again. His weight was bothering him. His feet were tired, and his bunions had started to heat up and ache a little. He set the bottle of RC Cola he was carrying home to Rosie down on the pavement so he could unlock the big iron padlock hooked through the U-bolt on the doorjamb. A swarm of candle flies and big gray moths worried around the electric light hanging just above his head. His shirt was open at the neck and wet with perspiration, and some of the pests flew down into his bosom and crawled around the top of his stomach, while others buzzed at his ears or tried to hide in his nose. Guts slapped at the bugs a time or two, and pranced delicately back and forth like a bull elephant trying to outguess a swarm of tsetse flies. Finally, he got the lock off, threw the hasp, and snapped it back through the U-bolt again.

The Blue Flame was closed. The day was over. It was nine o'clock. "On time," Guts mumbled to himself, and bent over to retrieve the RC he was taking home to Rosie. When he straightened up again, he sighed once more, turned himself around, and headed up The Avenue to Rosie and a hot tub to soak his burning feet.

The Blue Flame was the only eating place in Clayton City for colored people, and there was a sign above the front door announcing to all and sundry that Mr. Ben Gallimore was the proprietor. You couldn't see the sign so well at night because the drop light that hung down in front of the door of the café was only forty watts and encrusted with grime and dead candle flies. But everybody knew that Mr. Gallimore was the owner and that his establishment was clean and respectable. There were six booths in the front part of the Blue Flame, and if you were hungry, you could get a lard tray full of hot beef stew for fifteen cents. A couple of cinnamon rolls and a Nehi Grape or RC Cola would bring that to a quarter, with a couple of ready-roll cigarettes or three sticks of Doublemint chewing gum thrown in. A hamburger with everything cost a dime, and you could wash it down with a cold glass of buttermilk for a nickel more. Guts himself did all the cooking and much of the eating, as was attested by the three hundred pounds of flab that hung from his squat, square frame.

The Back Room of the Blue Flame had been cleaned out and outfitted with a Wurlitzer jukebox and a few benches scattered along the walls. Someone had nailed a sign above the door proclaiming it to be "Club Boogie-Woogie," but Guts Gallimore had taken it down and burned it in the pot-bellied heater that stood in the corner in the wintertime. "Ain't gon' be no boogie-woogiein' here," he said. "This here is a decent Christian establishment." Decent it was, and Spartan. All the records on the jukebox were personally selected by Mr. Gallimore unless the Wurlitzer man was able to slip in one or two on his own when he came to service the machine. And while Guts was usually too busy frying hamburgers to spend much time in the Back Room, he kept a close eye on who went back there, and anybody who had a reputation for drinking or fighting or otherwise causing trouble was turned around before he even headed in that direction. There really wasn't much to do in the Back Room except to jitterbug to the numbers on the jukebox or to sit on the hard benches around the wall gay-catting and drinking pop. But the Blue Flame was the only nightlife on The Avenue, and for an hour or two, three or four nights a week, it was the recreational center for the West Side of Clayton City.

The Blue Flame closed at nine o'clock, and Guts always turned off the jukebox in the Back Room at eight-thirty to get everybody out so he could clean up and close up on time. Hardly anybody came in for anything to eat after seven-thirty anyway; but he liked to stay open to accommodate anybody who might be late getting off from work, and the young folks needed somewhere to get together besides church, so he stayed open a little longer than he needed to and considered that his contribution to the community. Guts reasoned that most of the young uns around Clayton City didn't go to church anyway, or if they did, he didn't see much evidence of its effect. As a senior deacon in the Burning Bush Baptist Church, Guts possibly harbored some secret notion that the Blue Flame could somehow help make up for what the church had been unable to accomplish. Secretly he yearned for a call to preach, but so far the divine summons had eluded him, and he would not let himself be lured into being a self-called jackleg. So over the years he had continued to wait patiently for the call from the Lord which would allow him to swap his greasy apron and the Blue Flame for a bug-back coat and a little church with a steeple on top. Nobody knew his secret ambition, not even Rosie. But any day now his call could come. Any day now he could go home and go to bed one night a businessman, and wake up next morning Rev. Ben T. Gallimore.

Each night the possibility that he was perhaps closing his establishment for the last time always raised Guts's spirits a little and gave him the extra energy he needed to trudge on up The Avenue to his wife and the hot tub she would have waiting for his tortured feet. In his fantasy he could see the look of admiration in Rosie's eyes when he woke her some morning and told her that the Lord had called him to preach. ''That'll sho' be one big gittin'-up morning,'' he chuckled to himself.

Suddenly the moths down his collar crawling around on his wet skin seemed less bothersome, and a breeze seemed to come from somewhere across the way to break up the heat that seemed to be suspended around his chest. Somewhere in the darkness across The Avenue a tree frog was cheeping, and the crickets that lived in the tall grass in the drainage ditch had taken up the challenge and added their own protests to the night sounds. Under the streetlight a few yards away the usual gaggle of teenaged boys and older youth had gathered for their nightly session of talkin' that talk, which was the principal version of fun and games available to them in Clayton City. The revelry was already under way, and Guts Gallimore sighed with renewed weariness as he suddenly realized that the bugs in his bosom were just as itchy and the heat was just as heavy and oppressive as it always was. The breeze he thought he felt just a few minutes before had gone back to wherever it came from. Guts hated to hear anybody talkin' that talk, and it distressed him particularly to see the colored youth of Clayton City spend their time in such foolishness instead of going off somewhere and trying to improve theirselves. It didn't look good for the race, and although he'd never heard of anyone talkin' that talk in front of the white folks, white folks had a way of finding out everything, especially when colored people were making a bunch of fools out of theirselves. He shook his head sadly. ''It's jest pitiful. Pitiful!'' he mumbled. He'd tried to give them a nice place in the Back Room where they could have a little fun like decent people, but here they were under the streetlight as soon as the Blue Flame closed down, night after night cutting the fool and talkin' that nasty talk. *Nasty talk!* It was a wonder God didn't send down a thunderbolt and clean up the air around that streetlight. If God ever called him to preach, Guts had already decided where to begin. It would be under the streetlight, right there on The Avenue. You didn't have to go off to the four corners of the earth to find sin; it would come looking for you. And there it was, right out there in front of his own eating establishment. It was pitiful. Jest pitiful.

Guts shook his head sadly as he could hear the unmistakable repartee of the dirty dozens above the clapping and the loud laughter which always somehow seemed to be louder and somehow more pitiful whenever they were talkin' that talk. Two quick-tongued contestants were already hacking away at each other's family tree, prodded on to ever more colorful and drastic allegations by the third-party agitators whose job it was to keep the verbal skirmish at high heat.

"Hey, man, your daddy's so funny he'd make a three-dollar bill look real!"

"Yeah! And your mama's so ugly that when she saw her reflection in the millpond, she thought it was a turtle an' jumped in an' tried to catch it!"

"That ain't nothin'. If your A'nt Letty was in a beauty contest with a buffalo and a bulldog, she'd be second runner-up."

"Around the bend came the L&N, an' it was loaded down with your mammy's men!"

"Well, your mammy's in the po'house; your daddy's in the jail. An' your sister's on the corner tryin' to work up a sale!"

"I'm gon' tell you 'bout *your* sister. She wears so many flour sack drawers she flapjacks twice a day!"

"Yeah! An' you-all eat so many black-eyed peas 'til if your mama had a baby, she'd have to shell it!"

"I hear that when your daddy opens his lunch box, all he finds in it is two air sandwiches an' a long drink of water!"

"The first time your daddy went to church they buried him!"

"Yeah. Now when God made Adam, He made him quick, but when God made your daddy, it made Him sick!"

"You better watch out. You know I don't play no dozens!"

"If you don't play, just lay dead an' pat your foot while me and your mama play!"

As Guts neared the circle of revelers, he could see a tall, skinny youth of light complexion moving around in a tight circle, cutting some kind of step to the handclap rhythm of nine or ten other boys gathered under the light. It was Finis Lee Jackson, Mamie Jackson's boy who dropped out of the Academy school to work for Mr. Bimbo loading rags and scrap iron down by the railroad. Guts couldn't hear what Finis Lee was saying, but he guessed it must have been nasty or the crowd wouldn't be whooping and hollering like they were. And he knew that as soon as Finis got through, somebody else would step into the ring and the show would go on. But he never did have a chance to find out what nastiness Finis was up to because somebody spotted him leaving the Flame and put the word out.

"Ol' Creeper comin'! Cool it."

The clapping stopped. There was a long moment of silence, and then Finis Lee, determined not to forfeit his time in the ring, took on a pious look like a Methodist preacher and intoned:

> Amazin' grace, how sweet the sound
> It done saved a wreck like me. . . .

"A-man! A-man!" came a chorus of responses liberally interposed with sniggles and suppressed whoops.

"Evening, Mr. Gallimore," one of the boys said as Guts shuffled on toward the circle.

"Don't be tryin' to 'good evening' me," Guts said, looking at nobody in particular. "An' ain't no use to try to git so holy all of a sudden an' mess up no church song jest because you see me comin'. I know what you been up to. I heard you talkin' that ol' nasty talk. It's jest a sin an' a shame before Jesus in His heaven. That's what it is!"

"That's right, Mr. Gallimore. You sho' right. I been tryin' to tell these ol' nasty-talkin' boys to shape up an' get on the ball!" It was Nero Banks, one of the younger boys who had only recently begun to hang out under the light.

Without bothering to even search him out in the crowd, Guts warned, "Boy, don't you play with me. I know who you is, an' I'm old enough to be your daddy twice if I wanna be, an' I don't take no sass. If you ain't got no respect for grown folks, try to have a little bit for yourself. That's the reason colored folks like you don't never git nowhere. You spend your time tryin' to impress a no-good passel of nasty-talkin' niggers an' you end up bein' jest like them—nasty an' good-for-nothin'-but-trouble!''

The circle gave way, and Guts Gallimore shuffled on up The Avenue to his wife, Rosie, and his hot tub to soak his feet and pray for a call to preach. But other calls echoed after him through the hot and steamy darkness.

''That's right, Mr. Gallimore! You're right 'til you're left, an' when you're left, right don't make no difference.''

''Good night, Guts. Don't let your meat loaf, your gravy might curdle!''

''So long, Mr. Gallimore, 'cause so short can't cut no mustard.''

The circle closed in again, and the talk continued as before, but with the dozens giving way to the manly pursuits of sex and violence.

''I had a girl once with a poontang like a snappin' turtle. Wouldn't let go 'til it thundered!''

''Ol' Luke asked his girl for the key to the kingdom an' she gave him a can opener.''

''Ain't nothin'. Uncle Bob got this, Uncle Bob got that; Uncle Bob got a peter like a baseball bat!''

''Don't tell that lie on Uncle Bob. If he got such a whanger, why can't he find it when he wants to pee?''

''You been lookin' for it, Juicy Fruit? If you had a mustache, there'd be flies in it!''

''Don't call me no Juicy Fruit. I'll jack open your mouth, settle on your tonsils, and bumble out your nose like a booger!''

''Yeah. An' I'll jump down your throat, tap-dance on your liver, and hang out your ass like a tail!''

''Whooo-ee! Sounds like somebody's fixin' to get cold-cocked!''

''Right! It's your mammy!''

The banter died down a little at the sound of a pair of footsteps coming from up The Avenue. When the couple came out of the shadows and under the pale glare of the streetlight, it turned out to be Joe Jipson, and a shout went up in anticipation of his joining in the fun for a while. Joe was the local wit, and he could talk that talk for hours and never repeat himself or even sound dirty. He was just a natural born hip cat; but tonight he was pushing Poochie, and since she couldn't hang around, probably he wouldn't either.

"Po' Jip! What you gon' say?"

"I'd say the boat's up the river and it won't come down. B'lieve to my soul that it's waterbound!"

"What's the good word?"

"The good word is for the monkeys, a bad word: 'Great is the power of cash!' Or to put it in the language of the people: If you ain't got no money, you ain't got no business here!"

Poochie skirted the circle and moved on down The Avenue to wait for Jip out of earshot. She knew that Jip would have to spend a few minutes with the boys but that he would be along as soon as he could.

"Well, you done give us the word, now give us the news. How come you pushin' Poochie? That's Jubal's woman. Everybody know that!"

"Everybody? Perhaps so. But what po' Jip knows for sure is that all cats look gray in the dark! And if the cat you catch ain't gray, you'll find it out come daylight. Right, my man? Right as Ripley. Believe it or not!"

"Jubal's cat ain't gray, an' you might find out a heap sooner'n daylight. Believe that or not!"

"Jubal's cat? If you're referrin' to Miss Poochie Pie, I'd say she's what you call a much right woman. She's got as much right to be mine as she has to be his. And you can plainly see, the lady is with me!"

"We hear you! Tell it like it is! Be hard on him, Jip."

"You got to be hard as lard and twice as greasy! The times require it. The circumstances demand it. What can I do?"

"One more thing you ain't told us: How come you're out gay-cattin' in the middle of the week? This ain't Saturday night."

"Yeah, man! You got your nose wide open an' your tail straight up. Only difference between you an' a coon dog is that when a coon dog trees, he'll bay, but you're cool as a preacher getting ready to lift the collection.''

"Your observation defies explanation, my man. Suppose we just say I take a little whiskey, I take a little gin, I take a little lovin' every-now-an'-then. In short, poontang's what I'm after, seven nights a week. Saturdays not excluded.''

"Go hard, Jip! It's your world! Go hard or go home!''

"Thank you, my man. It so happens that home is my present destination. There is no place like home. And with the proper amenities of good food, good drink, and the comforts of love unbounded, I do recommend it to you.''

"Yeah! It's nice work if you can get it, but ol' Pip can't get it. He's too short.''

"No problem. Bulls with short horns should stand close!'' Joe Jipson moved on through the little gathering with the air of a visiting prince and caught up with Poochie, waiting for him in the darkness a few yards away. If she paid any attention to the gibes under the streetlight, she said nothing about it. Jipson circled his arm around her waist, and they moved on toward her quarters on the white folks' yard in downtown Clayton City.

The talk under the streetlight went on.

"Hey, Red, let me hold something. Lay a quarter on me.''

"I feel for you, my man, but I can't reach you. I ain't puttin' out nothin' but old folks' eyes, an' I'm puttin' them out with a pitchfork!''

"Don't get your ass up on your shoulders just 'cause you're shit-colored. Lay a quarter on me 'til Saturday. We might open a keg a nails.''

"I'd rather be shit-colored and have a quarter than be blue-gummed an' be askin' for one. I'm your friend, not your father. I didn't take you to raise!''

"Both of you shut up! Anybody who'd lend either one of you a quarter may as well throw his money up a wild hog's ass an' holler soo-oo-ee!''

"Down, Fido! Somebody might ask you what *you* doin' to get so many quarters, or how come you always got flies in your mustache.''

"Don't pee on me! Every time you open your mouth you tear your ass."

"Yeah! And every time some frail shakes her drawers in your face, you sniff like a hound dog and cry like a ruptured rooster!"

The streetlight winked out. It was nine-thirty, the unofficial curfew for the colored people on the West Side of Clayton City. In another thirty minutes the lights downtown would go off, too. With the lights gone and no moon to speak of, the gang outside the Blue Flame reluctantly broke up and began to drift off in the darkness.

"See you steelheads!"

"See your mama!"

"All goin' my way join my class. All ain't kiss my big black ass."

"Let your mama kiss it!"

Somewhere in the darkness a song drifted off The Avenue:

Wake up! Wake up! Wake up, Baby. Meet your
Daddy coming home. I say wake up! Wake up, pretty
mama. Meet your Big Daddy coming home. Hang
your nightgown in the closet, but, Baby, put your wig
back on. Because I'm comin', Baby, comin'! Baby,
'cause your Daddy's comin' home. . . .

Diagonally across The Avenue almost opposite the Blue Flame, Dr. Walter Pinkney Tait sat in his porch swing and swung silently back and forth in the darkness. The streetlight did not carry to the old house with the big dormer window where he had lived ever since he'd been in Clayton City, and even if it had, his privacy would still have been protected by the fragrant vines of honeysuckle which hung from the latticework and screened his front porch from the street. It was his favorite place and one of his favorite hours. The other was early morning, when the day began to come alive. The Avenue was not the world in microcosm, but if one had a critical eye and an analytical mind, one could learn a great deal about that part of the world called Clayton City and how it intermeshed with the rest of reality just by seeing The Avenue in context. The principal learnings were from life, Dr. Tait had long since convinced himself, not from books. And life was the way people behaved toward themselves, toward each other under the watchful eye of God, whether real or imagined. Each night, as he sat on his porch behind the honeysuckle listening to a motley group of colored boys flagellate themselves talking that talk, as they called it, he learned more about them, more about Clayton City, and more about himself. The disjunctions were more artificial than real. He was a part of the "Flame Gang," as he had labeled the boys who gathered there under the streetlight. And though he never really understood the intricate dynamics of *how* and to what degree, he knew he was also a part of Clayton City, and he cursed himself for it. He could find nothing in the history of the town to which he could sensibly relate, and there was nothing in its cachet or in its self-perceived cultural mission to which he wanted to relate. Yet there he was, a vicarious participant in its fun-and-games for colored youth and a scarred and tragic symbol of what they could not and would not become.

In Dr. Tait's opinion, Clayton City was a metropolis not burdened with a history of great significance or with a future of probable consequences for the world beyond its borders. While it was true that the town owed its existence to the white people's willingness to contest what they had considered a great cause—the late War Between the States—neither the town nor its people figured prominently in the resolution of that cause. Indeed, Clayton's relation to the war was more or less incidental. Late in the conflict, as the ebb and flow of battle washed over the cotton plantations of the beleaguered South, a Confederate general named Calvin Clayton built a small redoubt between himself and the pursuing Yankees. In doing so, he bequeathed his name to history. After the war "Fort Clayton" became the point of identification for the whole area surrounding the small circle of abandoned trenches and breastworks, although the town itself grew up around a railhead some two miles to the east. In time the town came to be called "Clayton City," while the general's old stronghold, now claimed only by the wild birds, the honeysuckle, and the bullfrogs proliferating in the stagnant trenches, was referred to simply as "The Fort." By-and-by the Yankees came again—this time in the name of religion—and built a colored school on the very site of the old Confederate fortification. The Fort Academy, as it was called, was promptly burned to the ground. The Yankee missionaries put it back, and this time it stayed.

Downtown Clayton City was where the white people of privilege and status lived. In the common pattern of most southern towns and cities before the private automobile created suburbia, the houses of the privileged classes usually stood near the center of town, convenient to the business and service institutions required for their well-being and comfort. And in this tradition downtown Clayton City was laid out around a square marking the center of the interests of the ruling elite. Precisely in the center of the square stood the County Courthouse, a squat, massive structure of granite and bloodred brick. It had four entrances at the ground level, each one facing one of the cardinal points of the compass. The Ground Floor took on a cavernous appearance by reason of the huge double doors which marked each of the four entrances. Rounded at the top and reinforced with strappings and braces of wrought iron, the doors looked like nothing so much as the portals of some medieval dungeon. The walls were a foot thick as if they anticipated the day when the eerie scream of minnie balls and the thuck-a-thuck of grapeshot might once again signal the resurrection of a cause that had never been very deeply interred. Inside, where the public toilets and some of the minor county offices were located, it was cool, and in the summertime the Saturday crowds of country Negroes and poor whites sat on the long wooden benches on opposite sides of the long halls and chewed tobacco or nursed their babies as they whiled away the afternoon.

The Second Floor was where the courtrooms, the judges' chambers, the tax assessor's office, and most of the important offices of county administration were located. A man on his way to the Second Floor of the Courthouse was a man either in the toils of the Law or a man with important business to look after. In consequence, most of the people one saw up there were either grim-faced with worry or they were officious-looking and in the casual suspension between stasis and hurry traditional to the southern approach to doing business. Like the Ground Floor, the Second Floor also had four outside entrances. They could be reached by climbing the granite steps with the iron railings running up the center of each of the four sides of the building. Inside, there were curving staircases made of Tennessee marble embellished by brass railings mottled by the perspiration of the calloused hands that hauled at them year in and year out. The marble and the brass halted abruptly at the Third Floor landing, and on three sides the Third Floor entrances were bricked up and impassable. The remaining entrance on the east was barred by a heavy wooden door bearing a warning to "Keep Out" and secured by a massive iron lock. The Third Floor of the Courthouse had never been open to public use; but occasionally there were lights on up there at night, and men could be seen climbing the outside steps to the East Entrance as though some kind of meeting were in progress. Any Negroes who happened to be passing in the area at such times were told to move on, and they did.

The structure was crowned by a cupola housing the siren for the Clayton City Fire Department, which stood directly across the square to the west. A short block to the south on Jailhouse Hill the Clayton County Jail faced the Courthouse from the corner of Jefferson Street and Morrison Avenue, which running west, became simply "The Avenue" when the pavement ran out on Sumpter Hill twelve blocks away. The Courthouse lawn was completely encircled by a hitching rail about four inches in diameter, set in concrete, and interrupted only by the concrete walks leading to each of the four entrances of the Courthouse. On Saturdays the country folks tied their teams up at the rail and sprawled on the grassy lawn to feast on the watermelons they had brought with them. Or if it were cotton-picking time and they had money in their pockets, they would lounge nonchalantly against the hitching rail drinking Big Oranges and RC Colas, or dipping Garrett's Sweet Snuff, or chewing Brown Mule Tobacco.

The principal businesses of Clayton City were located on the four streets that made up Courthouse Square—Washington, Jefferson, Jackson, and Polk. Jefferson extended was also the major highway linking Clayton City to anywhere else. Running north and south, outside the city limits it became Jefferson Davis Pike and ran all the way to the state capital 180 miles to the south. Running north, it went 79 miles to the state line. East or west of Clayton City, there wasn't much of anywhere to go. Going west, the pavement stopped at the city limit. Minnie's Ferry Road picked up there, and after winding around through more than a dozen farms and plantations, it ended up at the ferry crossing once run by an old black woman named Minnie. But the river kept changing its course and the ferry stopped running after Minnie and a load of people were drowned during a spring flood. But that was thirty or forty years ago, and most people didn't remember ever seeing the ferry, let alone crossing the river on it. Years ago there had been talk of putting in a highway to run to the river, and a bridge across it, but the people in the next county wouldn't put up their share of the money. Some people said it was just politics, and that the real reason the folks across the river backed away from the project was because they didn't want to be dominated by the Butlers and the Spencers, who ran everything in Clayton County.

Over the years The Forks of the River had developed into a sort of dead-end rendezvous where the Negroes of Clayton County got together on Saturday night for their more clandestine entertainment. It was strictly off-limits for the Law, and except for very occasional whites described as "all right" and brought along by someone whose local stature could make "all right" good enough, few white men ever saw The Forks on a weekend. Those who did left their color back in Clayton City and soon found the desired anonymity in the clicking of the dice, the gurgle of moonshine whiskey, and the soft, persuasive laughter of the brown-skinned women who materialized out of the darkness. Sometimes there was an exchange of pistol fire, or the switchblades and razors arced through the upper reaches of the night. But by Sunday morning the evidence of what had taken place on Saturday night was either at the bottom of the river, or swathed in bandages after a late-night visit to Dr. Tait's office over on The Avenue, or laid out in the undertaking parlor run by the ever-accommodating Ferdy Frost. Saturday night belonged to the restive element, and what they did with it was their pleasure or their misfortune. Only when Monday morning came and the work crews began to form would it be known whether Saturday night's black misfortune was also going to be Monday morning's white inconvenience.

There was a little church at The Forks called Minnie's Chapel, standing in a small clearing on the bluffs above the river. Minnie's Chapel hadn't had a regular pastor since the ferry quit running, but in the summertime it always managed one or two weeks of hell-shaking revivals to help keep the devil off-balance. People came from miles around in their trucks and wagons to spread dinner on the ground and to relax in the groves and hollows between 'round-the-clock sessions of prayer and preaching. When it was all over, those who had tarried faithfully on the moaners' bench until they finally got religion were marched down to the river and baptized amidst much shouting and crying and congratulations from those who had already crossed over into the kingdom of righteousness. Then the trucks and wagons loaded up again and took everybody back to the farms and plantations. The end of the revivals meant that lay-by was over, and although a goodly passel of souls may have been harvested in the name of Jesus, the white man's cotton still had to be picked in the name of survival, and saints and sinners alike found a speedy common deployment in the ubiquitous fields of fluffy "white gold" shimmering beneath the Clayton County sun.

Recreation and entertainment were limited options in Clayton City. The small public swimming pool was reserved for whites only, of course, but the local theater admitted colored patrons to its balcony, known colloquially as "Nigger Heaven" and reserved especially for colored citizens. Seasonal events, such as the revivals held in the summer during lay-by time and the Clayton County Fair, which came in the fall when the cotton picking was over, were occasions to be savored in anticipation, and relived and talked about long after they were over. The County Fair was divided into two parts: five days for the white fair and three days for the colored. The same carnival attractions usually played both segments, and in the interest of good business whites and blacks were permitted to attend both fairs but could not compete with each other in sporting events, 4-H Club or Future Farmer competitions, bake-offs, or the like. But the Colored Fair belonged to the colored people, and because it did, it was the principal occasion for relations who had gone to live in the North to make the annual pilgrimage home to be with the kinfolks. It was also a time for swapping experiences about the hazards of driving a "big car" Down South and risking the envy and hostility of the local whites in the towns along the way. There were no hotels or rest rooms black travelers could use, and frequently they were refused gasoline or repairs. Some local sheriffs made it a practice to hold all Negroes driving Cadillacs or Buicks or other big cars through their jurisdictions as suspicious persons until the ownership of their vehicles could be verified. Sometimes this used up two or three days of the carefully hoarded vacation time intended to be spent with the home folks.

On other occasions black travelers were given false directions or told to be out of town before dark. Practically nowhere below the Mason-Dixon Line could a black traveler find hotel accommodations, eat in a restaurant, or use the toilet at the service station where he stopped for gas, except in the rare instance of a "colored hotel." But colored hotels were few and far between. In order to circumvent such inconvenience, various strategies and techniques had to be developed. "Driving through," which meant driving nonstop from the point of departure in some city up North to the final destination in some southern hamlet, was considered the best way to avoid trouble. Sleeping in graveyards or other isolated places when fatigue would not be denied was another stratagem to which homebound expatriates also resorted. Wearing a chauffeur's cap and pretending to be delivering the car to "the boss" was another way of getting through the worst towns unmolested. Some of the adventures were indeed bizarre, and some were inevitably embellished and exaggerated. But the recounting of such experiences, and the vicarious participation they made possible, were in themselves an important form of recreation for the black people of Clayton City.

The most important year-round activity was churchgoing, and some of the older folks might attend two or three services at as many different churches on a single Sunday. Some of the services were enlivened by footwashings, visiting evangelists, singing groups, rallies, or all-day preaching with dinner-on-the-ground. Funerals had a definite recreational aspect, requiring that those attending be excused from work and providing an opportunity for special adornment and ritual participation. The need for pallbearers, soloists, persons to read the obituary, the condolences, and requiem poems or elegies, and others to prepare and serve the food for the bereaved and the funeral party transcended the somberness of the occasion and brought together friends and relatives in a not unwelcome interlude of socializing. Sometimes the fraternal orders like the Masons or the Eastern Stars would turn out in their regalia to march in the funeral processions, making the occasion almost festive. But most of the old folks who kept the fraternal orders alive had died out, and now it was difficult to get enough able bodies to make a successful turnout possible.

Night life in Clayton City meant the Blue Flame, the café on the Lower End of The Avenue, on the ground floor of the old Masonic Hall. That ancient building had long since been condemned as unsafe, but there was nowhere else for a colored business, so the Clayton City Fire Department obligingly closed up the upper story and the Blue Flame was left in peace. Guts Gallimore made a living out of it, and the West Side was a little less deprived because it was there, for after the churches and the Fort Academy, the Blue Flame was all there was.

That was the Clayton City Dr. Tait had come to know, by experience and by observation. And it had long been Tait's custom to conclude his professional services for the day in good time to catch the evening ritual under the streetlight after the Blue Flame had closed. He kept his office light on until seven-thirty so that the folks who couldn't wait until Saturday could stop by to see him on the way home after work. There wouldn't be many—he learned early in his practice that black folks can't afford to be sick during the week. So after one or two visits calling for pills and bandages he could usually pull the shade on his door down to OFFICE CLOSED and turn the light off an hour or more before Guts Gallimore backed out of the Blue Flame Café and headed up The Avenue.

The little patch of sidewalk under the streetlight in front of the Flame was the only public recreation facility Clayton City afforded for the convenience of its colored citizens. But for Dr. Tait it was more than fortuitous and more than a place for the boys to cut the fool, as Gallimore had described it. For the doctor it was a place to learn. It was clear to him that there in the narrow circle of pale light cast by the streetlamp the black youth of Clayton City learned from each other about who they were. More important, they learned who they were not, though they seldom learned why. But the most intense learning was that experienced by the doctor himself, for in the narrow ambit of the streetlight fun of a motley crowd of colored boys, he learned a lot about the meaning of being black and the torture of no way out.

He also learned a vocabulary he would scarcely have occasion to share with anyone he knew. With whom could he ever share the joy and enthusiasm of "opening a keg of nails," for example, which meant to have on hand an unlimited supply of corn whiskey? And what would he do if someone "shook her drawers in his face," challenging him to a sexual showdown? And if someone made an embarrassing faux pas, would he tell him that he had just "cut a hog"? Or if the error was irreparable and likely to produce retaliatory consequences, how could he communicate to that unlucky person that he had "up and tore his ass"? Some girls, he learned, had hair "as long as black pepper." Every homosexual's name was "Juicy Fruit." A girl who could be persuaded to "shake 'em on down" was preparing to "give up a piece of poontang." And the man who was suspected of oral sex was accused of "slopping at the hog trough" or "eating at the Y." But it was playing the dozens that perplexed and worried Dr. Tait the most of all when he first tuned in on what went on under the streetlight. Surely it required the grossest level of depravity to indulge in such willfull vulgarity. He had thought at first that Guts Gallimore's appraisal of talking that talk as "nasty" was too generous to be useful. In the early days of his listening and learning the doctor's sensibilities were particularly oppressed by a popular but unusually vicious bit of doggerel called a "drag." Dragging was a variation of the dozens, and it usually required a vulgarity so gross that when it was addressed to all the members of the group, those who claimed exemption from its allegations would hasten to give up their anonymity, yelling out, "Hold on! I caught that drag!" But in catching the drag, they inadvertently admitted being vulnerable to its claims. The drag Dr. Tait considered the supreme vulgarity was usually heard several times in the evening's program of obscenities:

> A nigger I know didn't get here fair
> I drove a Cadillac through his mammy's ass
> And he hung on the spare!

Tait hated the wanton perverseness of the very idea. For one black boy to call another a "nigger" was bad enough, but to bracket that most despicable of all epithets with so brutal and so vulgar a notion as that expressed in the drag was beyond his understanding. Or so he thought. But the truth of the matter was that in spite of his disgust, the twin insights of agony and intellection had eventually paid off, for suddenly not only the language but the logic of the whole streetlight ritual finally became clear to him. What he was observing from the safety and the anonymity of his cloistered front porch was nothing less than a teenage rite of passage. A very critical *black* rite of passage! How could he not have recognized it for so long? The public deprecation of black men and women was, of course, taken for granted in Clayton City, and everywhere else within the experience of the Flame Gang. But when those black men and women were one's fathers, mothers, and sisters, how could one approaching manhood accept that deprecation and live with it? To be a *man* implied responsiblities no colored man in Clayton City could meet, so the best way to deal with the contradiction was to deny it. Talkin' that talk—that is, disparaging one's loved ones within the in-group—was an obvious expression of self-hatred, but it also undercut the white man's style of black denigration by presupposing it, and to some degree narcotizing the black boys who were on the way to manhood from the pain of their impotence. After all, *they had said it first!* Playing the dozens, Tait reasoned, was an effort to prepare one to be able to "take it." Anyone who refused to play the dozens was unrealistic, for the dozens were a fact of life for every black man. They were implicit in the very structure of black-white relations, and if one didn't "play," he could "pat his foot" while the play went on, over and around him. No one could exempt himself from the cultural vulgarity of black debasement, no matter how offensive it might be. Cutting the fool was no less a part of the same rite of passage. It was the symbolic rejection of manhood, the public demonstration that one was still a child and unready to be a man in a world where manhood was impossible.

The streetlight was out. The fun and games were over. The revelers had dispersed into the joyless night, and Dr. Walter Pinkney Tait was alone with his learning, his lore, and his reverie. Tomorrow would be another day. And after that another. Each one as inexorable and as perplexing as the one before.

House Calls

*I*T WAS six-thirty in the morning, and Ramona Tait had
already served her husband his soft-boiled egg and oatmeal and gone back to bed. But for Dr. Tait the day
had truly begun, and if he was not prepared to savor it, he
was at least prepared to meet it, and not altogether by default.
The doctor was a creature of habit, and it was his custom to
rise early and avail himself of whatever small advantages
chance might throw his way which could help to offset somewhat the imbalance of his peculiar vulnerabilities. Watching
the West Side of Clayton City come to life was a principal
reward of his industry. The West Side was where the colored
people of Clayton were concentrated, and The Avenue was
the West Side umbilical. It was the only street in the colored
section of town with sidewalks, although the street itself was
not paved, and there were no gutters. The pavement ran out
at the top of Sumpter Hill, the last hill leaving downtown,
and the street name changed suddenly from West Morrison
to The Avenue. Only white people lived on the paved, Morrison Street end of it, and only Blacks lived on the unpaved
section called The Avenue.

Actually, the official name of The Avenue was Booker T.
Washington Avenue, for somewhere back in the dim recesses

of the past a benign city administration had favored its colored citizens with a street named for one of their own. But nobody ever used the official name. Possibly it was because Booker T. Washington Avenue was too cumbersome for ordinary conversation. Possibly it was because nobody ever saw Booker T. Washington painted on the curbstones at the intersection, because there were no curbstones on The Avenue. The curbing stopped where Morrison Street left off. On the other hand, The Avenue may have been more than a kind of local shorthand for the principal street in the black community. After all, it was The Avenue, the *only* avenue, and it had a mystique and a catchet all its own. So the white section of the thoroughfare was simply called Morrison Street, and the black section was known as The Avenue, and nobody got confused.

To Dr. Tait The Avenue was a charade, a pantomime. He lived there, and he had his office there; but he never thought of The Avenue except as a memory of some other way of life which itself may well have been hallucinatory. There it was, a depressing, ridiculous strip of graveled road with sidewalks! No curbs, no gutters, no pavement, and bordered by ditches three feet deep and full of weeds. A haven for snakes and toads and bullfrogs. A repository for Coca-Cola bottles, spent fifths and paper sacks and whatever other jetsam the bone-weary Negroes trudging home from downtown Clayton City had an impulse to discard.

But to most of the colored people of Clayton The Avenue was their most important symbol of status and elevation. All three of the brick houses and the only two-story house owned by colored people stood on The Avenue, as did the Congregational Church and the parsonage of the Congregational minister. All of the town's colored businesses were located there, and the only colored doctor in town lived on The Avenue and had his office in his residence. An involuntary grimace pulled at the corners of the doctor's mouth as his silent soliloquy included himself among the burgesses of The Avenue and made him a part of its distinction.

You could call The Avenue the umbilical of the West Side because it was the main artery linking the black and white communities in that peculiar symbiosis so characteristic of southern towns. The principals nurtured each other, fed on each other, and shared the most intimate physical relations every day, but invented and acted out the most extravagant fictions to deny what was apparent by simple observation. Like lovers, Tait mused to himself. Like lovers with all the nuances of feeling and emotion that fall within the spectrum of love-and-hate, trust-and-suspicion, sadism-and-masochism, acceptance-and-denial, sacrifice-and-exploitation. Out there on the street in front of him, since the first crack of dawn, the traffic had been moving along The Avenue toward town. Clayton City came awake in stages. Black Clayton had been up and moving for more than an hour. First out on The Avenue were the black cooks and maids hurrying in to cook the white folks' breakfasts, to clean the white folks' houses, make the beds, dress the children, and finally to wake the white folks themselves so that the day could officially begin. Next came the porters, janitors, and delivery boys of all ages to mop the stores and sweep the alleys around Courthouse Square and to have the places of business ready for the white folks to open up when they finished their sausages and grits and hot biscuits sopped in rich, amber country sorghum.

Following close behind the porters and janitors were the trashmen and the yard boys. At nine dollars a week the trashmen were the best-paid black laborers in town. Their job was to collect the garbage and get it off the streets before the sun could heat it up and saturate the morning air with unpleasantness, and before the big blue flies could lay the shaggy gray eggs which seemed to hatch out fat, squirming maggots in a matter of minutes. By nine o'clock all the garbage within a four-block radius of Courthouse Square would be burning at the town dump adjacent to the colored cemetery, and the next day's collection would already be accumulating in the shops and stores and kitchens and backyards of that element of Clayton City with something worth throwing away. Just a few years back the trashmen included the "honey squad," an elite order of Negroes charged with cleaning out the outdoor toilets and hauling away their contents in a big horse-drawn tank called the "honey wagon." It was a grimy, smelly way to earn a living, and when progress finally caught up with Clayton City and the last honey wagon rumbled into oblivion, few people cared enough to wonder where it went. But the honey squad forfeited the extra dollar a week it earned as special pay.

It was the yard boys who kept the lawns and gardens of downtown Clayton beautiful and in bloom. Some of them, like Josh Redus, were quite venerable and had long since been given the honorific title of "Uncle." Yet curiously, they remained boys, *yard* boys. Some of them were accomplished gardeners, and Dr. Tait thought of all the loveliness they had been responsible for and hoped that somehow the satisfactions they derived from digging in the soil and bringing forth life and beauty would be for them their primary compensation—not the four or five dollars a week they were paid or the fringe benefits of old clothes, broken furniture, and the daily handouts from the white folks' kitchens.

It was nearly seven o'clock now, and the traffic on The Avenue was steady and growing. From the side streets and by well-beaten footpaths across the dew-drenched fields the black men and women who serviced Clayton converged on The Avenue and made their way toward town. Practically all of them were on foot. As they caught up with each other, they paired off or walked together in clumps of three or four. Such conversation as there was was subdued as all hands went hurrying along, anxious to be on the job on time. In the evening they would return spent and wasted from the day's labor, but their progress home would be more casual, and the give-and-take of conversation would be considerably less restrained. Occasionally someone in a delivery truck belonging to the white folks would come speeding along and, with a great screeching of brakes and squealing of tires, would stop to load up as many as could get on. Few of the black people of Clayton owned cars, and those who did did not often risk driving them to work. It was not considered the right thing to do.

It was neither polite nor politic. If you worked for the white folks, you were expected to walk. Certainly that understanding was implicit in the unwritten code which structured white-black relations in Clayton and elsewhere in the small towns south of the Mason-Dixon Line. And if that weren't enough, it was spelled out quite clearly in the wages the colored retainers were handed each Saturday morning. Joe Jipson once said that it was not that the white folks didn't want black folks to ride; it was only that the white folks wanted to ride them. But Jipson's wisdom was variously interpreted, as indeed, he intended it to be. The practice of occasionally driving the more venerable family cooks home after dinner had been served, the dishes washed, and the kitchen swept was well established among the better class of white folks. And the black cook with her sacks and bundles and her bucket of leftovers, sitting alone and regal like a *grande dame* on the back seat of a shiny automobile being chauffeured through the streets by the white boss, was one of the less painful ironies of the conventions of the period. Perhaps this is what Jipson was talking about. Perhaps not. There are ways and *ways* for people to ride people, and though Joe Jipson was a clown, he was far from being a fool.

Again the shadow of a smile rolled fleetingly over the doctor's countenance and hardened the lines around his eyes for a second, causing him to squint. Dr. Tait had an acute sense of the impossible contradictions which seemed to him to illustrate the human condition, and he had developed his own peculiar mechanism for dealing with them. First of all, he lived in a private world of thoughts and feelings, appraisals and conclusions not often shared with any other human being. Possibly it was because he had no counterpart in Clayton City precisely capable of recognizing and responding to the nuances and the vagaries of the human comedy as sensitively as he. Perhaps his own personality, his own peculiar conditioning made it impossible for anyone to break through the thick crust of his personal suppositions to discover and relate to the strange and sensitive man inside. Perhaps it was because there were at least two distinct persons in him sharing the name of Tait. Possibly there were more, but at a minimum there was *Dr. Tait*, he of the finely tuned mind, the acute sensitivity, the precise articulation. This was the Tait who required solitude, gray spats, and hickory striped pants, the Tait who stood apart from that segment of the impossible scenario that was Clayton City because he found it contradictory and ridiculous, yet who felt compelled to observe it and to make it the constant subject of his reflection and his soliloquizing because he found it fascinating, intriguing, and perhaps intimidating as well. This was Dr. Tait, the philosopher by necessity, for how else could he stand outside the world he chose to monitor with no other world to hold on to and call his own?

But then there was also the Tait who was not *Dr.* Tait at all. It was a primordial self, a kind of indistinct, ubiquitous existence which seemed somehow to identify him firmly and irrevocably with a people and a culture he knew well, even though he regarded them with ambivalence. Even in this world he felt a kind of remoteness, a kind of aloofness which permitted him the role of commentator and interpreter. A sort of elder statesman; a respected archive of the wisdom, the trivia, the conventions, the significant experiences by which the meager existence of the black people of Clayton City was patterned. Sometimes he recounted all this in their idiom with the perfection of a tribal griot. But only in soliloquy. Only for his own divertissement.

To the Negroes of Clayton City Dr. Tait simply had ''funny ways,'' a description which meant simply that they did not understand him, but accepted him with respect, and then dismissed him as unimportant beyond his role as doctor. In a more sophisticated setting he would have been described as a very, very private person—sharing little, confiding less, asking nothing. When he laughed, which was not often, he laughed to himself, and his laughter had no necessary relation to whatever may or may not have seemed amusing to others. Indeed, he gave many the uncomfortable feeling that when he laughed, he was somehow laughing at them, even though they may have been laughing at something else.

Dr. Tait did not find life very funny; he did find it ludicrous, which is not the same thing. The behavior of human beings in their jockeying and posturing and in their constant efforts to take advantage of each other, he found most ludicrous of all. Humans, like chameleons and crocodiles, ought not to be taken too seriously. What lengths of lying and deceit, counterlying and counterdeceit they would go to to accomplish some obscure and dubious end would probably never be established with finality. He was thinking just now of the horde of Blacks descending on downtown Clayton City to secure the comfort and convenience of the white middle class, still blissfully asleep in the full confidence that the Blacks would come to do the work and that they would be there on time, no matter the vicissitudes of weather or personal circumstance. Yet at the same time they knew that some worn-out cooks would oversleep, some maids would have problems with the health and welfare of their own children, and some yard boys were so broken down with age and rheumatism that on a given day ten percent of the colored work force would be late. This proved the common understanding that Negroes in general were lazy and unreliable, given to carousing all night with no regard for the next day's responsibilities. Their individual cooks and maids and yard boys were exceptions, whose occasional lapses were overlooked. It was black workers as a class, Negroes as a race at whom the convention was directed. Negroes were expected to walk to work because possession of an automobile implied a defect in an arrangement intended, among other things, to make them pay for the privilege of working; to deny their ability to save and plan; to deny their need for such luxury; and, of course, to keep the economic and the status differential between white and black visible, pronounced, and unmistakable.

Take the case of Coretta Wiggins. Coretta made six dollars a week cooking for the Romines; but Coretta's husband, Jimboy, shot dice on the weekend, and sometimes Jimboy brought home more money on Sunday morning than the two of them could earn in six months working for the white folks. Coretta and Jimboy lived about two miles from downtown Clayton City, and in spite of herself, she was occasionally late getting to Mrs. Romine's kitchen. So Coretta and Jimboy saved up and bought a new Ford. After getting the car, she dropped Jimboy off at the Texaco station each morning and then drove herself to the Romines—being careful to park the Ford three blocks away on Courthouse Square. Now she was at work half an hour earlier than before. When she came out of the Romines' kitchen at a quarter past seven each evening, she walked to her car, picked up Jimboy at the Texaco station, and drove home. It was inevitable that the Romines should find out about the car, of course, and when they did, Coretta was discharged. There was no explanation, no mention of motive or reason. When Mrs. Romine paid her off on Saturday morning, she also told Coretta not to come back on Monday. The next week the Romines traded in their Ford and bought a Buick.

By seven-thirty the traffic along The Avenue had slackened, and except for an occasional washerwoman with a big basket of clothes on her head, the black service contingent bound for downtown Clayton City had gradually dwindled away. Soon the black schoolchildren whose parents lived on the yard downtown would come trooping along The Avenue in the opposite direction, bound for the colored school inside the fort. The seven-fifteen bell had rung minutes before, and school took in at eight. In the back of the house Dr. Tait could hear his daughter, Makeda, scrambling around the kitchen and banging the doors to the cabinets as she hurried through the routine of getting off to school. Fortunately she would not have far to walk, and in a fleeting moment of reminiscence Tait wished that she were once more at an age when he could walk with her. But alas! That was never to be again. Makeda was almost eighteen, and with a little luck she would graduate in May. It was the contingency of a little luck that had preyed constantly on the doctor's mind for the past few days. Makeda was pregnant. If she were lucky, those old maids at the Academy would not find out in time to prevent her graduating with her class. If she were not, he didn't know what would happen. One thing he did know, Clayton City would never be quite the same in either case. He had known about Makeda's condition for several weeks, ever since he had noticed the gentle rounding of her body and then the telltale signs of morning sickness. But he had not elected to do anything about it just then. His visions of what he ought to do and what he wanted to do were still in conflict.

It was possible, even probable that only he and Makeda knew the awesome, damnable truth. There was going to be a reckoning, of course, but the shape it would assume was not yet clear. He was grateful that neither Makeda nor her mother had said anything to him about the situation. If Ramona did know, he was glad for the extra time her little conspiracy of silence gave him to make the determination he knew he had to make. But he doubted that Ramona even knew, or knew why, or cared very much one way or the other if she did. Makeda and her mother were not close. They lived in the same house, but that was all. Now the fall of his house was imminent, and like the fall of the House of Usher, it would be cataclysmic and conclusive. His was a house of cards, he confessed grimly to himself. Without substantiality. Without reality, really, if one thought about it. A *no* thing! And in that nonreality, that elusive cosmos of nothingness, he himself was the principal illusion. But whatever his personal validity or lack of it, his thoughts were real. And if life itself were mere pantomime, it could at least be thought about, even as the play went on. He was the doctor, real or imaginary, and sooner or later he would need to take up his scalpel and expose something malignant, malodorous, and unclean, yet something that was somehow magnificent and necessary to his own corporeality, his own sense of being, his own recognition, even as a set piece in the charade they called life.

Walter Eldridge Pinkney Tait, M.D., studied medicine and took up his practice in Clayton City. That was about as much as anyone knew of him. It wasn't known for certain just where he took his medical degree, or even if he had one, for that matter; but he said he was a doctor, and since none of the white folks ever bothered to look into it, the colored let it alone. It is not necessarily that there was a presumption of doubt. One can imagine that somewhere on one of the walls of the dingy office in his house on The Avenue there must have hung the copies of the credentials necessary to his profession. But nobody ever remembered seeing them, or if any-body saw them, nobody could seem to remember what they said. The knowledgeable Negroes in Clayton City assumed that he was a product of Meharry or else Howard Medical School. They made that assumption quite logically, since these were the only two medical schools they knew about which were in the business of training colored doctors. Dr. Tait just sort of materialized in Clayton City when nobody was paying much attention, and stayed on. Clayton had once had another black doctor, a Dr. Weems, but he moved on a year or two before Dr. Tait came, and everybody was glad Dr. Tait was there to take his place. Those who remembered him said that Dr. Weems was a very good doctor, good as any *white* doctor. But he was old and ready to retire when he moved away from Clayton City.

It must have been nineteen or twenty years back that Tait had commenced his practice. He brought a wife with him, and this to the possible dismay of a handful of mothers and daughters who might be presumptuous enough to visualize a doctor in one of Clayton City's more respectable black fam-ilies. There would not be many, certainly not more than one or two who'd spend much time thinking about it. For the most part the colored citizens of Clayton City had a firm grasp on reality, and the real for them did not run to doctors in the family. If there had been a doctor available, he would have been preempted by the Goddards or the Binniwaters or the McVeys. They represented the black aristocracy, or the "Big Niggers" as they were called. Although the boys in their families quit school and went to work like everybody else, the Big Niggers had girls in college, and some to even finish places like Talladega and Fisk and Tougaloo. But Tait was not asking Clayton City for a bride. He brought his own.

There was nothing particularly impressive about Ramona Tait unless you are impressed by black women who look half-white. Some people are, of course, and there are many towns in the South quite liberally endowed with the proof of this contention. Clayton City was neither better nor worse than the norm. It had its share of black-white children, and they all lived with their black mothers and black daddies, and nobody got excited about it. It was part of an established tradition bequeathed by slavery and hardly interrupted since the Civil War. Half-white is not a precise term. In the common understanding it usually meant that an immediate parent was white and the other was black without reference to the possibility of any previous intermixture.

Mrs. Tait was obviously half-white, but beyond that not much more was known about her. Her reclusive tendencies kept her indoors. She was never known to go to church, for example, or to visit from house to house—the two prevailing social activities in Clayton City. It seemed that after a few years in Clayton Ramona had started to drink; but few people on The Avenue knew about it, and though there might have been a kind of hushed speculation, practically nobody could say exactly when or why she took to the bottle. The doctor knew, perhaps, but the doctor kept his own counsel. He had long since stopped keeping any form of alcohol or alcohol-based medicines in his office, and though he knew she had developed her own source of supply, he preferred for reasons of his own dignity not to speculate on what that source might be.

Sometimes Ramona could be heard playing a piano somewhere in the interior of the house the doctor bought on The Avenue, and on rare occasions one might catch a glimpse of a shadowy figure peering through the organdy curtains of the front parlor opposite the doctor's office. She wore her hair plaited in two long braids, Indian style, and gossip had it that indeed she was part Indian in addition to being half-white. It was possible. A lot of Negroes in the country around Clayton City were mixed African-Indian-White, but so long as they accepted membership in the black community, they were considered Negroes. The unmixed Indians and the half-white or "blue-eyed" Indians posed a more difficult question in social relations. They weren't Negroes and they weren't white people, so they didn't fit into the prevailing pattern of understanding and identification. For example, the blue-eyed Indians who came to town on Saturdays were shunned by whites and left alone by Blacks. The white merchants, who as a class traditionally assumed the responsibility of caste regulation, often recognized a venerable Negro customer by name and with the noblesse oblige proper to that situation would put themselves out to help a familiar black retainer with his sacks and bundles. But then, such Negroes were assumed to know their place, and recognizing them implied no breach of social distance. The problem with the Indians, especially the blue-eyed ones, was they *had* no place. They were an appendage to the defined and accepted order of things.

So if Mrs. Tait was, in fact, part Indian, that fact alone would have been no barrier to her complete acceptance by the black community, provided, of course, that she was also part black. Being part black made one *all* Negro, for "Negro" is a comprehensive term naming all people in America of African descent of whatever degree. For countless generations the Blacks, Whites, and Indians of the southeastern United States have enjoyed a certain understanding, the ultimate result of which has been the steady growth of the "Negro" population, externally assisted. Still, the Indians around Clayton, as elsewhere, frequently stood aloof from the black community lest they compromise their identity as Indians in the sight of the ruling whites. But the Blacks were flexible as well as understanding. If the Indians came to them, they accepted them; if the Indians kept to themselves, they accepted that, too. In slavery times, thousands of Blacks had escaped the white man to throw in their lot with the Indians, and among certain tribes the African infusion is still visibly pronounced. Blacks and Indians have an age-old understanding, so if Mrs. Tait was part Indian, that was an unlikely reason for her reclusion, for being part Indian in the black community is just another variable of being all Negro.

One popular explanation was that Ramona Tait was the yard child of a former governor of the state of South Carolina whose political reputation was made on his public abuse of Negroes. A few people who had seen her close up, like Guts Gallimore who ran the Blue Flame, declared her to be the governor's "spitting image." The complement to that story was that Dr. Tait himself was the black son of a distinguished white family in South Carolina and that his medical education had been paid for by that family on the condition that he alter the spelling of his name and that he not return to that state to practice. These stories may well have been factual, but the genius of such stories, factual or not, is that they assemble the informal data of those larger truths transcending the particular individuals to whom they claim to refer. The Tait stories were undoubtedly *culturally* true, and as such they were adequate explanations for whatever gaps there were in the factual histories of the individuals to whom they were applied. Whether or not the details were true, they were well within the conventional cultural format, and having some of the required characteristics, Dr. Tait and his wife were matched to patterns already established as normative. This made them easier to understand and relate to, and defined their place and their status in the prevailing scheme of things.

The nature of social relations in Clayton depended upon a high degree of ritualization and personal mystique. It was far easier to deal with the "what" than the "who" of the individual, Dr. Tait decided, for "what" was the critical factor which determined the style of any possible relationship, and "what" was first of all a question of race. It was a question of white or black, a determination absolutely necessary to any perspective on whether one was a genius or a fool, a saint or a sinner, or worth being concerned about one way or the other. The question of his professional competence, for example, could not arise until his racial identity was first resolved. Once that was disposed of, for the white people of Clayton City his professional competence could never become an issue at all, for a black doctor was a logical contradiction. It was not that black doctors did not exist or could not exist. They could and did in the same sense that there were black preachers and black teachers. But the reality of all this was both shadowy and mystical and anchored in a category of existence with no substantiality for any white man. Dr. Tait knew that he could practice a thousand years, but to the white people of Clayton City he would never be more than "Doc"—the *colored* doctor, a kind of shaman in black bow tie and striped pants. And if any white people of Clayton should ever find it necessary to seek his services—

an occasion not unheard of in the area, he had to admit—it would be for his magic and not for his science, and it would be only after the best available efforts of the white professionals had been exhausted.

Dr. Tait's personal style did little to discourage the notion that he might have been engaged in some sort of professional masquerade. Obviously he did not characterize the behavior of all black doctors, even in the limited experience of a town like Clayton City. For a dozen years before Tait came, Dr. Weems had practiced medicine and moved about Clayton with an air not distinctly different from his white counterparts, but it was a *colored* aura, even though some white people claimed they sometimes forgot Weems was black— an intended compliment to his competence no less than to his style. There were stories of how Dr. Weems had been called in to treat old Miss Della Russell, a prominent white spinster. It was said that Dr. Weems had "put Miss Della back on her feet" when all the white doctors had said she couldn't live. She did live—longer than some of her doctors. But Weems never forgot he was black. Nor did the white doctors who failed in what he had accomplished. And despite the legends of his prowess, his professional competence was never good enough to earn him membership in the County Medical Society, or to permit him to practice in the local hospital, or to have the white townspeople refer to him as "Doctor" rather than "Doc." But he did enjoy the *available* respect of most people who knew him, and the white doctor who headed the County Medical Society referred to "Old Doc Weems" as "the finest colored doctor in the state."

Now Dr. Tait was distinctly his own man. Even in a less restricted environment he probably would have been a loner. He was not what you would call "of the people," and like many professional men, he prided himself on the order and structure of his personal life. He arose promptly each morning at six, dressed himself meticulously in black shoes, gray spats, hickory trousers, and white shirt, with a black bow tie to match his black silk socks. And when he went out, he invariably wore a black derby and black pigskin gloves. Now it was nine o'clock, and The Avenue was deserted. The world of Clayton City Downtown was turning predictably, and on schedule. Now it was time for him to attend that world available to him. At nine o'clock in the morning his was a residual world, depopulated and denuded by the urgencies of the world downtown, and left to him by a curious default.

Dr. Tait pulled the string on the roller shade that hung inside his front door until the sign saying THE DOCTOR IS OUT was centered in the middle of the door glass. He then pulled on his gloves, picked up his battered satchel, fitted his derby deftly on his head, and went around the house to the garage. A few moments later he drove out in his ancient black De Soto and turned into The Avenue heading west. Just before the sidewalks ended, he turned off into Brandon's Lane, and skirting the corner of Nap Jones's vegetable garden, he pulled up before a neat little cottage framed by two giant elms towering high above it. Miss Inis Wells sat on the porch, taking the morning air and impatiently waiting for the doctor. "Sis' Inis," as she was called by her neighbors, was eighty-seven years old, and although she had no specific ailments she could point to, she coveted the attention "her doctor" gave her, and apparently thrived on it. Her eyes sparkled as Tait turned off the engine and stepped from the running board of the battered old De Soto.

"Well, bless my soul!" she exclaimed. "I knowed you wouldn't forgit Sis' Inis. The Lord bless you!"

It would have been easy to get the impression that the doctor's visits with Sis' Inis were somewhat rarer than was in fact the case. The fact was that Tait saw her nearly every day, the very first patient on his round of calls unless there was some emergency which prevented it. He had been treating Miss Inis for years. Mostly they just sat in the swing on her front porch and talked. Occasionally he had to give her an aspirin or a little seltzer to settle her stomach, but she never was sick enough to be confined to bed. All her children were dead except for a grandson "up in the North." She lived alone, but there was no sign that she was waiting to die. Her vital signs were good, and her enthusiasm for life was quite evident. "My doctor done told me I'm gwine prob'ly live forever," she confided to the neighbors, "but I'm gwine fool him one of these days. I aims to live a heap longer'n that!"

The doctor sat down beside Miss Inis in the swing and wondered what wisdom the world had lost because she was born black in a world full of white folks. She told him once in her soft, unhurried dialect, "I was bo'n befo' de War. My mammy was bo'n befo' me, and she saw the stars what fell on de State of Alabama. Yes, she did! But I saw ol' Gen'l Sherman come a-prancin' through de valley on his hoss, a-freein' de niggers faster'n you could cut a shoat, an' my mammy ain't seen *nothin'* like that! But *I* seen it. *I* was dere!"

Miss Inis shuffled off into the house after first commanding Tait to "Jest settle yourself down 'til I come back, 'cause it look to me like you lookin' kinda po'ly this mornin'. Somebody got to take care of you so you can take care of the rest of us," she reasoned, "and I guess the Lawd done 'pointed me!" Her voice trailed off into the little kitchen at the back of the cottage. Presently she returned with two thick mugs of homemade peach brandy. She handed one to the doctor and plopped down in the swing beside him. "Now drink this, suh!" she commanded. "It's good for what's ailing you. An' ain't no use to tell me you's up to snuff, 'cause if you was, you wouldn't have them wrinkles standin' up there betwix your eyes. An' yo' skin is pale as a cup of blue-hohn! You might not know it, Doctor, but the Good Lawd got a mortgage on de doctor same as he got on everybody else. So drink your tea and make your payments. You'll live a heap longer'n the rest of 'em, jest like ol' Sis' Inis."

Dr. Tait looked at the old woman with mixed affection and admiration. "Some tea," he scolded gently. "Miss Inis, how many times have I told you you're not supposed to drink alcohol? How many times?"

"Ain't no alcohol," she corrected him. "This here's brandy, peach brandy! Made from the fruit of the tree. God give me the peaches, an' I been makin' it and drinkin' it for lo these many years, an' it ain't never hurt me none. You jest shet your mouth, suh! An' do like somebody tell you sometime! De doctor don't know everything! I was making this here toddy befo' you was even a shimmy in yo' mammy's behind, and I'm still here. And gon' be here long as de Lawd see fit to tol'rate me,'' she added as an afterthought. Suddenly she rapped the doctor on his knee with the knuckles of her tiny fist. "No, suh! you jest pay 'tention to yo' business and let Sis' Inis's business alone! When you gits to be as old as I is,'' she continued, measuring her words for effect, ''yo' business is with yo' Jesus an' not with yo' doctor. I done sent for you to look after my health, not to meddle in my business, Mr. Doctuh Man!''

"Whoa! Wait a minute," the doctor interrupted. He drained the heavy mug and stood up. "Just catch your breath a minute. And by the way, let me remind you, young lady, I am the doctor, you are the patient, no matter what side arrangements you may or may not have with Jesus. Just now your business is my business and Jesus is holding me responsible. You understand that? What is more, madam, you didn't send for me, I came voluntarily, like I always do. I have to come by here every day, because if I don't, you're bound to get sassy and misbehave. Now you just stay out of that old crock you've got back there in the kitchen, or I'm gonna send you back where you came from—if there is such a place!''

"Where I come from ain't none of your business!" She shook her fist at him. "Ain't none o' your business, you young whelp!" But Tait had already climbed into the car and was headed back out toward The Avenue.

His next stop was at Good Jelly's just before The Avenue curved into Minnie's Ferry Road.

Good Jelly was in bad shape. Very bad shape. They said he'd gotten himself cut up in a dice game Saturday night down at The Forks of the River. Nobody was saying much about it because Good Jelly never did like for anybody to put his business in the street. Good Jelly had two fists like two ham hocks, and he had been known to coldcock a full-grown mule by hitting him between the eyes with his fist, *one time*! Once he mangled up two men in a fight like they were hog sausage, and then shot one of them with his own gun. Good Jelly weighed nearly four hundred pounds, and all the time he was hitting you, his big belly, which hung 'way down over his belt, would be shaking and jumping like a coon in a croker sack. It was a funny thing, though; Good Jelly loved children, anybody's children. When he walked down The Avenue, the little kids would run out and holler, "Jelly Belly!" And Good Jelly would growl like a big black bear and pretend to chase them. When he caught two or three of them, he'd scoop up an armful and take them to the Blue Flame and buy them all ice cream and soda pop.

Good Jelly was in the bed when Dr. Tait knocked on the door. His wife, Ruby, was off working for the white folks, but Baboon was there to look after Good Jelly until she got back. Baboon came from somewhere out in the country, and he must have been kin to either Ruby or Good Jelly, because they looked after him like he was their own son. People considered him not right bright, which is probably why he was called Baboon. But he had long, dangling arms that reached almost to his knees, and even though he was only fifteen years old, he had been known to hold up the back end of a truck while Good Jelly changed a tire on it.

They had brought Good Jelly to Dr. Tait's house a little after midnight Saturday, and it took four or five men and a considerable commotion to get him off the pickup truck and up on the front porch. The doctor's office was closed, and they say he didn't want to let them in; but when they told him it was Good Jelly, and him bleeding so bad and all, the doctor finally opened the door. They had a lot of trouble getting him up on the examining table, and when they finally got him up there, they say Good Jelly was so fat he hung over on both sides. Good Jelly is tall, too, so they had to pull up another little table for something to put his feet on, although his feet don't seem so big for a man his size. Not like Big Walkin' Man, for instance. Big Walkin' Man is a sure 'nuff big man and got big feet to prove it. Big Walkin' Man wears a seventeen- or eighteen-D-size shoe, but Good Jelly's just got average-sized feet, even though he is six foot of fat and muscle, maybe more.

Nobody was saying much about it, but it was out that it was Lil' Andy that put Good Jelly in such bad shape. Some say Good Jelly tried to take advantage of Lil' Andy, but before he could so much as get ahold of him, Lil' Andy had cut him every-which-way but loose. Good Jelly tried to pull his gun, but Lil' Andy hopped up on the table, jumped on his back, and cut him so fast he forgot where his gun was. Then he jumped down and stomped on Jelly's corn and cut him on the sole of his foot. Now they say, "Good Jelly can't sit down, can't lay down, can't wear no shoes and no hat! He's real messed up!"

Dr. Tait knocked on Jelly's door and Baboon opened it. Baboon had never seen a doctor before. He stared at Tait and at his medical bag, not knowing what to do or what to say. The doctor sized up the boy, noting especially his long, powerful arms and his barrellike chest. "I'll be damned," he exclaimed, under his breath.

"Suh?"

"I said what's your name?" the doctor said.

"My name's 'Boon," the boy said without emotion. "My name's Baboon."

Appropriate, the doctor thought to himself. It could just as easily be Pithecanthropus. Aloud he said, "Well, 'Boon, I'm the doctor. I came to see Mr. Good Jelly."

The boy let him in and showed him into the bedroom, where Good Jelly lay among a pile of feather pillows. The bed sagged almost to the floor from his great weight. The pillows were bloodstained, and the big man was obviously in pain. His dark brown skin had taken on an ashen cast. Now Dr. Tait had a distinct distaste for what he called "nigger violence" and for any one who got caught up in it. Good Jelly was no exception. There he lay, four hundred pounds of lard cut to ribbons by some other Saturday night character swinging a razor over some imagined wrong with a market value of fifty cents, probably. If that much. He'd had to take seventy-two stitches in Good Jelly to stop the blood, and it was still possible that Good Jelly wouldn't make it. He needed a transfusion very badly; but they wouldn't take him at the local hospital, and there was nowhere else to go. They only kept four beds for colored patients, and even if they weren't all occupied, the practice was not to admit any cut-and-shoot cases on the weekend. The rationale seemed to be that if the niggers in Clayton wanted to slaughter each other every Saturday night, that was their business, but the County wasn't going to encourage it by picking up the bill. The four beds in the County Hospital were kept available for the decent colored people who might get hurt on the job or who might catch a spell of pneumonia going to and from the job in the weather. Or something like that.

Dr. Tait changed Good Jelly's dressings, wrote out a prescription for him, and left. On thinking about it, he was annoyed with himself for agreeing so nearly with the white attitude toward Negroes who got themselves cut up or shot. They didn't *have* to gamble. They didn't *have* to get drunk and feud and fight every Saturday night. He spent more time and energy on cases of senseless violence than on all the other ailments in the community combined. Every weekend somebody got his head bashed in, or his guts shot out, or his throat cut, or his heart punctured with an ice pick. Or somebody was blinded or paralyzed from drinking bad whiskey. Added to that, the local police supplemented the mayhem by shooting somebody from time to time to keep the niggers cognizant of a nigger's place. For a small community, there was too much violence. And yet the remarkable thing was that no matter what happened on the weekend, come Monday, things went on exactly as before. After those who got maimed or slaughtered were patched up by the doctor or funeralized by Ferdy Frost, they took their places in the tales and legends of the town—as part of the folklore of survival. There always seemed to be another gambler, another bad nigger, another yardman, cook, bootlegger, or janitor to take the place of the one who got killed or put out of action.

So it would be with Good Jelly. If he died, the people would remember how he could bust your face with his fist, how he loved children, and how he sold whiskey for the white folks and never got arrested. And people would talk about Lil' Andy, too—how he climbed up on a table and cut Good Jelly down to his own size. But how long would it be before Lil' Andy turned up on the doctor's table or paid his last dues to Ferdy Frost?

Tait didn't really want to think about it. Deep inside he knew, or he thought he knew, that circumstances in which all black people were caught up were so much bigger than they, so much more complex than they'd ever have resources to cope with or even knowledge to understand. Still, there was a pebble of doubt that never quite let itself be answered to his satisfaction. He was his own best evidence, and he knew he wasn't like the rest of the Negroes in Clayton City. What was the difference that made him different and left most of the others *just a bunch of* niggers? It was an uncomfortable question, and he tried hard to put it out of his mind.

His thoughts came back to settle on Baboon. Odd-looking fellow if he'd ever seen one. A real troglodyte. But then, wasn't the whole town of Clayton a community of troglodytes, himself included? Sometime before the sun went down he would know more about himself than he had ever known. Possibly more than he truly wanted to know.

Dr. Tait had turned off The Avenue and was running along Giles Street headed north. If he went far enough on Giles, he'd pass the old cotton mill and come out at the fairgrounds. The mill had been closed longer than most folks could remember. The windows were all broken out, but the rusty old machinery inside the redbrick walls was still intact as though awaiting some divine decree to start up again. But the mill would never run again. That was the general consensus in Clayton City. When the cotton mill was operating, too many folks had money, and you couldn't get anyone to work in the white folks' kitchens or around the stores on Courthouse Square unless you paid them something close to what the people working in the mill were getting. Besides that, there were a lot of people coming into Clayton City with strange names and even stranger ideas about things. White and colored women were put to work side by side, and people began to talk about labor unions and such. So they closed down the mill and the strangers left town, and things went back to the way they were, some said the way they were supposed to be. Anyhow, Clayton City never permitted any outside industry after that. All the little businesses were run by folks who grew up with each other and went to church with each other and married into each other's families. Most of the poor whites who'd come in from the country to work in the mill went back where they came from, and the folks with the funny names and strange accents who'd set the mill up in the first place tried to sell out and get out. Nobody would buy the long rows of redbrick buildings or the machines that went with them, so they were just left standing there. The outsiders who owned them just sort of vanished, and the local folks soon forgot they'd been there, everybody, that is, except Lawyer Leakes. He kept in touch with the mill folks, wherever they were, and handled anything that came up about their abandoned property.

Tait turned off Giles Street three blocks before he got to the high chain-link fence surrounding the mill complex and drove a block and a half down Blossom Street. When he came to number 73, he made a U-turn and pulled the De Soto up on the side of the road before a neat yellow cottage with saffron yellow trim. Blossom Street was not paved, and it was only two blocks long; but all the houses on the street and most of those on the same stretch of Peachtree Street a block north were neat and well kept. Together the two short streets made up what was called Blossom Village, a small black enclave entirely surrounded by whites. The way it happened was that years ago the mill people had bought land right in the middle of the black community on the north fringe of town. They built the mill and then built houses for the white workers on the land they had left. The two little sections of Peachtree and Blossom Streets were all that was left of the black community caught between the tree-shaded lawns of the downtown whites on the south and some of the white millworkers who hung on to the drab company row houses on the north after the mill was closed.

The Negroes who lived in Blossom Village were for the most part domestics. Each morning they walked to their jobs at the white folks', and in the evenings they came home again to take up the responsibilities owed their families. On Saturday they dug in their little vegetable gardens and visited from house to house to fill each other in on the news. On Sunday they went across town to stroll on The Avenue in their Sunday clothes after the preaching was over in their favorite churches. But for the most part, during the week the streets were quiet and there was no one about except an occasional stoop sitter too old or too feeble to make a day in the kitchen or on the yard downtown.

Addie Ferguson was not exactly typical of the folks who lived in Blossom Village. First of all, Addie let it be known that she had never spent a day in anybody's kitchen except her own. She cooked, she said, for Mr. Ferguson. And she washed for Mr. Ferguson. And she slept with Mr. Ferguson. Period. Tending to Mr. Ferguson, she said, took all the time she had. She never called her husband by his first name, even when addressing him directly, but always referred to him as "Mr. Ferguson." Bonus—that was his name—had long since come to accept her style as he accepted Addie, and they had lived peacefully in the little cottage on Blossom Street ever since they were married.

Bonus Ferguson was the chief cook at the town's only real restaurant. The restaurant was run by a Greek everybody called Nick, and it was on the east side of Courthouse Square between Clayton County Hardware Store and H. W. Phillips Drugstore. Nobody seemed to know where Nick came from, or when; but he was the only Greek in town, and he lived by himself in a little apartment above the back of his restaurant and didn't get into whatever was going on in Clayton City. Besides Bonus, he had a second cook, also black. All his waiters and busboys were black, too. Nick served good food, and Nick's Restaurant was the only place to go for a good breakfast or a businessman's lunch. The only competition was the Bus Station Café but the Bus Station Café only served short orders, and it was a hangout for hillbillies and transients.

Bonus had worked for Nick since before he met Addie, and he had a secret pride in the fact that he was one of the few colored men in town whose wife could sit down at home while he worked. In the local idiom of the day, "Mighty few white folks and no niggers a'tall" could manage that in Clayton—unless they were bootlegging whiskey or stealing.

Bonus and Addie had been married for five years when

Addie came under the care of Dr. Tait. She had had two miscarriages and had gone to Tait in desperation. Her problem was compounded by the fact that Bonus was nineteen years older than she, and she sensed his expectation that she was going to have some children for him. She wanted to, but it just didn't turn out that way. After her third miscarriage Tait had recommended a hysterectomy and had succeeded in having it done at the University Hospital eighty miles away. Since Addie didn't work for anyone in Clayton, she might have had a hard time getting into the County Hospital there at home. It was true that Bonus worked, of course, and it was true, too, that his reputation for being sober, steady, and reliable was hard to match. But it was also true that Bonus worked for the Greek, and that was not the same as working for the real white folks who ran things in Clayton. Still, if Nick had talked to one of the businessmen who ate in his restaurant, things could probably have been taken care of for Bonus's wife to be put up at the hospital as a favor to Nick. But Nick kept his business to himself, and none of the colored people who worked in his restaurant ever had any reason to complain about the way Mr. Nick looked after them. Once Nick had a colored woman named Rachel who kept house for him ten or twelve years. Her boyfriend finally came back from Chicago and married her, and when she got ready to go to Chicago to live with her husband, Nick paid her train fare and gave her extra money to spend. She left two boys who looked a lot like Nick with her mother to raise for her until she got settled Up North, and while nobody openly claimed he was their daddy, Nick regularly sent something to Big Mama to help take care of the boys. Maybe it was a gesture to their mother's looking after Nick so faithfully when she lived in Clayton. Maybe not. But no matter how you looked at it, he didn't have to do it. Most of the white men in Clayton City who had colored children didn't even know their names and didn't want to know them.

When Addie got down sick the last time, Nick gave Bonus the money he needed. But Bonus couldn't be spared from his job, so the doctor drove Addie up to the University Hospital in his De Soto and went back and got her three days later. Nobody knew where they went, or why, but then it was nobody's business to know. But so many miscarriages followed by an operation left Addie in doubtful health and under the continuous care of Dr. Tait. As for Bonus, he was grateful that the doctor thought enough of his wife to stop by and see her almost every day without sending him a big bill at the end of every month. Not many doctors could be counted on to do that kind of thing. Most of the other women in the village worked, and since he had to be at Nick's all day, it was a real blessing to have somebody like Dr. Tait look in on Addie if only to pass the time of day, since she had to spend so much time by herself. You don't ever really get over the kind of operation Addie had; but Dr. Tait kept her feeling pretty good most of the time, and he kept her spirits up, even though she wasn't ever going to have any of the children she wanted for Bonus Ferguson.

Bonus had to be at work every morning by six-thirty in order to open up the restaurant and supervise breakfast for the Courthouse Square people who'd rather eat at Nick's than face their wives in the early-morning light. Bonus had a reputation for his buttermilk battercakes and country sausage which had earned Nick a steady clientele over the years, and breakfast at Nick's was as much a status symbol for the Clayton business community as closing up on Wednesday afternoon to go fishing. Bonus was always up by five-thirty, and Addie always had his breakfast on the table when he came out of the bathroom. When she sat down to eat with him, she was always fully dressed, her hair combed neatly into a ball at the back of her head and a fresh apron over the print dress she had chosen for the day. In all their years of marriage Bonus had never seen Addie looking sloppy or unkempt. It could be added that he had never seen her undressed either, and the little games he devised to try to catch her in the bathtub or dressing in the clothes closet lent spice and adventure to his married life. His schemes never worked, and Addie never let on that she knew what he was up to. In his fantasies Bonus imagined she must be a pretty thing under her clothes, but he never found out because if the lights weren't out, there was always something between him and what he wanted most to see. He lived with the perennial hope that tomorrow, or the next day, he would be more lucky, or more clever. Surely someday, as he pretended to doze in the rocker by the fireplace, she would drop her guard, or drop *something*, and he'd catch a vision of her secret loveliness. Such a hope was a mighty factor in getting him through the day at Nick's and getting him promptly home to Blossom Street again when his work at Nick's was done.

Bonus left the house promptly at six o'clock, allowing himself a leisurely stroll over the ten or twelve blocks to Courthouse Square. Addie walked him up to Giles Street, waving to the neighbors as they hurried into the street bound for the yards and kitchens downtown. When she came back, she washed the breakfast dishes and tidied the house. Since she kept it clean all the time, tidying up was never a chore. By eight o'clock, when the sun had dried away most of the dew, she was ready to work in her flower garden at the front of the house. The postman went by around ten, and usually that was her signal to put the hoe and the rake away. She would need to get back into the house to tidy herself and rest up for the doctor, who usually came at eleven.

Dr. Tait stepped from his car and paused for a minute to straighten his bow tie with the help of the side-view mirror. Then he tugged at the sleeves of his morning coat, glanced down at his black patent leather shoes, and dusted his hickory-striped trousers by slapping them gently with his pigskin gloves. Finally satisfied with his presentability, he reached for his bag and closed the car door with scarcely more than a click. He then stepped quickly and with professional purpose along the short walk made of old bricks and bordered with buttercups that led to the porch so lately swept and dusted by Addie Ferguson, and rang the bell. When he heard no response, he rang again and then opened the door and stepped into a small front hall filled with flowers and bric-a-brac and sundry relics of times past.

"Is that you, Doctor?" It was Addie calling from the rear of the house. In a moment Dr. Tait had framed himself in the doorway of the bedroom, where she lay resting among a clutch of feather pillows on an old four-poster bed gleaming and redolent of O'Cedar furniture polish. The pillowcases were trimmed with pink and green lace. The curtains at the two windows were of some kind of white fluffy material trimmed with pink, and the geraniums in the window boxes outside were strong and green and freshly blooming. There was a small fireplace neatly covered by a folded card table, now that it was spring, and painted on the table was a picture of an Indian maiden with long black braids paddling a birch-bark canoe across a quiet lake where a pair of white-tailed deer grazed peacefully on the farther shore. A rocking chair with embroidered cushions and back covers stood on either side of the fireplace, and a handmade oval rag rug measured the distance between the rocking chairs and spread out to anchor the foot of the poster bed in a line with the redbrick hearth. The counterpane on the bed was of green chenille fringed with the same pink cotton balls as the curtains at the windows.

"I heard you ask if it was the doctor," Tait said, "so behold, fair lady, I present myself in the flesh. And I make so bold as to ask whom else you could be expecting at this select hour of this beautiful morning?"

Addie laughed at the doctor's humor. His English was so precise, and nobody else had a voice like his when he was teasing her.

"Whom else?" she mimicked. "Well, you *could* have been the trashman!"

"Could have been. *Could* have been! But you're lucky today, it's not the trashman who comes to steal your time. It's the doctor."

"There isn't such a great difference." Addie laughed and sat up. "One talks trash and the other hauls it. Sometimes it's hard to say which is which. But if you're the doctor man instead of the trashman, then why don't you come on over here and see what ails me?" She pushed the bedclothes down around her waist to show off the newly embroidered gown she was wearing. She had made it especially for the doctor's visits, and she had spent hours on the needlework which adorned the deep neckline and the little puffed sleeves which accented her golden brown arms to such advantage. She waved impatiently to the doctor, and Tait left the doorway and sat down on the side of the bed and felt for her hand. A gentle hint of lilacs drifted up from her bosom and met his nostrils, causing him to rest his chin instinctively in the embroidered V of her new gown.

"Uhmmm," he said, "you smell good."

"With your shoes on how can you tell?" she murmured. They laughed at that together.

"In that case," he said, "I'll take my shoes off."

It was one o'clock when Dr. Tait left Addie Ferguson and headed for downtown Clayton. There was no traffic to speak of, and as the side streets drifted past the windows of his machine, his thoughts were on the woman who had become for him the only significant reward for his participation in Clayton City's human comedy. A magnificent woman, he mused. And a wasted one. A woman wasted by all those contradictions of living designed to frustrate any notion she might have of happiness or fulfillment. Or even usefulness. She was a black woman, and her intelligence, her wisdom, her humor, even her affections would ultimately count for nothing in this world. He himself represented the only contact she had with a reality she sensed but could never even dream about. And nobody knew better than he how warped and cracked, how unreal was the reality she was groping for through him, for he himself was the bitterest of human contradictions. The difference between himself and Addie Ferguson was that he knew and understood, and had to live with what he knew, while she only sensed that there was an order of being and living beyond the one she knew. Her meticulous cleanliness and neatness; her careful shyness and deference in her relationship with Bonus; her gardening, cooking, sewing—all of which she enjoyed and none of which was contrived—were her instinctual responses to society's demands for respectability. But respectability gave her no rewards. Respectability left her suspended between worlds. Even he was a part of her unconscious struggle to be respectable. A professional man, a *doctor*, his respectability seemed to her automatic, and through her public claims on him as her doctor and her private claims as her lover she sought to share in some small way his own respectableness, his own authenticity. But in his own mind he was not respectable. He was not authentic, not in Clayton City. The Negroes of Clayton and elsewhere wanted to be respectable *colored* people, which meant that they had already accepted unrespectability. He grunted audibly to himself as he recalled a phrase much favored in the obituaries of Clayton's more venerable colored retainers: "loved and respected by black and white alike." For him, to be "loved and respected by black and white alike" was itself a logical contradiction, an impossibility, for what it took to make a black man respectable would outrage all the whites he'd ever known, and the kind of love whites had for blacks was disrespectful on its face. It was the kind of love one has for a thing or for a favorite animal. It was not the kind of love white people meant when they talked about loving each other.

At the corner of Crockett and Webster streets Dr. Tait was forced to give way to a funeral procession moving east on Crockett Street in the direction of the Burning Bush Baptist Church. That would be Lucy Lunceford, or at least her earthly remains, in Ferdy Frost's old hearse at the head of the procession. Tait had signed Lucy's death certificate three days ago—complications of old age—but in his concern for Good Jelly over the weekend, and what with his personal concerns occupying his mind, he had managed to forget about Lucy's funeral, which was scheduled for one-thirty at Burning Bush. He suddenly felt a certain remorse, perhaps even a slight sense of guilt or shame that he had not included Lucy's funeral among the things to which he wanted to give his attention that day.

Lucy Lunceford was the person Tait admired most in Clayton City for selflessness and for integrity. While he himself was not much on religion, he admired her for her faith and for the way she expressed it in trying to relieve the pain, the ignorance, and the resignation which sucked remorselessly at black existence in Clayton City. She had used her whole life as an opportunity to try to lift people who didn't want to be or didn't deserve to be lifted, Tait commented bitterly to himself. And she had probably gone to her grave worrying about the welfare of a sorry lot of niggers who didn't have the grace to worry about themselves. In spite of all that, he decided, Lucy Lunceford was as authentic an institution in Clayton City as any black person could be, and his own sense of decency required his presence at her last rites. As the last car in the procession passed, Dr. Tait turned in behind and followed it to Burning Bush Baptist Church.

Coley's Hand

*C*OLEY lay on a low iron cot next to the window. He could see a good piece down the road without much trouble, and if any of his regulars should be coming, he could just reach under the bed and have his order ready by the time he got up to the window. On weekdays most people just wanted half-a-man to get them through the day. Beginning late Friday evening, business stepped up right nicely, and sometimes Coley really had to exert himself to keep from working. But today was Monday, and business was slow. Coley knew just about everybody who would be calling at the window at the side of his house. Jay Dee had already come by to get himself a taste to go to bed with. Jay Dee worked all night at the ice plant, and since Monday was his day off, he always stopped by Coley's on his way home to get a little something to help him sleep. It was about seven-thirty when Jay Dee was there. A little after that Velma Ray woke him up bamming on the front door as though she thought she was somebody important. As a matter of fact, she was. Velma Ray could ask a favor of most any of the white men downtown and get it. She could help you, or she could hurt you, depending on how you treated her. That was why Coley didn't say too much about her waking him up bamming on his door, even though she knew perfectly damn well that he didn't do no business inside his house. Only at the window. He just didn't want any trouble with any woman that close to white folks nohow. It could be bad for his business. But he let Velma Ray in, and after she'd had a toddy, she'd gone to the kitchen and fried up some salt pork and potatoes. Coley took a plateful and set it on the floor beside the iron bed. Velma Ray ate what she wanted and left after reminding Coley she had other fish to fry, an' she didn't mean no wore-out ol' crawfish like him! "I hear you, Boss Lady!" Coley grinned, waving her through the front door. "You know I need you, Baby, but I jest don't have the price!" He turned over on the iron cot to watch Velma Ray strutting on off down the road toward town. "She got to have a whole lot of poontang," he said aloud, " 'cause she got a whole lot of box to tote it in." All ass and no class, he mused. Nothing like Queenie. Queenie got it all. Still, he admitted to himself, Velma Ray did look good going away; it was coming toward you where her equipment broke down.

Coley was glad she was gone. He had a lot on his mind, and having a woman around, especially if she's not your woman, interferes with hard thinking, and hard thinking was what Coley wanted very much to do this particular Monday morning. Coley had his eye on The Avenue, but he was being messed up by a shitass named Roosevelt. He was thinking hard about Roosevelt and how he could get him out of his way. Not only was Roosevelt messing up his plans for The Avenue; but Roosevelt was ahead of him to the tune of $8, and try as he might, Coley hadn't been able to figure out a way to get any of his money or to keep Roosevelt from taking further advantage of him. Just thinking about Roosevelt made his head ache. His feet, too. In the first place, Roosevelt had made him violate his business principles. Coley didn't do no business on credit; that's how he had gotten where he was. Roosevelt knew that. Why, then, would he put him in a position which required him to break his own rules! Every one of those $8 Roosevelt was owing him was a dollar against everything Coley imagined himself to be. He was a businessman. If you want a man, or half-a-man, then pay your

THE AVENUE, CLAYTON CITY   53

$3, or your $1.50, and get your whiskey. That's the way to do business! But no, Roosevelt had to take advantage of the fact that Queenie was his sister, and Queenie was the one woman in the world right now that Coley wanted to be his woman.

Coley's bitter reflections on Roosevelt were interrupted by a sharp rap at the front door. He glanced at the Waterbury clock on the mantel. Ten-thirty. He had been so absorbed in the trouble Roosevelt was causing him that he hadn't even heard the car drive up to his door. But he knew who would be in it, and when Velma Ray left, he had left the latch off the door in anticipation. Someone knocked again, this time with authority.

"Come on in," Coley shouted. "This here is Coley's house!"

The Clayton City Police Department, consisting of the chief and his deputy, strode through the front door and on into Coley's bedroom.

"Coley," jibed the chief, looking down at the iron bed where Coley languished, "I hear tell you been sick."

"Yes, suh, Chief," Coley strained himself to reply, "I've been right po'ly. Right po'ly. And I'm sho' obliged y'all come out here to see ol' po'ly Coley. Sho' is, suh!"

"I also hear," continued the chief with a grin and a wink, "that you been selling whiskey!" At that all three men burst into laughter and Coley swung his long bare feet to the floor, the better to slap his skinny black thighs.

He reached under the bed and brought out a quart jar of lethal-looking clear corn whiskey and handed it to the chief. "Well, this here's to prove Coley ain't selling nothing." He grinned. "Ol' Coley's giving it away, white folks. Giving it away!"

The two white men sniffed at the jar and bobbed their heads in approval. Then they headed for the front door. On the way out the chief paused long enough to run his fingers into the brown faded Limit Life Insurance Company envelope hanging on the wall near the door. He removed the ten-dollar bill Coley always left there for him and stomped across the wooden porch after his deputy.

Lots of folks called Coley a "nigger" because of his whitemouthing to the police, but that didn't bother him too much. After all, he was a bootlegger, and bootlegging was his business. And if you're gonna do business, you have to do what the trade demands. A man had to make a living, and the less strain involved in the process, the sweeter life was bound to be. Life was a matter of energy. "Juice" Coley called it, and if you put all your juice into working, there wouldn't be any left for enjoying what you worked for, and that wouldn't make sense. No sense a'tall. The trick was to put out a little juice, decorate it with a little bullshit, and set back and let nature take its course. That way your back wouldn't be aching, your bones wouldn't be creaking, and you wouldn't have any knots on your head when it came time to enjoy yourself. Now the white man had the right idea, Coley thought: Get the niggers to do the work, get the niggers to de-juice themselves on your projects while you lay back in the shade and prosper.

Coley never denied that he was a nigger—that'd be mighty hard to sell, him being both black and humble—but Coley always believed that he was a nigger in a class by himself. He knew he was smarter than the average colored man he'd ever seen, or heard about, and half the white folks who thought he was a coon were going to wake up someday and learn he was a fox. For all his smartness, the average white man is still stupid. All you have to do is call him "boss" and cut the fool for him, and he'll give you the gravy off his grits. Coley had a way with white folks. Most of the ignorant niggers in Clayton cut the fool for nothing, but every time Coley cut the fool, it was another dollar in his bucket. That's business.

It was 10:38. Roosevelt would be coming as soon as he got off for lunch, and just as sure as his name was Roosevelt he was going to try to put the arm on Coley for half-a-man. It wasn't the money so much, but Coley just didn't like for anybody to owe him. He didn't do no business on credit. Roosevelt *knew* that. He didn't like for anybody to put anything over on him either, especially a chickenshit punk like Roosevelt. That just naturally made him mad. Roosevelt had somehow managed to make things hard for him. If Roosevelt had the guts to get married or just go on Up North, or something, Queenie wouldn't have to look after him and do his cooking and washing. If Roosevelt would go about his business like a grown man ought to, maybe Queenie would cook and wash for Coley. Yeah. He could move his business over to Queenie's house on The Avenue. Yeah. True, Queenie wasn't going to have any and everybody coming to her house buying whiskey. You see, he could understand that, he could live with it. He could fix things up to get around that problem. He could build him a little place out in the backyard, off a piece from Queenie's brick house. She got a big yard. Yeah. And a big behind, he remembered with satisfaction. He could fix it.

Now Queenie thought a lot of herself. She didn't have much education, but she had class. She knew how to wear her clothes and how to furnish a house off nice, to bring out the best. When Queenie came back to Clayton City when her mama died—she'd been off living in Chicago and big-time places like that—when she came back to Clayton to get young Roosevelt and take him with her back to Chicago, the white folks up and bought their old home place out in Fairmont for cash money and put up an electric station there. When she got the money, Queenie changed her mind about going back to Chicago and built her and Roosevelt a brick veneer house right smack on the Upper End of The Avenue! Right there with the McVeys and the Goddards and all the other Big Niggers. That's one of the things that made Roosevelt such a pain in the ass. Roosevelt thought that because he *lived* on The Avenue, he *belonged* on The Avenue. Shit! Who the hell was Roosevelt—a grown-ass man driving a silly-looking goddamn three-wheeled motorcycle around picking up cars for Jack Romine's automobile laundry! What made it so bad was that he dressed up in a leather cap, big black goggles, and leather gloves and all that shit like he thought he was a speed cop, or something. Putting on his funky airs! Smoking a big cigar! Ain't that a bitch? He better watch out; one of these days one of them crackers up there around Courthouse Square might snatch him off that motorcycle and kick his ass 'til it ropes like jelly. Coley figgered to do it himself if it wasn't for Queenie. Roosevelt wasn't shit and he wasn't worth a shit! He was just a two-bit hustler, and right now he was hustling Coley, and there ain't been no nigger born who could hustle Coley and get away with it. Mighty few white folks—and no niggers at all—could take Coley for his money.

Yeah! White folks got their hustle, too. Ol' Chief Evans and his po'-assed deputy came there every Monday morning like clockwork. Looking for whiskey. Looking for money. They always find a quart of corn and they take that away for "evidence." But long as Ol' Chief find ten dollars in the insurance envelope, the evidence always disappears before him and that dumb-ass deputy he got get back to town. One of these days the insurance man might get there first and get the money and Ol' Chief might have to *present* his evidence. "But if he do," Coley mused aloud, "they'll have to pump it out of his belly. Won't that be a bitch! But that Roosevelt. He's gon' be a pain in the ass long as grass is green and shit stinks. Roosevelt got to go.

Coley's thoughts were broken off by the sound of somebody marching down the road to a brisk military cadence. The approach was from the other side of the house from where Coley lay looking out of the window, but he knew that in a second or two Shelly Mahaley would march into his line of sight. Hut! Hut! Huh-Won-Who-Free-Four! Hut! Hut! The cadence grew louder, and he could hear Shelly's boots crunching the loose gravel at the edge of the road. A moment later he popped into sight, swinging along the road, looking to neither right nor left. He was in full battle dress, from canteen to gas mask, all of 1918 vintage, except that over his shoulder he carried a Civil War musket complete with bayonet affixed. The world war uniform was his own; the musket he had found on one of his forays into the trenches at the fort where he went to dig almost every day. Shelly was a casualty of the war. Shell-shocked in the trenches of Argonne, he was mustered out a corporal and sent home. His experiences in France remained his last consistent contact with reality, and over the years people had gotten accustomed to seeing him marching up and down the road counting cadence or singing the war songs of 1918. This morning was like any other. Shelly was going to the fort to dig for the money he believed the Germans had buried there. Probably he would not find any, and even if he did, it would more likely be Confederate money than German. But there were other treasures he had taken from his years of digging—cannonballs, muskets, arrowheads, bayonets, helmets, and even an occasional skull.

Coley watched Shelly march on down the road, and the germ of an idea creased his black, shiny forehead. Suddenly he leaned as far out the window as he could and yelled: "Shelly!"

Shelly Mahaley continued to march. Coley yelled again, his hoarse voice cracking with the effort.

"Shelly! Hey, Shelly!"

Shelly gave no sign of hearing. The crunch, crunch, crunch of his boots remained steady and determined. Coley cursed him and spat his disgust through the window. Suddenly it came to him that since Shelly thought he was still in the army, he might respond to an army command.

"Corp'al Mahaley! Halt!" Shelly took two steps and stood stock-still. Coley grinned with satisfaction. Now ain't that a bitch? "About face!" he ordered. "Now march on over here to my front door!" he commanded. Up to now Coley had not had time to figure out just what he wanted Shelly to do, although he was certain that his luck had sent Shelly to be the answer to his problems with Roosevelt. "Po" Jip always said, *If money lasts, luck has got to change!* And Coley believed in luck. Some people had it and some didn't, and some who had it didn't know how to take advantage of it. But Coley always knew he had a good hand, and he expected to come out on top ninety percent of the time, whatever it was he was after. He was lucky with the women. He managed to stay out of jail most of the time. And he had a molasses bucket full of money buried under his house—all of which was proof that he had a hand. Now his luck was rising again. He could feel it. He was going to get rid of Roosevelt and move into that big house with Queenie. On The Avenue.

Shelly was turning into the front yard. Coley could hear

him still counting cadence: A-hut! Hut! Huh-Won-Who-Free-Four! When he heard Shelly come clomping up on the porch, Coley got up off the bed and yelled through the door; "Detail, halt!" Shelly stomped to a standstill, and Coley made some effort at hurrying about preparing for his reception. He slipped his long, bony feet into a pair of old shoes with the heels cut out, put on a wrinkled white shirt, and rummaged in the closet for an old chauffeur's cap he used to wear before he went into business for himself. He then ordered Shelly in through the front door, being careful to look up and down the road to make certain that no one had seen him enter.

Shelly Mahaley was a small, wiry man, in his middle forties now, but with muscles still as powerful as spring steel, conditioned no doubt by daily calisthenics and digging in the trenches of the fort. His uniform, though somewhat tattered by years of wear, was clean and neatly patched, and his ancient musket glittered from the meticulous care of the professional soldier. Shelly had been a volunteer, one of the first men to leave Clayton when the United States finally joined the conflagration of 1914–18. In the early days of the war he had fought under French command, as many American officers at the time considered it demeaning to be assigned to officer black combat troops. As the war neared its end, Shelly was a seasoned combat veteran, and he was transferred to a regular American army unit along with hundreds of other blacks who had fought under the French. Shortly afterwards, following three months of exposure to sustained enemy bombardment, he was shipped home suffering from extreme battle fatigue. Shell-shocked. Coley, too, had been briefly in uniform, but after ninety days of training he had been discharged "for the good of the service." Now the military experience he had hated so much more than twenty years ago was finally about to become very useful to him. At the moment Coley was about to feature himself as an officer of the United States Army. He savored the thought, and for the first time ever he wished he had kept his uniform. But, no matter, the chauffeur's cap was enough. It would do. His hand was bound to hold, and in a few hours he would be on his way to new levels of personal success.

Coley was tempted to tell Shelly to sit down on the old overstuffed sofa by the door, but then he realized that that would be unbecoming to an officer–enlisted man relationship. Instead, he ordered, "Parade rest!" and Shelly set the butt of his musket on the floor, tilted the bayonet forward, and spread his feet eighteen inches apart. Coley was ecstatic. He had a one-man army under his control. He had power. He reached under the bed for a pint bottle he kept handy for his personal use and took a long swig from it. The corn whiskey was hot. Raw. It coursed like fire through his frail body and shook him like a small clap of thunder. Then a warm, tingling sensation flowed over him, and suddenly he felt very wise. The secret of a man handling his whiskey rather than being handled by it is in never drinking enough to make you stupid. A man's whiskey ought to serve him. If whiskey is going to be the boss, a man ought to leave it alone. Right now Coley knew he was boss. He slipped the pint bottle into his hip pocket, wiped his mouth on his sleeve, and looked sidelong at Shelly. If the old soldier had any thoughts about Coley's behavior, no sign showed on his face. He stood rigidly at parade rest, his gaze transfixed on some point in space far beyond the walls of Coley's house. Coley adjusted his chauffeur's cap and moved directly into Shelly's line of vision.

"Corp'al," he said in as grave a tone as he could muster, "Corp'al, we army men have to stick together. We got to fight for each other. That's the law. You listening at what I say, Corp'al?"

For the first time Shelly seemed to look directly at Coley. There was a dull gleam in his eyes that startled Coley for a minute. After all, he remembered, Shelly was not all there. Shell-shocked. Coley straightened his chauffeur's cap and tried to assume an air of military authority. His hand felt nervously for the pint bottle in his hip pocket, but upon being reassured that it was still there, Coley resisted the urge to strengthen his confidence with another drink. Shelly was saying something. He seemed to be looking through Coley rather than at him.

"The krauts are our natural enemies," Shelly announced

simply. Coley was immensely relieved. He had gotten Shelly to say something. Now he was ready to proceed with the plan taking shape in his mind. He looked at his watch. It was 11:47. Roosevelt would be there in thirty minutes or less. Shelly was talking about krauts. Germans. That was the angle he ought to push. The shortest distance between two trees is apt to be through the bushes. He cleared his throat and rocked back on his heels the way he imagined a general would do.

"Krauts. You got to be right, Corp'al. Them krauts is our natural enemies. They's downright hard on colored people. They don't 'low no colored to even live over there! You got to be right."

"We are Americans," Shelly announced. "The Yanks are here to make the world safe for decent people to live in. Safe for democracy. We will destroy the Germans. God is on our side. God is for the right!"

"Yeah. Yeah!" agreed Coley. "Them goddamn German krauts got to go! We gon' kill all of 'em. Roundhead bastards trying to take our democracy. God sho' don't like no ugly, do he? Naw, sir. He sho' don't! Now looka here, Corp'al, you an' me can stop them krauts cold, see? They out here every day. They got spies riding around on motorcycles— you know, like them German officers do in the movies— course, you don't have to see no picture shows 'cause you done been there for yourself. But you know what I mean? They come out here on them damn noisy-ass motorcycles messin' with our democracy every day. We got to put a stop to that shit!"

"We defy their bombs and their warplanes," Shelly cried, his voice now rising with a strange anxiety. "We ain't scared of their bombs. We ain't scared of their planes! We will shoot their warplanes out of the sky!" His face was contorted and strained as though he were reliving the scream of artillery shells and the whine of aircraft on some far-off battlefield. He brought his musket sharply to his right shoulder and began to march rhythmically in place to some ethereal cadence. Coley's apprehension increased. His inclination was to put as much space between himself and Shelly as he could, but his annoyance with Roosevelt made him stick it out.

"Jest be cool! Papa," he said to Shelly, "be cool! We got them krauts by the short hair. If you listen to me, you gon' be a big hero. Now listen: You see them German pilots bail out of them warplanes wearing them black caps and them big goggles so you can't tell who they is? Well, they right here sneaking around trying to get back to their units across the lines. Now here's what: When they come 'round here today, we got to stop 'em. If you help me, you'll git one of them medals. I'll see to it." He led Shelly into the kitchen and pointed through the back window. "You see that well out there? Well, them kraut bastards gon' come sneakin' 'round that well there. They lookin' for secret guv'ment documents to steal and to take back to them roundhead generals. Now if you lay down in the grass behind the woodshed over there, you can guard the whole area. You can stop 'em cold. When you see one of 'em trying' to pull something out of the well, or somethin', Corp'al, do your duty! Do your duty! We got to destroy them German krauts. God don't like ugly, and God despises them roguish krauts. When you hear one of 'em on his motorcycle, get ready. It'll be your time to win that medal and wear it on your uniform. Now, detail, take cover!"

Shelly trotted across the backyard and flattened out on his stomach in the weeds behind the woodshed. He spread his legs apart and trained his musket on the well where he expected the enemy to appear. But from time to time he swept the weapon back and forth, covering the whole pie-shaped space between himself and Coley's house. He was ready.

Coley went back into his bedroom, took off his shoes, and lay down on the iron bed by the window. He had been lucky. Shell-shocked Shelly was like a letter from home. In about an hour now Coley would have to go and tell Queenie about how Shelly went crazy all of a sudden and killed Roosevelt. Soon as the funeral was over, he'd move into her place on The Avenue to keep her from being so lonely all by herself in that big house. Business ought to pick up if he was on The Avenue. Luck is a funny thing. When he woke up this morning, all he had was trouble. Now his troubles were about over, and all he'd had to do was to be smart enough to use his luck. It's one thing to have a hand. It's another to know what to do with it.

The crunching of gravel and the squeak of dusty brake linings let him know that a car had pulled up in front of his house. He looked anxiously at his watch: 12:12. Roosevelt would be due any minute now, and whoever it was out front was going to be in the way. The car door slammed shut, and Joe Jipson came around to the window. Joe was one of Coley's regular customers, but Joe liked to joke too much and carry on a lot of stuff all the time. It got in the way of business. Sometimes Coley would exchange gibes with Joe, but he wasn't in the mood for a lot of foolishness today. He hoped that Joe Jipson would just get his man and go on about his business.

On seeing Coley's head protruding from the window, Jipson broke into laughter. "Well, if it ain't Po'ly Coley, the crummy mummy! Your head looks like an eight ball on a black toothpick, and if you don't get back in the window, a passing breeze could cause you to sneeze and break you neck! What say, my man!"

"Stuff's here!" Coley answered. "This is Coley's house, an' we got what you got to have! If our stuff can't drive your blues away, you may as well dig a hole and send for Ferdy Frost! How come you so sharp today? This here's Monday."

"I'm hip to your liver lip, but don't you try to jive po' Jip!" Jipson said. "If you plan to be seen, then you got to be clean, an' that ain't just on Sunday. If you're good-looking, you ought to be looking good. Every day. You owe it to your public. But then, I doubt that you ever need to worry, since you have missed the first requirement."

"I hear you, Bossman," Coley said with an exaggerated deferential nod. He didn't want to swap gibes with Joe Jipson all morning. Best thing to do was to let him win and maybe he'd get on out of the way before Roosevelt came up on his motorcycle.

But Jipson was not going to be put off so easily. He twirled at the toothpick he wore in the corner of his mouth and laughed again.

"Bossman? If I was your boss, I'd have you in a cotton field with rows so long folks behind you'd be plantin' before you got through pickin'! And if you complain, I'd put a bull ring in your nose, and hook it to your toes, and roll you 'round like the spare tire off a Hupmobile! Let me have a man."

Coley fumbled quickly under the bed and withdrew a pint of corn whiskey. "With all the stuff you got," he told Jipson, "you don't need a man, you need a jug to burn your mouth out. You full of shit as a Christmas turkey!"

Jipson grinned with satisfaction. He knew he had wounded Coley, and he was waiting for the next cue. He took the pint bottle and placed it carefully in the inside pocket of his jacket; then, holding on to the windowsill with both hands, he peered past Coley into the semidarkness of the bedroom. Coley eyed him suspiciously. Now that their transaction was complete, he was ready for Joe Jipson to move on.

"What the hell you looking for? Ain't nothing in here belongs to you!"

"Pears to me ain't much in there that belongs to you either," Joe retorted. "If you had to go by the furniture, you couldn't tell what lived in there—people or possums. If you ever cleared out that rat's nest, I'll bet your dear old mother would roll over in her grave in natural disbelief!"

Coley raised himself to a rare sitting position. As Joe withdrew hastily from the window, holding his nose, Coley pointed a long, bony finger at him and warned: "You can leave my mama out of this. You know damn-good-and-well I don't play no dozens. Jiving around is one thing; talking 'bout my mama is something else. I can joke with anybody, but enough is enough and too much stinks!" He was angry, and the words tumbled out so fast that he was sputtering and spraying spittle in all directions. "Now, while you carryin' on all that foolishness, don't forget to pay me for that man you have put in your pocket." He hoped desperately that Jipson would give him the money and go. Talking about his messy housekeeping hit a sore nerve. And besides, Roosevelt was due. But there was a day coming when neither Joe Jipson nor anybody else could talk about the way his house was kept, because somebody else was gonna be keeping house for him, and it wouldn't be in the little shotgun shanty he was living in now.

Joe Jipson retreated across the yard in mock fear. "Don't spray me, Po'ly Coley. You'll poison me for sure!" he pleaded. "I'd heap rather have you break my leg. But if you think you're a polecat, you shootin' from the wrong end. That ain't legal unless you shave off your mustache!"

Having delivered himself of that information, Joe Jipson stepped delicately back toward the window and paused to flick an imaginary fleck of dust from the front of his spotless jacket. He then dusted the toes of his glistening two-tone shoes by buffing each in turn against the back of the leg of his flawlessly pressed trousers and reached for his wallet. Coley's eyes followed him without moving. He dreaded these sessions with Joe Jipson; at the same time he could hardly conceal his admiration for Joe's stinging wit. Joe always had a comeback, but he liked to play too much to be a grown-ass man. A man ought to act like a man. But then, on the other hand, Joe Jipson always had money, and he was sharp. His clothes always looked nice on him. To have money and to be sharp, that's part of what it took to be a man. *If you ain't got no money, you ain't got no business here!* That was Joe Jipson's byword, and Coley had made it his gospel.

The staccato sound of a motorcycle throttling down interrupted Coley's flow of generous feelings about Joe Jipson. Damn! Coley thought. It was that chickenshit Roosevelt now, and Joe Jipson was still hanging around the window. He grabbed the five-dollar bill offered him by Jipson and pushed two crumpled singles at him with an air of dismissal.

It was too late. Roosevelt drove the three-wheeler into the side yard directly opposite Coley's window, revved it up a couple of times, and cut the motor off. In addition to being annoyed by the noise—he'd told Roosevelt a dozen times not to drive that damn thing up under his window—Coley was in a near state of panic. Shelly was back there layin' for Roosevelt, and nobody could predict exactly what he might do.

Shelly was shell-shocked. Nobody had counted on Joe Jipson being there in the way when Roosevelt came. Now Jipson was already sounding on Roosevelt. He might *never* go away.

"Twiddle-dee-dee and twiddle-dee-dum," Jipson was saying, "you mash one bug and his brother'll come! Oh, but excuse me, peoples, if you please, it's brother-in-law, in this case."

Roosevelt sat on the motorcycle, his legs spread apart, his black leather cap and goggles still in place. He rolled a cheap, cold cigar around in his mouth and looked at Joe Jipson. "I don't reckon you talking to me," he said. "I ain't got no kinfolks over this way you coulda' been mashin', in law or outa law!"

"Why don't you mind your own business?" Coley said to Jipson. "You jest like a big ol' catfish, all mouth and no brains. Roosevelt and me is friends. We don't claim to be nothing else. An' if we ever do, that will also be our business. Ain't that right, Roosevelt?"

"Right," Roosevelt said, thinking about the hype he aimed to put on Coley for half-a-man.

Joe Jipson twirled his toothpick and looked critically at Roosevelt while he burnished his fingernails against the lapel of his sports jacket. Roosevelt looked helplessly off into space, waiting for Jipson to demolish him.

"Booker T. Washington Frederick Douglass Robert E. Lee Roosevelt Jones," Joe Jipson begin, circling Roosevelt to get a better look at him. "My good man, aside from having the same name as the president of the commonwealth, just what is your claim to fame anyhow? You don't stand on the corner, you don't score with the wimmin, and you don't have the price of a Coca-Cola, so tell me, my man, just what do you do for sport?" Roosevelt swallowed hard and began digging a hole in the gravel with the toe of his shoe. He couldn't get any comeback words to come into his mouth; it was too dry. Jipson stepped back for a different perspective. "Uhmm," he continued. "Now it comes clear to me, my man. When you on your motorcycle and got your big goggles on and a champ cigar resting on your tonsils, you's the biggest sport of all! All you have to do is go poot-poot-poot up The Avenue and I bet the wimmin run out in the street to clip your fingernails for souvenirs!''

It was not because of Roosevelt's discomfort that Coley interrupted Joe Jipson's needling. There were bigger things at stake. Shelly was out there in back somewhere, and Jipson was just getting warmed up. Things had gone too far for Coley to call it off now, and he probably couldn't call it off if he tried. How do you stop a crazy man from being crazy if he decides to do something? If Joe Jipson didn't have sense enough to leave and go on about his business, then maybe it was meant for him to stay. Coley knew he had a hand, and his hand was smoking. He had to move while his luck was with him. As a matter of fact, maybe Jipson was a part of his hand. He could be a lot of help in case anything went wrong. Yeah. If you got a good hand, play it.

''Roosevelt!'' Coley broke into Jipson's monologue as though his sole interest were to rescue Roosevelt. ''Roosevelt, if you tired of Joe Jipson, tell him that how you run your business ain't no business of his. And listen here, I got me some good home brew cooling in the well out in the backyard. You go git a bottle for me, and one for you and one for Ol' Big Mouth Joe. As usual, he got his bowels in his mouth, and maybe some home brew'll dry him up.''

For once Roosevelt was glad to hear Coley call his name. ''Where you say that beer is, Coley?'' he asked gratefully. ''I'll go get it for you. Right now.'' He started removing his leather gloves. Coley was dismayed. It was important that Roosevelt keep his regalia intact.

''I got it in the well back there,'' Coley said hastily. ''I got it tied up in a croker sack an' hangin' on a long ol' chain. You better keep your gloves on so you won't mess your hands up. That ol' chain is rusty.''

''The world is got to be coming to an end,'' exclaimed Jipson. ''Coldhearted Coley is going to give away somethin' besides bad breath and body odor. There's got to be a catch to it.''

Roosevelt's first inclination was to ride his motorcycle right on around to the well. He loved the commanding throb of the engine between his legs, and he seldom walked where he could ride. But he knew he'd be criticized by both Joe Jipson and Coley if he should start up the motor again. He didn't care about Coley, Coley could go to hell, but Joe Jipson could make you feel like a fool sometimes. He didn't want to give Joe any more ammunition than he had to. In fact, when he got back with the home brew, if he could somehow get Joe's attention focused on Coley, Coley would be so frustrated he'd more than likely turn loose the half-pint Roosevelt intended to ask for on credit without too much trouble.

He climbed off the motorcycle and pushed it carefully to one side of the driveway; then he tugged at his black leather gloves, glanced down at his shiny black leggins, and sauntered toward the rear of the house. The gloves and leggins and the leather cap and goggles he wore all contributed to his sense of importance. He was short and not too big, and whenever he wore regular clothes, like on Sunday, nobody seemed to even see him. But when he was riding his motorcycle, everybody heard him and saw him and knew it was Roosevelt. Whenever he passed somebody on the street, he always threw up his hand and they always waved back. He was Roosevelt. In his fantasies he was a speed cop patrolling up and down the highway like he'd seen at the picture show. If he ever really got to be a speed cop, he'd sure as hell pull a raid on Coley. Coley was stingy as hell. There he was, calling hisself liking a man's sister and too damn stingy to credit her own brother for a drink now and then. To tell the truth, he didn't really drink Coley's white lightning—Queenie'd put him out of the house if he did—but every pint he got from Coley, he sold to some of the boys working around Courthouse Square for a little change to keep his motorcycle looking good. Trouble was that when it came time to pay Coley, he'd already spent the money. But Coley thought he was trying to deadbeat him just because Queenie was his sister. Maybe he ought not to even worry about paying him. Coley was so damn conniving and stingy. And if Queenie was to marry him, which he hoped and prayed she wouldn't, he'd get his money back with interest.

Roosevelt turned the corner and sauntered over to the well. It had a brick housing shaped like a barrel standing about three feet above the ground. The housing was once topped by a wooden frame from which there had hung a well wheel or pulley in times past. Now only a single two-by-four upright remained, and to this was fastened a rusty chain secured by a bent nail. The other end of the chain was lost in the darkness of the well itself. Roosevelt leaned over the housing and peered down into the gloom. The well was quite deep, and he could see nothing. He tugged at the chain. Whatever was on the other end of it was heavy. Coley must have a dozen bottles of beer in that sack, the cheap bastard. But he was glad Coley told him to wear his gloves. He leaned over the well and started hauling in the chain.

Behind the woodshed Corporal Shelly Mahaley lay concealed in the tall grass and weeds. He lay on his stomach, his legs spread apart, his rifle ready. He checked his gas mask. It was ready if he needed it. He had heard the motorcycle drive up several minutes ago, and he watched carefully as the uniformed kraut came down the side of the house and headed for the well. He could have shot him then, but he wanted to see if there were others. Shelly couldn't exactly tell whether the man he was about to kill was a downed pilot trying to get back across the lines or a courier trying to get some message through to his superiors. But he was a kraut, he was sure of that. And Corporal Mahaley had him in his sights. The German peered into the well. His back was to Corporal Mahaley, so he waited for his target to straighten up. He aimed at the base of his skull and squeezed the trigger.

"Zap!" The old musket misfired. Corporal Mahaley squeezed again.

"Zap!" Corporal Mahaley checked his bayonet. Suddenly he was on his feet and in a half crouch. "C-h-a-r-r-ge!" he screamed, and hurtled across the yard toward the well.

Roosevelt was hauling the sack of beer up from the bottom of the well, hand over hand, when he heard the blood-chilling scream. Instinctively he let go the chain as he saw the madman charging toward him with fixed bayonet. The sack of beer plummeted to the bottom of the well, followed by the long chain wrenched loose from the rusty nail that held it to the rotting two-by-four. Roosevelt was frozen with fear, his back against the well housing. But even in his fright he recognized the figure charging down on him as Shelly—shell-shocked Shelly, gone completely crazy! He screamed and tore off his black leather cap and goggles.

"Shelly! For God's sake, man! It's me—Roosevelt! Shelly! Don't kill me, man!" It was too late. With a second cry of "Ch-ar-r-rge" Shelly was already at the well. He twirled his rifle, and the butt caught Roosevelt squarely under the chin, lifting him from the ground and sprawling him backwards across the mouth of the well. A split second later Roosevelt caught the full thrust of the bayonet in the left side of his chest. As the bayonet was withdrawn, Roosevelt's body shuddered for a brief moment and then slipped into the well. A long second later there was a splash, and then silence.

Joe Jipson rounded the corner of the house just in time to see somebody in an old soldier suit stick Roosevelt with a bayonet and disappear in the weeds beyond the woodshed. It looked like Shelly Mahaley, shell-shocked Shelly. Both he and Coley had heard screams a moment before. When neither Roosevelt nor Joe came back after several minutes, Coley put his shoes on and went to the back door. Jipson was peering down into the well and calling Roosevelt.

"What happened, man?" Coley wanted to know as he hurried across the backyard, stuffing his shirttail inside the wrinkled, dirty pants he had on.

"Roosevelt's in the well," Jipson said simply. "I think

he's dead. Shelly Mahaley went crazy and stuck him with a bayonet.''

"Goddamn!" Coley said with convincing disbelief. "Now ain't that a bitch? I always said that crazy-ass Shelly was gonna kill somebody! Now he's done it. We better git the Law, 'cause he'll probably kill somebody else if they don't catch him. He still fighting them Germans in the war. You know that?''

"I always heard he was shell-shocked," said Jipson.

"We better git the Law," Coley urged. "You git in your car an' go on downtown and git the police. And if you don't mind, stop on by Queenie's and tell her. I'll stay here with the body." Jipson was halfway to the street when Coley called out to him, "Say, man, which way old Shelly go?''

Jipson shook his head. "I don't know. I don't know which way he went. He just sort of disappeared." He got in his car and drove off to get the police.

Coley said aloud, "He sure is shook up over Roosevelt. First time I ever saw him let five minutes go by without a lot of foolishness.''

A sudden silence descended on Coley's place as the sound of Joe Jipson's automobile traced around the corner a half block away and faded into the distance. What started off as a routine day for Coley had developed into a busy morning. A lot of things had happened, and his hand was holding. He walked toward the well where Roosevelt was supposed to be. Spying Roosevelt's black leather cap on the ground, Coley picked it up and let it hang from his finger. "Now ain't that a bitch?" he said half aloud. "The way he loved this cap, and he couldn't even take it with him partway. Now ain't that a bitch?" He examined the cap, snapping and unsnapping the goggles attached to it. Finally, he put it on and pulled the goggles down over his eyes and fastened them. This was the way Roosevelt liked to look, but Roosevelt was gone now. Coley leaned over the well and peered in to see if he could see anything through Roosevelt's goggles.

"Ch-a-r-r-r-ge!" came a cry that sounded like some demon from hell itself. Coley turned just in time to see the wild, piercing eyes of Shelly Mahaley zooming at him through space. He caught the full thrust of the bayonet in the pit of his stomach. As he lay slumped and dying on the well housing, he managed to pull off the leather cap that used to belong to Roosevelt. It hung from his finger for a moment and then dropped off into the darkness.

Nish

ONESIMUS GREENLEAF MOORE hunched his shoulders forward and allowed himself to break into a dogtrot. He didn't especially mind hurrying to the job at three-thirty in the morning; it gave him time to think. The streets were deserted, and the plop-plop of his sneakers on the gravel made a friendly sound for company. Besides, he liked to run. It was three miles from his gramma's house to downtown Clayton City, where he was going, and if he did it at a trot, the time passed faster and he'd be there long before daylight. Old Man Gilligan raised hell whenever he was late, and once or twice had gone off on his milk route without him. But he didn't pay too much attention to Mr. Zebbie Dee, that's what everybody called Mr. Gilligan. He raised hell and shouted all over the place at everybody except his wife. Maude said ol' Zebbie Dee was nothing but a po' white cracker in the first place, and that he had married out of his class. That's why he went around bellowing and raising hell all the time—trying to make people think he was somebody. But Mr. Zebbie Dee just didn't have it in him to be what Maude called quality folks, no matter how hard he tried. Or how loud he cursed. He was still nothing but a redneck cracker; that's all.

One day, for instance, Mr. Gilligan made Nish—that's what everybody called Onesimus—Mr. Zebbie Dee made Nish catch two of Mr. Charlie Morgan's big Rhode Island Reds that had come through a broken picket and were scratching around Miss Molly's roses. "Goddamn!" Mr. Zebbie Dee hollered. "Nish, goddammit, get out there and catch them goddamn hens! I'm goddamn tired of feeding other folks' chickens!" He made Nish kill the hens and pluck them before Miss Molly knew what was happening, but when she asked Nish where he got the chickens, before he could answer, Mr. Zebbie Dee started hollering about Nish heating the water too hot and pulling all the skin off the goddamn hens like he was skinning them! He then grabbed both chickens by the feet and flung them out into the alley and stomped off to Courthouse Square without saying anything more to anyone.

Well, Mr. Gilligan was like that. At times he'd do most anything for you, Maude said—and she ought to know, she'd cooked for him and Miss Molly for nineteen years, and for Miss Molly's family ten years before that. At other times, when the cracker came out in him, Maude said, he was downright trash. None of the Dobbins family—those were Miss Molly's people—ever really liked him or had much to do with him.

Miss Molly was the youngest of three sisters and the only one to get married, and that late in life; and the great big old house her two sisters lived in stood right up the street from Mr. Gilligan's house and seemed to be sort of frowning down on it all the time as if in perpetual disapproval of Mr. Gilligan and all that he stood for. But then Mr. Gilligan had his own reservations about who and what was acceptable. As he saw it, a whole lot of God's creations were of doubtful benefit to anybody, and he often wondered whether their sole reason for being was to afflict him with their presence. Among those whose existence outraged him most were no-'count niggers and thieving Jews, but of the two crosses he felt destined to bear, it was the Jews who burdened him most heavily. A nigger will work sometimes, Mr. Gilligan reasoned. You give him enough to eat, supply him with a good mule, put him with a good woman, and keep your foot up his ass, he'll

THE AVENUE, CLAYTON CITY   75

make you a good crop year after year and be faithful to you 'til he dies. On the other hand, a Jew is a Jew and can't ever be anything else. He'll rob you blind and jolly you along with a funny story the whole time he's slicking you out of your money. "Why God figgered we needed Jews," Mr. Gilligan told Nish, "I guess I'll never understand. We already have rattlesnakes and lizards."

That was the time when Zebbie Boy brought his fiancée home from the university. Well, actually it wasn't really his fiancée, but that's what Zebbie Boy had in mind, and before it was all over, Mr. Gilligan came pretty close to busting a gut and probably laying up in the County Hospital for a spell. You see, Zebbie Boy was Mr. Gilligan's only son— only *child*, for that matter, he and Miss Molly having married so late. He was named for his daddy—Zebulun DeWitt Gilligan III was his real name, but everybody called him "Zebbie Boy," just like they called Mr. Gilligan "Zebbie Dee" for short.

Nish remembered that Miss Molly bounced into the kitchen for about the thirtieth or fortieth time that morning. It was a misty, overcast day in December, and the odds were that before the sun came out, there was going to be some rain or maybe even a little snow. It was the possibility of rain that was agitating Miss Molly. This was the day that Zebbie Boy was coming home from the university for the Christmas holidays. This called for a double celebration, because Zebbie Boy was the only child born to Miss Molly and Mr. Zebbie Dee in twenty-five years of marriage, and he was bringing someone with him who might one day be his wife and carry on the family name. That's what was uppermost in Mr. Gilligan's mind, and he had been crowing about it around Courthouse Square for a week. But the family included Miss Molly's two sisters—both older than she and both spinsters—who lived in the big rambling two-story gray house a few doors up the street. As a matter of fact, Miss Laura and Miss Lila considered Zebbie Boy to be as much theirs as Sister Molly's—with as little mention of Mr. Zebbie Dee as could be managed. The three sisters had always been inseparable—that is, until Mr. Gilligan came along. And even after Miss Molly married, Miss Laura and Miss Lila tried to suffer his intrusion with as much grace as possible.

Well, here it was nearly Christmas, and Zebbie Boy was bringing the girl he intended to marry home to meet the family. He called her his fiancée, but Miss Laura had written him a letter and cautioned him about that. Good manners, she told him, did not permit the use of formal categories for casual relations, and until the girl he liked had been received by the family, his attachment to her must remain in perspective. What she meant was that she and her sisters had to give their approval before there could be any talk about marriage. She didn't say anything at all about Mr. Zebbie Dee's approval, or lack of it.

But it turned out to be Mr. Zebbie Dee who had the last say on the matter. He said that when he went to the depot to meet Old Number Four, he knew the minute Zebbie Boy and Miss Barbara got off the train that something was wrong. "She just didn't look right," he told Miss Molly. "Her eyes were too close together, and she had that sneaky look about her, the way they all do. You know, like they've either murdered somebody, or plan to. And why in the hell Zebbie Boy couldn't see through her for what she was, I can't understand. Why, god-a-mighty, she was a Jewess—plain as the nose on her face! A painted-up conniving Jewess. Hell! You'd think anybody who had sense enough to go to college coulda seen that!

But Zebbie Boy hadn't seen it, or if he had, it hadn't made any difference to him, because here she was in Clayton City and she was going to be the houseguest of the Gilligans for about a week—over the whole Christmas holiday. As soon as Mr. Zebbie Dee got home from the station and had a hot word with Miss Molly in the kitchen, Maude was hustled out of the back door to fetch Miss Laura and Miss Lila. It was plain to see that some sort of real crisis was in the air because Mr. Zebbie Dee was blowing his nose and spraying spit in all directions, a good sign that he was too mad to talk. It was all Miss Molly could do to get him out of the back door and headed toward the barn, where he could cool off a little bit fooling around with his cows. In the meantime, Miss Molly followed the slow-footed Maude across the neighbor's back-yard and overtook her before she got to Miss Laura's and sent her on back to the kitchen. Dinner had to be cooked, and on time, no matter what, or nobody could predict what kind of fit Mr. Zebbie Dee would throw.

In the meantime, Zebbie Boy and Miss Barbara were sitting in the parlor, looking at the family album and waiting for the family to gather so that everybody could be introduced. Since everybody else seemed to have gone off in one direction or another, Nish decided that this would be as good a time as any for him to see Zebbie Boy's girl and to say hello to Zebbie Boy. Before Zebbie Boy went off to college, he and Nish used to play together and to hunt and fish with each other just about every chance they got. Zebbie Boy had a .22 rifle and a bicycle and baseballs and gloves and things, but Nish used them whenever he wanted to and sometimes kept them at his house until Mr. Gilligan found out about it and made him bring them back. As a matter of fact, Zebbie Boy sometimes stayed at Nish's house when they were going on a fishing expedition, and Mama Lucy always set them down at the same table just like there was no difference between them—which as far as they were concerned, there wasn't, except that Zebbie Boy was a little older, but Nish was almost as big.

But all this came to a sudden halt when Zebbie Boy got to be fifteen. Zebbie Boy didn't go swimming or fishing with Nish anymore, and whenever Nish asked for him in the kitchen, he was always studying, or that's what Maude said Miss Molly said to tell Nish. Finally, Mr. Zebbie Dee came right out and told Nish that Mr. Zebbie didn't have time to be fooling around, and to stop asking for him. It was hard to give up such a good friend, but Nish got accustomed to not seeing him around much, and then Zebbie Boy had gone off to college and Nish found other friends and interests. But he never did call Zebbie Boy "Mr. Zebbie" like Mr. Gilligan wanted him to. He just didn't call him anything at all.

Now Zebbie Boy had come home with a girl, and every-body was in a big to-do over it for some reason. With Maude out of the kitchen and Miss Molly gone up to her sisters' house, it looked like a good time to find out what was going on. Nish sauntered through the kitchen and on through the dining room to the parlor. The floors had been newly waxed, and the furniture carefully rubbed with oil until it glistened and gave off the pleasant aroma of an evergreen forest. Every pane in the French doors had been washed and polished, and the scatter rugs had been beaten and cleaned and carefully spaced with the bare oak floors framing them like pictures. There was a small Christmas tree in the corner near the piano, and in the opposite corner the Victrola with the picture of the dog listening for his master's voice stood ready with the lid up in case anybody wanted to hear one of the thick wax records Miss Molly kept in the burnished cabinet underneath. Zebbie Boy and Miss Barbara were sitting on the old Duncan Phyfe settee with the family album between them on the matching coffee table.

"Oh, hello, Nish," Zebbie Boy said when he heard Nish come in from the dining room. "I was wondering if you were around. Barbara, this is Nish. He works for my daddy in the dairy. He goes to school, too—out there where he lives."

"Well hello, Nish," the girl said with a smile. "You do go to school? That's very nice. What grade are you? School is such fun, isn't it?" she said. He liked Miss Barbara instinctively. She was kind of pretty, he thought. But not as pretty as Coy. And she had brown hair. Coy's hair was yellow. He wondered what part of the country she came from. She didn't sound much like the people around Clayton City. Maybe she was a Yankee from Up North. Maybe that was why Mr. Gilligan was so mad—Zebbie Boy had brought home a Yankee. Nish realized that he was staring at the girl and that he'd run out of things to say. Suddenly he spied her suitcase in the front hall off the parlor.

"I'll put your suitcase in the guest room," he said, and hurried down the hall with the bag before he had to say anything else.

"Thank you, Nish," she called after him. "Thank you very much."

Maude was coming up the back steps to the kitchen and spied Nish as he turned into the kitchen from the hall. "What

you doing up in the front of this house?'' she demanded.
''You know you ain't got no business up there nohow. I done
jest about wore myself out cleanin' and waxin' and polishin'
for near 'bout a week, an' I ain't working myself to death for
you to go 'round messin' up everything soon as my back is
turned. What you doin' up there anyhow? Ain't nobody come
here to see you!''

''I just went up to get Miss Barbara's suitcase and put it
in the guest room,'' Nish alibied. He could see that Maude
was already mad at somebody, and he didn't want her to take
it out on him. When Maude got a mad on and started pouting
and slinging things around the kitchen, even Mr. Gilligan
found somewhere else to be. And Maude could stay mad for
a week.

''You march yourself back in there an' get that suitcase
and put it right back where you found it,'' she ordered. ''Ain't
nobody asked you to be so fast-assy an' meddle in what you
don't know nothing about. Put it right back where it was, an'
you better be quick about it before Miss Molly gets back
here! It ain't none of your business—an' mine neither—but
if you jest got to know, she ain't staying here tonight.'' With
that Maude swept on into the kitchen and began ominously
rattling the dishes piled in the sink. Nish knew that that meant
the conversation was over and that Maude was far from satisfied with whatever it was that was going on in Mr. Gilligan's house. He decided to chance one more question but
was careful to position himself near the back door in case
Maude ran completely out of patience.

''You mean Miss Barbara isn't supposed to stay here?''
he said with a show of disbelief. ''But she's Zebbie Boy's
girl. She's his guest!''

''You don't know nothin' 'bout *what* she is,'' Maude
snapped. ''An' I don't neither. An' it ain't my business nohow. If these white folks want to act like they actin', well, I
reckon that's white folks' business. That's between them and
the Lord, an' I ain't got nothin' to do with it. I'm just they
colored cook. But I tell you one thing, what they doin' ain't
right, an' God don't like ugly. Don't care what color you is
or how much money you got, God don't like no ugly!''

"Here comes Miss Molly," Nish said, looking across the backyard as he heard the latch fall on the gate.

"I don't care who's comin'!" Maude grumbled. "Jesus Christ is comin' one day, too, an' some folks ain't liable to be ready. Here!" She thrust a panful of sweet potatoes at him. "Set out there on the back porch out of my way an' peel these potatoes. I guess we still going to have to eat sometime today!" Nish took the potatoes, got a paring knife from the kitchen, and sat down at a small table on the back porch to do as Maude had ordered him. He was glad that it wasn't really him she was angry with, and he hoped she'd forgotten about Miss Barbara's suitcase sitting on the bed in the guest room.

Miss Molly didn't even seem to see Nish as she hurried across the screened-in porch and into the kitchen, where Maude was still rattling the china and humming an old Negro spiritual with unusual preoccupation. "Well, Maude," Miss Molly confided, "it's a very trying situation, but I think we've worked things out the best way for everybody."

"Yes'm," Maude said, continuing to hum over the dishes in the sink.

"Now the problem is how to tell Zebbie Boy. He's so young and so innocent. He didn't know what he was doing, and we're all concerned not to hurt him. But we don't want to let him hurt himself either."

"Yes'm."

"I guess I'll have to tell him before Mr. Zebbie Dee takes it upon himself. We've arranged for Miss Barbara to spend the night at Laura's. Sister Laura and Sister Lila are going to come down to meet her in a little while and invite her to be their overnight guest."

"Yes'm," Maude said without turning from the kitchen sink. "When you had me cleanin' up an' gittin' things ready, I thought you told me she was goin' to stay in the guest room an' that she was goin' to be here for a week," she said peevishly.

"That true," Miss Molly said with some exasperation. "But that was before Mr. Dubbie Dee found out that Miss Barbara is a Jewess."

"A who?" Maude demanded, turning away from the sink the better to see what Miss Molly was talking about.

"A Jewess," Miss Molly repeated, and she blushed bright red with annoyance with Maude for not understanding the difficulty that raised for the Gilligan family. "She's a Jewess," she repeated with finality, "and we don't want to create the wrong impression about her relationship to Zebbie Boy." With that she ran up the hall to her bedroom and closed the door. She couldn't afford to let her colored cook know that she was crying.

Later that evening, when Mr. Zebbie Dee blustered into the kitchen after spending the day at O. Spencer's commissary store, it was plain to see that he was still mad at the world. He glared at Maude as if she were the cause of all his unhappiness and demanded to know if that woman was still in the house. But Maude glared back at him. "You talkin' 'bout Miss Barbara?" she asked.

"I'm talking about that woman that came home with Zebbie Boy. That little Jewess," he sputtered. "Is she still here?"

"I reckon she is," Maude told him. "I ain't seen her leave. I got to be cookin' y'all's dinner, an' I ain't got no time to be runnin' up behind no 'Jewess' to see if she gone or not. That's y'all's business. Anyhow, I don't know what no 'Jewess' is. I doubt if I ever seen one in my whole life."

"Well, you seen one this morning, sure as you're born," Mr. Zebbie Dee told her. "You know what a Jew is, don't you? Well, a Jewess is a female Jew. That is what she is. And I'm just not gonna stand for one to be messing around with Zebbie Boy. God-a-mighty! She could be the ruination of that boy before he's even grown! And I want her out of here! Now I told Molly to take care of it before I got home this evening. Now is she gone or not?"

Maude had started humming again, but now she stopped and looked directly at the glowering white man. "Mr. Zebbie Dee, ain't you the one what went to the depot this mornin' an' brought Miss Barbara out here?"

"Yes, goddammit, I brought her here," he admitted. "But I didn't know until I saw her what she was! God-a-mighty! You'd think Zebbie Boy would have had more sense! Wouldn't you think so? Why, Maude, even you would have figgered out what she's after! Now wouldn't you?''

''Yes, sir,'' Maude said automatically. ''What's she after? How come it so bad for her to be a—what you call her—a female Jew?''

''Because all them damn Jews are alike, that's why. Male, female, and in between. Don't make no difference a'tall if it's a Jew. They're not Christian. They're not American. And they're not white. That's why. They're just Jews. Damned gypsies, that's all.''

''I don't know nothing about they bein' Christian,'' Maude said. ''Whole lot of folks claim to be Christians an' ain't. An' if they ain't Americans, I reckon the guv'ment will take care of that. But I don't understand how come you say they ain't white—they sho' looks white to me! One thing for certain, they ain't black! Is they?''

''There's more'n a little bit about the world that you don't understand and ain't going to ever understand,'' Mr. Zebbie Dee said. He was getting mighty peevish with Maude because she acted so stupid. ''Everybody with any sense knows the Jews were in Egypt for four or five hundred years. The Bible tells you that. Well, Egypt is in Africa, if you please, and every African I ever saw or heard about was black. So it stands to reason that even if they weren't black when they went in there, they were black when they came out—or mighty near black, as any fool can plainly see!''

''Well, I guess I can't see plain, 'cause Miss Barbara sho' don't look colored to me. An' if she a Jewdess, or whatever that is you call her—she must be jest like Mr. Sol what runs the shoe store. They call him a Jew.''

''Exactly, Maude. Exactly!'' Mr. Zebbie Dee exclaimed. ''Now you're beginning to look bright a little.''

''Well, Mr. Sol ain't colored,'' Maude said, '' 'cause if he was, he wouldn't have no store right downtown on the square like he do. An' he sho' wouldn't be livin' in no big house over yonder next to Jedge Potter's like he white folks. I sho' don't understand that.''

''Shit-an'-be-damned with what you don't understand!'' Mr. Zebbie Dee fumed. ''If this country had to depend on the level of your understanding, we'd be living in trees and have a monkey for president. One thing I bet you would understand: If you ever went to work for one of them Jews, you wouldn't stay very long because they wouldn't keep you in sausage and pork chops like I do. They don't eat them. And they don't give out no Santa Claus this time of year either. They got their Sunday on Saturday, when they can get the most money from folks like you! Do you think you might understand that?''

''Well, it says in the Bible that the Lord Jesus was a Jew,'' Maude said. ''I understand *that*. Now do that make His mama the same thing you calling Miss Barbara? If it do, it sho' would be pitiful 'round this time of year if she'd come 'round here trying to have a baby. Manger or no manger. Pitiful.''

''Aw, shit!'' Mr. Zebbie Dee retorted. ''Why Molly puts up with somebody like you is something *I* don't understand. God-a-mighty! Shit!'' And he stomped on off to find Miss Molly to see what had been done about the Jewess in his house.

After dinner Miss Barbara spent the night as the houseguest of Miss Laura and Miss Lila. The next morning they put her on the train headed away from Clayton City, and after that nobody in the Gilligan household ever mentioned her name again.

If it ever occurred to Mr. Zebbie Dee that *he* might not be entirely acceptable, it did not seem to bother him. He went about his affairs with a peculiar zestfulness that left little occasion for deploring what others might perceive as his shortcomings. There were more important things to think about. He was, for example, the manager of O. Spencer and Sons commissary store. Mr. Spencer was a big man in Clayton County, and more than half of the farmers and sharecroppers in the county had to come by O. Spencer and Sons for some portion of their supplies. In fact, most of the plantation owners in the county maintained regular accounts at the commissary for the croppers who lived on their land and worked for them. Doing business with O. Spencer was more convenient for a busy planter than maintaining his own commissary. And Zebbie Dee could be counted on to allow the requisite flexibility in his books that would enable the share-cropping system to sustain itself in the traditional manner with the least inconvenience to the landowners who kept O. Spencer and Sons in business. Business at the commissary was light during the week, and most of the customers then were townsfolk looking for side meat or heavy shoes or other items of nostalgic reference to former times. But on Saturdays the store stayed open late to fill the orders of the country croppers who came to buy cornmeal, kerosene, molasses, dress goods, lamps, overalls, union suits, side meat, lard, and suchlike necessities to keep them eating and working until they could get to town again. No money changed hands on these transactions, but they were all entered in a ledger Mr. Gilligan kept for each landowner and each of his croppers authorized to take up supplies at the store. After the crops were in in the fall, Mr. Gilligan would supply each planter with the record of what his hands had bought. The planter would pay O. Spencer and Sons off with a loan from the bank (also controlled by the Spencers) and then settle up with his croppers in terms of their other obligations to him, such as the provision of livestock, housing, personal loans, and other assorted amenities built into the tenant-farmer relationship. That the sharecroppers and their families seldom ended up with anything to show for the year's labor and had to borrow from the planters against the next year's crop, which would end the same way, was a feature of the arrangement which did not trouble Mr. Gilligan. His job was to mete out the necessary dry goods and staples according to his instructions from the landowners and to keep the books accordingly. This he did, and in consequence he became the indispensable middleman between the planters and their tenants, and from this he derived his sense of prestige and power. The fortunes of many, both black and white, were in his hands, and if he fudged a bit to cover his personal needs or to offer an occasional present of dress goods or a brace of kerosene lamps for the sexual favors he routinely exacted of certain of his customers in the stockroom of O. Spencer and Sons, then that was no more than he deserved for all the bother of looking after the welfare of so many people.

About once a month, before it was fairly daylight, Mr. Zebbie Dee would park his milk truck in the alley behind the commissary and help himself to sugar, coffee, flour, and whatever other staples Maude might be needing in the kitchen. He would also restock himself with B.V.D.'s and shirts and would sometimes bring out a pair or two of over-all pants, or a pair of brogans for Nish to wear to school. He had even given Nish the tennis shoes he liked so much. O. Spencer and Sons didn't usually carry tennis shoes, but now a lot of country people were wearing them, especially in the summer. Their thick rubber soles made stomping snakes turned up by the plow a lot less hazardous than stomping them barefooted. But Mr. Gilligan said that if enough people wore his tennis shoes to church on a hot Sunday, it would sure as hell discourage the devil from sniffing around the pews because they smelled so bad.

Nish's long reverie on the doings of Mr. Gilligan brought him at length to The Avenue. Now he slowed down to walk a little, and his thoughts left Mr. Gilligan to settle on a care-fully folded sheet of notebook paper he had in his pocket. That was why he'd been thinking about the white man in the first place. If Mr. Gilligan knew what he was up to, there'd be no telling what he might do. When he came to the street-light guarding the Blue Flame, Nish took the paper from his pocket and carefully unfolded it. The light was out, of course, but the sun was just beginning to crash the darkness on The Avenue, and it seemed that being near the light would help a little, even though he knew the lines on the paper by heart, having worked on them through most of his afternoon classes at the Academy.

> Fair maid with flaxen hair,
> I lay me at your feet
> And if perchance you care
> Life ne'er will be more sweet.
> Oh, I wouldst take they hand
> And hold it to my breast.
> Oh, willst thou understand
> And bless my sacred quest?

On and on it went in such a vein for almost a whole page. The poem was signed "O.G.M.—The Black Knight," and a shield bearing the letters *O.G.M.* was traced in the lower right-hand corner of the sheet. Nish had never liked the name Onesimus—it came from the Bible and meant "obedient servant," Reverend Rusoe had told his gramma when he was born. His middle initial, *G*, had originally stood for "George," but since only Mama Lucy knew the difference, he changed it to "Greenleaf" when he read about the New England poets in the seventh grade. By the time the change caught up with him at home, it was too late to do anything about it. He was in fact, in his more pleasant fantasies, O. Greenleaf Moore. But everybody still called him Nish. Everyone but Coy. She didn't call him anything, but he knew that inside her there must be a name for him. A good name. A special name. He felt it.

Nish was glad to be a poet. There was no other way he could adequately express his feelings about people who meant a lot to him. He thought about Miss Edgarson. She had been principal at the Fort Academy school longer than most folks could remember—thirty-seven years, they said at her retirement. She had taught him to appreciate poetry and to try to express himself in that medium. As a matter of fact, he wrote the official poem read at her retirement. It was called "Flowers in Autumn," and it tried to express the beauty of what Miss Edgarson had accomplished during her long service to the colored people of Clayton City.

Nish's reverie was shattered by the blat! blat! blat! of an automobile horn. He jumped at the sound and hastily folded the paper he had been fondling and put it back into his pocket. It was Buford Atkins, the post office janitor, sitting in the mail truck blowing at him. "Hey, boy!" Buford said. "You goin' to work, or you jest gon' stand there under that dead light reading the funny paper? That light ain't comin' on. Don't you know the city don't furnish no lights for you to read no funny papers?"

"I wasn't reading the funny papers," Nish said grudgingly as he went around the front of the truck and got in beside Buford. "There are other things people read besides funny papers." Nish didn't like Buford, and he would have passed up riding with him except that sometimes in the winter when Buford picked him up he was glad to get the ride. He didn't like the way Buford was always slapping him on the leg and forgetting to take his hand away. Speaking of funny papers, Nish grunted to himself, there were some funny people in the world, too. He moved as far away from Buford as he could.

"Well, what was so important you was reading then? I seen you put it in your pocket." Buford put the truck in gear and drove on toward town.

"It's something personal," mumbled Nish. "It's my personal business."

"Boy, where *you* come from?" Buford exclaimed. "Niggers ain't got no personal business! You show me a nigger that'll tell a white man he got some personal business, and I'll show you the tree where they hung his ass!"

"Umph!" Nish mumbled again. "I didn't know you had changed color. When did you get to be a white man?"

"You don't have to be mumblin' nothing under your breath," Buford said. "I heard what you said. You're one of them smart-assed niggers. You don't know how to act around grown people. Somebody gon' teach you some manners one of these days! Anything I can't stand is a smart-ass nigger that don't know how to talk to people." They rode in silence. Nish wanted to get out of the truck and slam the door and tell Buford Atkins to go to hell. But he knew he'd never do it. He had been taught never to be disrespectful of grown people, and even though Buford probably wasn't worth much respect, he was a grown man with children older than Nish. Besides, if somebody ain't worth respecting, Gramma always said, then you got to respect yourself. They rode on awhile in silence. Nish was glad he didn't have to talk anymore, but the silence didn't last. Suddenly Buford chuckled softly to himself as if he were remembering a private joke. He turned toward Nish and grinned at him in the darkness to signal the passing of his anger. "Boy," he said, his voice now grown soft and confidential, "where your mama at?"

Nish turned toward the window and drew himself up as

small as he could. He really wanted to get out of the truck now because he sensed that Buford was going to push him too far. It was a dirty game no real man would play with a boy; but Buford had done it before, and Nish knew no way to fight him back short of hitting him with something. Finally, he said, "If you don't mind, Mr. Atkins, I want to get out here and walk the rest of the way."

"Walk?" Buford pretended to be insulted. "You glad enough to ride when it's raining or when I pick you up an' it's cold. Whassa matter? I jest asked you where your mama is." He drove on. "Ain't no harm in that."

"I don't see why you need to know," Nish said. "My mama is at home. In bed. 'Sleep."

"Aw, you know I ain't talking 'bout your gramma," Buford said, joshing him in the ribs. "I'm talking 'bout your real mama. Man, I sho' would like to know," he insisted. "She was one good-looking woman! You ain't never gonna look as good as she do, wherever she is at," he said, reaching over again and slapping Nish on the thigh as if to force him to join in the joke. Nish waited a second trying to control himself until Buford moved his hand. When Buford began gently squeezing his leg instead, Nish flung his hand aside with such force as to frighten the older man and make the truck swerve to the far side of the road.

"Ain't no use to git your ass up on your shoulders," Buford complained when he got the truck back under control. "All I said was you got a good-looking mama. Ain't nothing wrong with that. I'll say *that* again."

"And you got a good-looking daughter," Nish blurted out. "And ain't nothing wrong with that." Nobody said anything after that. In a few minutes they came to the corner where Nish got off to go to Mr. Gilligan's. Buford halted the truck and Nish got out; then he gunned the motor and drove off without waiting to see if Nish was going to thank him for the ride. As for Nish, his heart was pounding with excitement and remorse. He had hurt Buford without really intending to. He didn't know why the words came out as they did; they just came—up and out. He didn't know either that Roxie Lee Atkins, Buford's fifteen-year-old daughter, was six months pregnant. But Buford did. It was still dark, and Nish was glad he couldn't see the expression on Buford's face. He was sorry he had said what he did about Roxie Lee—he didn't like being smart with adults, even stupid ones like Buford—but Buford had it coming. And anyway, what was done was done, and there was no way he could call back the words. He was a few minutes early, thanks to the ride, so he sauntered along the edge of the yard toward the little dairy in back of Mr. Gilligan's house. Mr. Gilligan was pouring the morning's milk over a big tin cone filled with ice, to cool it. After that he caught the milk in thick glass bottles of varying sizes and capped them with paper disks. Nish pushed the door open behind Mr. Gilligan and stepped inside the little milk house. He was still trying to put Buford Atkins out of his mind when Mr. Gilligan snapped at him without even turning to see who had entered. "Well, good afternoon!" he barked as sarcastically as he could. "Well, hell, come on in! Don't just stand there in the door letting the flies in. Hell, we got enough flies in the world without you inviting more. Shit! Shake the lead out of your butt and get that milk loaded. We ain't got no time to be dreaming. Hell! Let's go! Hell! If you got the dreamie-weemies, I suggest that you go on back home and dream in the bed. *I* can't do that. *Me*, I got to work for a living!"

Nish picked up one of the big wire crates filled with twelve quarts of fresh milk and carried it out to the Ford pickup waiting in the driveway between the dairy and the barn. His intended "Good-morning!" to Mr. Gilligan had been lost in the white man's tirade. But Nish didn't mind particularly. He was accustomed to Mr. Zebbie Dee's fits of ill temper. Being mad in the morning was a part of his preparation for the day. Screaming and yelling all over the place, that was just his way, and most times the people who worked around him didn't pay him any attention at all after they got used to it. But Nish didn't like to be screamed at, or cussed at, and although he knew Mr. Gilligan probably didn't mean any harm, he wished he would act more like Fess McClain at the Academy or some of the other white men he had come to know.

By the time all the milk had been loaded into the pickup, dawn was breaking over the east side of town beyond the waterworks. The east side was precisely where Nish was wanting to go, but it would be an hour before they worked their way over to Mason Lane, where Coy lived. As he settled in the old Ford beside the hulking form of Mr. Gilligan, Nish had finally forgotten Buford and the unpleasantness of their exchange a half hour earlier, but the constant stream of words that came from the white man passed over him like a rainstorm over an underground cavern. Mr. Zebbie Dee was given to telling off-color jokes, and most of the time the butt of his jokes turned out to be colored people. As they drove along, Nish vaguely heard the white man saying something about a "nigger who was so ugly his face hurt," but the joke never really registered. Nish's mind was on Mason Lane, and over and over in his mind he was repeating to himself:

> Fair maid with flaxen hair,
> I lay me at your feet. . . .

Suddenly he became aware that Mr. Gilligan was saying something to him that required some kind of response.

"Sir?" he came to attention, ashamed at being caught dreaming again.

"What I said was," Mr. Gilligan was speaking in a low voice freighted with his usual sarcasm, "that if you don't care to deliver any milk this morning, why, I'll just put my truck and my time at Your Black Majesty's disposal and ride you around the city of Clayton 'til breakfast time. Then, if you feel like waking up, and if you happen to have energy enough to eat, why, I'll have Maude cook you up a big breakfast of ham and eggs and serve it to you in my dining room! But if you do aim to do some work for the money I'm paying you, then get off your ass and take two quarts of milk across the street to Miz MacIntosh. Hell! I suppose she'd like to have her milk for breakfast sometime before noon! Don't you reckon so?"

By this time Mr. Gilligan was screaming again, and Nish was halfway across the street trotting toward the front porch where Mrs. MacIntosh did indeed stand waiting for the milk to pour over her oatmeal.

"Good morning, boy," she said cheerily. "I'm here a-waiting on you—waiting on the milkman! You have to get up mighty early to miss me, don't you, boy?"

"Yes, ma'am," Nish agreed. "Mighty early."

"Well, here's what I owe you for last week," Mrs. MacIntosh said, handing him some money in a folded-up envelope. "Now you go straight on and give it to Zebbie Dee, you hear me?"

"Yes, ma'am," said Nish. He took the envelope and trotted back to the truck.

Mr. Gilligan took the money and crammed it into his pocket. "Hot damn!" he exclaimed. "Good as gold and right on the minute every week. Why, that old woman is the only person in Clayton City who gets out of bed early to pay her bills! It ain't much; but she pays on time, and that's more than you can say for most folks. Mighty few white folks and no niggers a'tall go to any trouble to pay you what they owe you! That right, Perfessor?"

"Yes, sir," said Nish. He was glad that Mr. Gilligan had forgotten to be mad for a moment.

After they left Green Street, where Mrs. MacIntosh lived, they worked the neighborhood south of Courthouse Square and then headed east. They passed the Clayton City Dairy truck twice while they were delivering on the Southside. Mr. Gilligan always waved at the Clayton City man and passed the day with him, but he said privately that Clayton City milk was contaminated and ought to be kept off the streets. Clayton City Dairy controlled about eighty percent of the dairy business in Clayton, supplying all the stores and most of the homes. Mr. Gilligan and another small home dairy owned by Jack Poindexter divided what was left. The Clayton City Dairy was run by the Butler family, but Mr. Zebbie Dee said they were fronting for a Jew syndicate from the North. He often blamed the Jew syndicate for whatever annoyed him at the moment, like when Mr. Billy Henderson lost the election for mayor. Mr. Gilligan said the Jew syndicate had bought and paid for the opposition. Once Nish asked what the Jew syndicate was, but the only answer he got was that they were a bunch of foreigners trying to invade the South and stir up trouble. They were the ones who owned those old mills in North Clayton, and everybody knew they wanted to open them up again. He warned Nish that he'd better stay away from them if he wanted to keep his job. Nish wasn't bothered about losing his job on that account. He didn't know anything about Jew syndicates, and if they had any boys his age, he hadn't met them.

The sun was bright now, and the streets were beginning to come alive as Mr. Gilligan finally swung the old Ford truck into Mason Lane and headed for the McCoys', the only customer they had on Mason. It was a pretty long drive out to Mason Lane, out past the white folks' cemetery and almost to where the new highway was being cut through to the state line. To Nish, the drive seemed longer than ever. He fumbled with the poem folded tightly in his pocket and worried about whether Coy would come to the door for the milk or whether she might be asleep. Or her mother might come out to speak to Mr. Gilligan, as she sometimes did. He worried, too, about whether he would have nerve enough to give the poem to Coy, even if everything else went off all right. The hand gripping the poem in his pocket began to sweat and to be clammy. He withdrew it and examined it absently, his mind still racing with all the possibilities that would shape the next few minutes of his life.

Mr. Gilligan saw him looking at his hand. "What's wrong with it?" he demanded. "It ain't worth a damn for holding milk bottles, that's for sure, but I betcha it'll still hold a pork chop!" He guffawed at his own humor. "Hot damn!" he exclaimed. "There ain't nothing in this world a nigger likes more'n a pork chop, unless it's two pork chops and a sweet potato!"

Nish winced. He had never thought of himself as a nigger. He was colored, but that was different. Ordinarily he paid no attention to Mr. Zebbie Dee's gibes, but for some reason the word "nigger" struck him this morning in a way it never had before. Niggers and pork chops, he thought to himself. I guess they're supposed to go together. In his pocket the poem he had spent almost a day writing and polishing suddenly seemed foolish and unimportant. Flaxen hair, niggers, and pork chops—they didn't go together, and probably never would. He felt like dying. Maybe he really ought to be thankful to Mr. Zebbie Dee for keeping him from making a fool of himself.

The white man sensed that something was wrong with the black boy on the seat beside him, but it never occurred to him that he was in any way involved. He had forgotten what he said to Nish about niggers and pork chops even before he said it, and even if he had thought about it, he could never conceive of such a statement giving offense to anybody. Most niggers were all right in their place. They couldn't help being niggers. He looked closely at Nish.

"Nish, you sick, Perfessor?" he said.

"No, sir," Nish said flatly. "I think I was, but I'm not sick anymore!"

"Hot damn!" said Mr. Gilligan. "You got what they call rabbit fever. It comes and goes. It comes when you come and goes when you go! Now that ain't no ordinary ailment. Nothing but preachers, perfessors, and bootleggers can manage to have that. Boy, you're something! Why, I once knew a colored woman to have rabbit fever and she looked like two baboons trying to mate!"

They had come to the McCoys' house. It was on the far side of the street, a modest clapboard bungalow standing on the side of a low hill. To get to it, you had to climb a flight of concrete steps from the street level and go down a short walk to the steps of the front porch. Nish took a quart of milk from one of the crates in the back of the truck and started across the street. Mr. Gilligan got out a cigarette and pushed the automatic lighter button on the dashboard and got out of the truck to count the remaining bottles of milk in the back. They were almost through, and only a dozen or so bottles were left. In just a few minutes now he could sit down to Maude's hot biscuits and scrapple before going off to work in Otis Spencer's commissary off Courthouse Square. He got back into the truck, leaned back away from the steering wheel, and closed his eyes while a gray-blue cloud of smoke drifted from his nostrils and wafted itself out the window.

In the meantime, Nish struggled with the crisis Mr. Zebbie Dee's remarks had introduced into his own life. He had always been vaguely aware that white people and black people were somehow different. He didn't know how they were different, or exactly why, but there always seemed to have been a kind of general understanding that being black was not the same as being white. Nobody ever had to tell you. It was an understanding that came with existence. But in the day-to-day business of living in Clayton, Nish had seldom been faced with the full implications of what it meant to be black instead of white. Until he was eleven or twelve, he had played with white kids and black kids—anybody who wanted to play, whatever race or sex—and there had been nothing said or done to make him feel a limitation in his blackness. Now, as a teenager, it was true, now that he thought about it, almost all of his friends were black, like himself, and his only remaining contact with white boys was at the swimming hole under the railroad trestle two miles out of town. Even this was not always peaceful. There were frequent fights with one group chasing the other out of the water or wetting each other's clothes and tying them in knots. But this was, on the whole, a not unfriendly kind of rivalry, and nobody ever got hurt seriously. It seemed kind of the expected or natural thing to do. If the white boys had more muscle on their side, they took over the swimming hole and chased the blacks away. If the blacks were stronger, they routed the whites. Whether you were white or black was just a way of deciding which gang you belonged to and who you had to fight.

Now, suddenly, it was becoming clear to Nish that being white or black involved a great deal more than that. Twice within a few hours he had been told in effect that to be black was to be automatically considered less than a man. Maybe less than human. Buford Atkins's words haunted him: ''Show me a nigger what'll tell a white man he got some personal business and I'll show you the tree where they hung his ass.'' Now, right after that, Mr. Zebbie Dee comes along and makes his remark about niggers and pork chops. He had never before been stung by anything Mr. Gilligan had said. Everybody—Mama Lucy, Maude, even Mrs. Gilligan herself—had given him to understand that whatever Mr. Gilligan said that might be offensive to colored people if it was said by someone else was not to be taken too seriously if Mr. Gilligan said it. That was just his way. Mr. Gilligan *had* to like colored people, because he dealt with so many of them, and more than once he did things for them he didn't have to do. For example, Mr. Gilligan would more than likely slip them a little extra food when they came into the store if he thought they needed it—a piece of salt pork here, a bucket of molasses there, or maybe an extra pound or two of cornmeal. And he always outfitted Nish for school at the beginning of September, driving his Ford pickup down the alley behind the store before sunup and bringing out the carefully wrapped packages of blue denims, long johns, and brogan shoes he had stashed aside the evening before. Nevertheless, he called all of the colored people who did business with him "niggers," even those he befriended.

They said it was just his way, but now Nish was not quite so sure. Maybe Mr. Zebbie Dee had been trying to tell him and all the others something in his way all the time: that they were all niggers and that there was nothing in the real world for a nigger to do except the white man's work and to provide for the white man's amusement and gratification. And maybe doing a little for the niggers now and then, even stealing for them, was only a way of showing how helpless they were and how powerful he was. Sometimes Mr. Zebbie Dee acted like he thought he was God. Nish thought about how Mr. Gilligan often came into the kitchen and stood behind the table where Maude gave him his breakfast after the milk had been delivered. "Hot damn!" the white man would say. "Why Maud, look at that nigger eat! Here, give him some more!" and he would scoop more grits onto Nish's plate like he was fattening a shoat, or something. Now Nish knew why: To Mr. Zebbie Dee, at least, niggers and shoats were not substantially different. That's why niggers and pork chops belonged together.

If pork chops and niggers belonged together, where did

love and poetry fit in? Nish felt foolish now when he thought of the poem folded tightly in his pocket. For the first time he began to see Coy as a *white* girl, not just some beautiful apparition with flaxen hair who happened to be in the same grade as he—albeit in a different school far from the West Side of Clayton and where no black kids had ever been allowed to attend. Why hadn't he thought of it? She was not a nigger, and he was—that's why they were separated in the first place. They were not just blocks apart or miles apart; they were worlds apart. She would never see him run for a touchdown or hit a home run or play Othello, or any of the things he wanted to do to impress her, because he was just somebody who went together with pork chops and sweet potatoes. Now it was clear what Miss Edgarson at the Academy had in mind when she had once assembled the football team in her office to pray for Christian success and to advise the boys that when they went abroad in the city, to "avert the eyes should they encounter temptation." They had laughed at Miss Edgarson for her quaintness, but nobody had really understood what she meant. They thought she had pilfering in mind. But now that he recalled it, Mama Lucy had been even more explicit in her warning to him. Shortly after he had turned fourteen, one day while commenting on how big and tall he was, she abruptly ordered him to stay away from downtown unless he had business there. When he had business there, she told him, "Go and do your business and come on home. And don't pay no 'tention to the white trash you see down there flouncing around with long hair and short dresses." He hadn't thought of it before, but his gramma and Miss Edgarson had been trying to tell him the same thing, each in her own way. Was it the same thing that Mr. Zebbie Dee was trying to tell him in his own way? And what of Fess McClain? He was smarter than most people, but he had never said anything at all to make Nish think of himself as being all that different. Or had he?

The climb up the embankment to Coy's house was like climbing a mountain in leg irons. His feet were weighted, and the quart of milk he was carrying was burdensome. In all his fantasies before he had imagined Coy's house to be a forbidden castle perched high on some tortuous crag that he must conquer each day in order to hold her hand and keep alive her hopes of rescue. She was a princess shut away from the world by the magic of some evil spell that only he could break. That was why he signed himself the "Black Knight." It was his destiny to rescue the flaxen-haired maiden and carry her off to some happy ever after. Maybe an enchanted house he might build on The Avenue. Now, toiling up the concrete steps, he knew how foolish his fantasy had been.

"Nish!" Mr. Zebbie Dee was hollering after him. "Shake the lead out and get that milk on up there to Miz McCoy! Hell-god-a-mighty, we ain't got all day!"

"Yes, sir!" Nish answered woodenly, and stumbled on up the steps and out of sight of the white man waiting below in the pickup.

There was no one in sight at the McCoy place. Nish was relieved. Coy usually came out on the porch to take the milk in. That was how they had met in the first place. That was a year ago. Sometimes she lingered a minute to exchange stories about school experiences. That was how they got to know each other. Finally, he had written her a poem, and after three or four anxious days had passed, he had written the one he carried in his pocket. He knew now that she was not going to answer him. And now he knew why. He was black and she was white, and somehow that made a difference. All the difference. Come to think of it, they didn't really even know each other. How could they? They lived in different worlds. He had never seen her except on the front porch of her house. Now he hoped he would never have to see her again. She must know how foolish he had been, and probably she had been trying to make him a bigger fool. He set the milk on the edge of the porch and turned to hurry away. As he did so, he heard the screen door open and he knew that he was caught.

"Nish?" He turned slowly, feeling very much like a thief in the night. It was Coy McCoy. It was Coy, standing there in a blue robe and red pajamas, her golden hair cascading down about her shoulders. She stood there with an empty milk bottle in her hand, and she looked very much the princess he dreamed about in his fantasies and wrote poems about whenever he could escape into his other world. And she had called his name! Instinctively he felt at the poem in his pocket: *Fair maid with flaxen hair!* How apt it was, and how true. But now he had doubts about even his other world. He knew now that even his other world was not her world. He was just a nigger, a nigger that went together with pork chops. Mr. Gilligan had said it, and although Mr. Gilligan often played the fool, the fool he played was real. If he wasn't, then nothing in Clayton was real.

"Nish! Please wait a minute," the girl called again, ever so softly. "Please take this bottle with you." He walked slowly back to the porch. "There's a note in it," she said. "A poem. I wrote it for you. I'm not as good a poet as you, but I wanted you to have it."

She handed him the milk bottle, and as she did so, she managed to squeeze his hand for an imperceptible, unforgettable second.

Impulsively he reached into his pocket and handed her the poem he'd written for her. She took it quickly, smiled, and pressed it to her lips for an instant. Then she turned and was gone, her slippers plopping soundlessly across the wooden porch.

Nish stood there for a few seconds, trying to reconcile all the conflicting thoughts and passions that tore at him. For the moment he was sure of one thing: Whatever Buford Atkins had said, whatever Mr. Zebbie Dee had said, whatever the whole world might say about him, they were wrong. His feelings told him that he was a man; a somebody. A poet even! Being black had nothing to do with what he was and could be. And now Coy, the most beautiful princess in the world, had confirmed what he had always taken for granted until today. He shook the note from the bottle and put it into his pocket.

"Nish! Goddammit! You planning to come back anytime this morning? God-a-mighty!" It was Mr. Gilligan. He had climbed the bank and was yelling at him from the edge of the yard.

"Coming!" Nish said, praying silently that Coy was nowhere in sight. He struck a trot and was seated in the truck before Mr. Gilligan could get back across the street. He wanted to sing. To shout. To tell someone what he had just discovered about himself. But quite as suddenly he felt subdued and frightened because of what he had just learned about life. Mr. Gilligan started the truck and swung it around into the pike and headed across town.

"What the hell were you doing so long up there at Widow McCoy's?" he demanded. "Hot dammit! I bet you were up there dreaming like you've been doing all morning."

Nish drew a long breath and looked down the pike ahead of him to where the houses on either side finally converged into one at the horizon. "Yes, sir," he said, "I guess I was. Just dreaming. Just dreaming around about nothing.

Inside the Fort

*T*HE tall, dignified white woman with the horn-rimmed glasses and the iron gray hair looked out over the small sea of black faces in the audience below her and brushed a tear from her soft blue eyes with her white linen handkerchief. These were her people, and they had come to bid her good-bye. Washed and scrubbed and shining, some in gingham or overalls, some in their Sunday best, but all equally dear to her. Some of them had tears in their eyes, too. It was a time for crying because it was a time of parting. For thirty-seven years she had been a part of these people, she remembered, and they had been a part of her. Could it really have been so long? It must have been, for at that very moment she was hearing the gentleman at the podium intone her virtues: "For nigh on to forty years, save three, Miss Susan Harpeth Edgarson has taught us and taught our children and our children's children, opening up to us the grand vistas of truth and learning, without which no people, whatever their color, can enjoy the felicities of our democracy."

The speaker was Angus McVey, the leading colored citizen in Clayton City. Angus had been one of her earliest students, and one of the brightest. From Fort Academy he had gone on to finish Tuskegee, where he became a friend and a disciple of Dr. Washington's. He had made a fine career—returning to Clayton to teach several years at the Academy and then giving full time to the development of his agricultural interests. And there on the other end of the platform, wearing a corsage in her honor, was Angus's lovely wife, Clara Sue. She was a Fisk graduate and had traveled to Europe with the famous colored singers from Fisk to raise money with their voices for that institution. The McVeys were such dear friends, and they had both gone to Fort Academy, just as had their lovely daughter, Sarah. Now Angus was giving the principal address, paying tribute to her years at the Academy. She would miss them when she returned to New England in retirement, but she would never forget their courtesies to her in their lovely home on the Upper End of The Avenue. Nor would she forget the fine example they had set for the others in the colored community of Clayton City. There Angus was again, his rich baritone filling the auditorium with praise of her work: ". . . and I say to you that never in the history of our fair city has anyone done more to heal the rift between the races, to bring God into this community, to set an example of the highest moral standards, to give hope to the generations of our children yet unborn than this gracious, magnificent noblewoman who came to us thirty-seven years ago from the inhospitable but uniquely, superbly productive shores of Massachusetts Bay."

Miss Edgarson smiled graciously at the applause and wiped at another tear. Angus had always had a facility with words. Even now she still remembered bits of the stirring valedictory address he had given on his graduation from the Academy almost thirty years ago. What a fine political leader he might have been for his people—for his country even, if he had lived in some other period of history. Or if only he had not been a black man. Life was so ironic. Actually Angus wasn't black at all, except by designation. His skin was as white as her own, and his dear wife and daughter were only slightly darker. Back in New England nobody would have challenged them on racial grounds. They were a lot fairer than some of the Italians and Portuguese who worked in the shipyards and factories she knew when she was growing up. Her reverie was interrupted by a final round of applause for Mr. McVey. She glanced at the neatly typed program she held in her hand. The Reverend Ruffin Rusoe was scheduled to speak next for the West Side community, and then Miss McAlphin for the faculty. Onesimus Moore was going to read an original poem on behalf of the student body. Onesimus was a fine, bright young man, who was prone to be somewhat adventurous but who had the strong guidance and discipline of his dear grandmother, Mrs. Lucy Lunceford. Yes, there Mrs. Lunceford was, seated in the second row. She was very proud of her boy and had undoubtedly come as much to hear him recite his poetry as she had to say farewell. That was as it should be. The march of progress ought to take the young and the old along in tandem.

After Onesimus, Mr. Butler, the postmaster, would speak on behalf of the city of Clayton. Mr. Butler had not yet arrived, she noted. But there was a chair reserved for him on the platform next to where Angus McVey was sitting. Perhaps he would be along soon. White friends from downtown had visited the Academy from time to time to hear the FACS—or the Fort Academy Chorus—sing the spirituals that colored people did so well. Music was surely their forte, and the Negro spirituals were their most precious heritage. Perhaps arrangements could be made with the new principal to have the FACS sing in some of the New England churches to raise money for tuition scholarships. She must remember to take it up with him before her departure. She would be glad to continue as a kind of "Friend of the Academy," representing its interests even in her retirement. Following Mr. Butler's remarks, it would be her turn to respond and to thank all these dear people for the opportunity they had afforded her for relevance—for the chance to be a part of the coming of God's kingdom through the instrument of education. Then she would accept a corsage from Clara McVey and present the charter of the Academy to her successor, Mr. Roger McClain, who had come down from New York City for the occasion. Then it would be over. Thirty-seven years! Over and done!

Already the relentless clock of history was ticking away. Racing on, it seemed. She could hear the measured cadences of Mr. Rusoe as he thanked God "for this wonderful woman who was sent to us by a benevolent hand to help us roll back the darkness and walk in the light." She hoped that she had somehow been worthy of at least some of the beautiful things that were being said about her. She hoped that she had made a difference. Even a small one. The Reverend Rusoe finished up his tribute to Miss Edgarson, and the program moved on according to schedule. Onesimus Moore drew loud applause and a series of amens from the older folk, who, knowing that he was one of Lucy Lunceford's children, had expected the best of him. When Nish, as he was called on less formal occasions, was about halfway through his poem, Mr. Butler entered the auditorium, followed by Buford Atkins, the post office janitor who had driven him out to the Academy in the mail truck. Mr. Butler did not take the chair set aside for him on the platform but stood in the back of the room just inside the entrance until it was time for him to speak. When he did not come forward, Reverend Rusoe left the platform to escort the postmaster directly to the podium. Their passage down the aisle was somewhat uncertain, Miss Edgarson noted to herself. And Mr. Butler did seem to have a certain glow about his countenance. She hoped he would not be ill. Mr. Butler's remarks were as brief as they were perfunctory. He praised Miss Edgarson as "as fine a Yankee lady as the Nawth has produced or is likely to produce." She had "never given the city of Clayton one minute of trouble," he said, and she could come back to Clayton City anytime she took a notion to do it. He then left the hall without ever sitting down and without speaking to anyone on the platform, including Miss Edgarson.

When Miss Edgarson got up to go to the speaker's stand to deliver her response to the tributes made to her, the whole auditorium stood with her. When the applause finally died away, she gave a short, simple address, as restrained of emotion as she could manage, reviewing the highlights of her years at Fort Academy and mentioning by name some of the individuals who had helped to make those years the most meaningful period of her life. When she could no longer hold back the tears, she stopped talking. Sarah McVey hurried to the lectern to pin a corsage of red roses on her, and Roger McClain came forward to receive a copy of the charter of Fort Academy, dated in 1866. It was her final act, and with it went a prayer that it had all been worthwhile and in accordance with the Divine Plan.

As a matter of fact, Miss Edgarson had had the satisfaction of seeing three complete school generations of colored children enter the first grade and graduate from the twelfth. At least some of them graduated. The standards at the Academy were not at all arbitrary, but Miss Edgarson truly believed that if faith could move mountains, then no matter how limited the child, the requisite amount of faith in God could accomplish miracles of learning. Religion and academics went hand in hand, and Miss Edgarson always said it was doubtful that learning in the absence of faith could have any useful outcome anyway.

Miss Edgarson was of old Puritan stock dating back to the *Mayflower*, and her notion of the mutual reinforcement of religion and learning might well have been taken for granted by anyone who knew anything about the New England Puritan. But if tradition was not enough, four years of professional service in New England Congregationalist churches before she came to Clayton City had set the mold and etched in the pattern. Gentle but firm, gracious but demanding, friendly but mindful of the necessary distance that must be kept to maintain respect and insure authority. She came to serve the colored people of Clayton because that is what God had ordained her to do. As for the colored people of Clayton, they accepted Miss Edgarson like they accepted all else that was imposed upon them by the mysterious white powers which controlled their lives and the circumstances of their existence. That she came to Clayton City on a mission of mercy and in the interest of their spiritual and moral enlightenment and of their intellectual uplift was notwithstanding. In a sense, she could just as well have come to restore them to bondage, for they had nothing to say about her coming. Or going. Such decisions were made outside their community by the people they cooked for or swept the streets for or sometimes by people in far-off places they had never seen, but who, like the white folks downtown, always seemed to know what was good for them. But as it turned out, Miss Edgarson proved to be of such Christian character and development, and so ardent in her efforts to elicit a like behavior from the colored people among whom she labored, she was not only accepted but in time referred to with genuine love and reference as "Saint Sue," albeit behind her back. Miss Edgarson was also called the "BIG SHE," in recognition of her acronym and her status, also behind her back. To her face she was "Miss Edgarson," never "Miss Susan," for she never accepted the prevailing southern custom which made every white woman of quality a "Miss," using her first name, whether or not she was married.

When Miss Edgarson first came to Clayton, she had had little experience with white southerners and practically none at all with Blacks of any description. "There was a Negro girl at Holyoke," she remembered fondly, "who, except for having a dark skin, was no different from the rest of us." Nor could she think of any reason why the colored people of Clayton should be any different, except, of course, that they had been more deprived by the circumstances of their previous bondage. They were, in a word, *unsettled*, and because they were unsettled, their moral and aesthetic sensibilities had had no proper opportunity to flower. That could be remedied with patience and persistence. One of her New England kinsmen named Cotton Mather had said of Negroes almost two hundred years before that "If they be dull, teach them!" Teach them she would, and did: Homer, Virgil, Shakespeare, Scott, Milton, Whittier, Longfellow, and the Bible. Above all, the Bible. As for the white southerners who might object to the alleged waste of time and money teaching Negroes, her mission was not to quarrel with them. In their spiritual blindness they had transgressed the Divine Law and violated the very principles of the human law they had helped to put together and under which they had agreed to live. But justice had prevailed, as indeed it always must; the Union had been restored. The South had been chastened, and Mr.

Lincoln had admonished both sides that they should bind up their wounds. So in the spirit of Cotton Mather and Abraham Lincoln, Miss Edgarson was there to teach and to heal. The war had been over for nearly eighty years. It was time to forgive and forget, and she had forgiven and forgotten. In the long run, her work with the colored people would be a service to the South, to America, and to God. She was certain of that. No one benefits when one-tenth of the population is in the darkness of ignorance. Ignorance is depravity, a special kind of sinfulness.

The years went by, and if the students at the Academy didn't take too well to the classics, they did learn the Bible, and they could recite long passages of Scripture as evidence of their learning. That was understandable, Miss Edgarson reasoned. After all, religion was etched very deeply in the cultural experiences of southern Negroes; art and literature were not. They could communicate with their parents and friends about the Bible, but finding someone to share an interest in Euripides or Sibelius or Titian would, of course, be more difficult. Nevertheless, education is its own justification. In time there would be a vast community of educated Negroes, and then they could share with each other!

On the whole, some of the black children at the Academy got better educations through a superior curriculum and patient follow-up than did some of their white counterparts across town, but if it made a difference in their life chances, or even their personal satisfaction, that difference was not always apparent. A few girls like Sarah McVey and Olivia Johnson went away to college. When they came back by-and-by, they got appointed to teach in one of the isolated county schools for thirty dollars a month for seven months, which was the full school year for the Clayton County colored schools.

The teachers who taught at the Academy were almost all white New Englanders, like Miss Edgarson. There was, for example, Miss McAlphin, a tall Scottish lady who taught mathematics and doubled as librarian. Miss McAlphin had flaming red hair, which she wore cascading over her shoulders like a cape. She spoke with a bit of a burr, and she brooked no nonsense. From the outset she advised her students that if they couldn't get math, they might as well get married. Some took her at her word, but the Academy girls seemed to satisfy Miss McAlphin's math requirements a lot more easily than the boys. And it was said that the more attractive the girl and the more often she went to Miss McAlphin's quarters for special tutoring, the more certain she was of finishing the course near the top of the class.

There was Miss Burberry, who was unique in that she was the daughter of a wealthy Alabama planter, but whose Christian commitment was stronger than her cultural and family affinities. When she came to teach at the Fort Academy, she was disowned and disinherited by her family. And of course, there was Miss Farnham, who came from Boston and who spoke with a brogue so thick that mimicking her was a favorite pastime of the boys who worked in the school gardens to help pay their tuition of $2.50 a month. Miss Farnham was short and full of bulges in spite of the fact that she played tennis practically every day. When she was not playing tennis, she could usually be found wandering around the campus looking for a big purple cat she called Felicia. The campus work crews were under the direction of a colored man named Cunningham, who also doubled in brass as janitor, gardener, shop instructor, and campus wit. Since Felicia was missing every day, it was not beyond suspicion that some of the boys working for Jasper Cunningham may have conspired in Felicia's disappearance from time to time. In any case, almost every evening after her tennis match with Miss McAlphin, Miss Farnham's search for her cat would begin. And inevitably she would find the groundskeeper to ask in her rich Boston brogue: "Mr. Cunningham, have you seen my pussy today?"

And just as inevitably Jasper would answer in solemnly measured tones: "No, ma'am, Miss Farnham, not today!" This curious exchange always left the boys on the work crew doubled up with suppressed sniggles, which exploded into the most raucous kind of laughter as soon as Miss Farnham had waddled out of sight.

All of the women who taught there accepted spinsterhood

as normative, and none had any reason to be disappointed on that score. In consequence, all of their energies were available for their common commitment to the education and uplift of their colored charges, and in the spirit of their principal, they gave of themselves in the name of the Lord. Nish had profited handsomely as a result of this spirit, and now at fifteen he had a perspective on the world that was highly inconsistent with his time and place. This perspective was sharply expanded by the arrival of Roger McClain, who came to be principal of the Academy upon the retirement of Miss Edgarson.

Professor McClain, as he was immediately entitled, came from New York City. His coming to Clayton, he confessed, was an accident but not necessarily, he hoped, a fatal one. He had received a letter at the university he was attending addressed to someone with the same name as his own, inviting that other Roger McClain to apply for the principalship of a missionary school for Negroes in a place called Clayton City, somewhere Down South. He applied and got the job and interrupted his doctoral studies in New York. The rest was history. Certainly it was the beginning of a new era at the Academy. Professor McClain, if he was anything, was different, and he was certain to leave a different impression on the colored people of Clayton City, if he lived long enough.

Neither McClain nor his young wife of seven months had ever been in the South, to say nothing of having lived among southerners. Their notions about proper human relations were as novel as the strange foods they ate or the strange music Mrs. McClain played on her Hammond organ. Two days after the McClains arrived in Clayton, they were paid a courtesy call by Mayor Jody Pickens and Chief of Police Cody Evans at the Faculty House, where they were quartered with several other teachers on the Academy campus. They had heard they were in town, the mayor said to the McClains, and they wanted them to know how glad the folks of Clayton City were that such a fine Christian gentleman had come to help out in training the colored people to be good workers and to stop stealing and lying; to stop fornicating, laying off the job, and cutting and shooting and ice-picking each other to death. But in spite of their natural instincts to laziness, to kill each other, and to steal and tell lies, the mayor said that the colored people of Clayton City got on well with the white people, because the white people of Clayton understood them and took care of them. They would continue to do so, of course. The colored people knew their place and were happy doing what God and nature intended them to do. The mayor said that he and the chief were right satisfied that Professor McClain would cooperate with them in every way in their public and private effort to maintain the fine relations between the white people and the colored people of Clayton City for the good of all concerned. Then the mayor and the chief scratched their backsides and bowed slightly in the manner of southern gentlemen and left Professor McClain to get on with the legacy left him by Miss Edgarson.

Clayton City found out early that Fess McClain had some ideas and plans of his own. In the first place, he was forty years younger than Miss Edgarson. And he was a man. This made the first difference, and a very important one in a small southern town with very distinctive notions about sexual role assignment. But more than that, Professor McClain's philosophy of education made no allowances for the improbables of race and color. He saw no reason why the educational task at the Academy should be different from any other serious-minded secondary school. The procedures for teaching and the preparation for learning were the same. Or they ought to be, and after four years of John Dewey's progressive education at Columbia he felt uniquely equipped to get things moving in that direction.

As starters, he encouraged his teachers and their students to aim at the total integration of all learning experiences. Buying groceries on Saturday was just as valid an experience in economics and math as were formal class sessions in these subjects. Their day-to-day relationships were to be practical experiences in history, civics, geography, art, and the like. A good way to learn about physics and chemistry was not only to read about them but also to have the experience, say, of electrifying a rural home or school or painting and fixing up some of the dilapidated houses the students lived in on the West Side of Clayton City. One could learn a lot about geography by drawing maps of the county which showed the location of schools, streams, rural churches, and farms and then testing the maps for accuracy by visiting these places. One project in civics had to be abandoned when the professor took his senior class to the County Courthouse to observe the trial of a white man accused of keeping a colored worker on his farm against his will. Judge Carson said the whole thing was something drummed up by the same bunch of Communists from out of state who were behind the Scottsboro niggers. He told Professor McClain rather pointedly that he sure hoped there weren't any Communist agitators living among the colored people in Clayton County, because if there were, and if they ever came before his court, as was quite likely, they could expect to do some time. A lot of time. Because any white man who'd stoop so low as to stir up the niggers against his own kind deserved the worst he could get. "You take these negra chillun on back out there and put them to work," the judge advised, "or I'll put them in jail for loitering. And I'll put you in jail for incitement and contempt of court and contributing to the delinquency of a bunch of minors. White and colored don't go to court together in Clayton County." When the professor tried to explain that he was the principal at the Academy and that the nine students with him were there to learn about civic affairs, Judge Carson told him that he knew who he was already, and he was not sure he liked what he knew. But it was time for the professor to know that civic affairs of whatever sort were the business of white people, not negras, and that if the professor expected to stay on in Clayton City, it behooved him to learn that, and in a hurry.

Fess McClain's new-style progressive education got a more sympathetic ear from the county extension agent, a Mr. Wills. Mr. Wills not only agreed to come out to the Academy and talk about how to raise better crops through proper use of fertilizers and crop rotation, he also agreed to give two of the older boys on-the-job training in how to butcher hogs, cure fresh meat, and improve the health of most farm animals. But after one visit to the school the extension agent said that he had to cancel this program because it interfered with his official obligations elsewhere.

Unlike Miss Edgarson, Professor McClain didn't call for much public help from God, but he did demand a lot of hard work on the part of everybody else. Some of his teachers— the first one was Miss McAlphin—quit, but to the delight of his students and the fear and misgivings of practically everybody else, Fess McClain went out and hired black teachers to replace those who left, and the students seemed to take on new pride in themselves and their work.

Nish Moore had come to the professor's attention early, and they had become great friends. In fact, whenever Nish was not working for Mr. Zebbie Dee or doing things around the house for Mama Lucy, you could likely find him at the McClains' quarters in the Faculty House, listening to Mrs. McClain play the Hammond or talking with Fess McClain about the strange new world being opened up to him. Mrs. McClain explained the themes and the movements of the great symphonies to him, and permitted him to play the recordings for himself on her high-fidelity system. At a time when most of his friends knew only the music of the popular radio and jukebox celebrities, Nish spent hours absorbed in the intricate works of Ravel, Bach, Beethoven, Rachmaninoff, and Rimsky-Korsakov. He had always been an avid reader, and now he had at his disposal what seemed to him to be an unlimited library of strange and fascinating books. Fess McClain let him take whatever he wanted home with him to read by the small kerosene lamp that stood on the mantel above the fireplace. There were books by H. G. Wells, John Dewey, Karl Marx, David Thoreau, V. I. Lenin, Max Weber, Plato, Machiavelli, W. E. B. Du Bois, and Carter G. Woodson, the black historian. And when Nish showed Fess some of his poetry, Fess McClain brought back from a trip to New York some books of poetry by Langston Hughes, Claude McKay, and Countee Cullen. These, he explained, were famous Negro poets who lived and wrote in an all-Negro city called Harlem. Perhaps Nish would be as well known as they someday, Fess McClain told him. Nish fervently hoped so. Mama Lucy would be proud of him, and he would be very proud of himself! Practically everyone around home expected him to be a preacher, like Reverend Ruffin Rusoe. Some even thought he might grow up and be a doctor like Dr. Weems or Dr. Tait. But Nish didn't want to be a preacher, and Fess McClain didn't seem to be too impressed by Dr. Tait, although he never came right out and said it. Fess just said that Dr. Tait and the Hippocratic oath seemed to be strangers to each other. His counsel to Nish was that he could be whatever he wanted to be if he was willing to pay the price of his aspirations. Nish thought about what Fess McClain had said. If he meant being willing to study hard and work hard, then he knew that someday he *would* be somebody, and that somebody would be a poet. Maybe even up in Harlem with Langston Hughes and the other great Negro writers.

But there were others besides Nish whose lives took on a markedly different patina because of the McClains. There was Ocie Mae, for example, who came from somewhere out in the country to live with relatives in Clayton City when her widowed mother died of tuberculosis and left Ocie Mae at fourteen to raise two younger sisters. Such situations were not unheard of in Clayton County; but Ocie Mae's relatives had nine children of their own, and it had already been determined that she would have to be hired out to the white folks in order to contribute something to the family economy, which was already precarious before she and her sisters were taken in. Since she had only recently come to Clayton City, the nearest white folks she knew about were those at the Fort Academy, where several of her cousins went every day except during cotton-picking time. Accordingly Ocie Mae scrubbed herself until she glistened, cornrowed her hair in short plaits, put on her Sunday dress, and turned up at the back door of the Faculty House at nine o'clock of a Monday morning.

Audrey McClain went to answer the timid rapping at the kitchen door with some degree of annoyance. She hoped it would not turn out to be another black student, because she had repeatedly announced that as long as she was the principal's wife and the mistress of Faculty House, anyone wanting to see her would come to the front door, regardless of race. The word spread quickly enough, and so did the rumor that the professor's wife was a little bit "off." She was aware of the rumors—and the resistance—but she insisted, and by-and-by one or two of her black neighbors had ventured through the front door to pay their respects. The first had been Clara McVey. But then Clara quickly let it be known that *she* had *always* used the front entrance whenever she came to call on Miss Edgarson. But then she and Miss Edgarson were *personal* friends for just years and years, she explained, and Miss Edgarson always knew what was fitting for people who carried themselves well and deserved respect.

Audrey told Clara that while Miss Edgarson's waiver of custom on the basis of personal friendship was indeed refreshing, she thought that just being human was fitting enough for some courtesies and that being admitted through the front door of the Faculty House was one of them. As a matter of fact, Audrey considered most of the racial customs of Clayton City to be nothing less than barbaric, and the requirement that black people must always use the back door while whites came to the front seemed particularly ridiculous to her.

If colored people were so contaminating or so despicable, why let them in at all? As far as she was concerned, one part of her house was no more sacred than another, and in her native Montana her folks would certainly not have put up with any such nonsense. Anyway, if there was such a big difference between white people and colored people in the South, she had been unable to detect it in the few months she had been in Clayton City—except that the colored people seemed more subdued. But nearly everybody was polite, and everybody moved slowly and wraithlike, as if it pained them, and whether black or white, to speak a simple sentence seemed to take forever as the thoughts unwound themselves through the tortured labyrinth of a mystic drawl. Besides that, it was often difficult for her unpracticed eye to tell who was white and who was colored anyway. Chester Hines, who was the delivery boy for the meat market downtown, was as white as anybody she'd seen in Clayton, yet everybody but her seemed to know that he was colored and treated him accordingly. Then there were the Toomer children at the Academy. All four of them looked so white to her that the first time she saw them in assembly she asked her husband if he was challenging the segregation laws by accepting white students. On the other hand, Nick the Greek who ran the restaurant downtown was several shades darker than a number of colored people she'd seen in the West Side community, and so was the pastor of the white Presbyterian church who had come out to visit the Academy shortly after her husband took it over.

All in all, it was an annoying, demeaning, confusing, un-American custom, and not the least thing wrong with it was that it was inconvenient. If she were practicing at her organ in the parlor, as indeed she was this morning, she had to pass through the parlor and right by the front door to answer someone knocking at the back door. She hurried through the kitchen with a sigh of resignation and opened the door.

It was Ocie Mae. Mrs. McClain did not remember ever seeing her before. "Good morning," she said to the short, dark-skinned girl standing on the kitchen steps. "Won't you come in?"

"No'm," the girl said, "I come to see Miss Audrey."

"Well, I'm Mrs. McClain," the white woman said. "I guess that sort of makes me 'Miss Audrey.' Come in and tell me what you wanted to see me about."

"I come to do some work for you," the girl announced, without moving from the back stoop. "Y'all got some work you want anybody to do for you? I'm lookin' to do some work."

"Well, come in," the white woman said again. She stood aside and opened the door as wide as it would swing as if to give the girl plenty of room to step into the kitchen. Ocie searched the older woman's face, hesitated a few seconds more, and stepped timidly across the threshold. "A little bit further," the woman urged her. "There now! We can shut the door and go into the parlor and have a talk." She led the way out of the kitchen and up the hall to the big formal parlor, which now housed a grand piano and a Hammond organ and Professor McClain's Scott stereo system in gleaming chrome, as well as the glistening mahogany Victrola left by Miss Edgarson when she retired. Ocie followed reluctantly, her eyes and ears drinking in the strange panorama of objects and sounds she had never experienced before. "Now, we can just sit down here," Mrs. McClain said as she motioned toward a small settee, "and you can tell me about the work you want to do."

Ocie sat gingerly on the edge of the settee but bounced up automatically when the white woman sat down beside her. Sensing the girl's uneasiness in what must have seemed to her a very novel and threatening situation, Mrs. McClain tried to put her at ease or to at least assure her that her discomfort was shared by herself. "Oops!" she said. "I should have warned you that the cushions on this old sofa are too soft. Every time somebody sits here they sink down so far they think they're going to keep on going, and they sort of bounce up like you did to sort of save themselves. Why don't you just sit on the chair over there? It's probably more comfortable. There now. Tell me your name. I'm Mrs. McClain.

"My name's Ocie Mae."

"Well, Ocie Mae, you just relax and make yourself at home, and we'll see what we can do to help you. What is your last name? Do you go to school at the Academy?"

"Griffin. No'm."

For a moment Mrs McClain was puzzled. "Griffin-nome," she repeated. "Griffin-nome is your last name?"

"No'm," the girl said. "Just Griffin. My name's Ocie Mae Griffin."

"Oh! I think I see now! Your last name is Griffin, and 'No, ma'am,' you don't go to school! Is that right? How stupid of me. I asked you two questions and you gave me two answers. I'm sorry. I'm kind of slow to catch on, but I'll keep on trying until I make it." They both laughed a little at that, and for a moment Ocie Mae seemed to lose a little of her uneasiness. Mrs. McClain got on with the interview. Somehow her heart went out to this simple black girl sitting there fidgeting with her fingers and waiting for her to make some decision about her future. It was she who now felt uncomfortable, for suddenly she realized that she was involved in a real-life drama of a magnitude she had never known before. She had never hired anybody. At home in Montana the women did their own housework. Besides that, the girl before her couldn't be more than fourteen or fifteen, and it was probably illegal to hire anyone that young anyway. More than that, she hadn't the slightest idea about what Ocie Mae was equipped to do, but she sensed that for Ocie Mae, doing *something* was most urgent. For a moment she wished Roger were there to help her, but immediately banished the very thought as nonsensical. She could handle it herself.

"Tell me, Ocie, what kind of work would you like to do?"

"Anything."

"Anything?"

"Yes'm."

"Well, what kind of work have you been doing lately?"

"I work in the field."

"In the field? Doing what?"

"I hoe cotton. Pick cotton. Cut cane. Plow the mules. I do most anything, I reckon." Here for the first time a note of pride crept into Ocie Mae's voice, and a smile dared to lighten her plain black face.

"You can plow mules?" The white woman gasped. "Incredible! How old are you, Ocie? Did you even go to school?"

"Yes'm. I plow mules. My daddy 'cropped for Mr. Whitney 'til he died. Mr. Whitney had a whole lot of mules. I reckon I plowed about all of 'em, one time or another."

"How old are you?"

"I'm fourteen goin' on fifteen my next birthday. My a'nt Bet says I'm about grown as I'm gon' git, she reckons."

"I see. School. Do you go to school?"

"Yes'm, I guess I mean no'm. I used to go to school 'til my mama died when I was in the sixth. We lived in the country, and I went to school all the time when I wasn't in the field. I can yet read real good, but now I have to take care of Dinky and Dory. That's how come I want to work for you." Ocie was finally beginning to open up a little. More and more fascinated by this child who was already "grown as she was going to get" at fourteen, Audrey, who was only twenty-six herself, and had never been close to a mule, to say nothing of having plowed one, pressed to learn more.

"Dinky and Dory, who're they?"

"My little baby sisters. I'm the oldest one. I got to help take care of them."

"You live with Aunt Betty? Who is she?"

"A'nt Bet? A'nt Bet Griffin. That's my daddy's brother's wife. That's my uncle Renfro's wife and my cousin Robert Lee's mama. Robert Lee goes to y'all's school. Annie Mae, Rosie, Hark, an' Ernie do, too. An' Doodie. He just started. Dinky and Dory, they're too little, but Dinky'll be wanting to go next year, I reckon, if I can help send her," she added, and there was that note of subdued pride and determination in her voice again.

When Roger McClain came home for lunch, Audrey had already made some determinations about Ocie Mae Griffin. She had written them down and placed the sheet of paper under Roger's napkin at the dinner table so that he could see them as he sat down. "Who in the world is Ocie Mae Griffin?" he asked, chewing on a stalk of celery. "Did you have some sort of celestial visitation this morning?"

"No," she admitted. "But I did have a revelation, and Ocie Mae Griffin is it. She's cousin to Robert Lee and Annie Mae Griffin, already over there in your school. And I want her in school, too. She's fourteen and very bright, I think, if you can scrape off the encrustation of plowing mules and being a cropper for some white man named Mr. Whitney. I want her to have a chance. She deserves it."

"All right! Of course, she belongs in school if she's only fourteen. That's no problem. We'll find her a scholarship if necessary."

"Well, of course, I knew you'd say that, Roger," Audrey interrupted, trying hard to restrain her impatience and let her husband work things out in his usual calm and reasoned way.

"But there is a problem. Ocie Mae is an orphan, and there's Dinky and Dory. She feels responsible for them."

"Dinky and Dory? Who're they? We'll give them scholarships, too. None of these people have any money, and I'll just have to go up to New York and see what I can scrape up among our friends and maybe from one of the foundations. You just don't worry about it. We'll find a way to take care of Ocie Mae and Dinky and Dory, too. I'm hungry. What's for lunch besides celery and Ocie Mae Griffin?"

The next day after an interview with Roger McClain, Ocie Mae Griffin enrolled in the Academy in the eighth grade. The work was hard, much harder than she had experienced when she lived in the country, but she worked at her assignments with a single-minded devotion. She learned from her cousins and anyone else who was willing to help her catch up, including Audrey McClain, whom she helped with various chores around the Faculty House mornings and evenings to earn a little money to help take care of Dinky and Dory. In little more than six months she was helping the cousins who had previously helped her, and she was playing simple hymns on the Hammond organ besides, even though she had never seen one, or had a music lesson, before she met Mrs. McClain. She learned to make clothes for herself and her sisters and eventually announced to her friends at the Faculty House that she was planning on going away to college to become a home economics teacher when she finished the Academy. Nobody had any doubt about whether she could do it. Least of all Ocie Mae.

Geraldine Wilkins was another student at the Academy with whom the McClains became personally involved during their first year in Clayton City. Unlike Ocie Mae, Geraldine had lived in Clayton City all her life, and she was due to graduate from the Academy at the end of the spring term following Ocie Mae's enrollment. She was eighteen, and she was also pregnant. The whispers began right after school opened in September, and by the end of the month her condition was hardly a matter of speculation anymore, the evidence being more than convincing. She was, in streetlight parlance, "knocked up," and something had to be done about it. Miss McAlphin, who taught mathematics, decided that since the headmaster didn't seem to be able to see what was quite obvious to everybody else, it was her obligation to inform him. After all, he had a responsibility to the school and to the community, and he had a duty to perform before things got any worse. As a matter of fact, she decided, Geraldine's condition was, or ought to be, a matter of concern to the whole faculty, so rather than speak with the principal about it in his office, she decided on another strategy which would assure the situation the prompt attention it deserved.

One night at the dinner table at the Faculty House, as Ocie Mae was in the process of serving the sweet potato cobbler for which she had become famous, Henrietta McAlphin cleared her throat for attention, took the startled girl by the wrist, and demanded: "Ocie Mae, whose child is that Geraldine Wilkins is carrying?"

"Ma'am?" Miss McAlphin's behavior was so unexpected that Ocie almost dropped the hot dish of sweet potato cobbler in her lap.

"Oh, never mind," Miss McAlphin said, having gotten the rapt attention she wanted from the whole table. "Never mind. You wouldn't know anyway, even if it were you instead of Geraldine." She then looked directly at the principal seated at the head of the table. "Professor McClain," she said pointedly, "have you seen Geraldine Wilkins lately?"

"Why, yes," the principal answered, "as a matter of fact, I saw her this morning. Is there something wrong?"

"Well, not if being three or four months pregnant out of wedlock isn't wrong. Am I to assume that you don't know that she is pregnant?"

"Well, I can't say that I have any direct evidence, not having been a participant in bringing about such a condition, if it in fact exists."

"Well, I can assure you, if you don't in fact know, it does in fact exist," Miss McAlphin shot back.

"Maybe it's something else—something she ate, maybe," Roger gibed.

"She'd be better off if she had," Miss McAlphin insisted. She was not amused. "It's not something she ate; it's something she did, and would probably still be doing if she weren't temporarily incapacitated. You know as well as I do that once they get started, they don't quit until nature takes a hand and stops them. And as soon as they get over the temporary inconvenience of pregnancy and childbirth, they go right back at it. That's why they're in the condition they're in."

"Well, if it's nature that starts them, whoever you mean by 'they,' I guess it's fitting and proper for nature to stop them," Joe Fischer, the economics teacher, chimed in, trying to soften the tenseness he sensed developing around the table. "Hail! Hail! Mother Nature! She turns us on, and then she turns us off again. Whatta fount of wisdom!"

"I fail to see any humor whatever in your remarks, Mr. Fischer," Miss McAlphin said icily. "We've got a pregnant girl in this church-sponsored school, and her presence here is a mockery of all we're supposed to be teaching. It's hardly an example I think we'd want to have set for our less promiscuous students. Now the question is what are we going to do about it, not what Mother Nature may or may not do about it. It's up to you, Professor McClain. You're principal here, and I say it's past time for this unsavory situation to be resolved. Send her home. She would have been expelled weeks ago if Miss Edgarson had been in charge."

Roger McClain folded his napkin and let his gaze sweep slowly around the table. "I think Henrietta McAlphin has a point we ought to consider," he said. "Instead of waiting for nature to take its course, our responsibility is to see that justice takes its course. Miss McAlphin, when Geraldine Wilkins attends your class tomorrow, and when that class is over, please ask her to stop by the office to see me. There are some things we need to discuss. In the meantime, this southern delicacy that Ocie Mae has put together for us this evening is getting cold, and I intend to eat mine while it's hot."

The next day the principal of Fort Academy spent an hour behind closed doors talking with Geraldine. When she left his office, he sent for Billy "Boll Weevil" Mercer, quarterback on the Academy football team. That evening after supper Professor McClain and Audrey dropped in for a visit with the Wilkins family on Acorn Street off the Lower End of The Avenue. From there they swung over to Jones Street three blocks away to sit for a while on the front porch with Ola Mercer, the widowed mother of Billy the Weevil and five other youngsters. Mrs. Mercer was a large jovial woman who greeted her guests with a hearty "Y'all come on in. Billy done tol' me to be expectin' you, so I come out here to try to cool off a little bit to git ready to run my mouth awhile. It's so hot, running my mouth is 'bout all I got the energy to do after I been cookin' an' scrubbin' for my white folks all day! Y'all come on in an' set a spell! Jest set yourselfs down in that ol' swing over there an' maybe you can stir up a little air. I been settin' here in this here ol' rocker, but rockin' it ain't doing nothin' but wearing me out an' makin' me hotter than I was. Now ain't that a mess! Set down, y'all.''

The front door to the little shotgun house was open, and by the feeble glow of the kerosene lamp on the mantel the outline of a porch swing could barely be made out. The McClains made for the swing but Roger managed to trip over what must have been a hound dog, which had been sleeping peacefully near the edge of the porch. By the time the frightened animal stopped yelping, three or four small children were crowding the front door screen to see what the commotion was all about. One of them sidled out onto the front porch and climbed furtively into its mother's lap. It was hard to tell in the half-light of the oil lamp whether it was a boy or a girl.

"This here's Boo," Mrs. Mercer said with a chuckle. "I can't say he's my last one, 'cause that's bad luck. But he's my latest one, an' spoiled to death! I got a passel of 'em back there, an' they done jest about ruint him 'til he ain't fit for nothing but for his mammy to rock him.'' It was easy to see that she liked children.

The McClains stayed an hour with Mrs. Mercer, during the course of which they learned that Boo wanted something more than to be rocked. He had not been on his mother's lap long before he began to fumble at the buttons of her housedress. At first she slapped at his hands and threatened to put him off her lap and send him back into the house. When he persisted in his quest, she finally opened her dress and he nestled into her very ample bosom and began to nurse at her breast. "Now ain't that a mess!" she exclaimed. "Here asking for tit, an' him goin' on five years old!"

"Why is he nursing so long?" Audrey McClain finally asked when she got her voice working again. She was pregnant herself, and suddenly she had visions of a five-year-old pulling at the buttons of her blouse and "asking for tit." Incredible.

"It's mostly my fault, I reckon," Ola Mercer explained. "When Dave went off—that's his daddy—when Dave went off an' I got to be a widder woman—I'm what you call a grass widder—but anyhow, when Dave went off, lil' ol' Boo wasn't but about a year old, so I just put him in the bed with me and never did take him out. So he never yet stopped suckin'! Now, Lord Jesus, ain't he a mess!"

The next morning word had already spread across the West Side that somebody at the Academy was going to be expelled, and the campus buzzed with the anticipation of calamity. The names of at least four or five different students were being bandied about, and even the teachers were not exempt from speculation. About ten o'clock the Reverend Rusoe arrived at the principal's office and asked to see Professor McClain. He was shown in immediately, nervously clasping the brim of his derby hat with both hands.

"Good morning, Mr. Rusoe." The principal extended his hand in greeting and pointed the clergyman to a seat. "This is a pleasant surprise, and very welcome. I was just about to send one of the boys to ask you to come over for a few minutes."

"Uh, yes, sir, Professor McClain. Reverend Rusoe is right here," the preacher said, anxious to get his title properly established with the new principal. "I come right over from the Burning Bush Baptist Church, where I, uh, have the privilege of being the pastor for the last twenty-one years to see if I could be of service just as soon as I heard the unfortunate news."

"News?" said the principal. "What unfortunate news?"

"Well, uh, uh, I'm given to understand that we have at our school here two wayward, misguided young people who have ignored the teachings of God's church and fallen into the way of sin and lust and degradation and who must be rooted out from among the innocents at this God-fearing institution lest this entire generation be counted as a generation of vipers. Yes, it was our dear neighbor, our fellow laborer in the vineyard of grace and righteousness, who came to the parsonage early this morning to tell me what the Lord had laid on her heart."

"Just which one of your beloved neighbors was that, Reverend?" McClain wanted to know.

"Why, uh, Sister Mahalia, of course. Mahalia Crenshaw. A fine Christian woman I'll tell you, in case you haven't met her yet. A guardian of the morals of this community and a pillar of the church, God bless her! If only this community afforded more souls like Sister Crenshaw, how quickly and how magnificently we would rise above our present station in this valley of dry bones and tribulation. Why, Sister Cren—"

"Reverend Rusoe, is that the same lady some of the students around here complain about for getting them into trouble by sometimes seeing more than she sees and hearing more than she hears?" the principal interrupted.

"I have not heard that report." Reverend Rusoe was emphatic. "But I wouldn't be at all surprised if that kind of slander was put out by that element in this community who would do just about anything to confuse the issue of their dereliction. But I'll tell you, Professor, God don't like ugly, and the truth will out. If no man (and I include the women) dares to pull the cover off of evil, then the very stones will cry out. Now I believe that because God said it—not Sister Crenshaw, mind you. And that's why I'm here to offer you my humble services: to root out this evil which has befallen this great institution; to let it be known that things done in the darkness will be brought to light and that the wages of sin must be paid. Amen. That's what the Book says."

"Amen," the professor echoed. "Now, Reverend Rusoe, I'm glad you're here. We're going to root out some evil around here, and we're going to try to turn some darkness into light. Maybe we can even change some of the wages of sin by changing some of its consequences. But I need your help. Are you willing to lend a hand?''

"Professor McClain, you call on me and I'll call on my Jesus. And with Him to support me, I know we'll claim a victory. We'll make clean all that is unclean. We'll make straight the crooked. We'll—''

"Well, that's just what I want to hear you say," McClain said, coming from behind his desk to shake the reverend's hand again. "Reverend Rusoe, you're all wool and a yard wide. You are truly a man of God. Now what we're going to do is have a wedding, and you will have the honor of performing the ceremony.

"Wedding?'' The reverend was startled. "Professor McClain! Surely you ain't aimin' to marry those miserable young fornicators? Sister Crenshaw says the girl is seven or eight months pregnant. We can't do nothin' like that. Why, the church wouldn't have it. I come over here to help you make an example that might save some other young soul from temptation. I can't help you glorify their sin. My church won't have it. That's blasphemy!''

"An example, Reverend Rusoe, is exactly what I'm after. Only I want a positive example. Doesn't it say in the Bible somewhere that if you stumble, you ought not to just lie there and wallow?''

"It says that. It do.''

"And doesn't the Bible say that a person who has done wrong ought to be forgiven?''

"Yes, sir. Seven times seven.''

"And isn't there a story in the Bible about a woman taken in adultery, where Jesus himself intervened and said something about letting him without sin cast the first stone?''

"Yes, sir. John, eight-and-seven. That's what the Scripture says. It says that. It says that.''

Roger McClain sat down on the corner of his desk directly in front of the increasingly troubled and uneasy pastor. He looked earnestly at the unhappy cleric and said in his most confidential tone: "Reverend Rusoe, when you were a young man, were you ever somewhat addicted to the pursuit of girls? Maybe in a kind of heavenly way, perhaps?'' The preacher's face turned ashy gray. He began to perspire, and large beads of sweat formed on his brow and trickled down the sides of his face. Suddenly the man began to tremble uncontrollably. His jaw dropped and his mouth sagged open as if his face had suddenly come unhinged. Surely he could not have heard what he thought he had heard. Not from the principal of Fort Academy. Not from some white Yankee a few months out of Up North. Not from anybody. Nobody had *ever* asked him what he'd thought he'd just heard!

''Sir?'' he managed in a small voice when he could finally get his lips to stop shaking and form a word. ''I don't think I heard you right.''

''I said,'' Roger continued, pressing his advantage, ''did you ever get sort of restless, you know, with your nose open and your tail up and your feet itchy for the trail? I mean, when you were younger, of course. Now I may not have it just exactly right, but I've overheard enough of that talk, and there's enough graffiti in the boys' washroom for me to have a pretty good notion of what it's all about. I believe you know what I'm talking about. Certainly your friend Mrs. Crenshaw would know.'' Reverend Rusoe startled at the mention of Mrs. Crenshaw's name. What a terrible old woman to have strewing lies and gossip up and down the street about somebody else's business. The very thought shook him all over again, and the professor had to put his hand on his shoulder to steady him. ''I don't really want you to answer my question,'' McClain continued, ''because it really isn't any business of mine. Or of Mrs. Crenshaw's, for that matter. But I do want you to think about it, and if in your mind people who fall into such errors merit God's forgiveness as that Bible you are carrying seems to be telling us, then I want you to think again about two of our students who may have been in error but are now willing to make up for it.

''In that passage of Scripture you quoted from John, I believe it also says that Jesus told the adulterous woman that he did not accuse her and that she should go and sin no more.''

The next Friday morning Geraldine Wilkins and Billy Mercer were married at the assembly hour in the auditorium of Fort Academy. Audrey McClain played the organ, Professor McClain gave the bride away, and the Reverend Rusoe officiated. After the ceremony there was a reception in the cafeteria attended by all of the students at the Academy and as many adults from the community as could be spared from the kitchens and yards downtown. Conspicuously absent was Miss Henrietta McAlphin, who turned in her resignation the next day, effective at the closing of the school year. A honeymoon pot was collected, and the newlyweds took a bus trip to the state capital for the weekend. When they came back, Geraldine and Boll Weevil continued in school as before, until they graduated the following June.

Geraldine's misadventure provided a unique opportunity for learning something positive about sex and its consequences. And Audrey McClain, with the help of Constance Carter, the home economics teacher, soon set up a well-baby clinic at the school. It was the only one in Clayton County, possibly in the state. The local churches were invited to help raise money to equip the clinic, and Principal McClain cadged the rest from friends in New York. He also persuaded the Clayton County Health Office to send a nurse out a half day on Saturdays so that the people in the community could come in and learn about nutrition and child care. A few months later Billy Roger Ruffin Mercer made his eight-pound-four-ounce debut into the life of Clayton City, and Geraldine found her destined niche in one of the kitchens off Jefferson Street, downtown. Billy Boll Weevil caught a freight train headed north with a solemn promise to send for his family as soon as he could get a job. And Widder Ola Mercer, now elevated to the status of Big Mama by the arrival of her grandchild, inherited another young un to add to that previous passel that kept her so busy and gave her so much pleasure.

Reverend Ruffin Rusoe preached at Minnie's Chapel down at The Forks of the River the third Sunday afternoon in each month following his regular Sunday morning service at

Burning Bush Baptist. Services at the chapel began at three o'clock, allowing him plenty of time to get there in time for a meal with one of his members and for one or two visits with the sick before returning home after the services were over. It was late September, and the fields were white with cotton as far as the eye could see once you got outside Clayton City. The armies of black laborers who had hoed the fields clean of crabgrass and jimsonweed in the spring for seventy-five cents a day were back now to pick the lint for seventy-five cents per hundred pounds. Can (see) to can't (see)—sunup to sundown, six days a week the rickety old trucks and buses combed the West Side long before daybreak every morning, gathering the cotton pickers for ten to twelve hours in the fields. Black men and black women. Black boys and black girls from six years old to any age still able to drag a sack and rob a boll. It was a phenomenon Roger McClain had read about and heard about, and when Reverend Rusoe invited him to ride out to see the cotton fields and to say a few words at his church, he quickly agreed to go. The clergyman was delighted. The professor would be the first white man ever to grace the pulpit of Minnie's Chapel, the reverend told him. In fact, he would be one of the very few white folks to ever be in that community on Sunday afternoon.

"The folks down here is kinda different," Rusoe explained. "They don't act much like the regular colored folks you been used to around Clayton City."

"What's so different about them?" the professor wanted to know. "My experience has been that people are pretty much people wherever you go. Wouldn't you agree to that?"

"Well, yes, sir, and no, sir," the reverend said slowly, weighing his response carefully as he searched for a fuller explanation of what he meant. "Take me, for example," he continued. "These folks let me come in here and preach for them once a month. That's all right. But they don't want me hanging 'round too much after that, getting in the way or telling them how to run their business. What I mean is, they ain't what you would call bad folks; they just like to be left alone."

"What do they do?" McClain asked.

"Well, mainly they're farmers. But to tell you the truth, I expect one or two of 'em might make a little moonshine now and then. Course, that's been going on for years and years. But then, folks make moonshine all over the county, black as well as white. But it ain't the moonshine what makes these folks so different. It's the history, I reckon you'd say."

"What is it about their history that makes them different from the rest of the colored people?" the white man insisted. "They are colored, aren't they? Or are they Indian?"

"Well, to tell you the truth," the reverend replied, "they's a little of both, I reckon. But they's mainly African, *mean* African. They don't take no stuff. From nobody. Black or white. My daddy used to tell us that a long time ago they had slave hands that wouldn't take no whipping, and if the ol' overseer tried it, they'd kill him like as not, and run off to the woods 'round The Forks of the River and lay out there. As time went along, it got to be so many of 'em and they was so mean that you couldn't pay nobody to go in there and try to catch 'em or run 'em out. Some of 'em married up with the Indians, and some didn't. But they been in there ever since, and don't nobody bother 'em. Even the Law don't go in there!"

The principal of Fort Academy went in with Reverend Rusoe, of course, and he came out again a chastened man. It was not that the people at Minnie's Chapel did anything to make him feel uncomfortable. They were cordial enough. They listened politely to his brief talk about the value of an education for their children, and they clapped a little and said amen! when he sat down, allowing them to get on with the business at hand, the soul-fire preaching of Reverend Ruffin Rusoe.

It was after the service was over that the incident occurred which broadened considerably the principal's perspectives on human achievement and introduced him to a kind of black self-confidence he had rarely seen in Clayton City or anywhere else. When they left Minnie's Chapel, Reverend Rusoe decided to make his customary visit to some member who was sick, or shut in. Deacon Cain wasn't actually sick himself, the preacher explained; but one of his mules was down, and the deacon wouldn't leave her, even to come to church until she was back on her feet. Deacon Cain was like that. "A mighty stubborn man," the preacher said. "Now he'll risk his salvation for what he believes in, and he believes in that ol' mule! But the deacon's a mighty good man," he added as an afterthought. "He's been a deacon at Minnie's Chapel for fifty years, I guess, and he don't usually miss coming unless it's something mighty, mighty serious—like his mule being down."

They drove through the woods for what seemed to McClain to be a long time, only rarely passing a house or any sign of human presence. Abruptly the forestation gave way to open, cultivated countryside, and in the middle of a vast tract of glistening white cotton there was a large ramshackle two-story house. The single track road they were following dead-ended in the front yard a quarter mile away. As they drew nearer, Reverend Rusoe explained that Deacon Cain had built the house himself, adding to it from time to time according to the demands of his family. A lone oak tree towered above the old house like some rugged old sentinel that had been on duty for centuries, its massive branches pockmarked with memories and recollections. If trees could talk, McClain mused to himself, I'll bet this one would have some amazing tales to tell.

They finally drove into the yard surrounding the old house, passing a large vegetable garden near the side of the road. It had cabbages as big as a lard bucket and cucumbers as long as a man's forearm. There were also tomatoes, green beans, collards, okra, and a large patch of turnip greens. "They eat good," Reverend Rusoe commented, noticing the professor's preoccupation with the garden. More fascinating than the garden was the old man who greeted them as they got out of Reverend Rusoe's dusty old Chevrolet. Seated in a cane-bottomed chair propped securely against the oak tree was the blackest man the professor had ever seen. His skin actually glistened like polished ebony, and his teeth, which despite his advanced age seemed to all be in place, were as white as alabaster. His hair, too, was white, as white and as woolly as a merino ram. It gave way along the angle of his jaw to long white sideburns framing his ebony features and ending in a short white beard. The old man had a kind of regal bearing about him that somehow suggested the trappings of royalty and the habit of command. Deeply embedded somewhere in his lineage and in his mien was the bold denial of the appropriateness of his present circumstances. He sat there propped against the tree in the warm sun of the September afternoon, wearing only his long white drawers and a faded deck of blue denim overalls. The deacon kept to his chair and gave a perfunctory wave as Reverend Rusoe ushered the white man toward where he sat. "Come on in, Reverend," he said simply. "Y'all git out and come on in. Who's this you got travelin' with you?"

"Deacon Cain," Rusoe announced, "why, this here is Professor Roger McClain. He's the new president, ah, that is to say, the principal, the head man at the colored school in the city of Clayton, that's who this is travelin' with me today! He done spoke at your church this afternoon, and since you couldn't be there to hear him—your mule being down and all—why, I just brought him on over here to meet our senior deacon. That's what I done! Now Professor McClain here, he comes from Up North—up in New York City as a matter of fact. He's got four or five dee-grees from them big colleges they got up there, and he's qualified to teach anything he takes a notion to and even to preach if the Lord takes a notion to call him. He's got him a wife that plays the piano, the organ, and just about any other musical contraption you can think of. And he gets wrote up in the newspaper near 'bout every time he makes a big speech somewhere. Why, Professor McClain here is—"

"Wait! Wait a minute!" the deacon interrupted. He unpropped his chair and stood up with the deliberate movements of a man who had something to say and who expected to be heard. When he had gained his feet, he stuck out his right hand to shake Roger McClain's. "Welcome, Perfessor," he said, dismissing the preacher and his windy testimonial with an impatient wave of his hand. "Now, Perfessor," he continued, as if they had suddenly been relieved of some noisome presence, "I want you to look all around you. You see dat land? Well, dat's *my* land!"

His long black fingers gently grasping the professor's elbow, the old man waved his free arm back and forth across a vast panorama of land planted to cotton and corn and sorghum. The deacon's intense brown eyes sought the professor's blue ones and held them. "Dat's my land," he said again. "Ain't no mortgage on it. Ain't *nobody* holdin' no papers on it but me! Ain't no rocks in it. Ain't no gullies in it, 'cause I done got 'em all out! You see dat cotton?" He swept the horizon with his arm again. "Well, dat's *my* cotton," he said softly, almost wistfully. "Ain't no crabgrass in it; ain't no boll weevils in it, 'cause it can't be no crabgrass an' no boll weevils where I'm at. I been here seventy-leb'n years an' I done made seventy-leb'n crops, I reckon. Come drought in the summer, come flood in the winter, come hellfire an' tornadoes in between, I ain't *never* missed no crop! I done raised sebenteen boys an' 'leben gals, an' ain't a one of them boys ever spent a night in jail. An' ain't a one of them gals never toted no bundle of joy before it had a name on it to say where it come from. I done wore out me four wives an' I got the fifth one twenty-seven years old in there ready on the pallet waiting for you to leave so I can come on in the house! Now 'scuse me, Perfessor, but what's that the preacher said *you* done?"

Deacon Cain's question turned out to be both rhetorical and predictive of things to come as the professor's name began to turn up more and more often on the lips of people not necessarily sympathetic to his presence in Clayton. The work projects his students carried out in the rural areas did not always sit well with the powers that liked to keep things the way they were, and already the newly installed electric wiring in one rural school had been yanked out in the middle of the night by persons unknown. The county school superintendent immediately cancelled any further cooperation with the lighting program. There had been complaints, too, about a developing "bad attitude" among the Academy students. It was alleged that it was increasingly hard to get them to stay out of school to pick cotton, and with the picking season at its peak things could get critical if all the hands available didn't go to the fields before the fall rains set in. There were open complaints about the new teachers the professor had brought with him from New York, especially Joe Fischer, who was accused by a merchant of "flying around town in his Ford convertible with a carload of niggers of both sexes hollering and laughing and creating a general nuisance." What wasn't said quite so openly was that Mr. Fischer was suspected of being a Jew, and probably a Communist Jew at that. But the heaviest lot would fall eventually upon the frail shoulders of Hiroshi Yoshida, an obvious foreigner, but who was for the moment more of a curiosity than a perceived threat to the Clayton City scheme of things. One thing seemed clear: Professor McClain's new style of dealing with old problems looked more and more like a subtle challenge to the efficacy, if not the morality, of some of the conventional ways of doing things. Rumblings of annoyance from the downtown power structure were already being transmitted through the domestic servant grapevine as a first warning that not everyone was happy about the New York crowd at the colored Academy and that the professor's grace period for learning the local rules was in danger of running out. The mayor and the postmaster and the chief of police had all come out to see him when he first arrived and had given him a conditional welcome along with the ground rules for his success and their support, which amounted to the same thing. But the rumors heard downtown and elsewhere in the county raised some doubts as to whether the Yankee schoolteacher had heard what they said. Perhaps that was one of the reasons Reverend Ruffin Rusoe had invited him to drive with him to Minnie's Chapel that Sunday afternoon. Somebody needed to have a talk with the professor. But then, the professor had his own way about him. He was not an easy man to talk to about what he didn't want to hear, and he was given to asking more questions than he answered.

Hiroshi Yoshida was one of the new teachers who had come along with Roger McClain to help him launch his new experiment in education at Fort Academy. The other was Joe

Fischer in economics. Hiroshi, who had a seminary degree and was the son of a Congregational minister, was at first given the title of school chaplain and put in charge of counseling and religious life. This proved to be a misapprehension of his talent as well as of his interest. Hiroshi's spiritual style did not catch on well at the Academy, and he felt somewhat ill equipped by training and experience to function effectively as spiritual leader for a constituency whose spirit eluded him. But Hiroshi, whose own spirit could only be described as blithe, languished in the chaplaincy for all of two weeks before his fate was redetermined by his friend the principal after a talk about other possibilities. It turned out that Hiroshi's real interests had always been music and art and that although he had come to America to study for the ministry, it was out of duty and loyalty to his father, who presided over a small Christian mission at home in his native Japan and who lived for the day when his American-educated son would return home at last to help him make the mission blossom and grow.

Hiroshi had accepted that expectation as both proper and inexorable, but until his moment of truth was finally upon him, he just wanted to paint and dream. Accordingly McClain let him organize an art department at the Academy, and he put his spiritual commitments on ice until he could return to Japan. In the meantime, it was arranged for the Reverend Ruffin Rusoe to lead religious services at the Academy on Friday morning and to offer spiritual counseling between times as might be necessary on a temporary basis.

The news from Japan was not encouraging. Letters from Hiroshi's older brother, Toru, told how all of the young men of Hiroshi's age were being conscripted and how those who refused service on whatever grounds were routinely shot. It was not a good time to think of going home, even to work in a church mission, so when Fess McClain had invited him to become a part of his educational experiment in Clayton City, Hiroshi leaped at the opportunity. Once he arrived in Clayton City, he was immediately in love with everything he saw or encountered. Color fascinated him, and the people on the West Side came in every shade and hue. Even the people who were supposed to be white were often tobacco brown or turkey red. The white cotton, the red clay, the green woods filled with all kinds of exotic vines and flowers were a source of endless delight, and with his ever-handy sketchbook he tried to capture it all. Because he liked people so much, he never noticed the stares he drew when he ambled along the streets of downtown Clayton gawking with friendly anticipation at the strange world of color he saw there in the people, the animals, the gardens, and objects. Hiroshi was happy, and although he sometimes felt a twinge or two of guilt when he thought of his father waiting for his return to help with the mission, those twinges were always allayed by the probability that his American seminary degree would count for nothing at home in Japan, and he would almost certainly be hustled into the military should he return home.

Hiroshi quickly became the most popular teacher at the Academy, practically losing his professional identity as well as his racial identity in the process. Barely five and a half feet tall, and weighing about 120 pounds or so, he was towered over by most of those he taught. At first the students were somewhat hesitant, not knowing exactly where he was to be fitted into the rather rigid racial scheme of things in Clayton City. White folks they knew, both real and po' white trash. And although only a few of them had any direct relations with the handful of Indians who lived in the county, the Indian presence was common enough, and the proper attitudes toward them were well established in the local conventions. But probably nobody in Clayton City, white or black, had ever even seen a Japanese, and there were no guidelines for dealing with them. None of this bothered Hiroshi. He loved people the way he loved art and music, and his own openness and spontaneity simply would not be ignored. In practically no time at all "Hiroshi" was shortened to "Hero," and he was seldom without an entourage wherever he went. His students were concerned about his diminutiveness and promptly set about trying to fatten him by sharing with him the lunches they brought from home—or by taking him home with them on occasion. Before he came to Clayton, his diet had run to such things as crisp green salads and fresh fruits with an occasional bit of raw fish. He was soon introduced to ham hocks and turnip greens, butter beans and rice, and chitlins and cornpone. Hero took to this new gustatory experience with apparent enthusiasm but with no apparent results. He looked as underfed as always, to the great disappointment of his friends.

Hiroshi showed his gratitude by doing sketches of his young benefactors and caricatures of their teachers, including himself. Among the most popular caricatures hanging in the hall that served as an art gallery were sketches of Fess McClain digging in the sewer in cap and gown and Reverend Ruffin Rusoe, Bible aloft, staving off the devil in front of the Burning Bush Baptist Church. His student friends competed for his attention as models, and half the homes on the West Side would very likely have had drawings or sketches by Hero Yoshida had his stay in Clayton not come to such an abrupt and unusual conclusion.

His troubles began when Louella and Gouchie Peebles started having trouble with ha'nts in their house off the Lower End of The Avenue on Porter Lane. Porter Lane wasn't much of a street to speak of, being only a half block long, running off The Avenue and dead-ending in the alley behind Coman's Mortuary. The Peebles' house was the only one on the lane, and it had once been the carriage house for the old Porter mansion fronting on Porter Street, which ran parallel to The Avenue. Gouchie's daddy, Jim, had worked for old Colonel Porter until he died forty or more years ago, and the colonel had left Jim Peebles the old carriage house and a garden plot to help ease his own transition toward that better life in heaven where the colonel expected to resume his relationship with his faithful old retainer. When Daddy Jim died, the carriage house and the garden plot passed to Gouchie. He and Louella fixed it up with a pine floor and a brick fireplace and turned it into a four-room cottage. They had lived there peacefully for twenty-five years until the ha'nts started giving them trouble.

After Colonel Porter died, the old mansion bearing his name changed hands several times, as none of his children wanted to live in it. It was a grand two-story house—classic Georgian, with tall white columns and tall, narrow, green-shuttered windows strung out across a wide veranda on three sides. The surrounding gardens were kept lush and beautiful by Jim Peebles as long as the colonel was alive, but after that the subsequent chain of owners let the grounds fall into decay, and over the years they were claimed by crabgrass, catbirds, and honeysuckle. Eventually a man named Charley Coman bought the property and turned it into a funeral home. He tried to buy the old carriage house, too, but Gouchie and Louella, having fixed it up and lived there so long, figured to stay put. Their children were all grown and scattered, and moving to anywhere had no attraction for them. "Mr. Charley Coman, he say I could git me a house on The Avenue," Gouchie confided to his friends. "But what I want a house on The Avenue for! If I turn my house around from where it sits, I'll be smack on The Avenue anyhow, an' then everybody be coming through my front yard! Like it is, I'm on The Avenue when I want to be, an' I'm off The Avenue when I don't want to be. What I need to move for?"

Hiroshi Yoshida discovered the old Porter mansion one day on one of his roamings about the West Side, looking for something exciting to add to the growing collection of sketches he intended to take back to Japan with him. He often stood across the street from the Blue Flame, sketch pad in hand, recording the life that came and went along The Avenue. At first the people stared at him, but soon they were taking deliberate poses, hoping that he would notice them and maybe give them a likeness to take home. From his vantage point in front of Dr. Tait's office Hiroshi could catch the patrons going in and out of the Blue Flame. And if it happened to be a Sunday afternoon, the strollers out on The Avenue had been to church and were still dressed in their Sunday best, providing an interesting contrast of color and movement against the drab background of Mr. Gallimore's little café.

It was late fall, and the sun was partially behind him. As he shifted about to take advantage of the light, Hiroshi suddenly noticed for the first time the bold white and green gables of the Old Porter mansion standing starkly among the elm trees and sycamores which shielded it from the alien life of The Avenue a short block away. His restless curiosity aroused, Hiroshi folded his sketchbook, crossed The Avenue, and made his way through a gap in the thick barrier of second-growth trees and bushes that marked the entrance to Porter Lane.

It was a little like entering the back side of a new world. The imposing façade of the Porter mansion dominated the view, of course, even from the rear, but the only structure on the lane itself was the converted carriage house. A small porch had been built against the center of the front side of the house for summertime sitting, and three slat-bottomed rockers with fat cushions were spaced out across it in anticipation. Gouchie Peebles was digging potatoes in the little garden beside his house when the diminutive Hiroshi suddenly appeared with his sketchbook and easel.

"Hello! Hello! Mr. Garden Man," he said with a wide, toothy grin. "I am Hiroshi Yoshida. Also Hero to my friends. Please, what is your name?"

Gouchie had not seen him come up. He straightened up and pressed his back into alignment again with his left hand while he looked at the little brown man with the warm, friendly voice. He liked him right off. "My name's Gouchie," he said, still staring. "Who you say you is again?"

"Hiroshi! Hi-ro-shi!" came the answer. "Please call me Hero. I am sorry my name is complicated for you. It is too difficult. Please say Hero to me, Mr. Gouchie, and let us be friends." He advanced a few steps into the garden to shake hands with the tall black man, and Gouchie dropped the garden fork he was still holding in his right hand and reached around a dead tomato bush to take the small brown hand reaching out for his.

By the time Louella got home from church Gouchie and Hero had become fast friends. They were both gentle souls, and there was a mutual fascination that drew the hulking black man in hobnails and overalls and the little art lover from the other side of the world toward each other. Gouchie told Hero all about the old Porter place and how his daddy, Jim, had waited on the old colonel until he died. He walked his new friend down the alley behind the old mansion and back up Porter Street so that he could see it from the front. The gardens had not been restored, but since Mr. Coman had bought it and turned it into a funeral home, the mansion was beginning to look something like it did in former times. The only thing wrong was that Mr. Coman didn't have anywhere to keep his hearses, so he wanted to buy Gouchie's house so that he could reconvert it into the old carriage house that originally went with the mansion.

After their first meeting Hero came often to do sketches of the Porter mansion, or the converted carriage house, or just to sit and talk with Louella and Gouchie. He liked to pick the green vegetables still left in their garden and eat them fresh from the earth, and Louella was always cooking something exotic in the big kitchen at the back of the house and not letting him leave until his small stomach protruded like he'd swallowed a cantaloupe. In return, Hero brought them exotic teas from Japan and filled the walls of their living room with sketches and paintings of all the exotic objects and people and landscapes that made his life in America so exciting. He held them spellbound with simple stories about life and culture in Japan and promised to send them souvenirs of all he had talked about when he went home again. But the Peebleses had already come to dread the time he'd be leaving, for to them he had become the son of their old age, a blessing sent by the Lord to comfort their declining years— sent to them all the way from a world they'd never heard about before.

That was about the situation on Porter Lane when the ha'nts or spirits, or whatever they were, infested the Peebles house and started giving them trouble—a whole lot of trouble. Gouchie didn't go to church much and hadn't given much thought to ha'nts and spirits one way or the other. Louella went to church "every time the bell rang and the door swung open," her husband said, but Louella believed all good Christians were immune to any harm that dead folks could do. So while she believed in spirits— "God is a spirit, you know; it says so in the Bible"—she had no reason to feel vulnerable or concerned. And then it happened.

It was a cool fall evening, and Louella and Hero and Gouchie were sitting on the front porch, enjoying the fat-cushioned rockers after a good Sunday dinner of baked guinea hen and cornbread dressing. Suddenly the lamp in the living room took off and smashed against the floor. Thinking a stray cat must have gotten into the house, Gouchie leaped up and hurried inside to chase it out before it did more damage. But as soon as he entered the door and reached for the wall switch controlling the ceiling light, something smashed against his head, and he staggered back onto the front porch.

"What's the matter, Gouchie?" Louella demanded as she leaped up to steady him. "What's the matter? You want me to get Dr. Tait?"

"Something hit me," Gouchie said. He sounded more puzzled than hurt as he sank down into his rocking chair to sort things out. "Something hit me 'side the head. It don't hurt much, but it stunned me a little. I'm gon' see what it was." He got up and reached inside the front door again and flicked on the ceiling light. At his feet near the door lay the family Bible. That must have been what hit him on the head. Across the room on the floor near the fireplace was what was left of the porcelain lamp he had given Louella years ago when they first got electricity. It had been knocked from the mantel and shattered against the brick hearth. He walked on into the room, followed by Louella and Hero, who were anxious to see what had happened. Gouchie picked up the Bible and laid it on the end table by the davenport. Suddenly the lights went out again, and there was the distinct sensation of things flying through the air in all directions, like bats in a dark cave. Hero, who was last to enter the room and nearest the door, instinctively reached for the wall switch, but light flooded the room before he could touch it. A cushion from the sofa was lying against the wall on the far side of the room. An umbrella which always stood in the corner behind the door was lying in the hallway, ten or twelve feet away, and the Bible was lying on the hearth near the broken lamp. All this had occurred in the space of a few seconds.

"Oh, Lord, have mercy! Look at that, Jesus!" Louella exclaimed. "Come on, y'all, let's get away from here 'cause something here ain't right!"

Hero crossed the room and picked up the Bible. "How can this be?" he said as he examined the book. "It was on the table, Gouchie. I myself saw you put it there. This is very strange!"

"Well, it may be strange," Gouchie said, "but I aim to find out what it is. One thing's for sho', bet' not be nobody messin' 'round in this house, 'cause I ain't gonna stand for it. I'm gettin' ready to search every room in this house, right now!" He reached for the long iron poker resting against the fireplace to arm himself, but suddenly the air in the house seemed to quiver as though someone were shaking a bowl of Jell-O. The poker stood out from the wall, at first leaning at crazy angles like a nail between the poles of a horseshoe magnet. Then suddenly it began to vibrate violently, dancing about the hearth, then taking off through the air, it flew around the room end over end and crashed through the window and out into the night. Immediately the air stopped quivering. It was as though whatever might have been present in the room had escaped through the shattered windowpane. Louella had crumpled into a heap on the living room floor the moment the poker had detached itself from the fireplace wall. Hero helped Gouchie lay her on the sofa and ran across The Avenue to get Dr. Tait.

When the doctor arrived a few minutes later, Louella had recovered somewhat and was sitting up on the sofa, staring into the emptiness of the fireplace. Dr. Tait checked her over for bruises and, finding none, decided that except for a high pulse rate caused be extreme fright, she was all right. Gouchie explained what had happened and asked the doctor if he believed his house was ha'nted. "It may be," the doctor said cryptically, "but not by anybody dead." He then declined Louella's suggestion that he help them search the premises, saying that that was the job of the Law. Then he picked up his satchel and went back to the swing on his porch across The Avenue. Gouchie and Hero searched the other three rooms of the old carriage house but found nothing amiss. With the help of a lantern they found the iron poker sticking in the ground about thirty feet from the broken window through which it had flown. They left it there for the police to see and went back inside to check on Louella. She had fallen into a deep sleep on the sofa, so Hero said good night and made his way back to the Faculty House at the Academy.

The next day the word had spread all over the West Side that Louella and Gouchie had ha'nts in the old carriage house where they lived. The police had come out and searched the place and found nothing but a broken lamp that had probably fallen off the mantel, and an iron poker some one had left sticking in the ground in the side yard. Chief Evans dismissed the whole thing as "probably somebody's imagination from inside a whiskey bottle." But neither Louella nor Gouchie drank whiskey, and while folks were a little uncertain about Mr. Hiroshi, they had to admit that he didn't look much like a drinking man. Then what *was* the trouble? Louella and Gouchie had lived in the community all their lives, and nobody ever remembered either of them to ever cook up a bunch of outright lies about anything. They were just regular people, working every day like everybody else and minding their own business living back there on Porter Lane by themselves.

Speaking of Porter Lane, there was that big funeral home backed up to their property—Coman's Mortuary—and people began to speculate whether some white ha'nts from the funeral home might be trying to run the colored people away from their home back there. And what about living in that old carriage house anyway? Maybe old Colonel Porter didn't like the way they'd changed it around and made a regular house out of it. Or maybe some of his dead descendants didn't want them in there. And didn't the old folks use to tell a story about a slave being whipped to death out in the carriage house by his red-necked overseer? Maybe the dead slave wanted somebody to tell the colonel so he could rest in peace. Maybe that was it. Anyhow, *something* was going on. Something mighty funny. *Mighty* funny!

In spite of the Sunday night happenings and the speculations about them, nothing else unusual took place at the Peebles house until the end of the next week. Gouchie stayed home on Monday to be on hand for the police. But on Tuesday, and every day for the rest of the week, he went to his job at the brickyard, and Louella went to hers at the Clayton Star Laundry. When they came home in the evening everything was in place as if they had never had any trouble. But on Saturday morning things heated up again, and word spread rapidly around the colored community that ha'nts and spirits had taken over the Peebles house in broad daylight. Lucy Lunceford was busy sweeping her front porch when Mahalia Crenshaw stopped by to tell her what was going on.

Now Mama Lucy didn't believe in ha'nts, not actually having seen one for herself. She had heard tell of people who had "seen something" or who *thought* they'd seen something, but nobody in Clayton had ever stood up to her face and told her they'd seen a ha'nt without backing down and admitting that they didn't know *what* they saw if indeed they'd seen anything at all. Folks are prone to tell lies anyway, Mama Lucy said, and the folks with the biggest mouths tell the biggest lies, and Mahalia Crenshaw had a big mouth so she had to be a born liar. Here she was now standing on the front porch telling Mama Lucy that Old Man Jim Peebles—dead and buried for lo these many years—had come back to ha'nt his own house and was throwing teacups and plates and such at his own chillun. "Ain't no way you can get me to believe Jim done anything like that," she said to Mahalia. "Them people over there on Porter Lane tryin' their best to live decent like Daddy Jim taught 'em, and if anything is wrong over there, it's just some jackleg up to some kind of devilment. You can put your foot down on that! There ain't no such-a-thing as a ha'nt, and you know it well as I do. And even if there was, Jim Peebles wouldn't be one 'cause he had too much sense for that kind of foolishness. Now I got my work to do—and if you had anything worthwhile to do, you wouldn't be standin' here wastin' my time!"

Mahalia tried to interrupt, but Mama Lucy urged her toward the steps by making sweeping motions with her broom. "I ain't comin' over there," she said with finality, "because there ain't nothin' to it."

Mahalia limped across the front porch and down the wooden steps and across the front yard. When she was safely into the street, she turned around and said: "Lucy, God knows I don't aim to 'spute your word or git in no kind of argument with you. But I just now come from over there, and God knows that house is *full* of ha'nts! I seen it with my own eyes!"

"Ha'nts your foot!" Mama Lucy shook her broom at her. "And don't put God in it. God don't know nothin' about it. Did *you* see the ha'nts? You were there, you say."

"Naw, I didn't see no ha'nts. But I seen what they did, and everybody said to come git you because you'd know what to do to stop it."

"Well, I ain't comin'. There ain't no such-a-thing as a ha'nt! And the thing to do is for y'all to go on home and mind your own business. Saturday ain't no time for a whole lot of foolishness. Folks got work to do. Go on home, and I expect your ha'nts'll do the same!"

By the time Mahalia got back to Porter Lane the Peebles yard was full of people who had come to see the ha'nts. Chief Evans and his deputy were making their way through the crowd. "Whatever is going on here, we aim to put a stop to it—and this morning!" the chief said, patting his holster. "Now move back, everybody, so you won't get shot in case a ha'nt runs by you and I or my deputy have to take a crack at him." There was some cautious laughter, but not much. Gouchie had had a chair knocked from under him as he tried to sit at the kitchen table to have breakfast with Louella and Hiroshi Yoshida. A cup of hot coffee cracked for no apparent reason and spilled into Louella's lap, scalding her legs, and when Louella ran from the house for help, she was chased by a soup bowl that launched itself at her from the cupboard where she kept her dishes. After that there had been a short period of sustained pandemonium. People coming in from The Avenue to help, or to look, were met with flying silverware, pots and pans, or any other loose objects. As before, the air seemed to quiver or vibrate before some object flew across the room, and the lights flashed on and off even when no one was near the switch.

As the police entered the house, followed by Gouchie and Hero, the door to the kitchen suddenly slammed shut. Just as suddenly it swung open again, and an ironing board which had stood behind the door in the kitchen hurtled through the air, striking the chief in his midriff and knocking the wind out of him. At the same instant a dinner plate grazed the deputy, knocking his cap off and bearing it on through the living room and out the front door. People scattered in all directions to give the ha'nts the room they seemed to require. Gouchie and Hero helped the frightened chief of police to his feet while the deputy ran out the front door, ostensibly in search of his officer's cap. Chief Evans flushed beet red with fright and confusion, brushed himself off, and noticed Hiroshi Yoshida for the first time. "Who the hell are you?" he demanded, fingering his holster in his embarrassment.

"Oh, me?" Hiroshi smiled and extended his hand. "I am Hiroshi Yoshida. I am friend of Mr. Peebles and also Mrs. Peebles. I am called Hero. Please call me that. I am sorry my name may be difficult for you."

Chief Evans ignored the outstretched hand of the little man smiling up at him. "Well, let me tell you one thing, Hero, or whatever your name is," he said. "This ain't your house and you ain't got no business in here. I want you to get on back out there in the yard with the rest of 'em before you get shot.''

"Yes, sir.'' Hero smiled again and backed toward the door. "Where you work at anyway? You don't look like you're from around here.''

"Oh, I am not from here,'' Hero explained. "I am not of this city, which is so beautiful. I am the teacher of art at the Fort Academy. That is where I work, and I have come here from New York with Professor McClain, who is also my friend. To New York I come from Japan.'' Hero smiled, bowed slightly and again extended his hand.

"Japan?'' the chief asked incredulously. "You a Jap? I didn't think you looked like any of our colored people around here! If you work up there at the Academy, I want you to stay up there where you belong.'' As Chief Evans was speaking, the air suddenly began to quiver again and a heavy iron skillet on the stove began to shake and clatter. A few seconds later it rose straight up a foot or more above the surface of the stove, spun around, and sailed through the kitchen window. The chief drew his gun, but by the time it cleared the holster there was nothing to shoot at.

On his way out Hero met the deputy on his way back to the kitchen. He had retrieved his cap, and like the chief, he now had his gun drawn. "Deputy,'' the chief ordered, "go back up there and lock the front door. And tell all them people out there to go on home. I don't want a one of 'em in sight when I come back out there. We gonna git to the bottom of this thing, and I mean rat now.''

"My wife, Louella, she's still out there,'' Gouchie said. "You want her to come in?''

"We don't need Louella,'' the chief replied somewhat testily. "Let her go on off somewhere with the rest of 'em.'' When the deputy returned to the kitchen, the chief ordered Gouchie to open every cabinet and every drawer in the room, while the two white men searched with the guns at the ready. They turned the kitchen table upside down. They looked in the oven, the firebox, the flour bin, and they examined the pots and pans, all without result.

They searched the sparsely furnished bedrooms, looking carefully under the mattresses and between the homemade quilts, in the closets and under the beds. Still, there was no evidence of ha'nts or spirits or anything else unusual. They searched the front room again, going through the Bible several times and shaking it to see if anything was concealed between the pages. Finally, they searched the yard and the vegetable garden, and except for the plate which had grazed the deputy, and the iron skillet that flew out of the window, they found nothing.

Finally, Chief Evans and his deputy got in the Clayton City police car and prepared to drive off. The chief called Gouchie to the car for a bit of farewell advice. "Boy," he said, "if there's anything in your house, we aint' seen it. Now, I don't know exactly what I did see, but it wasn't no ha'nt 'cause there ain't no such thing. Now you been living back here a long time. I knowed your daddy. He ain't never give nobody no trouble, not to my knowledge, and you ain't either. And I don't *want* no trouble, and I don't think you do either. So my advice to you is that if it looks like you gonna have trouble living back here, git rid of this place and move off somewhere else. And keep that Jap away from here. He ain't no kin to you. I don't want to have to come out here no more. Understand?"

"Yes, sir, Chief Evans, I understand," Gouchie said, and went off to find Louella.

The deputy pressed the starter button, and the police car belched into life, turned right on The Avenue, and headed back downtown.

Early one Monday morning a few weeks later there was a loud authoritative knock on the front door of the Faculty House at the Fort Academy. It was exactly six o'clock, Roger McClain noted as he stumbled down the stairs to see who could be calling so early in the morning. When he opened the door, he was amazed to see Chief Evans and his deputy standing on the porch with guns drawn. The Clayton City officers were flanked by two strangers in plain clothes who wore slouch hats and who waved FBI badges in his face before the chief shoved him back inside the house. In the oval driveway there were the chief's police cruiser and two large black limousines bearing out-of-town license plates and more men in slouch hats.

"Step back inside," the chief ordered. "We come out here to git that little Jap you harboring over here. We aim to put him in custody rat now an' I don't mean afterwhile! Now you git him down here, an' you git him down here quick! Move!" He waved his police special toward the stairs. "Move rat now!"

McClain could see that the chief was in a high state of excitement and that he had been drinking. He didn't trust either Mr. Evans or his deputy in the presence of liquor and firearms. Anything could happen with that mix. But the FBI agents could probably be relied upon to provide some semblance of order in the presence of so much Law, he concluded in afterthought. There was no real danger.

"I'm in charge here at Fort Academy, Chief Evans, as I believe you know," McClain said without moving. "Would you mind telling me just why you want to place Mr. Yoshida in custody? What has he done?"

"Well, Perfessor," the chief said, floating a cloud of alcohol directly at the professor's face, "we don't know exactly what he done yet, but we sho' as hell aim to find out. But maybe *you* know. You ain't got that big overseas radio settin' in your living room with all that wire strung across your roof just for no music. Why, it don't take all that to git Nashville. Didn't you have it turned on yesterday when them other sneaky-ass Japs was bombing our boys at Pearl Harbor? We got a war, and it 'pears to me like you been frat'nizing with the enemy. Now you git that little slant-eyed bastard down here!"

At that moment Hero Yoshida appeared at the top of the stairs, rubbing the sleep out of his eyes and trying to make sense of the commotion at the door which had roused him from his sleep. In his oversized Japanese pajamas he looked very much like a sleepy nine-year-old about to stumble down the stairs for breakfast. "Ah, gentlemen." He smiled. "Good morning. I am—"

"That's him! That's the Jap," the chief shouted. "Don't let the little bastard get away!"

With gun drawn the deputy rushed up the stairs and dragged the bewildered Hero down to the front door. The FBI men looked on as he was searched and hustled out and placed in one of the waiting limousines. Then the officers went upstairs to search his room. When they came down again, Chief Evans holstered his gun and confronted McClain once more as he followed the government agents out the front door.

"I expect I'll be seein' you again, Perfessor," he snarled. "The war ain't over yet. Not by a damn sight it ain't! An' I ain't jest talkin' about the one that started yesterday!

When God Messed Over Vernon

*P*ANK HALL came out on the front porch of his house on the Upper End of The Avenue and sat down heavily in the old hickory swing that gave him command of the traffic in the street. There wasn't much, just an occasional straggler late getting out of her white folks' kitchen and headed on down the road to Fairmore. It was Saturday afternoon, and 'most everybody was gone to the ball game in the field back of Bullock's Store down at the crossroads. Or gone fishing. Or gone somewhere. *Must* be gone *somewhere*, Pank mused. There sho' ain't nobody 'round here! In a little while Lizzie came out of the house and sat beside him in the swing. She caught up the front of her dress and flounced it a time or two, trying to stir up some kind of breeze around her legs. It was hot back there in the kitchen, where she had been canning peaches all day.

" 'S hot," she said. "Hot! Hot!"

"Yeah," Pank agreed without enthusiasm. "Sho', it's hot." Then he tapped the floor with his foot and leaned back in the old hickory swing to start it to moving back and forth. Slowly. He didn't have much energy to put out on swinging. But the old swing moved to and fro with a pleasant creaking that seemed for a moment to make the afternoon a little more tolerable.

Pank spent a lot of time these days just kind of thinking about things and wondering what else life might have in store for him. The occasional cooks trudging on to Fairmore and bearing their carefully wrapped pans full of leftovers from the kitchens downtown reminded him that he used to live in Fairmore before he came up on The Avenue. He was lucky, he thought to himself. Five years ago he and Lizzie were living in a two-room shack in Fairmore. Now they had a five-room bungalow, with a built-in toilet to boot—smack-dab on The Avenue!

"We been lucky," he said to Lizzie. "Lucky to be up here sittin' on our own front porch lookin' at the folks go on over the hill."

"I reckon we been lucky, too," Lizzie said simply, joining in his reverie. "We been lucky, but we got God to thank for everything. Everything."

Pank was silent after that. He was ready to admit that they had God to thank for everything, but he was sometimes troubled by the thought that some of the things God sent their way were pretty hard to be thankful for. He was even tempted to think that sometimes God oversported his hand. But what kind of a thought was that? He tensed his ears to try to squeeze it from his mind as he stole a glance at his wife to see if maybe she had heard what he was thinking. But Lizzie was already off on her own private soliloquy. Dozing on the edge of consciousness in the shade of her front porch with the old swing creaking a lazy cadence, she was humming almost inaudibly the lines of an old Negro spiritual:

> If it wasn't for the Lord
> Tell me what would I do
> Tell me what would I do
> Tell me what would I do?
> If it wasn't for the Lord
> Tell me what would I do—
> He is everything to me.

Pank grunted his satisfaction that the slipup in his thinking had gone undetected, and returned to his reverie. Inevitably his thoughts turned to Vernon. Vernon Banks. Vernon was Lizzie's nephew, but from the start Pank had always thought of him as his own son—he and Lizzie not having any children of their own. When they moved up on The Avenue four or five years ago, with nobody to fill up their five rooms but themselves, the first thing they thought about was getting one of Lizzie's sister's children to come and live with them and be company for them when they got to be old.

The way it all came about was that when the word got out that the TVA was hiring people, white and colored, to clear the land for the big dams and reservoirs they were going to build, Pank was lucky enough to be one of the first ones called to get on and to get called up to go to work. Right away he quit his job at the brickyard and caught a ride with Sonny Lee in his pickup out to where they were building the dam, seventy miles away, crossing two counties. Sonny Lee covered over the back of his truck with slabs and tar paper and put two benches in it to hold the eight riders he hauled back and forth with him every day. In the wintertime he put in a charcoal bucket to help keep out the cold. Sonny charged everybody a dollar a day to take them and bring them, but everybody who worked for the TVA was making good money, so a dollar a day didn't seem like too much to pay to get to and from the job. Sonny Lee worked on the dam, too, and pretty soon he built a house on The Avenue and bought another truck and fixed it up so that his wife, Ellie Mae, could haul a crew to the dam alongside him every day. She said it was better than cooking for the white folks, but she soon went to work in a café close to where the men were working to keep busy until time to load up and come back to Clayton City. She made twice as much working in the café as she made when she was cooking on the yard in Clayton City.

Pank rode every day with Sonny Lee from the time he first got on at the dam. They left Clayton City before daylight every morning, and it was past dark when they got back, five days a week. They didn't usually work on Saturdays unless the weather threw them behind, and then they got overtime pay. The weather turned pretty bad in the wintertime, sometimes, but Pank worked all the overtime he could get for three years. No matter how cold or sloppy it was, "If the truck leaves, Pank gonna be on it," he used to say. And he was. That's how he got to be on The Avenue. That's how he got to be where he was today. Working hard and not wasting his paycheck.

Pank Hall reached into the bib pocket of his overalls and pulled out a sack of Bull Durham. Lizzie was dozing fitfully, her arm stretched across the back of the old swing, her head slumped forward above her ample bosom, and her two long plaits hanging Indian-style across her breast and almost down to her waist. "Look at that." Pank grinned to himself. "She's gone for the afternoon!" He rolled his cigarette and eased out of the swing to sit on the edge of the porch. He didn't want his smoke to be a bother. "Just looka there," he said softly, and there was unrepressed tenderness and pride in his voice. He was glad he married Lizzie. Glad he had left the brickyard and gone to work for the TVA, no matter how cold it got and no matter how tired he was every night when he came home. He was glad they'd scrimped and saved and bought a house on The Avenue. Five rooms and some peach trees. It wasn't all that much; but it was theirs, and Lizzie was proud of it and proud of him. She was right. God had been good to them. "Well, most ways, anyhow," he admitted. That afterthought just wouldn't leave him alone, no matter how hard he tried to ban it from his mind. He knew he was grateful for all the Lord had done for him. And for Lizzie. He *had* to be, but somehow it seemed like there was always something nagging at him that wouldn't let him just be altogether satisfied with what God did for him the way he wanted to be.

Since Lizzie had gone to sleep on him, Pank decided to run it all back through his mind to see if he could clear things up a little. He felt guilty to think that he was hiding something from his wife, especially since he knew that she put all her dependence on the Lord and didn't ever question anything He did. Actually Pank wanted to be like that, too, but he just didn't seem to be able to come up to one hundred percent understanding the way Lizzie did, and after what happened to Vernon, Pank stayed away from the church, and it was mighty hard to get him to say much about the Lord, one way or the other. Yes, come to think of it, it was Lizzie's nephew, not his, that got in trouble and started Pank to thinking like he did in the first place. "Look like she ought to be the one to wonder about things 'stead of me," he said half aloud. But that thought brought no real relief. After all, he loved Vernon as much as Lizzie did, he admitted. Maybe more.

It all started, Pank remembered, when he and Lizzie moved up on The Avenue out of Fairmore, and sent for Vernon. Vernon wanted to get on at the TVA so he could send back and get Evalena, the girl he'd been intending to marry ever since they weren't nothing but tadpoles. Well, he'd got Vernon a chance to talk with the boss down at the dam; but they had slowed down the hiring right then, and Vernon couldn't get on right away. The man told him to come back in about three months, so Vernon went to work washing dishes and cleaning up at the Bus Station Café while he waited to get on at the TVA. He never did like it at the Bus Station. He said it was too close an' hot in there and that he'd rather be outdoors somewhere where he could get his breath better. Truth is, there was too many young hoogies hanging out at the Bus Station an' pickin' at the colored an' all, all the time, to suit Vernon. So he quit an' got hisself a job at Bledsoe's Good Gulf Service Station. He worked mighty hard for Mr. Bledsoe, pumpin' gas, fixin' tires, washin' cars, an' stuff like that. But Mr. Bledsoe died, an' the new boss let Vernon go and hired all white to run the station.

Funny thing about Vernon, he never did git no discouragement, an' he never did talk about goin' back home out in the country in the next county where he came from. An' even when he was laid off, he never did run in the streets or hang out with no bad crowd. The girls he ran into on The Avenue didn't change his mind about nothin', an' he never did talk about any of them except Evalena, and she 'way down in the country. Vernon didn't talk a whole lot nohow, but when he did say somethin', it was most likely about how he hoped to buy him a farm one day and raise a crop an' have plenty of cows an' hawgs an' chickens to feed all the chillun he an' Evalena expected to have. That's what he talked about when he talked, so naturally when he heard they was lookin' for hands on Mr. Milton Rogers's plantation, he just shook The Avenue dust off his feet and walked on out to the plantation. It was thirteen miles, but that didn't bother Vernon none. He had Evalena and them chillun on his mind.

Mr. Milton took him on. Lizzie wanted him to stay here, but then, she figgered it was the Lord's will, so she never did fight against it. I guess it hurt me more than it did her. Vernon wasn't here a great long time, but after he left, I just never did feel sure 'nuff satisfied no more. For a little while he'd come back over here near 'bout every Sunday to go to church an' eat Sunday dinner with me an' his a'nt Lizzie. But then, that Boss Tilman was workin' him so hard, I guess he was jest too wore out to git over here after a while; so whenever I could catch a ride, I'd go out to see him on Saturday afternoon an' take him some preserves or something his a'ntie cooked up for him.

Come to think of it, it was a Saturday afternoon a whole lot like this when all the trouble started. It was smack in the middle of August, and the heat felt like it was just pushin' down on you every time you tried to stir 'round a little bit. The cotton done all been laid by, and most folks wuz jest restin' up 'til pickin' time. Dog days had come, and even the catfish had sense enough to lay low 'til the heat slackened up a little. The mules just bunched up under the mulberry trees switchin' flies and dozin', and the blue jays kept to the thickest part of the fence rows, gapin' for air instead of screamin' and fightin' like jaybirds always do. Hot? It was *sho' nuff* hot. An' dry! That ol' hot dry weather made the cotton balls swell up tight. In two, three weeks they would bust open like popcorn and the fields would be black and white far as you could see—white with cotton and black with the niggers pickin' it. But right now everybody was trying to get a little rest 'cause it wuz already the middle of layin'-by time, and come the first of September you ain't got time to mash a bedbug 'til the cotton gits all in.

Out yonder on Mr. Milton Rogers's place they don't take no time off after they lay by. Mr. Jim Tilman—he the overseer—he always say that the best time to get a nigger to work is while he's workin', not after he done quit. So all of Mr. Milton's hands was ditchin', an' cuttin' cordwood, an' puttin' in fences while everybody else wuz tryin' to rest a little bit to git ready for the pickin'. It look like a real good year for the cotton crop, an' they gon' need every hand they can git to git it in the barn afore the rain come down.

Now Mr. Milton got Vernon over there workin'. Six foot two, he was, an' tall; big hands like a crawfish. Now Vernon worked for Mr. Jim, but Vernon had his own ideas about what to do with his time after his cotton done been laid by. He hadn't been raised in Clayton, an' he didn't seem to care enough about who he had to look up to an' who he didn't to please Boss Tilman. Fact is, Vernon ain't looked up far to nobody. He always do his work, mind his own business, an' that's the best he can do, I reckon. Some of the white folks (mostly it was white trash, not the real white folks) look like they had it in for Vernon. Seemed like they thought he ought to be learned a lesson 'fore he got too far out of his place. But the fact is, Vernon stayed so close and kept out of the way of trouble so good, wasn't nobody ever able to catch him in nothin', mainly because he didn't do nothin'. When he worked, which was most all the time, he worked steady an' he worked hard. Mr. Milton say he was worth two good niggers an' three, four no-'count hillbillies. But Mr. Jim, he the overseer, Mr. Jim say he didn't like Vernon's attitude. You see, when Vernon wasn't workin' for Mr. Milton, he was always tryin' to do somethin' for hisself. That's what caused all the commotion. If you work for the other man, seem like he jest naturally against your tryin' to help yourself. Seem like he ain't never satisfied with less than all you got. That's the way it was with Mr. Jim Tilman. He didn't jest want your body. He want your soul, too.

Well, Vernon lived by hisself 'way back off the road in a little ol' cabin he rent from Mr. Milton. He try to buy the cabin an' one or two acres, but Mr. Milton say naw, he ain't gonna sell it. But he say long as Vernon work for him an' don't give him no trouble, he rent it to him cheap. Vernon want his own place, so he could marry Evalena, but that was the best he could do right then, so he move in an' go to work for Mr. Milton. He knocked up a chicken house out of some boxes an' stuff an' bought some layin' hens. Next thing, he save his money and bought him a heifer cow. Now he had chickens to eat, an' butter an' eggs an' milk. He let it out that he might be lookin' around for him somebody to marry soon as he was in a little better shape. Funny thing, he was already in better shape than most of Mr. Milton's hands, an' some of 'em had been there on the place ever since they saw the light of day. Truth of the matter was, Vernon never did like being no hand. He figured hisself to be a real farmer. All he needed was a farm. An' in his own way he aimed to git one sooner or later.

That ol' cabin Mr. Milton let Vernon live in wasn't but two little bitty rooms an' a lean-to. Remind me of the shanty Lizzie and me lived in in Fairmore before we moved up on The Avenue. It leak in both of the rooms, an' the ol' chimney was fallin' down in the fireplace; but Vernon fix it up an' got the leaks stopped. Then he got him some slabs from over at the sawmill an' built him a closet down the hill a little ways, 'cause even though he live by hisself, he say he never did believe in jest goin' to nature out in the field like some dog or somethin'. He was funny like that—always try to carry hisself with respect. He had him some slabs left over, so he takes 'em an' nails 'em onto the back side of that ol' lean-to to kind of keep the weather off his cow 'til he can do better. Come lay-by time, when he expect to have him some time off, he plan to get him some more slabs from the mill an' build him a little shed for the cow joined onto his chicken coop. That way he'd have hisself a little barn, kind of. He never did intend to let that cow stay in that lil' ol' lean-to perm'entlike, though some woulda done it. But Vernon aimed to make him a kitchen out of that ol' lean-to soon's he got on his feet good, 'cause like I say, he might get married to Evalena if things worked out.

But that's where all the trouble s'posed to have started, 'cause he had a cow in that lean-to next to his house. Mr. Jim Tilman, he's the overseer for Mr. Milton, like I say—well, it come up lay-by time an' Mr. Jim don't see Vernon show up Monday morn'n' with the rest of the hands to git ready for ditchin' and such, so he asked Mr. Milton if he done let Vernon off. Mr. Milton say he didn't, so Mr. Jim, he got in his pickup and run on over to where Vernon live. He call him out an' asked him how come he didn't show up that mornin' with the other niggers.

Now Vernon don't like bein' called no nigger, so he jest stood there for a little while an' thought 'bout how he better answer his boss. Mr. Jim asked him if he hear him, since he kinda slow answerin', and Vernon tell him yes, sir, he hear him. He say his cotton was all laid by, and he was tryin' to git his cow out of the shed 'fore pickin' time, 'cause then he won't have no more time 'til up in November. Mr. Tilman want to know how come he got a gawddam cow in his house in the first place an' ask him don't he know that house belong to Mr. Milton? An' don't he know his time belong to him (Mr. Jim, that is) 'til the last lint been rolled up in a booger? He say Vernon ain't got no business with no cow nohow, and he done a lot of rarin' an' cussin' an' told Vernon he'll kick his black ass to kingdom come if he don' git it up there on the job. And he mean rat now, an' he don't mean afterwhile!

Well, now Vernon don't like that kind of talk, an' he don't take to being cussed; but he look at his cabin he done fixed, and he look at his chickens out there in the yard, an' his heifer cow, an' he thought about how he might git married. So he hold hisself in an' don't sass Mr. Jim none. He jest tell him he done laid by his crop, and he need jest a lil' bit of time to fix a decent place for his cow, an' then he be on up there with the rest of the hands. But he don't make no move to git in the truck an' go rat now, so Mr. Jim yell at him and ask him, "Nigger, is you married to that gawddam cow?" Vernon tell him naw, sir, he ain't. Mr. Jim spit his terbacker out the window of the pickup an' tell him well, gawddammit, he gonna be if he ain't careful. So he crank up his truck an' kick up a lot of dust an' run on into Clayton madder'n a rattlesnake in a beehive.

Funny thing, when you think about it, Mr. Jim didn't never git out of his truck the whole time he talk to Vernon, an' he got a reputation for knockin' an' kickin' his colored hands 'round if they even a lil' slow to do jest like he say do. Another thing, Vernon mighty careful 'bout what he say and how he say it, but he don't back up for nobody, white nor black. Reckon Mr. Jim had a feelin' 'bout Vernon—he not bein' from 'round here, an' all. Anyhow, he let him alone after he seen how Vernon didn't shuffle 'round like no hambone nigger. But he went on back to town an' make a lot of trouble for Vernon jest the same.

It was about two o'clock the next afternoon two deputies from the Clayton County Sheriff's Office come out an' 'rested Vernon and his cow and took 'em in to the Clayton County Jail, riding in the back of a pickup truck. Ol' Sheriff Jesse Dunn, he went on ahead of 'em, driving his patrol car with the siren wide open all the way through town. Soon's they got to the jail, folks commenced to crowd around to see what was goin' on. Well, when they backed the truck in the jail-yard, they unloaded Vernon an' his cow, with po' Vernon handcuffed to the cow's halter. Ol' Deputy Wilson Riner got out of the truck and took charge of everything. He took Vernon and the Je'sey cow up to the back door of the jail, holding a pistol on Vernon like he was some kind of highway robber or something. It was jest pitiful. Pitiful. Wasn't no cause in the world for them to treat Vernon like that.

The folks watching everything was mostly white, it being a Tuesday an' all the colored was most at work. But there was considerable excitement just the same as folks tried to figure out how come Mr. Wilson had Vernon handcuffed to a heifer and was holding a pistol on him. Now they had a big ol' green and red parrot in a homemade cage hanging on the back porch of the jail, all screened in. That ol' bird been at the jail there for twenty or twenty-five years an every time a colored person pass on the street he'll holler, "Nigger stealing! Nigger stealing! Nigger stealing!" An' that's just what he did when he saw Vernon. It sho' was pitiful, all them crackers laughin' an' whoopin' at Vernon. An' him ain't done nothin' a'tall to be up there at that jail. Pretty soon the jailer come to the back door and talked a minute with Sheriff Dunn. They unhitched Vernon from the cow and led him on into the jail by hisself, still handcuffed. When they took him on off, his heifer got lonesome an' commenced to lowin' "Moo-ooo!" an' everybody jest broke up laughin' 'til they turned the cow loose to eat some grass in the jailyard. After that everybody drifted on off, but inside the jail they booked Vernon on the charge of cohabitin' with a cow. Trial was set for ten o'clock that Friday morning. It wasn't nothin' but a disgrace before the Lawd. It was a shame.

Pretty soon word spread that a colored man had been jailed for livin' with a cow and that the cow had also been jailed for protective custidy, as they called it. The whole county heard about it, and by Friday every wagon and pickup truck that could roll was headed for Clayton City. Like I said, the cotton was laid by and the people had a little time on their hands. The trial would give 'em something to do besides going to revival meetings in the brush harbors and sideshow tents. Them revivals was the only thing to keep folks out of devilment until fair time, an' that didn't come until October, when all the cotton pickin' was jest about over an' settle-up time had done come for most folks.

The way it turned out, though, they never did have no trial. Po' Vernon, he got tried all right, but not by the Law. He got tried by a bunch of po' white trash that couldn't spell "Law" if you wrote it on a plate of grits. It was just a big mess.

Early Friday morning, before the case of the State against Vernon Banks come up, Mr. Milton drove in town to see the judge. He told ol' Judge Carson that Boss Tilman, his overseer, had jest been aiming to learn Vernon a little respect but had let it git out of hand. Course, the judge knew all the time what kind of fellow Boss Tilman was, so he wasn't surprised none. Mr. Milton told the judge that Vernon was a hard worker but had to be handled different from most niggers. Now if things didn't go right at the trial, he said, he could have trouble with his other hands, and with nearly a thousand acres of cotton to be picked, if any of the niggers got scared and run off, that could be real trouble for him and the other planters in the county. Besides that, Vernon wasn't making him a dime sitting up there in jail eating on the county. His policy, he told the judge, was to deal with troublemakers after the work was all done—in the winter.

They called the sheriff in, and Vernon walked out free, like he ought to have been all the time. They got his cow loaded in the back of Mr. Milton's pickup and drove on back to the plantation before anybody even knew he was gone. Mr. Milton told Vernon that since it was Friday, he could have the rest of the week off, but he wanted to see him report to Mr. Jim Tilman early Monday morning. And in the future, he told him, he didn't expect to hear of him giving Mr. Tilman no trouble whatsoever. Vernon said, "Yes, sir," and Mr. Milton drove on back to his compound, cussin' Jim Tilman for being a po'-ass cracker too dumb to pour piss out of a boot.

Funny thing 'bout white folks—like I said before, look like they don't never want the colored to have nothin' or to git ahead even a lil' bit. They jest seem to natcherally resent it if a colored man shows any disposition to better hisself. Long as you got dependence on him to put clothes on your back an' somethin'-to-eat in your stomach, the white man act like your friend. Try to do somethin' for yourself, an' right away he your worst enemy. That's all it was that got Vernon in trouble. He was movin' too fast an' wasn't askin' nobody for nothin'. They try to scare him with big talk; but he don't scare, an' he was too smart to sass 'em. But they figgered out what he was thinkin', an' since they didn't want to mess with him theyselves, they put the Law on him and tried to make him look like a fool. But the Law don't scare him neither, an' they let him go 'fore all the other niggers got restless an' run off 'fore the pickin' start. That shows you how fast the white man thinks. He's like the farmer with the tater. He'll plant you now, but he gon' dig you later. *An' roast your behind* if you ain't mighty careful! No matter what Vernon done or supposed to have done, it was all right so long as he come on back an' pick that cotton an' don't get the other niggers riled up. That's white folks' thinkin'.

Now, Mr. Milton had done gone over Boss Tilman's head and handled it hisself, but that wasn't gon' be the end of it. Even if the ignorant rednecks had stayed out of it, what most likely would've happened is that when it come time to settle up, Mr. Milton would've docked Vernon for the days he took off an' charged him interest. Then he would've charged Vernon for damage to his cabin by nailin' them slabs onto that lean-to an' puttin' his cow in there. Right behind that he would've charged him for keepin' chickens on the place, an' on like that. When he got through chargin' him for all this an' all that, an' for the provisions he got at the commissary, Vernon would natcherally end up owin' Mr. Milton instead of Mr. Milton owin' him. That's the way they do, they out-count you every time. Now if Vernon couldn't pay up, which you know he couldn't, why, then Mr. Milton would order him to vacate the cabin an' git off the place. An' he'd have to leave his chickens an' his cow to pay on what he owed. That's the way they handle niggers what gits out of line and cause 'em trouble. If you lucky, they jest take whatever you done 'cumulated an' force you to leave. If your luck runnin' against you, or if you got a real mean boss man or overseer, they notify the high sheriff an' he hold you in jail an' rent you out to work off what they say you owe at fifty or seventy-five cents a day. Now if you got a family, well, they got to go an' make a crop for anybody who'll take 'em 'til you git out of jail, which may be a long time. Lucky for Vernon, he didn't have no family to worry 'bout but me and Lizzie. But then he wasn't so lucky after all, you might say, 'cause before it was all over he did a whole lot of sufferin' for nothin'.

It come about like this: All them rednecks an' hoogies what come into town to see the trial, well, they wasn't 'bout to go home 'til some po' nigger had been made to suffer for their inconvenience and disappointment. Didn't make no difference which nigger, an' didn't make no difference whether he was in court or out; some nigger or other was bound to pay for their comin' out of the woods an' off them clay patches into Clayton City. You could count on that. The white folks downtown didn't want 'em there. They have to tolerate them crackers, but the real white folks ain't got no use for 'em. It's lay-by time, like I said, an' them rednecks ain't got no money, so they ain't spendin' nothin' nohow. Ain't got nothin' to spend. If there's anybody po'rer'n a nigger, it's a po' white cracker at lay-by time. Why, they's as mis'able as a jaybird with a plucked behind. An' when they gits mis'able, they gits mean.

But the real white folks downtown don't want no disturbment in Clayton City. It's bad for business an' it upsets the colored help. You don't see it, an' I don't see it; but there's a strain goin' on most all the time between the business folks what run Clayton City an' the hoogies an' rednecks what live out in the county. For twenty years them hoogies been tryin' to vote in a judge an' a solicitor so they could come on in an' take over. They finally got 'em a sheriff. Why, ol' man Jesse Dunn jest as soon shoot a nigger as to spit on a snake. Sooner, I reckon.

Well, them ol' rednecks got the word that Mr. Milton done come in an' got Vernon, so they jump on them ol' raggedy-assed trucks some of 'em got—you seen 'em with the rifles and shotguns hangin' in the back windows to scare the niggers—an' tore off down the road for Mr. Milton's place. Ol' Howard Hargis was leadin' 'em—he's the nephew of one of them deputy sheriffs. He ain't hardly full grown, but he already a sho'nuff cracker jest like his ol' daddy an' his daddy's daddy before him. Well, young Hargis led all them blood-suckers 'round through the back side of the plantation so they don't have to go by Mr. Milton's compound, an' they bust out in the clearin' 'round Vernon's cabin not long after Mr. Milton drop him off there. Young Hargis kicked in his door an' point a gun at him, an' three or four of 'em grab Vernon and brung him out.

He ask 'em what they want with him, an' they ask him ain't he the nigger been in jail for fornicatin' on a cow? He tell 'em he been in jail all right, but he ain't never done nothin' like what they talkin' 'bout, an' that the high sheriff let him out this mornin' with no charges 'gainst him. They jest tell him he the nigger they want all right, an' they got some charges. Then they drag him on out an' put him up on a truck so all them hoogies can get a look at him. They ask him where his cow is, an' he tell 'em she in the lean-to back of his house. One of them rednecks run to git the cow and bring her out on the trot an' tie her to the truck where they got Vernon.

After that things quiet down a minute while they likker up an' decide what other devilment to do. Some of 'em want to lynch Vernon straight out; but they on Mr. Milton's place, an' he ain't gon' like that if they do. Finally, Hargis tell 'em that since Vernon been livin' in the house with that heifer an' fornicatin' her, he ought to marry her an' make it legal. A big whoop went up when he told 'em that, an' all them ol' redneck rebels got ready for the ceremony. Two, three of 'em went to be lookouts in case Mr. Milton or the sheriff was to come, but the lookouts say they ain't never seen a nigger married to a cow before, so they come on back after checkin' the road once or twice. Then they all git to likkerin' up some more on the moonshine they keep in them ol' trucks, an' the rebel party is on.

Howard Hargis say he was gon' be the preacher, so while he gittin' hisself together, some of the rest of 'em got restless an' start lookin' 'round for some other devilment to do. One of 'em named Joe Poole, he grab the heifer by the tail an' look at her hind parts an' say that whoever been fornicatin' on that cow must have one hell of a whanger. That start everybody to hollerin' an' laughin', an' young Poole take another swig from his jug an' raise the heifer's tail an' spread her open to see if she was pregnant. He say she shore is, an' two, three of them rebels sittin' up on the truck start to joshin' Vernon an' cuffin' him 'round an' congratulatin' him 'cause he was gon' be a daddy, they say. By this time everybody is drinkin' heavy, givin' them ol' rebel yells an' havin' a good time. Everybody but Vernon.

Finally, they got they nerve up, an' young Hargis say he ready to proceed with the weddin', so they git Vernon off the truck an' make him stand by the tailgate near the heifer. Hargis ask, "Who giveth this Je'sey heifer in marriage to this here nigger?" an' Joe Poole jump up on the tailgate an' say he do, but first he want to see proof that Vernon in fact the one who done violated that bovine. "That po' cow is ruint," he say, lookin' under her tail, an' he didn't believe no man coulda done it, so maybe Vernon was accused unjestly. Joe Poole he called for Vernon to be examined to see if he had a whanger big enough to ruin a heifer like he say this'n ruint. They told Vernon to take off his pants, an' when he wouldn't, they knock him down an' tore 'em off him an' stand him back up on the tailgate with nothin' on but his shirt to hide his nakedness. Joe Poole look at Vernon's private parts an' say, "Great-god-a-mighty, he got to be the one!" He poke Vernon's business with his rifle barrel an' say he sho' felt sorry for that heifer to have to stand up to a misery like that.

Hargis say he ready to go on with the marriage ceremony, but somebody in the crowd say he ain't yet satisfied with the evidence, an' that if the marriage was gonna be legal, they ought to see the nigger do it to the cow, not jest speculate 'bout it. That make 'em all whoop again, so Hargis tell Vernon to git down off the truck an' salute his bride-to-be from the rear. Vernon tell 'em he could't do nothin' like that, it bein' a sin in the Bible. So they knock him down again an' kick him 'round two, three times an' tell him they gon' lynch his black ass right then an' there if he don't cooperate with the marriage consummation. Well, Vernon got up an' wipe some of the blood off him, an' then that funny look come in his eye like when he thinkin' deep, an' he tell Mr. Hargis he need him a drink to get his steam up. Everybody hollered at that, an' somebody give him a quart jar about half full of corn whiskey. He tell 'em that his cow was nervous, an' would they please give her a lil' room for some air?

Well, them ignorant hoogies really thought they were 'bout to see a nigger go up on a cow, so they all run to climb up on the trucks so they could git a better look at what they thought Vernon was about to do. Young Hargis, he stand by with his rifle in case Vernon tried to run off. This jest exactly what Vernon want him to do. He took him a long swig from the fruit jar to steady his nerve, an' while them hoogies was still scramblin' up on them trucks so they could see better, he smash the jar 'cross Hargis's face, pick up the rifle that ol' rebel drop, an' shot him right 'twixt the eyes. Vernon then turn round an' kill Joe Poole an' another redneck name Cecil Long. When they see that nigger with a gun in his hand, them hoogies run off in all directions like roaches at sunup. They leave they trucks, they whiskey, they shotguns, an' everythin' an' take off duckin' an' dodgin' through the bushes while Vernon steady bustin' caps up they ass with ol' Hargis's thirty-ought-thirty. He kill him two, three of 'em an' shoot up three, four more, but they too mean an' stubborn to go ahead an' die, 'cause it was a nigger what shot 'em.

Well, it be 'bout a hour 'fore they come back, an' they got every redneck hoogie in the county comin' with 'em. The high sheriff was in the lead, an' he'd done swore 'em all in to be deputies so they can lynch Vernon legal. Ol' man Lamon Hargis—he young Hargis's ol' daddy—he in the crowd with two pistols strapped on him an' totin' a twelve-gauge. An' there was Deputy Willis Hargraves. He in the crowd cussin' every nigger to ever walk the face of the earth. He already killed him four, five niggers an' got the notches cut in his pistol butt to prove it. That was jest some of 'em, but to tell you the truth, them woods was jest 'bout filled with hoogies of one description or another. Every ol' pickup truck an' rattletrap Ford with four wheels was bustin' down the dirt road to where Vernon live in that lil' ol' bitty cabin on the edge of the woods. Some of 'em even started cuttin' cross the fields, but Mr. Jim Tilman, he right on 'em 'bout that. He tell 'em he want that nigger dead worse'n any of 'em, but any son of a bitch what mash down one stalk of cotton gonna have to answer to Mr. Milton, an' Mr. Milton don't take no shit. They got careful after that an' stayed in the road.

It was a sight to see—all them hoogies hollerin' an' shoutin' an' goin' on like that. They brung them two big ol' bloodhounds from the County Jail to run Vernon down with, 'cause they figgered he'd done already took off in the woods. An' some of 'em brought they own personal huntin' dogs; they had coon hounds, possum hounds, and rabbit hounds— anythin' what could smell a nigger and yap about it, them hoogies brung it. They had every kind of gun they got in the store, an' one of 'em even had an ol' Confederate sword. But the part that makes you feel so bad was that a whole lot of church people was in the crowd. They was having this big revival up there at the Oak Grove Tabernacle at the junction not far from the plantation, an' when the word got out 'bout the shootin', why, that meetin' jest broke up like ice under a wagon wheel. The preacher dismissed one and all to the loving care of his personal Savior, and then everybody in the church, includin' the preacher an' the sinners on the moaners' bench, left out of there to go nigger huntin'.

Well, the way it turned out, they didn't need to put theyselves to so much trouble. They could've left the dogs at home, an' the preacher could have stayed at the church takin' care of the Lord's business—if he had any up there with them redneck sinners, because you see Vernon didn't go nowhere. Nowhere but in his cabin. He didn't run off in the swamps to be run down like some kind of wild animal. An' he didn't set 'round on his tail a-whimperin' an' waitin' for them hoogies to come an' lynch him on no tree or pour gas on him an' set him afire. Naw. Not Vernon, he was funny like that. When he commenced shootin', an' them hoogies jump up an' run off in the bushes an' give him a few minutes peace, why, he knowed already that his time to labor an' to suffer in this valley was jest about over. So he jest unhooked the gate to his chicken coop an' shooed out his chickens. An' he untied his cow an' told her to go on off an' enjoy herself in Mr. Milton's cornfield. Then Vernon went on in the cabin and closed the door.

Pretty soon the woods 'round Vernon's cabin was full of hoogies an' rednecks an' bloodhounds a-yellin' an' bayin' at each other. First they held off an' didn't get too close to Vernon's cabin, bein' that he might of shot two, three more of them with the rifle he took from young Hargis. But them ugly ol' bloodhounds was steady runnin' back an' forth up to the door an' bayin' like they'd treed a coon, or somethin'. They is the most ugliest and the meaniest dogs you'll ever see, an' they jest seem to hate anybody black. Anyhow, them old dogs kept on a-bayin' an' a-whinin', so they knowed po' Vernon was in there. They call Vernon to come on out so they could git to him, but he ain't said a mumblin' word. Finally, they shoot out his window an' put enough lead in that ol' cabin to sink a battleship, but they still don't hear nothin' from Vernon. Finally, ol' Lamon Hargis—his boy's the one what started it all and got hisself killed—ol' Lamon Hargis got 'em to throw up a lot of brush an' stuff 'round the cabin an' pour gasoline on it. Then they set fire to it an' burned that shack plumb to the ground. An' Mr. Tilman, the one Vernon was workin' for, jest sat in his pickup truck pickin' his teeth an' watchin' it burn. Funny thing though. They never did find no evidence of po' Vernon in the ashes of that ol' shack. Nothin' a'tall.

Pank had talked himself out in a soliloquy meant for nobody in particular. He felt purged. Lizzie was napping peacefully in the old hickory swing he'd brought with him when he moved up on The Avenue from Fairmore. He looked at his wife with a certain contentment as his nose picked up the smell of hot peaches cooling in the kitchen of his five-room house. Then he got up from the porch and stretched himself, bringing his reverie to a sudden end. He glanced quickly at Lizzie once more as if to make certain that she would not hear the thought that he knew was about to come into his mind. She was right, of course. Suddenly he heard himself saying, "God had been mighty good to them, *but God sho' messed over Vernon!*" There it had finally come out. Pank stood gaping in horror at the blasphemy that had come involuntarily from his lips. He put his hand to his mouth as if to recapture the dirty words and force them back down his throat—back into the inner recesses of his being; back into his guts, his bowels which had harbored them all these years. Back. Back. Back. But like gnats escaping from a bag of stale bananas, they had mixed with the air and vanished. Gone. Like Vernon.

Pank looked frantically at his bungalow as if to see if it was still there. It seemed intact. He could still see the peach trees in the back and smell the canned fruit cooling in the kitchen. Lizzie was still sleeping in the old hickory swing. Suddenly Pank leaped upon the porch and shook his wife into grudging wakefulness. "Git up, Lizzie," he said, "and come on in the house."

Lizzie blinked at him and then got quickly to her feet when she saw the urgency in Pank's eyes. "What we goin' in the house for, Pank?" she wondered aloud as she followed him through the screen door.

"To pray," he said simply. "Before God strikes me dead and sends you back to Fairmore."

Lil' Un

*B*IG WALKING MAN soaped his head generously with the hunk of soap Ma Lou had given him. At the first sign of water his hair had drawn up into hard little curls against his scalp, and the cut of lye soap bumped pleasantly against the successive rows of springy black wool which contoured his head. He laughed to himself at the pleasant sensation of the stiff, pungent lather hissing and popping as he worked it into his scalp with his long, powerful fingers. Rabbit hair, he mused to himself. "Run an' squat! Run an' squat! Ha!" he ejaculated aloud. " 'S *my* hair! All I got. The devil on who don't like it!" He laughed again, his big chest heaving and rumbling with the sound of his laughter. Lil' Un, he mused, she ain't never found no fault with it, an' she got more sense than most folks. Course, that ol' gal like about everything if it got anything to do with me! He cuffed the top of his head vigorously with the satisfaction the thought afforded him and then rubbed the lye soap even more vigorously into his scalp as if to underscore his defiance. Now he was working his armpits with the strong gray soap and a course rag cut from the leg of some long-forgotten union suit. He reached his arms straight up to the sky as he scrubbed and wiped, and the big muscles rippled and gleamed like dark ribbons of steel in the sunlight of early afternoon. As he looked toward the sky, his eye caught the nervous movement of a gray dove fluttering back and forth in the oak tree over his head. "Hah!" he said, "I see you, Miss Dove. See your nest, too. Ain't gon' bother you. But if you don't go back an' set on them eggs, yo' chillun gon' come up missin'! G'wan back an' set down, ol' Walkin' Man jest gittin' hisself a rinse-off! Git!" Standing wide-legged in the shallow creek, he looked like a black colossus as he flung his arms against the sky to urge the dove back to her nest. His stomach was flat and muscular; his thighs were long, tapering down to slim black knees and calves that disappeared in the swirls of soap suds dripping from his laundering. Now he sat down on a convenient rock in the middle of the stream and finished washing himself, scrubbing his feet meticulously with a mixture of sand and soap. He looked appraisingly at his long black feet with the thick toenails and orange-white soles. Feet, he mused, you an' me belong together. Let's go home 'cause we got us a lil' walkin' to do 'fore dark.

As if on his own cue, Big Walking Man got up and waded a few yards upstream to where the creek deepened into a quiet pool overhung with oaks and alders. He shied a rock or two toward a pocket where the water was deepest and the growth of the weeds and bushes along the bank provided heavy cover for the muskrats and snakes and other water life that shared the stream with him and with the old black women who came almost daily with cane poles and croker sacks to fish for the catfish and goggle-eyed perch hiding under the bank. "Look out, ol' moccasins!" he warned, beating the water with his arms. "Comin' to rinse off, an' don't want no comp'ny, an' don't want no competition! So look out!" He swam the length of the pool a few times, diving deep under the surface to wash the lye soap out of his hair. On the way out he instinctively ran his hand into one of the holes under the bank and brought out a foot-long catfish which had been hiding there. "Ha!" he exclaimed as he flung the bullhead into the tall grass away from the edge of the bank. "Caught you! Caught you, you slick black rascal! You and Lil' Un gon' have some supper together. All meat and no bones!"

Back home Big Walking Man cleaned the catfish, salted it, and wrapped it in corn shucks and a paper sack. Then he put on a fresh deck of overalls, blacked his brogans with a damp biscuit dipped in chimney soot, and prepared to walk on into Clayton City, nine miles away.

"Josiah!" It was Ma Lou calling him from the kitchen, where she was picking and washing a bucket of poke salad. "Josiah! You goin' off before dinner?"

"Yes'm, Ma Lou. Goin' on into town, I reckon."

"You goin' go by to see Cousin Irene, suh, I reckon?"

"Yes'm. Gon' see Cousin Irene, shore's you born! Sho' is! 'Cause that's where Miss Lil' Un is at! Gon' take her a catfish, fresh caught an' no bones! Lil' Un, I'm talkin' 'bout."

"Well, I reckon Irene might like some, too," Ma Lou said. "After all, she's your cousin, you know. And you leave Lil' Un right there with Irene. I don't want you to bring her out here 'til you gots someplace fixed up fit for her to live in. You hear me?"

"I hear you, Ma Lou. Gonna build a house for Miss Lil' Un soon's the crop is in an' move her to the country. You watch an' see. I woulda done it already, but Irene say Lil' Un the only company she got right now. She takes it hard every time I tell her I want Lil' Un to be out here in the country with me where she belong. Why, I'd build ol' Lil' Un a house right smack on The Avenue if I thought that's what she wanted. But she's a country gal an' I'm a country boy. Only time we want to be on The Avenue is maybe when we die. An' that's a long ways off, I reckon."

"Well, suh, you have you'self, you hear me? An' if Irene ain't ready to let her go, you just have to wait."

"I hear you, Ma Lou. An' *you* behave while I'm off. Be back later. When you see me, look for me!"

"Don't you act mannish with me, boy!" Ma Lou confronted him as he clumped noisily through the kitchen on his way out. "Big ol' rascal that you is," she said proudly, "I can still take you 'cross my knee if you git outa your place! You comb your hair? You put on them clean underwear I put on your bed? Irene don't want you coming over there looking like you ain't got nobody to look after you. Lil' Un neither. I want you to look like you got folks when you go over there to Clayton City. Here! You take this sandwich to eat on the way.'' She thrust a big ham and cornbread sandwich garnished with freshly made chowchow and wrapped in clean brown paper at him. He slipped it into a pocket of his overalls. He and Lil' Un would eat it together.

''Ain't hungry,'' he said. ''Can't *be* hungry. Got Miss Lil' Un on my mind. Got to go.'' Bending over to kiss his mama on the top of the head, he tucked the shucked-up catfish in the bib of his faded blue overalls and clumped through the back door of the cabin. ''See you!'' Pausing briefly in the backyard, he went to his bucket of river rocks hanging near the doorjamb and slipped three or four of the smooth round stones into his pocket. ''Might see a rabbit,'' he said to himself. ''Miss Lil' Un near 'bout crazy 'bout rabbit as she is 'bout me!'' He guffawed at his own joke and felt the muscles in his stomach shimmy with approval. Big Walking Man was on his way.

He could have taken the wagon track that ran in front of the house and on up the hill to Mr. Grady's place and on down to the gravel road leading to the blacktop. But that would cost him an extra mile, and he was in a hurry. So out along the edge of Ma Lou's garden and down the path to the creek and across the foot log was quicker. Save me some time, he mused. But then he remembered that he would have to cross the lower end of Mr. Grady's cow pasture before he could come out of the woods and onto the blacktop pike that would take him on into Clayton City, and Mr. Grady had a new young bull that hadn't yet settled down to minding his own business. He had chased two or three folks cutting across the pasture to the creek, and he kept old A'nt Eula Morell treed in a sycamore 'til feeding time. Big Walking Man thought about that and chuckled to himself as he pictured A'nt Eula dropping her fishing poles and getting all her skirts and petticoats up a tree before the bull could get to her. ''Must have been a sight to see, A'nt Eula up a sycamore tree! Ha!''

When he came to the pasture, Big Walking Man let up a

moment to see if he could see the bull anywhere close around. Not a single cow was in sight, although Mr. Grady had to have twenty or thirty of them grazing around somewhere. Maybe they were all down at the pond on the far side of the pasture. After all, it was early afternoon, the time of day when cows have usually finished their first grazing; and are lazing around, chewing their cuds and trying to keep cool. Anyhow, Big Walking Man figured he didn't have time to worry about it, so he pressed the top strand of barbed wire down with the palm of his left hand and swung his right leg over the fence and planted it firmly inside the pasture. He was careful not to scuff his soot-blacked shoes on the rocks along the fence row because he wanted Lil' Un to know that he was all cleaned up and decked out just for her. Big Walking Man was six feet tall with three or four inches to spare, and straddling barbed-wire fences was no big problem for him. He swung his other leg over, tensed the muscles in back of his calf, and set off across the pasture. A covey of young quail ran silently through the tall grass ahead of him, almost invisible as they darted among the rocks and cow tracks for cover. "See you little rascals," he said with a chuckle, and reached instinctively for one of the river rocks he had in his pocket. But he was in too big a hurry to fool with the scurrying and darting wild chickens. They could lead you for miles and then disappear between your feet. "Later for you." He shrugged and lengthened his stride toward the far side of the pasture. Topping a slight ridge that drained the land into Mr. Grady's farm pond, he suddenly saw the missing cows. Some were standing silently in the shallows of the pond while others were resting themselves beneath the mulberries and the sycamores shading the water from the afternoon sun. Standing guard with his hindquarters to the cows and his massive head directed at any potential intruder was Bozo, the young bull Mr. Grady had recently bought from Cap Spencer to replace his old bull, who had been retired and butchered. "Ha!" said Big Walking Man. "I see you, ol' bull, and you look pretty ugly to me. But ne' mind, don't aim to give you no trouble, an' don't you give me none." He kept to the ridge, where he could keep the bull in sight, but veered his direction slightly so that he would reach the other side of the pasture a little quicker than he had planned. He'd probably lose a few minutes, but he'd give that up to Bozo for letting him cut across his pasture without asking him about it.

Bozo didn't seem to be of a mind to cooperate. The big red bull followed Big Walking Man's progress across his domain with beady eyes and increasing annoyance. Once or twice he snorted, pawed the ground, and shook his great head to let his heifers know that he was in control of the situation and that they were to stay put. Big Walking Man's slight change of direction must have seemed like a direct challenge to Bozo, and he made known his displeasure by a short warning bellow. Now he was pawing the ground furiously, his short tail sticking out like a gate latch. He shook his head angrily, and the sharp tips of his long curving horns glistened in the sunlight.

"Ha!" said Big Walking Man, increasing his stride again. He turned sharply down the ridge and headed for the nearest fence. That ol' Bozo, he decided, he aims to make me some trouble. Suddenly the bull galloped up the ridge from the pond and with a loud bellow charged down the other side toward the retreating figure he reckoned to be the cause of his unhappiness. There were no trees handy, and even with his long legs Big Walking Man knew that he could not reach the fence ahead of the rampaging bull. Again he reached into the right-hand pocket of his overalls, and this time he brought out a river rock about the size of a baseball and fitted it into the socket formed by his first two fingers and thumb. Then he fitted a second rock in his left hand—he could throw with either one—stopped still and turned around to face the maddened animal bearing down upon him at full speed. His left arm was cocked to throw. Suddenly the young bull stopped his charge some twenty yards away and stood pawing the ground and shaking his head with indecision. Then just as suddenly he charged again, and in the same instant Big Walking Man reared back and let go with the river rock in his left hand. The stone caught Bozo squarely between the eyes, and he dropped to his knees with a long, low groan. Big Walking

Man had already cocked his right arm to throw again, but when he saw that the bull was stunned, he turned and headed on out of the pasture and on toward the road. He straddled the fence and was over, pausing anxiously to see if maybe he had killed Mr. Grady's prize bull. What he saw was a mighty relief to him. Bozo was already back on his feet, shaking his head slowly and pawing listlessly at the turf in Mr. Grady's pasture. A minute or two later he gave a low, plaintive bellow and trotted slowly back over the ridge to where his heifers were.

Big Walking Man cut through a stand of timber that had grown up where the old Pearson plantation used to be, and lengthened his stride a little to get him on out to the road as soon as possible. In the wintertime he sometimes hunted on the old Pearson place, but he always felt a little uncomfortable whenever he was there. It was too quiet. Too still. The place was grown up in briars and honeysuckle and all kinds of trees; but the old grapevines, big as a man's arm, were still bearing, and over behind the old Big House were some twisted old apple trees and pear trees more than a hundred years old. There were persimmon trees, too, and mulberries, and a double line of old elms that must have marked the drive to the Big House. The house was still there; but the windows were knocked out, and the shutters had dropped off, and the doors were gone. People generally stayed away from the Pearson place, even though there was plenty of small game and even deer there in the winter. In the summer the fruit trees and grapevines were presided over by blue jays and squirrels, and what they left dropped to the ground to rot or to be eaten by the foxes and possums. Here and there a wild rose clambered around a long-dead oak tree, and a patch of rhododendrons or century plants pushed through the weeds and grass as if in solemn reminder of a departed era. There was a small graveyard surrounded by a wrought-iron fence off to the right of the dilapidated old mansion which seemed to frown down on the headstones there with some secret disapproval. Back in the woods was a graveyard for slaves, marked only by mounds of stones heaped at the head of each grave.

It was these abandoned graveyards that made Big Walking Man feel uncomfortable. Nobody ever talked about what happened to the Pearsons and why their plantation came to be abandoned. The white folks were mighty tight-lipped about it, and if the colored knew anything, they were afraid to say what they knew. They just clammed up, minded their own business, and stayed away from the Pearson plantation as much as possible. There were one or two white families in Clayton City named Pearson, but nobody ever said whether or not they had any connection with the Pearson place out in the country. Even more strange was the fact that there were no Negroes named Pearson around, although all of the other big plantation families in Clayton County had black counterparts whose forebears had been their slaves. "Ha!" Big Walking Man said aloud as he tried to put some more distance between him and the Pearson mystery. "Something mighty bad must have went on up there!" *Mighty bad!* his words seemed to echo from the gaping windows of the Big House, and again as he passed the overgrown slave cemetery with its tumbledown piles of field stones for grave markers. *Mighty Bad! Mighty bad!* He got the feeling that somebody was watching him; maybe a whole lot of somebodies. And was somebody calling him? Maybe somebody was trying to tell him something. If they were, Big Walking Man decided right off that he didn't have time to hear it today. It was Saturday afternoon, and he was on his way to see Lil' Un. Anybody wanting to talk to him about some ol' run-down plantation with two graveyards and a ha'nty-looking ol' house on it would have to catch him another time. It was that ugly ol' bull named Bozo that caused him to be over there in the first place. He hadn't intended to go nowhere near where he was, so Big Walking Man stretched his legs a little more with each stride and stepped up his pace. Jest pick 'em up an' jest put 'em down, he mused, and git the devil on away from here!

Pretty soon he came to a creek that marked the edge of the Pearson property. It was the same stream that ran near his house two miles or so on the other side of the woods, but since folks hardly ever let themselves stray over on the Pearson side, there was no regular way to get across the stream. No foot log, no bridge. Not even a rock jump in the shallows. Big Walking Man didn't lose any time over that. He sat down on the ground, took his shoes off, and waded across the creek without even thinking hard about it. A few minutes later, as he emerged from the woods into a clearing, he could see the dirt and gravel road where it topped the hill half a mile away. Two miles on the dirt road would take him to the blacktop, and that to the pike which would take him on into Clayton City. He put his shoes on again and settled into an easy rhythmic cadence, his long arms swinging him along almost effortlessly across the open field toward the old dirt road that had serviced the plantations and farms of West Clayton County for more than a century. Suddenly a rabbit jumped from its hiding place in the grass almost under his feet. Hardly breaking his stride, Big Walking Man felt in his right-hand pocket for a rock and waited a second or two for the fleeing cottontail to settle into its zigzag pattern. It was not a long run. Shifting his weight to his left foot and throwing with his right arm, Big Walking Man caught the young cottontail behind the ears with his rock about thirty yards from where he was jumped, and the unlucky animal was quickly gathered up and wrapped with the catfish inside the bib of Big Walking Man's overalls. "Ha! Lil' Un done hit the jackpot." He grinned to himself. "Catfish *an'* rabbit. An' me coming to check on her. She luckier'n anybody! 'Cept me, I reckon!''

Everything was quiet on the dirt road. Just about anybody who was going to Clayton City on Saturday had already gone by now, and it was too early for the wagons and trucks to be headed out again. It was late summer, and the plaza around the Courthouse would be crowded with teams hitched to the iron hitching rail that circled the big limestone building. The town stores wouldn't be doing much business because the country folks wouldn't have any money until cotton-picking time. But the Courthouse grass was probably covered with folks in black and white clumps, eating watermelon and chewing tobacco and just visiting with one another. They wouldn't be starting home for another hour or two—just in time to make it in and get unhitched before dark. Big Walking Man knew all about Saturday afternoon in downtown Clayton, because, growing up in the country, Clayton is where most of his Saturdays had been spent—unless he was fishing or hunting. Lil' Un liked to hunt even more than he did; but since she'd been staying in town with Irene, she didn't have a chance to get out in the country too often, and Big Walking Man was forced to hunt mostly by himself. But he was going to change all that. He was going to build a house for Lil' Un and bring her out in the country to stay. Irene would just have to make it by herself or maybe get one of her grandchildren to come and stay with her and keep her company. Big Walking Man wanted Lil' Un with him, and he didn't aim to put it off much longer. People teased him a lot about Lil' Un being undersized, but he didn't care. "She's better-lookin' than anything y'all got to show," he'd tell them, "an' if she ain't no bigger'n a booger, she's *some* little booger, an' you can put that in your pipe an' smoke it."

By now Big Walking Man had settled into the steady, ground-eating stride that got him his name. His mind was fixed on his plans for Lil' Un come settle-up time, and the fence posts along the side of the road marched steadily into the distance behind him. Just as he turned onto the blacktop, a pickup truck passed him and then stopped and waited for him to catch up. It was Mr. Jacob Lester, who rented a little piece of ground back down toward the river a few miles below Mr. Grady's place.

"Howdy, boy," Mr. Jacob said when he got even with the pickup. "You want a ride?"

"How you, Mr. Jacob? Sho' is a right nice day for a Saturday, ain't it?" There was another white man in the cab with Jacob Lester, and Big Walking Man could see a red and white yearling peeping through the side boards on the back of the truck. He didn't want to ride with no yearling and get himself all dirty and smelly before he got to Irene's house. Still, if he took the ride, he could get there quicker. But his mind wouldn't come together on it right away.

"Boy, you want a ride?" the white man said again. "I ain't got all day."

"Yes, sir. I mean, no, sir. I mean, I'm just going a lil' ol' piece down the road here. But I'm mighty obliged to you, Mr. Jacob.''

The pickup truck pulled off and disappeared over the next hill down the pike. Big Walking Man tried to pick up his cadence again, but he was still shaken by his encounter with Jacob Lester. He didn't mean to, but he had violated the code of manners he had been born with in Clayton County. If a white man offers you a ride, *you take it*, even if you don't want it or even if it takes you out of your way. He felt he hadn't heard the last of it, and he would be worried until he'd talked to Ma Lou or maybe Mr. Grady. But Mr. Grady didn't have any use for Jacob Lester. He didn't just come right out an' say so before his colored hands, but he hinted it mighty strong that he considered Jacob poor white trash. He suspected Jacob of stealing cows and hogs all up and down that part of the county and selling them for slaughter in Clayton. Now that he'd had time to think about it, it had suddenly come clearer to Big Walking Man the real reason he didn't want to ride into town with Mr. Jacob. If Mr. Jacob got into trouble over that yearling he had in the truck, it would be easy for him to put the blame on him if he was back there with the calf. That must have been the reason he offered him a ride in the first place!

With his mind eased somewhat by this new insight, Big Walking Man swung on down the pike at his old stride. In a little while he was approaching the outskirts of Clayton City, and traffic into and out of town began to pick up a little. Tom Scully driving his team of gray mules passed on the way back to the country and waved at him. Tom was mighty proud of his team of mules, and he was one of the few colored men around to own his own farm and the stock needed to work it. Big Walking Man waved back and kept on down the pike. Another mile and he was getting close to Fairmore. He could hear the shouting and yelling, so he knew there was a baseball game going on in the field behind Bullock's Store down at the crossroads. Now if there was anything Big Walking Man liked more than hunting and fishing, it was baseball, and when he got to the crossroads, he just naturally had to go down behind Bullock's to see who was playing. As soon as he turned the corner of the store, a yell went up from the losing team, and Booker Tee Jones came running up to get him to pitch for his side.

"Big Walkin' Man! Big Walkin' Man! You come just in time! We sho' need you bad, 'cause if you don't help us, ain't no way we can win. Come on and pitch for us."

Big Walking Man hesitated a little bit. Joe Wiley was getting ready to bat, and there was nothing he'd enjoy more than to see ol' Injun Joe swatting at the air where the ball *used* to be. But he was on his way to town, and he knew that if he stopped to play baseball, he wouldn't get there anytime soon. Besides, he had a catfish and a rabbit in his overalls bib, and he didn't want Lil' Un to have to wait for the present he was bringing her. Just about the time he was fixing to tell Booker Tee he had to get on down the road to Clayton City, somebody behind him clipped him on the shoulder and pulled him around.

"Well, I do believe it's my main man, the African! Also known locally among the folks as Big Walkin' Man, they tell me. What you gon' say, country boy!" It was Joe Jipson.

"What you say, Jip!" Big Walking Man returned the greeting. "You got the business!" He looked at the razor-sharp crease in Jipson's hickory-striped pegs and at the afternoon sunlight flashing off his gold wristwatch and the gleaming orange-brown Florsheim knobs that adorned his long narrow feet. "If I had your hand," he continued, "I'd throw mine in."

"For a clod of the sod, you're pretty hip with the lip, my man," Jipson told him. He was obviously pleased at having his Saturday afternoon finery noted right off by somebody from the sticks. "Take it from Po' Jip, an' it's for free! I suppose you gon' pitch some ball for these clowns, I suppose," he said with a grand sweep of the Coca-Cola he held in his left hand covering the growing knot of people who wanted to see Big Walking Man save the day for Booker Tee Jones's team. Jipson inserted a finger in the Coke bottle and shook it gently to raise a head of foam. Then he took a small sip, cleared his throat, and turned to the crowd. "Ladies and gentlemen," he announced, holding his Coca-Cola up high to get attention. "Ladies and gentlemen, it is my distinct pleasure to give you the pitching sensation of the American Nation. I give you Big Walkin' Man—the ladies' pet, the men's regret. And he'll win this game before sunset! I thank you one and all."

With everybody pushing and pulling and cheering at him, Big Walking Man never had a chance to say anything for himself before he found himself on the pitcher's mound with a baseball in his hand. "Ha!" he said to himself. "May as well make it quick and get on down the road." He looked up at the sky. It was still a long time before sundown. "Won't be long, Lil' Un," he promised himself on her behalf. "Won't be long."

To the intense delight of the crowd Big Walking Man fanned the first three batters to face him. The next inning he did the same thing; then he hit a home run so far it took several minutes to find the ball. With such encouragement, Booker Tee's team was hitting now, and the score was nearly even, but when it was time for him to take the pitcher's mound the third time, Big Walking Man was nowhere to be found. In the excitement of the change of fortune for Booker Tee Jones's team, their new pitcher had simply walked around the corner of Bullock's Store and disappeared. By the time he was missed he was on the Upper End of The Avenue in Clayton City and was headed for Cousin Irene's.

Irene lived off The Avenue on Brandon's Lane near Sis' Inis Wells. Folks said ol' Sis' Inis was the oldest person in Clayton City, or anywhere around, for that matter. She could remember back before the Civil War, when she and her folks were slaves, and she liked to tell about how the Yankees came by, freeing all the colored people but taking all the corn and the stock and the chickens so that there was nothing left for the people to eat. "But that was all right with me," Sis' Inis always told it. "Me, I could live on freedom! I'd heap rather have a bellyful of freedom any day than to have a bellyful of cornpone an' hoppin John with some ol' rebel calling hisself my master! I ain't never had no master but Jesus, and He don't press me none."

Sis' Inis was sitting in the swing on her front porch when

Big Walking Man passed on his way to Irene's. "You, suh!" she yelled at him. "Ain't that you, Big Walkin' Man?"

"Yes'm, Sis' Inis. This is me," he called back, turning into the path that led up to her front porch. "Sho is."

"Well, how come you was gon' strut on by here without so much as a howdy-do?" the old woman scolded him. "You ain't been raised like that. You come on up here an' set down an' tell me how your mammy is before I take a stick to you— you long-legged rascal, you!"

Big Walking Man had hoped Sis' Inis might be in the house when he passed. He liked to talk with her because she'd lived so long and knew so much, and she had her own way of saying things that always set him to laughing. But today he was trying to get on to Irene's to see Lil' Un, and he'd already been thrown off his time by that baseball game at the crossroads. Still, he knew that since Sis' Inis had caught him trying to sneak by, he'd have to stay and visit with her awhile. Ma Lou wouldn't let him back in the house if he didn't. Sis' Inis moved over in the swing so that he could sit beside her. "Set yourself down, you young whippersnapper," she commanded, "an' give account of your meanness. An' if you lookin' for Irene, she ain't at home, nohow. Passed here must be nigh on a hour ago. She an' that Lil' Un, they call her."

Hearing that Irene and Lil' Un weren't at home, Big Walking Man settled back in the swing and relaxed a little. "Where you think they went, Sis' Inis?"

"Ain't none of my business where they went," she scolded. "Nor yours either. You jest prepare to rest yourself com'table 'til they decide to come back. Then, if you so nosy, you ask them where they went. Don't ask me, 'cause it ain't none of my business."

"Well, tell me, how is she—Lil' Un, I mean?" He realized before the words were fully out of his mouth that Sis' Inis was really going to be put out with him now. And she was.

"Well, do Jesus!" she exclaimed, slapping her hands against her thighs to show her indignation. "You talkin' 'bout Lil' Un, ain't you? You ain't asking 'bout your cousin Irene!

Well, if that don't beat a mammy hen a-cluckin'! How is she? She jest like all the rest of 'em, far as I'm concerned, that's how she is. All right in her place, I reckon—long as she know her place an' don't git it mixed up with mine. Irene thinks the world of her, an' that's all right with me, 'cause she stays with Irene. She don't stay with me.''

"Don't be so hard on her.'' Big Walking Man grinned at the old woman and set the swing in motion by pushing his brogans against the floor. "She's all I got.''

"Well, I can't say you got a whole lot. How'd you say your mammy is anyhow? I ain't got no time to waste talkin' 'bout your foolishness.''

He told her again that Ma Lou was all right and added that the next time he came to town he was going to see if Mr. Grady would let him have a wagon so he could bring Ma Lou by to visit.

"Well, it's about time that gal come in here to see me,'' Sis' Inis complained. "Why, I knowed your mammy when she didn't have a tit fit to suck on! Why, she was jest a little bitty thing, puny as peckerwood when her mammy used to bring her in here to town years ago. But afterwhile, when they put her to work in the field, she commenced to eat an' flesh out a little bit, an' you could begin to tell she was gon' be a woman without havin' to ruminate your mind about it. Next thing you know, she'd up an' jumped the broom with your daddy and come up mighty soon after that with you, suh! Couldn't find no apron big enough to go 'round her when she was a-totin' you. That's how big you was. An' you come here from God-knows-where a-squallin' an' a-bawlin' like a catamount settin' on a anthill! Big as a Georgia watermelon, you was, an' you ain't stopped growin' yet, is you? You bring your mammy in here to see Sis' Inis, you big ol' double-sized scamp, you! I been knowin' you ever since you been here—an' your mammy and your mammy's mammy before you.

Sis' Inis was about out of breath from talking so much, so she stopped the back-and-forth motion of the swing long enough to bend over and pick up the mug of peach brandy she had set on the floor against the wall when Big Walking

Man first came up half an hour before. " 'S my medicine," she said defiantly. My doctor, he recommend I take a lil' toddy every day to keep off the miseries. But it ain't for no chillun," she warned. "So don't be whettin' up your goozle, 'spectin' me to give you none. It ain't for no chillun, and it ain't none of your business nohow."

Big Walking Man was getting anxious about Irene and Lil' Un. He'd been talking to Sis' Inis a long time, and they still hadn't come back from wherever it was they had gone. It was getting late, and he didn't like for Lil' Un to be in the streets after dark, even if she was with Cousin Irene. He got up from the swing, intending to go down the path to the street to see if they might be coming. "You come right back here an' set yourself down," Sis' Inis demanded between sips from the thick brown mug of peach brandy. "Irene's a-comin', an if you go traipsin' off out there in the street, you gon' miss 'em."

Big Walking Man sat down on the edge of the porch. "How do you know they're on the way, Sis' Inis? I don't see nobody."

"Don't have to see nobody to know when somebody's comin'," she told him. "Somethin' come to me an' said she's on the way, an' she is. I listens when things talk to me in my mind."

"You mean somebody's talkin' to you? Who? I don't hear nobody."

"You don't hear nothin' 'cause you ain't got nothin' to hear with. It comes to my mind, an' it ain't *nobody* that's talkin'. It's a spirit. That's what it is, a spirit."

"Well, if you gon' be talkin' to spirits, an' can't nobody hear 'em but you," Big Walking Man said, "I'm leavin'." He got up and brushed the seat of his overalls and looked carefully about him as if to see whether any of Sis' Inis's spirits were hanging around right then.

"Ain't no use to look," she said, shaking her empty mug at him. "You can't see no spirit, but they're here. My mammy what come from Af'ca used to talk to 'em all the time an' now they come to me. Now look out yonder in the road— who you think that is?"

A large woman carrying a bag of groceries turned into the yard and waddled up toward the porch. It was Irene. Following close behind her was a small black-and-tan rabbit hound with long, floppy ears and a tail like a willow switch. It was Lil' Un. "Hey, Josiah," Irene called out between pants as she heaved herself down into the swing beside Sis' Inis. "I expected you'd be coming in to town to see me today. How is Cousin Lou?"

If Big Walking Man heard her, he was too busy feeding his dog the catfish he brought for her. And the rabbit, as they sat side by side on Sis' Inis's front porch.

"Now ain't that a mess o' chitlins!" Sis' Inis said to nobody in particular, and shuffled off into the kitchen to fill up her toddy mug to help stave off the miseries while she talked with Irene.

A Tough Titty

*J*ELUS APPELBY looked at the girl twisting and turning on the bed in the corner of his three-room shack. He could not see her too well because there was only one small window in the room and it was away up near the ceiling. But by the way she was moaning and carrying on, he could tell that she was in trouble and he had to do something right away. The problem was that Jelus didn't know just what to do. He opened the front door so that he could see better. Maybe if he could just see a little better it would come to him what he ought to do. He walked to the edge of the rickety porch and spat a splat of tobacco juice across the yard. About that time the girl on the bed gave a loud holler that startled Jelus so bad that he almost fell off the porch and onto a pile of pine slabs he had been aiming to split up for stovewood. It wasn't that he hadn't seen anybody in labor before. As a matter of fact, he had seen his wife, Virgie, die in labor on that same iron bed, and that was probably part of what was troubling him so much just now. He spat out his wad of chewing tobacco and went back into the house, easing gingerly toward the bed as if he expected something to leap up and grab him by the throat. Finally, he leaned over a little to talk to the girl. She just had on some kind of old smock, and with half of the buttons gone he could see her stomach heaving about like a pumpkin in a washtub. And she was sweating, sweating all over, and Jelus couldn't tell whether her water had broken or whether she had just wetted up the mattress with sweat. He felt in his hip pocket for his dirty red handkerchief and sopped some of the water from her forehead.

"Paris?" he said. "Paris, this here's your daddy. You hear me, Paris?"

The girl didn't move or open her eyes, but finally, she whispered, "I hear you, Daddy." But then she was hit by a sudden volley of pains which set her screaming again. When the screaming stopped, she rolled over on her side as if she were dead.

Jelus put his hand on her forehead and then told one of the other children, Cora Jean it was, to "run fast down the road yonder an' git Preacher Yancey. Now hurry up and do what I tell you." In a short time that seemed like a very long time to Jelus, Preacher Yancey trotted into the yard on his mare mule with Cora Jean perched up behind him. Preacher Yancey was a tall, imposing-looking colored man with a subdued air of mystery, or maybe it was spirituality, about him, even when he wasn't wearing his preaching clothes. He slid off his mule and tied her to a convenient bush before stopping to help Cora Jean down from the animal's rump. "Have to be careful with this here critter," he explained as he reached up to help the girl. "She gits mighty spiteful sometimes, an' she'll kick anybody she ain't used to. Now where's your daddy?"

Before Cora Jean could answer, Jelus opened the door and hurried out on the porch. When he saw Preacher Yancey's mule tied up in his front yard, he forgot his troubles momentarily and climbed off the porch to examine the animal. "Rat nice-lookin' ol' mule you ridin' on, Preacher," he commented as he stroked the mule's neck admiringly and peered into her eyes.

"She'll do pretty good," the preacher admitted, trying to conceal his pride. "But you got to be careful 'round her. She ain't but four years old, an' she's still full of devilment. You don't want to git too close to her withers 'cause if you do, you bein' a stranger an' all, she's liable to kick you.''

"Shucks!" the white man exclaimed, prying open the mule's mouth to see if the preacher was telling the truth about her age. "I ain't never seen the jarhead I'd let kick me an' git away with it. The secret to handlin' a mule is to do it first; handle him before he handles you! Why, Preacher, I—"

A prolonged scream from Paris cut short Jelus Appelby's reflections on mule handling and thrust him back face-to-face with the reason he'd sent for Preacher Yancey in the first place. He let the mule alone and rushed into the cabin, followed closely by the preacher.

Cora Jean was already at the bedside, staring down at her sister but not knowing what to do to stop her from moaning and screaming. When Preacher Yancey saw Paris lying there like she was dead, but with her stomach jumping and jerking like a big ol' toad frog in a croker sack, he knew right away what the problem was, and he knew it needed attention. Right away. He pushed Cora Jean gently aside so that he could sit on the edge of the bed beside Paris. "Get me some water," he said, and Cora Jean fetched him the water bucket from the shelf inside the kitchen. The preacher's lips were working silently as he drew his handkerchief from the bib of his overalls, dipped it into the water, and began to bathe Paris's face. A minute or two later she opened her eyes and looked at Preacher Yancey as if she wanted to smile, but before the smile could form, another pain hit her, and she hollered in agony as her swollen body jumped halfway across the bed. Preacher Yancey laid his hand on the suffering girl's forehead to try to calm her. At the same time his eyes searched the room urgently as if he were looking for something to help his silent prayers to bring her some relief.

"Git me the ax to cut them labor pains," he said to Jelus, who stood leaning helplessly against the front of the bed.

"Git me the ax, one you chillun," Jelus echoed. "Git me the ax rat now so's we can cut them labor pains!"

Jelusie, ten years old and named for her daddy, detached herself from the far corner of the room where she had stood crying silently ever since Cora Jean had gone to get Preacher Yancey. She ran out into the front yard and got the big double-bitted ax from the slab pile and brought it in and handed it to Preacher Yancey. "Please don't hurt my sister with the ax," she said, a look of wonder tinged with terror in her soft brown eyes. "Please, Preacher Yancey, don't hurt Paris no more."

"Jelusie! You git on out o' here," Jelus screamed at her in his frustration. "Ain't nobody gon' do nothin' to Paris with no ax. You git on out from here! This is grown folks' business."

"No, sir," Preacher Yancey said gently. "We jest gon' put this ol' ax under the bed so Paris won't hurt so much. We ain't aimin' to harm her with it a'tall. Now you jest run on out an' play, like your daddy said. Your sister gon' be all right. Afterwhile." He patted the little girl on the head to reassure her, and she left the room to find Cora Jean.

When the ax was in place underneath the bed, Preacher Yancey got up and began to talk urgently with Jelus Appelby. "You better git a doctor, an' mighty quick," he told the frightened white man as they moved out on the porch to get out of earshot in case Paris was listening. "If you don't git a doctor, I 'spect your gal is liable to die. She is bad off sick, an' it don't look like to me she gon' be able to birth that child with no help. Well, now," the preacher added as an after-thought, "course, now I didn't mean she ain't got no help. She got the Livin' God, an' He's a mighty independent help when all other helpers is liable to fail. But right now I expect she needs all the help she can git, an' the Good Lord's more likely to help you if you try to help yourself. Now what you gon' do for that child in there?"

Jelus scratched his backside and looked off into the pine-woods. "Preacher Yancey," he said finally, "I'll jest have to tell you. I don't rightly know what I'm gonna do. I jest don't know what to do. That's how come I sent for you. You bein' a preacher an' all, I figgered you could help me think o' somethin'."

"Well, it look like to me you don't have to do a whole lot of thinkin'," the preacher replied. "That girl needs a doctor, an' she needs one right now. An' that's as plain as your nose on your face."

"I can't git no doctor," Jelus said flatly. "She ain't married!"

"That ain't none of the doctor's business," Preacher Yancey said. "That's between you an' her an' her Maker. You got to be in it 'cause you're responsible for raisin' her better, but the doctor ain't got nothin' to do but come on out here an' try to help her if he can. So you better crank up an' run on into town if that's all it is. I'll send for my wife, Maybelle, an' we'll stay here 'til you git back."

"Preacher, I jest cain't go in town an' bring no doctor out here to treat Paris. They probably wouldn't come anyhow." Jelus hedged, still looking off into the pine trees. "I jest can't do it."

"You ain't got no money?" the preacher asked. "That ain't supposed to get in the way of no sick call if you talkin' about a sho' nuff doctor. An' a sho' nuff doctor is what you need. You don't need no jackleg. Anyhow, Maybelle an' me can probably scrape up two or three dollars between us, an' that ought to do for a down payment. You go on an' git a doctor. Let me and the Master worry about how he gon' git paid. You go on."

"It ain't jest the money," Jelus said, finally looking directly at the preacher. "It's Po' Boy."

"Po' Boy? What's Po' Boy got to do with it?" the preacher said, a note of suspicion creeping into his voice.

"Po' Boy's got everything to do with it," Jelus said, his voice rising to show his indignation. "He's the one what done it. Po' Boy!"

"Well, I don't know nothin' a'tall about all that," Preacher Yancey said. "An' I don't want to know nothin' about it. But no matter who done it, your gal is in yonder a-moanin' an' a-groanin' an' mighty close to birthin' time. An' if she ain't never done it before, she ain't liable to make it."

There was a patch of silence during which Preacher Yancey was looking up into the sky as if for some sign or some word on what was to be done. Jelus just sat down on the steps in resignation and despair. After a while the preacher put his hand on Jelus's shoulder and shook him a little to get him thinking again. "You know Dr. Tait?" he asked Jelus as if an idea were coming into his mind.

"Cain't say I ever done heard of him," Jelus said, looking up without enthusiasm. "But it don't make no difference. I couldn't place no more confidence in him than I could the rest of 'em."

"Well, prob'ly not," the preacher admitted. "But he's a colored doctor. The only trouble with him is that they don't want him to work on no white folks. 'Specially no white women. But maybe he'll come out here an' do it anyway, your girl bein' so sick an' all. He got one white man what goes to him reg'lar, they say; but he's a special case, an' it ain't none of my business. But he *might* come out here for you, the Good Lord willin'!"

"Well, I'll sho' go see him," said Jelus, getting up from the stoop. "I ain't got a whole lot of money to pay him with like them fellers downtown, but the worse thing he can do to me is say naw, he ain't comin'. An' I jest don't b'lieve he'll do that, do you Preacher? Him bein' jest a colored doctor, an' all, you don't reckon he'll turn me down, do you?"

"Well, I don't know," the preacher admitted. "If he comes out here, he might be in trouble with the Law in more ways than one. But he *might*, God willing. He *might*. But now jest in case he don't, I want you to go see A'nt Malissy Hargrove, if he don't come. Now she's done retired from pulling babies, but she don't care much about what they say downtown since she brought most of 'em down there into this world. Now you hur'rup an' git on into town, an' if you can't do no business with Dr. Tait, you go on an' see A'nt Malissy an' tell her that Reverend Yancey done sent you."

Now Jelus had an old flatbed truck that he used to haul his slabs on when he went into Clayton City to sell them. The old truck wasn't good for much else, certainly not for riding on because the flatbed was full of nails and splinters, and there were no floorboards in the cab to put your feet on. Only a raggedy old buggy seat Jelus had managed to jam in there separated him and any passenger he might have from the ground. But the old truck ran pretty good when it got started, and Jelus and Po' Boy made regular trips with it hauling pine logs to the mill and pine slabs to Clayton City. He hurried out to crank the old Ford so that he could go on in to see Dr. Tait like Preacher Yancey had told him, but in his hurry to be off, the stubborn old crank kicked him and almost broke his arm. The preacher heard him hollering and cussing, so he hurried into the yard to tell Jelus to get in and choke the truck while he cranked. They got it started, and Jelus backed it around the big pile of slabs piled up in the yard so that he could head on out to Clayton City.

"Dr. Tait lives on The Avenue," Preacher Yancey shouted at him above the clatter of the Ford. "He got his office in his house right there on The Avenue 'cross the street from the Blue Flame Café. You can't miss it. Now if the doctor can't help us, you go on an' see A'nt Malissy. She don't live but a quarter mile off The Avenue from the doctor. You jest ask anybody you see. They'll tell you where she lives."

A loud scream from Paris sent the flatbed hustling out of the yard as fast as Jelus could manage it, and Preacher Yancey raced back into the house to see if his worst fears had been realized. Paris was wild-eyed with pain, and her alternate moans and screams tore mightily at the clergyman's heart, if not his confidence. He called Cora Jean and told her to run on down to the house and tell Maybelle to come on up to help him look after Paris until her daddy got back with the doctor, but first he wanted her and Jelusie to join with him in prayer. The preacher hitched up the only chair in the room to the side of the bed and began to pray, holding on to Paris's hand with one hand and to her younger sisters' hands with the other. The children were looking both sad and fearful, so the preacher squeezed their hands and told them that Jesus Christ was the Divine Healer and that Jesus Christ would take care of everything. He gazed at the ceiling and said that he was going to lift up his eyes to the same God that delivered Israel, and who touched the heart of Abraham Lincoln, and who raised Lazarus from the dead in olden times. Then he made the girls kneel with him on the floor by Paris's bed and say the Lord's Prayer with him. They had never heard it before, so he patiently lined it out to them and had them repeat what he said. When he said amen! they got up from their knees, and he shooed them on out and told them to go on and get his wife to help him tend to Paris. After the prayer he felt a little more satisfied, and even Paris seemed to be resting better, for she had dropped on off to sleep.

Jelus Appelby lived about nine miles in the country, not counting the three miles he had to go from back in the woods to get to the blacktop. He made his living cutting pine trees and hauling them in to the planing mill and selling the slabs that were left when the trees were cut into lumber for firewood. Nearly all of the people living in the area where he built his shack were colored people, but Jelus said that he was raised up around colored people, and being about the only white family for four or five miles didn't bother him.

At least it had never bothered him before, but right now it was bothering him a whole lot, all on account of Po' Boy. And Po' Boy was colored, not to just come on out and call him a nigger. As he drove toward town with his sore arm hanging out of the window of his Ford, his thoughts about Po' Boy grew increasingly bitter. He had never called Po' Boy a nigger before, but that's just about what he turned out to be, Jelus decided. And now because of Po' Boy, he stood to lose his business, his reputation, and maybe even his oldest girl back there at the house trying to birth Po' Boy's baby. He hated Po' Boy, he decided. He hated niggers, all except Reverend Yancey, an' maybe Dr. Tait.

It all started when Po' Boy helped Jelus unload some slabs in Clayton City one Saturday morning. Jelus liked his big muscles and the way he worked, so he told Po' Boy that if he'd come out in the country where he had his sawmill, he'd show him how to make hisself some good money. He gave Po' Boy the directions to his place, and first chance he got, Po' Boy just put his feet in the road and walked on out there. Well, Jelus didn't have what you could rightly call a sawmill, just an old saw blade he could hitch up to the hind wheel of his truck and cut slabs into stovewood was all he had. Po' Boy looked kind of disappointed, but since he'd walked all the way out there to work, he helped Jelus cut up a load of slabs and haul them into Clayton. Jelus gave him a dollar and promised that if he'd come back and work the next day, he'd give him another dollar for what he'd done already. When Po' Boy went back to get his other dollar, Jelus put him to work helping him to cut pine trees to take to the planing mill. From there one thing led to another, and pretty soon Po' Boy was working every day for Jelus Appelby. Jelus let him eat in the kitchen after he and the girls were through, and Po' Boy slept under an old tarpaulin hanging over the truck until he and Jelus built him a one-room slab cabin about a half mile back in the woods from Jelus's house.

Po' Boy made a whole lot of money for Jelus. He could cut more wood than two or three men, and he didn't lay around on the job or jack the dog like Jelus had expected he would when he had to be away on business. As a matter of fact, Jelus came to think a whole lot of Po' Boy for him to be a colored boy, and pretty soon he was even letting Po' Boy drive his truck into town on Saturday night to spend his money. But first thing you know, Po' Boy just didn't seem interested in going to town on Saturday nights anymore. He just hung around Jelus's place, splitting stovewood or working on a chicken house for Jelus, without even asking Jelus if he wanted him to do it. As time went along, when Jelus went off to take a drink or two on Saturday night, he didn't feel like he had to hurry back so quick because he knew that Po' Boy was around to take care of whatever might come up. It got so that Po' Boy would just stay on around Jelus's house every Saturday afternoon when he quit work, just sitting out on the porch 'til Jelus came home, no matter what time of night. Then, if Jelus had had too much corn likker, as happened right along, Po' Boy would help Paris get her daddy into bed before he went on off to his own shack.

Jelus never did say anything to Po' Boy about being around his house so late on Saturday night. Every Monday morning, when Po' Boy came to work, Jelus acted just like he hadn't seen him since Saturday noon. Then, when Paris got to looking so big and he asked her what the trouble was, she told him she was in a family way, and that Po' Boy had done it. Even then Jelus didn't put in for a lot of trouble like most people woulda done. He just looked at Paris and told her,

"You my own flesh an' blood, my oldest daughter, an' you know you ain't goin' to have no nigger baby in this house." She told him she didn't want to have any kind of baby, but that Po' Boy got her in a family way, so she guess she didn't have no choice.

"When that boy rape you?" Jelus asked her.

"He ain't never rape me," she told him. "He jest 'round here all the time an' we done it together."

"Ain't no white woman sleep with no nigger of her own free will," Jelus told her, but he didn't sound like he had his heart in what he said. She knew where his weak spot was, so she told him, "Well, Daddy, you work with him, and you eat with him, an' I done seen you try to get him to drink with you. I wasn't aimin' to do nothin' with him; but we 'way out here in the woods, an' I got to have me somebody, sometime. So since you like him so much, I figger it may as well be Po' Boy irregardless of him being colored, an' all."

When she said that, his fire come up, and he hauled off and slapped her down on the bed. The other children started hollering and crying, and Jelus stomped on out of the house and headed for Po' Boy's cabin. Po' Boy saw him coming and figured by the way Jelus was walking that something must of happened he didn't want to hear about. So he just slipped on his lumber jacket, picked up his ax, and cut out through the woods without Jelus so much as seeing which way he went.

Jelus went on back home and told Paris he'd run Po' Boy plumb out the county, and that she either had to go into town with him to tell the Law how Po' Boy had overpowered her, or she had to do something to git rid of what she was toting. "If folks find out you let a nigger knock you up of your own free will," he told her, "we'll be run out of town like dirt, an' that's for sho'." But Paris told him she wasn't going to sic the Law on Po' Boy and get him lynched after all he'd done for them, because she was as much to blame as he was. And she said she wasn't going to kill herself by trying to get rid of no baby when she was already better'n six months gone. She reminded him that she'd seen her mama die trying to get rid of a baby because he told her he couldn't feed no more young uns. Jelus slapped her down again an' went off to cut some pine slabs. But Jelus wasn't what you would call a mean man; he just didn't know what else to do.

Jelus never did seem to do much good after that. With Po' Boy gone, he wasn't cutting enough wood to make any money. He had aimed to put another room on the house, but he didn't have Po' Boy to help him, so he gave it up. And the chicken house Po' Boy was building never did git finished. Jelus halfway wished Po' Boy would come on back and help him out a little while; then he could run him off proper when things got better. But Po' Boy kept himself out of sight, and nobody seemed to know just where he went. But it was hard on Jelus, and by the time it came for Paris to get down to confinement, her daddy had just about come to the end of his rope. That's why he'd sent for Preacher Yancey, the colored preacher who lived about a half mile down the sand road from where Jelus had built his shack.

Jelus's arm was hurting him mighty bad where the crank on his old truck had kicked him, but he drove the old flatbed through the ruts and around the pine stumps like he never had a pain in his body. When he made it to the pike, he opened up the old Ford, and the fence posts went by so fast it would have given him a swimming in the head if his head had not been already aching with so many troubles. Jelus was in a hurry. He had to get on to Clayton City and find Dr. Tait's place on The Avenue because the preacher had already as much as told him his oldest gal was going to die if he don't get somebody to help her right away. Then, too, nigger babies generally come big, he'd always heard, and it wasn't natural anyway for a white woman to try to have one.

When Jelus got past the edge of town and his old truck clattered onto the Upper End of The Avenue, he slowed it down a little to watch out for the Blue Flame Café, but he had driven almost the total length of The Avenue before he saw it. When he recognized the Blue Flame, he suddenly remembered that he had dropped Po' Boy off there once or twice, and he was almost tempted to get out of his truck and go in there to see if maybe that's where Po' Boy was hiding out. The urgency of his mission in Clayton City wouldn't stand for any delay right now, though, he decided, so he went on past the Flame, made a U-turn, and pulled up in front of the house where the colored doctor must have his office. As he was getting out of his flatbed a United States Mail truck turned off The Avenue and parked behind the doctor's house, and a white man with tousled gray hair and a beet red face got out of the mail truck, entered the backyard, and disappeared. Jelus hoped the white man was not the special patient Preacher Yancey had mentioned, but if he was, he hoped that the doctor wouldn't have to spend too much time on him today. Paris was bad off, and he hoped to get the doctor to go with him back to the country right away.

Jelus couldn't read much, but when he walked up to the front of the doctor's office, the printing on the roller shade said THE DOCTOR IS OUT. He rang the doorbell and shook the doorknob until he figured it was going to drop off, but nobody answered. Finally, in desperation he walked around to the backyard where he had seen the white man disappear. Maybe he could tell him when the doctor would be back. He didn't see the white man, but there was a colored driver in the mail truck. It was Buford Atkins.

"You see a white man go in here?" he asked the colored man in the mail truck. "I'm lookin' for a colored doctor name of Tait."

"Naw, sir," Buford replied, "Me, I been 'sleep. I ain't seen nobody a'tall. But if you lookin' for Dr. Tait, I know he ain't here, an' won't be here 'til he opens up his office about two hours from now. An' now it ain't my business, but Dr. Tait don't take no white folks. You got the wrong doctor."

Jelus was very disappointed. He'd hoped to catch the doctor in his office and persuade him to go see Paris, even though Preacher Yancey had told him the doctor might not come. But he couldn't wait two more whole hours. He had to get some help, and right away. "Where ol' A'nt Malissy live?" he asked Buford. "I'll go see her."

"Go on back up The Avenue an' turn off to the left on Cooper Street. She live in a green house. But she ain't workin' no more. She done quit for good."

A few minutes later Jelus turned his truck off on Cooper Street, and pretty soon he pulled up in front of a little green clapboard house with a big chimney on each end. Old A'nt Malissy had lived there for more than fifty years, and she was sitting on the front porch in a big rocking chair just like she was waiting for him to drive up. Malissy was close to seventy-five years old, and she had brought ninety percent of all the colored children in Clayton County into the world, and a heap of white ones besides. But over the past few years her white practice had fallen off since they got the County Hospital, and the doctors on the Medical Board had been after her. But Malissy didn't pay any more attention to the Medical Board than she wanted to. She knew a lot more about delivering babies than most of them, even though she was a colored woman and black as sin. The best evidence of her success was the Medical Board itself. She'd delivered nearly everybody on it.

Jelus jumped out of the truck and started to tell the old woman about his daughter laying out there in the country in labor; but he talked so fast he tripped over his tongue, and A'nt Malissy just sat there rocking and looking at him and waiting for him to calm down so she could make out what his trouble was. When he finally stopped to catch his breath, she asked him what he'd said his name was. He told her, and she just said, "Umhumm," and kept on rocking as if she was studying the situation. But Jelus was in a hurry, so he asked her to get in the truck and come with him right away, because his daughter was bad off. But Malissy continued puffing calmly on her pipe and rocking until Jelus had exhausted himself. Suddenly she looked at him as if she saw him for the first time and demanded: "Now, suh. I don't know no Appelby like you call yo'self. Who sent you over here? You know I done retired. I git my bag for mighty few colored folks an' no white folks a'tall these days. I done looked after y'all for more'n fifty years, an' half the big folks what run this here town, I brung 'em here head first with these here ol' black hands. But now I done retired from the white folks; they don't need me no more."

Jelus told her he didn't know anything about all that, but

he sure did need her because he had a special case; and Preacher Yancey sent him to get her because nobody else could help him under the circumstances. When she heard him say Preacher Yancey sent him, she commenced to get herself together to get out of her rocking chair as fast as she could. But Malissy weighed close to three hundred pounds, and getting up and down she had to be careful and go kind of slow. She called her grandson Thornton out of the house, and he came out and gave her a hand to help her up on her feet. As soon as she was standing securely, she looked hard at Jelus and said, "Now, suh, you ought to done told me in the first place that Reverend Yancey done sent you over here. I don't know nothin' 'bout you, 'cept you livin' out yonder with the colored people. And I don't go off nowhere with no white folks I don't know. How come you livin' 'mongst the colored anyhow? If your gal in trouble, I suspect it's your own fault, an' now some po' colored boy is the one what's got to pay for it! That's how come you come to me, ain't it? Well, let's go before that child dies in labor. Thornton, git me my bag."

Jelus and Thornton helped Malissy down from the porch and out to the truck. But when she opened the door and saw there were no floorboards in the cab for her to put her feet on, she refused to get in.

"I ain't ridin' in that contraption," she told Jelus, " 'cause there ain't nowhere to ride."

Jelus looked as if he wanted to cry, he was so flustered by the way things were going. He said, "Goddamn!" But Malissy shook her finger at him and told him not to ever let her hear him blaspheme God while he was standing in her yard.

"I don't have nothing to do with no blasphemers," she said, "colored or white," and she turned around to go back and sit on her porch.

But Jelus had an idea all of a sudden. He ran up on the porch and grabbed her great big old rocker before she could occupy it and lifted it up on the truck bed. Then he ran his log chain through the chair to fasten it down and hold it steady. When he got it firmly anchored, he jumped up on the truck bed and tested it out. The old chair could rock back and forth just fine, but it couldn't slide off the truck on account of that heavy log chain Jelus had hitched it down with. He grinned triumphantly at Malissy and asked her to try it out to see if she liked it. He and Thornton helped her up on the truck, and she sat down in the old rocker and said she liked it fine. Jelus then hurried around the truck and got in the cab while Thornton cranked it for him, and they drove off down the road with old A'nt Malissy back there rocking on the flatbed like some kind of African queen sitting on a river barge.

Maybelle Yancey was putting on a pot of collards when the two white children knocked at her back door. She could see they were the Appelby children, and she reckoned they were looking for a bucket of milk or something their daddy sent them after. She told them to come in, but the biggest one—that would be Cora Jean—told her their sister Paris was bad sick, and that Preacher Yancey wanted her to come up there to the house right away. She looked at the girls and decided they hadn't had anything to eat, so she fixed each one of them a big sandwich of cornbread and side meat with homemade chowchow, and she was ready to go. As they walked up the sand road, Maybelle kept wondering what could be wrong with Paris, but the children were busy eating and she didn't get much information from them. Maybelle hoped it wasn't real bad, because the last time she was up there to Mr. Appelby's, po' Miz Appelby passed away in childbirth, although she'd done all she could for her. Maybelle had raised six or seven children of her own, so she knew something about it. But all her chillun were grown now, and living in Chicago and Detroit and places like that, she mused to herself. Ain't a one of 'em stayed home to be a comfort to me an' Preacher Yancey while we're gittin' on up in age. The grandchildren came to see them sometimes, but by the time they'd get attached to one his folks would send for him or come get him, so the old folks still didn't have anybody around to do for and to love. But they never complained, and Preacher Yancey always said that when God gets ready, God will play His hand. But most folks figured that there wasn't much God could do for two wore-out old colored folks like Preacher Yancey and Maybelle.

When Maybelle and the Appelby girls got halfway to the house, they could hear Paris a-screaming and a-hollering every few seconds like she was going by the clock. They didn't see Preacher Yancey anywhere until they got up on the porch, and then they could see him down on his knees by the bed, praying. He hadn't stopped praying since Jelus had been gone. Maybelle looked at Paris, and she knew right away what the trouble was. She made a fire in the kitchen stove and put on some water to boil. Then she asked Cora Jean for some clean rags. When they couldn't find any, she put the girls out and ripped up her muslin petticoat and got it ready. The Reverend had stopped praying for a minute, and she asked him how long Jelus been gone after the doctor. About that time they heard Jelus's old truck backfire when it came through the creek on the other side of the clearing, and Preacher Yancey ran out on the porch to see if he could see him coming and if he'd brought any help. The old truck was keeping up an awful racket as it came on out of the woods and around the edge of the clearing. Pretty soon Jelus drove on up into the yard, and the reverend could see old A'nt Malissy sitting up there on the flatbed, smoking her pipe as calm as you please. He closed his eyes and said, "Thank you, Jesus. Jesus, I thank you."

Jelus backed the flatbed up to the porch, and A'nt Malissy walked right off with no trouble at all and went directly into the house. She put her hand on Paris's stomach and talked with Maybelle for a minute; then she told the men and the children that she and the Lord would be in charge from then on, and she needed the room they were taking up. It was getting on toward dark, so Maybelle lit the kerosene lamp, shooed the men and the girls outdoors, and closed the door. Malissy sat down on the bed an' put both Paris's hands on her stomach. "Now, honey," she said, "when the next pain comes, push down. Push down hard!"

Reverend Yancey was standing outside the door, and he heard what she said, so he looked up in the sky where the stars were coming out and said, "Lord Jesus, when the next pain comes, push down. Push down hard!"

In a little while Paris started to grunt and holler and holler and grunt with almost every breath. When all of a sudden she stopped, it sounded like there was a baby crying somewhere in the house. In a minute or two Maybelle cracked the door and told Jelus and the preacher to come in. Fifteen minutes later the door opened again, and Maybelle went off down the sand road with a bundle in her arms, Reverend Yancey right beside her, leading his mare mule. Three days after that the Appelbys were gone. They just loaded everything they had on the old flatbed Ford and disappeared.

The next Sunday Reverend Yancey had a christening at his church. He looked out over the people and told them how the Lord works in mysterious ways. Then he read from the Bible where it says that unto you a son is given. An' unto you a child is born. When he got through reading, he took the baby from Maybelle and held him up for the people to see and said: "I called on the Lord an' He heard my prayer. In our old age, an' in His own wisdom, He done sent us a son. Until the Lord give him a better name, I name him Pee Bee Yancey. Blessed be the name of the Lord, an' let all the people say amen!" They all did and stomped their feet against the floor 'til it shook.

Now Pee Bee was the Reverend's secret way of naming the boy for his real daddy, the fellow they called Po' Boy, who used to cut slabs for Jelus Appelby. After he'd given the baby a name, Reverend Yancey gave him back to Maybelle, and she took him on back to where she'd been sitting on the front pew. A few minutes later she took out her breast and put Pee Bee to sucking and smacking just like he was her natural child. When all the people commenced to gape and stare when they saw the old woman long past sixty suckling a newborn child, the reverend just looked at them in a sort of compassionate way and said, "Marvel not, brothers and sisters. It's a mighty tough titty that won't give milk when God is in the plan." Then he closed his eyes and looked up in the sky and whispered, "Thank you, Jesus. Now push down hard, Lord, one more time!"

Mama Lucy

*S*HE was born on the six acre home place just west of the Old Fort, and there was always a certain security and a silent rejoicing in the Lunceford family that they had never had to rent from the white man. Not that they had anything, except the ground itself and the old house that stood on it—a house long since grown weary of the continuous assaults of the rain and the cold and the hot sun and too many children. But the land was theirs, and the house was theirs, and the right to be proud and independent on account of it all was theirs, too. At least, that was the way Mama Lucy saw it. Time after time she admonished the children under her roof and her protection, "You're as good as anybody—and you'd better act like it." She meant it. And by *anybody*, she meant white and colored, on or off The Avenue. Having your own land, and owning your own house, and being in good relations with the Lord went a long way toward self-respect. So Mama Lucy never had any problems with being who she was. Or who she wasn't. If God was pleased, she was satisfied. Whenever there was a need for her in the community, she was there for whoever needed her. She figured the Lord must have some satisfaction in who she was or He would have done something about it.

Folks called Mama Lucy a "Georgia woman" behind her back. It was not a term of disrespect; but it carried the connotation that she wasn't to be trifled with, and certainly that was true. It was true, too, that her folks, the Slaters, had got off a wagon train coming up from South Georgia en route to Kansas as part of the exodus of black people following the Civil War and the uncertainties of reestablishment in the South. According to the story handed down in the family, the wagon train had been hastily organized after a wave of anti-Black terrorism and had left Georgia without proper equipment or sufficient supplies. When it arrived in Clayton County, the decision was made to winter there in the ruins of the Old Fort and to push on to Kansas in the spring. But by the time spring had come, several of the migrants had decided to stay on in Clayton, and among them were Omar and Lucy Slater.

The Slaters bought six acres of land and built a three-room cabin on it. A year later they were blessed with the arrival of their first child. It was a girl, and they named her Lucy in honor of her mother, who was thenceforth called Big Lucy in the tradition of their culture, and the newcomer was, of course, called Little Lucy. At seventeen Little Lucy married Lucius Lunceford and went to work in the white folks' kitchens where she stayed for more than forty years. At nineteen, with one child of her own, she inherited the care of four younger brothers and sisters passed on to her when Big Lucy died in childbirth and Omar decided he had a call to go on to Kansas after all to preach to the black pilgrims from the South. Nobody knows if Omar ever made it to Kansas after he took up preaching, for he was never heard from after he left Clayton City. But Little Lucy raised his brood along with six of her own and an undetermined number of other orphans and strays the Lord and the circumstances sent her way, and nobody remembered when she ceased to be Little Lucy and became Mama Lucy to a whole community. When her children were all grown and she had only an occasional grandchild or stray to provide for, she left the white folks to do their own cooking and stayed home to rest her mind. She took in washings after that to keep clothes on the children's backs and bread on the kitchen table; but she did her washing at home—away from the strain of daily contact with the contradictory world of white folks who defined all reality in Clayton City. Gradually, and over the years, in the community where she lived Mama Lucy became something of a living legend known for a simplistic mixture of forthrightness and compassion, toughness and tenderness, wisdom and forbearance. She had certain expectations of herself, and it seemed incongruous to her that the people around her could think less and demand less of themselves. Yet those who failed to live up to what Mama Lucy thought was a reasonable standard of decency and self-respect were never for that reason excluded from her company or from her compassionate concern.

Mama Lucy was first and foremost a Christian woman, but one who spoke her mind (often in the most colorful language) inside and outside the church. She had no patience with the pretensions of form. The substance of action—"doing what you ought to be doing"—was the only convincing evidence of character she could understand. She believed that God would punish the evildoer, and sometimes when God was slow, she had been known to strike a blow on His behalf.

Lucius Lunceford was all the things his wife was not. A small, wiry, mild-mannered man, he was not given to controversy or conflict, and he went out of his way to avoid both. Physically he was dwarfed by Mama Lucy, who, though not a large woman, seemed to loom above her husband and cast him in a perpetual shadow. If Lucius ever had any thoughts about it, they must have long since been dulled by the years of being married to a woman he could never hope to fully understand, to say nothing of control. Yet on occasion he dared with some wistfulness to wish that she would let things alone a little bit and give him a little peace. But then, on such occasions, Lucius was more likely to find his own peace by hitching up his mule and escaping to the solitude of the cotton fields. He believed in God, but he was never known to enter a church. Nor did he ever talk about it. Lucius accepted Mama Lucy's and the children's churchgoing as a matter of course but showed no interest in what went on there. Yet his moral life seemed to be exemplary, and he was known everywhere for being hardworking and easy to get along with. To the children and grandchildren, "Papa Lucius" was a favorite refuge from the wrath and righteousness of Mama Lucy. When of an evening he propped his cane-bottomed chair against the wall for a nap on the front porch, even the neighborhood children would come to climb on his lap to marvel at the springy softness of his white woolly hair and the smooth chocolate color of his gentle face.

The white folks found Mama Lucy to be a puzzlement, sometimes to the point of exasperation, but never enough to compromise her value as a servant. She was an excellent cook, turning out extraordinary cakes and pies or Sally Lunn or Charlotte Russe with effortless perfection. Her pork roasts were succulent and done just right; her crackling bread was unrivaled, and her homemade sausage made every plate of hominy grits seem like a special event seven days a week. She kept an immaculate house, and she could work the arrival of unexpected guests into her routine without panicking or requiring extra supervision. All for six dollars a week. But Mama Lucy never did let the white folks know what was going on inside the private recesses of her mind. She didn't talk about what went on in the colored community either, and any effort to pry information out of her was apt to be met by the blunt declaration that since it wasn't none of her business, she had made no big effort to find out about it. Mama Lucy usually made her point, and when she had said all she wanted to say, she was apt to be let alone. She had a way of starting in to sing or hum snatches of some old spiritual, and this let it be known that the conversation was over.

On the other hand, when Mama Lucy felt called upon to speak her mind, she was terse and to the point. Once she was asked her frank opinion by a bedridden spinster for whom she worked as to whether she thought the stricken woman was going to die. "Yes'm," she said simply as she continued to polish the ornate mahogany bed in which the white woman languished. "Most folks do—colored and white."

On another occasion, when she cooked for the Gilligans and Mr. Gilligan was commenting on what he called the natural differences between white people and colored people, Mama Lucy said she didn't know if people were all that different. "Every ear of corn may look different," she told him, "but when they come out of the gristmill, grits is what you got. And grits ain't nothing but grits no matter how you cook 'em!"

It was in her own community that the wisdom and integrity of Lucy Lunceford were most respected and appreciated. Her notion of what was right and wrong never varied with the circumstances. She whipped her children when they were wrong, praised them when they were right, and she did as much as she could to protect them from the hazards of existence over which she had no reasonable control. The tired old house on Crockett Street usually had more than its share of her children, and anybody else's children who happened to need some place to stay. Mama Lucy treated them all alike. She took them to church, sent them to school, and fed them as best she could. She taught them how to work and then expected to see them work. She wept over them, rejoiced over them, and every night she gathered them around the hearthside and prayed over them. Her petition always concluded with the reminder that *"Now, Lord, these is your chillun. You made 'em and you made 'em black. So, Lord Jesus, in your name let them be black and beautiful. Let them stand the test. Amen!"*

But in spite of prayer and precept, Mama Lucy's children did not always measure up to what she hoped they'd be. The girls raised under her roof and her rule occasionally succumbed to the prevailing patterns of time and circumstance and had a child or two before they were finally married. While this was a routine mistake, and one that time would eventually heal, it grieved Mama Lucy that she could not single-handedly, as it were, hold back the convergence of social and economic forces she didn't even understand but which from time to time overrode her best efforts. She grieved over the rules that were broken, and she decried the weakness that opened the door to sin; but when the babies were born, she found space for them, and having added them to the family, she was glad that the Lord had seen fit to bless her with their presence. The new mothers usually settled down and found jobs cooking and nursing and cleaning for the white folks to support their new responsibilities. Now that they knew better, they were more wary, and as settled working girls, they were also more attractive as marriage partners. In a year or two most of them would have husbands. Some would marry their former boyfriends who had run away Up North in fright and shock at the sudden prospect of marriage and fatherhood. But having gotten a foothold in Chicago or Detroit, and having gotten over the initial intimidation of family responsibility, they often came back to claim the girl and the child who precipitated their sudden passage from pubescence to manhood.

Whenever this happened, Mama Lucy was apt to view it as a vindication of her faith—faith in God, who could change the meanest heart and who could bring light and strength and courage where before there was only ignorance and weakness and fear. She had faith in her children to do the right thing, even though it might take a little time for them to see the right with clarity and decision. She was willing to wait, if need be, for the change she always felt to be imminent in even the most stubborn miscreant. And she was decidedly impatient with people whose judgments and prejudgments allowed no room for error and no chance for reform.

Mahalia Crenshaw was a case in point. Mahalia was the perennial bucket of sour grapes. She was like an implacable thunderhead in perpetual contest with the sun whenever it tried to peep through the cultural smog that afflicted the colored people of Clayton City. As a matter of fact, it was a popular convention about town that if Mahalia ever said a pleasant word about anyone, it was either someone dead or someone about to die. Each morning after breakfast Mahalia took to the streets to distribute the somber news she had managed to accumulate during the previous twenty-four hours, and woe to the hapless individual who had made her news column for the day. Her route to her married daughter's house covered about four blocks, including two blocks along Crockett Street. As she waddled along, meandering from one side of the street to the other to capture an audience of passersby or of housewives sweeping their porches or digging in their yards, the warning went on before her by some invisible courier that *"The Black Banner is coming!"* This was the signal for the youngsters who feared Mahalia might have something to tell on them (and she usually did) to disappear and to try hard to get all the grown folks into the house and out of gossip's way. But the *Black Banner* was relentless, and many a disgusted mischief-maker was hauled forth to give account of misbehavior that would probably not have surfaced if Mahalia had minded her own business. But Mahalia made everybody's business her business, and while not everyone subscribed to the *Black Banner*, it was nonetheless a potent force for the information, or misinformation of discord as the case might be, on or off The Avenue in Clayton City.

Mama Lucy preferred to hear her news from more reliable and less vindictive sources, so she was annoyed and not a little surprised when Mahalia came rapping on the edge of her front porch one Saturday morning.

"Howdy, Mahalia," she offered when she saw who it was that summoned her to the front door. "You here to see me about something?"

"Well, I reckon so," the woman began is if she were about to announce a state secret. "And I'm so glad I got to you first, before everybody starts talking about it, you know." She eased her short, plushy frame down on the edge of the porch. "I'm mighty glad you happen to be at home. So many folks out in the street on Saturday morning, you know, when they ought to be at home cleaning up. Why, some of these houses are just plain nasty!" she declared. "But I knew you'd be at home! I jest—"

"Wait a minute, Mahalia," Mama Lucy said impatiently. "Jest wait a minute! You didn't walk all the way over here to tell me about somebody else's nasty house. At least I hope you didn't, because I ain't got time to listen to it. I'm busy trying to clean up my own. Now what is it you want with me?"

"Well, I didn't want to have nothing to do with it," Mahalia blurted out, "but I jest made it my business to come on and tell you anyhow! Well, yesterday evening late, it was, they done caught Sweet Feet and Carrie Sloan's little hussy, Lena Mae, that's her name, up yonder in the choir loft in the church. They got up and run; but they found her drawers, and here—you can see 'em for yourself!'' With that she pulled from a paper sack she had been clutching against her bosom a forlorn pair of cotton bloomers which she waved above her head.

At first, Mama Lucy just stared at the exhibit in unbelief. Finally, she said with unconcealed disgust, ''I don't think it's my place, nor yours either, to be out inspecting somebody's drawers on Saturday morning. But one thing about it I do know,'' she continued, ''Sweet Feet don't wear what you're holding, and if they don't belong to him, then it's somebody's else's business instead of mine. But since you have made it your business, maybe you ought to take that pitiful little sack of dirty drawers you got there, put your dirty little mind in there with 'em, and tie it around your dirty neck, 'cause I ain't got no time for such foolishness!'' With that she went back into the house, praying hard under her breath that the Lord would give her the strength to love Mahalia Crenshaw.

The Sweet Feet Mahalia had come to tattle to Mama Lucy about was her own child, at least in a way he was. While he was not blood of her blood and flesh of her flesh, there could have been no stronger bond of love between them had that been the case. Between them there was a fierce mutual pride and admiration as well. He was her boy; she was his Mama as long as she lived. But Sweet Feet seemed destined from the cradle, almost, to be a continuing source of anxiety for Mama Lucy and seldom far from the center of attention for everyone else who knew him.

People around Clayton City said he was star-crossed. Perhaps he was indeed singled out for some kind of special destiny, for he arrived at Mama Lucy's house one midsummer night in the midst of one of the worst storms folks around Clayton could remember: Mama Lucy heard the pounding on the front door above the crash and rumble of thunder, but by the time she'd got Lucius awake and shuffled off to the door, there was nobody in sight. But there was a shoe box, and in it was a baby boy wrapped in a tiny blanket made from calico and flour sacking. When she pulled the blanket back a little, there he was, waving his little feet and gazing confidently into the eyes of the woman who from that minute knew she was destined to be his Mama. "He jest got the sweetest little feet," Mama Lucy explained to the neighbor women who came the next day to look at him and speculate on his origins. "I guess the Lord jest naturally sent him here for me to look after." So it was that Sweet Feet came to live at the old house on Crockett Street and to take his place among the brood that Omar Slater had bequeathed to his oldest daughter when he decamped for Kansas to pursue his call to preach.

They gave Sweet Feet a proper Christian name, of course, but few people in Clayton ever knew what it was, or ever considered the possibility that the sobriquet by which they knew him was not the only name he had. Nicknames were as commonly used as Christian names, and while they were more prevalent among teenaged boys, for a man to be known by his nickname all his life was not at all unusual. The West Side of Clayton City had its share of such colorful and often descriptive appellations as "Realfoot," "Mallet Foot," "Snout," "Britches," "Guinea Meat," "Rail Head," "Booger Man," "Big Walking Man," "Wrinkle Belly," "Heap-o-Man," "Big Un," "Good Jelly," "Crip," "Dootsie," and "Blind Bates," to name a few. Many boys were simply known as "Son," or "Junior,', or "Little Ed," in which instance the father was advanced to "Big Ed," or "Big Jim," or "Big John," as the case may be. All the others seemed to be named either "Robert Lee," or "Booker Tee."

Sweet Feet himself was unusual, his name notwithstanding. Small for his age and mischievous, he was petted by his teachers and indulged by almost everyone else—partially, no doubt, because he was Mama Lucy's boy, but also because he was good-looking and he had a fine tenor voice. For a time he sang in the church choir and even over the radio in the next town as a member of a local quartet. Later on he sang to the women, too, and told them small lies and funny stories. "I'm a little weed," he would confess with an impish grin, "but, baby, I'm awful bitter!" But if the women found him bitter, it must have been *bittersweet* and irresistible as well, for they competed with each other in loving him, giving him presents, and worrying about who else he was singing to and being a bitter weed.

Sweet Feet was never known to do a deliberately mean thing to anyone, and he would rather run than fight—laughing as he ran. As a matter of fact, on more than one occasion Mama Lucy had to rescue him from the consequences of his nonintentions or when on occasion some of his humor backfired, such as the time he and his friends put a buggy astride the gable of the Burning Bush Church. Or the night he and June Bug and Bump got a full-grown heifer up two flights of stairs into the music room at the Fort Academy. The buggy stayed atop the church for two years, and the cow remained a feature of Miss Johnson's Senior Chorus until they could build a ramp to get her out through an opening cut through the window. But Sweet Feet's antics were generally harmless and amusing, and he managed to escape the knots and scars of that element of Clayton City that was intentionally bad, or went for bad, or that aroused the ire of those who turned out to be badder.

As for Mama Lucy, he bore her a kind of impish admiration so often expressed in a kiss or a hug or a reassuring squeeze of her hand that said: "That's my Mama!" And through all his misadventures, although she fussed and scolded and prayed and prophesied, his greatest assurance was the love he knew she bore him in return. Nevertheless, Mama Lucy longed for the time when he would grow up and be somebody, not so much as a reward for herself, but because she knew God's talent ought not to be wasted. And she knew by faith that Sweet Feet had something worthwhile to give the world if only he could discover it in time. In the meantime, she could only do her best to keep him morally solvent until that power greater than she took over.

A year or two before the choir loft incident broadcast by Mahalia Crenshaw, when Sweet Feet was fourteen or fifteen, he had his first introduction to the world beyond the confines of Mama Lucy's rules. A new café called the Shake It (But Don't Break It) opened up on the Upper End of The Avenue. Its arrival was probably brought on by the convergence of a number of events, not the least of which was the influx of TVA money into the town of Clayton. The TVA was building dams and impoundments all over the region, and while there were none being constructed in Clayton County, good jobs were to be had in the surrounding counties nearby. In fact, two or three men had managed to acquire pickup trucks which they converted to minibuses to haul the TVA workers in Clayton City sixty or seventy miles each day to the job sites. Suddenly the quiet little West Side community became a base for a sizable number of itinerant workers from the outside and for the women who followed them. Unlike the Blue Flame, where the school crowd hung out, the Shake It drew a rough-and-ready clientele not previously known in Clayton City, and on Saturday night it was filled with outside people mixed in with the less respectable elements of the local folk, all out for a good time. Fruit jars full of moonshine whiskey were featured on every table, and couples clutched in a kind of agonized ecstasy bumped and dragged to the gut-bucket syncopation blaring from the jukebox in the corner. The kitchen did a big business in pig feet, catfish, chitterlings, and cornbread, and the raucous laughter of the pleasure-filled diners and dancers could be heard in the byways a quarter mile away. Occasionally happiness turned into surliness, and switchblades flashed through the stale smoke that hung in tiers above the tables. But when the fight was over, new sawdust was sprinkled on the floor to cover the blood, and the fun went on. The police, who often ate their chitterlings, sampled the fruit jars, and indulged whatever additional interests they might have in the apartment behind the café, seldom bothered to arrest anyone. The problem was a lack of witnesses, they said. But after a disturbance they'd threaten to close the Shake It if the fighting didn't stop. Then they'd gather a few jars of whiskey for evidence should any witness come forward later, and go back to City Hall.

The excitement of the Shake It was something new to

Clayton, and hanging out there quickly became a fascinating and daring adventure for a handful of schoolboys who suddenly outgrew the less exotic offering of the Blue Flame. When word reached Mama Lucy that her boy was among those hanging around the Shake It, she put on a fresh apron and took her knotted oak walking stick from behind the front door and set out for The Avenue to see for herself. It was eight o'clock on Saturday night, and when she got to the Shake It, the evening was already humming, but the crowd was still sparse and still somewhat subdued. The jukebox was going full blast, and there were three or four couples on the floor being cheered on in their writhings by a group of boys on a bench along the wall. The center of attention was a large, voluptuous woman with a ragged scar on her cheek and long black hair streaming down to her waist. She danced with a kind of subtle, vulgar grace, her feet barely moving, her hips gyrating slowly to the easy rhythm with the deftness of a finely tuned engine. A wailing saxophone bumped by a bass drum and the frenetic flourishes of a steel guitar blared out from the inner recesses of the jukebox near the counter where the pile of fried sweet potato pies and boiled pig feet were displayed. The distressed baritone of a blues shouter moaned plaintively:

> Great big woman
> (Bump-de-bump)
> Built up fine, Lawd
> (Bump-de-bump)
> Got big sugar hangin'
> (Bump-de-bump)
> On her vine, Lawd
> (Bump-de-bump)
> That's sho' my weakness
> Yesss, that my scuppernong wine
> (De-bumpty-bumpity-bump-de-bump)
> Law-w-d my Big Mama
> (Bump-de-bump)
> My sweet sweet scuppernong wine!

The big woman swayed effortlessly to the compulsive syncopation. Her plump brown arms completely engulfed her small partner, leaving only the top of his head visible, his face lost in the cavern of her large, gently undulating bosom. The all but hidden dancing partner turned out to be Sweet Feet, and the heavily perfumed bosom in which he had taken temporary refuge from the world belonged to Big May Shake, a longtime madam and bootlegger from the next county, and now owner of the Shake It Café. Mama Lucy might not have seen Sweet Feet at all if one of the boys hadn't rushed over to warn him that his mama was standing in the doorway of the café. When the startled young scamp raised his head, he looked squarely into the eyes of Mama Lucy. He struggled frantically to get out of the powerful arms of Big May, but May Shake, her big brown eyes closed in her own private fantasy, was lost in the sensuous beat of the music, and the more the terrified youngster struggled, the tighter she clasped him to her.

"Sweet Little Daddy," she cooed to the top of his head as she crushed him ever closer, "hang on, Little Pepper, it gon' be all right! *All right!*"

But it wasn't going to be all right, and nobody knew that better than Sweet Feet, for he could clearly see the enraged visage of Mama Lucy advancing across the dance floor.

Mama Lucy shattered both the reverie and the impasse by giving Sweet Feet a sharp whack on the backside with her walking stick, followed by a punch with the same instrument to Big May's heaving midriff, which had been suddenly vacated by the struggling, terror-stricken Sweet Feet.

"You, suh!" she said to Sweet Feet. "Get your nasty self loose from that strumpet before I break my stick on your hind parts! Get on out from there! Get aloose right now!" she insisted, and she gave him a few more whacks, sharper than the first. Big May's big brown eyes flew open as she heard the blows and felt the jab in her stomach.

"What in the hell?" she rasped. "What the hell is going on?" she demanded. When she finally saw Mama Lucy, she moved as if to reach for the walking stick.

"I'm the hell what's going on," Mama Lucy told her,

standing her ground with one hand on her hip and the other shaking the stick at the big woman. "I'm the hell, and this here empty-headed young un you've been trying to squeeze the life out of happens to belong to me. An' I don't have to ask you who you is, 'cause it can't be nobody much! You ought to be ashamed of yourself, a old wore-out strumpet like you, taking advantage of these schoolboys!" She then turned to the thoroughly embarrassed and frightened Sweet Feet, who stood frozen beside Big May, and whacked him again. "March yourself out of that door, you little nasty, stinking rascal," she commanded. "And don't let up 'til you git home. And wash yourself!" she added. "Because you smell like something the buzzards picked up!"

As she started to follow Sweet Feet out of the door, her eyes fell on the other schoolboys cowering around the jukebox in the corner, trying to escape her attention. "You, suh," she said to one of them, "you, suh, Master Dickey, you nasty little possum! I see you. Now you git yourself on out of here and go on home to your mammy. An' when you git there, you tell her I sent you and I sent you right now!" With that she whacked the unhappy Dickey with her stick just as she had Sweet Feet. He hurried through the front door, the other boys fleeing ahead of him.

Having turned out the Shake It, Mama Lucy paused for a parting word with the management. "Whoever you may be and wherever you come from" she said to Big May, "it don't take a whole lot of effort to be a great big pile of trash. But if trash is what you want to be, you don't have to dump it on the chillun. God knows they got enough to contend with already without the likes of you!" With that, she rapped her walking stick against the floor a time or two and marched out into the night to go home to pray over the events of the last half hour.

When Mama Lucy left, the big woman with the scar on her cheek just stood there in the middle of the floor staring at the spot where Mama Lucy had stood arms akimbo, talking about how easy it was to be trash. She looked as if her mind was far away, focused on something she had long since forgotten about. "I'll be damned," she finally murmured.

"I'll just be goddammed!" Suddenly a large tear rolled over the ugly scar and tumbled down her cheek. When finally she could move, she walked over and pulled the plug on the jukebox and announced that the café was closed for the night. "Get on out!" she demanded in her low gutteral voice. "All of you. I'm closin' up!"

When Mama Lucy got home, there was a young girl of fourteen or fifteen sitting on the front porch waiting for her. It was hard to tell much about her in the dark, but if Mama Lucy could have seen her in the light she would have noticed that the girl was heavily made up and that the short skirt she wore was not designed to cover very much of whoever she was. She paused to greet the strange girl before going on into the house. "You looking for me, honey?"

"Yes, ma'am," the girl said simply. "My name's Lera, and that was my mama you were fussing with up at the Shake It. I want to stay with you."

"Come on in the house, child," Mama Lucy told her. "You're welcome. Come on in the house and wash yourself up. Then we'll see what the Good Lord wants us to do about you."

Lera stayed on with Mama Lucy until she gave up her earthly struggles and went to her heavenly reward. Mama Lucy found her to be a joy and a comfort as she reached her declining years, and she thanked God for the mystery of His ways that seemed to always turn out for the best. As for the Shake It, it never did reopen after the night Mama Lucy turned it out in her confrontation with Big May. But May Shake didn't just fade away into the landscape of Clayton City. About a month after the Shake It closed, a new sign went up over the front door of the former café. It said "Avenue Cash Grocery—May Shake Prop." Inside, behind the cash register, sat Big May beaming with pride at the modest display of canned goods on the shelves around the room and the bushel baskets of onions and potatoes on the floor in front of the meat counter. Three years later Big May's rich contralto could be heard regularly in the choir of the Burning Bush Baptist Church in dutiful support of the Reverend Ruffin Rusoe, whose wife she had come to be.

Sweet Feet had come out of his encounter at the Shake It with just enough misgivings to get him through his next two years at the Fort Academy, but it was obvious to anybody who bothered to notice that while he was as full of fun and mischief as always, he was changing. Somehow there was a different tone to his voice, and his shenanigans began to take on the quality of escapades. Gradually his attendance at church and at school diminished beyond the point of truancy. He was restless, and most of the time he seemed preoccupied with something he didn't talk to anyone about. His conversations with Mama Lucy became more and more infrequent and less and less informal. He took to staying out later and later at night, but with the Blue Flame closing at nine o'clock, and the Shake It turned into a grocery store, where could he be spending his time so late at night?

By the time Sweet Feet had turned twenty-one he had developed a decided appetite for fast cars and faster women. And women of all ages and stages liked him and made themselves available. If he didn't come to them, they came looking for him. He got the cars by working for Grigsby Gardner, the town electrician. Mr. Gardner weighed 340 pounds or so, and the diminutive Sweet Feet could fit handily into the corners and the tight places in the attics and closets Mr. Gardner could not hope to enter. He learned the electrician's trade quickly and was soon wiring houses all over Clayton County as the electric power from the new TVA works became available. He always gave Mama Lucy a part of what he earned, but he knew that money was the least thing she wanted of him. What he knew she wanted most, he seemed increasingly unable to give her. One night he woke her up to tell her that he was leaving to go Up North to live with her brother Cass. She knelt with him at the side of the bed for a few minutes to commend him to God's care, and then he was gone. Sweet Feet was now on his own, and Mama Lucy knew that only God could save him from himself from that point on.

Each year toward the end of the summer, when the cotton was laid by and the farm folk of the rural South had time on their hands, the roads from Up North would be burdened with struggling automobiles of uncertain vintage and value en route to the towns and villages of Dixie. They came from Detroit and Akron, and Cleveland and New York and Cincinnati, Pittsburgh, Rockford, Chicago, and a dozen other industrial cities. They came bearing the black expatriates who had quit the South to find a better living Up North but who longed to see, and be seen by, the folks they had left behind. It was hard driving, for there were no hotels or rest stops along the way for colored people. And the uncertain condition of the cars they drove, and the hostile attitudes of the lawmen they encountered along the way, made each trip an adventure that was equally uncertain and hostile.

Sometimes the homecomings were delayed until after the crops were in and the county fairs were in progress. Most people would have a little pocket money then, the cotton having been sold, and the fair offered something beyond just visiting the various kinfolks. Sweet Feet usually waited until fair time for his annual visit to see Mama Lucy. You could tell when it was getting close to fair time; there was something different in the air. People seemed less driven and more relaxed. And there was a sharp increase in the number of young women who stopped by to see how Mama Lucy was doing and to find out when Sweet Feet was coming home. Of course, Mama Lucy was not exactly deceived by the sudden upsurge of concern for her welfare from the young women of Clayton City, and she was likely to advise her callers straight out that Sweet Feet would be here today and gone tomorrow and that they would be a sight better off if they spent their time worrying about some local boy who would still be around when Sweet Feet had gone back to where he came from. She had little patience with the veiled inquiries that came from married women. "Sweet Feet is none of your business coming or going," she'd tell them. Or, "When did your husband come to be named Sweet Feet?"

But the young women of Clayton City weren't the only ones coming to see Mama Lucy as it got closer to the time for her wayward son to make his annual pilgrimage. Mr. Cody Evans, chief of police, usually got by to see her, too, to get a line on Sweet Feet's arrival. Like his cousin Grigsby,

Chief Evans was a heavyset man, so heavy, in fact, that it was always a chore for him to get out of his Chevrolet and struggle up on the front porch to settle down in Lucius's old cane-bottomed chair. But when he had made himself comfortable, Mama Lucy would bring him a big tin cup of cold buttermilk to help him cool off.

"Lucy, when's your boy Sweet Feet gonna be gittin' in here?" he'd ask as casually as he could.

"Mr. Evans, I just don't rightly know for certain," she'd answer with the same note of informality. "But it ought not to be too long from now."

"Well, when he do," the chief would be apt to say, "you want to be sure to tell him to come on by to see me *before* he gets his tail up. Not *after*! Thataway maybe we can take a little worry off you, and off us and the rest of Clayton City, if him and me can have a little understanding in the first place." Having delivered his message, the chief would drink another cup of buttermilk and take himself a snooze on the front porch before squeezing back into his machine for the drive back to the police station.

So it went for nearly twenty years or more. Sweet Feet never missed a summer without coming to see Mama Lucy, and each time he came his reception and his agenda in Clayton City were about the same. Chief Evans continued in his efforts at law enforcement between cups of buttermilk, and each summer the women of Clayton City would be waiting for Sweet Feet's arrival like honeybees waiting for the clover to bloom, no matter what strategies were devised to keep them innocent. Some of them were placed under quarantine or at least close surveillance by their husbands and boyfriends even before the big, ancient Buicks and Dodges Sweet Feet favored had rumbled into town. But each summer brought a new crop who had heard about the legendary Sweet Feet all their lives. They felt themselves ready to hear it from that lovable little man himself, who intrigued them so with his rakish tweed cap, his perennial cigar, and the taunting, impish smile that played around his face when he was fixing to be up to some devilment. Which was just about all the time.

Inevitably the time came when Sweet Feet made his last trip home. Mama Lucy was dead. She had passed peacefully in her sleep during a mild summer thunderstorm two nights before. Telegrams had been sent to all the relatives, and even now the living room was filled with kinfolks and neighbors drinking sassafras tea and talking in low tones. People came and went, their passage marked by the subdued bang of the screen door. Reverend Ruffin Rusoe had come and prayed for the spirit of the departed, and the women in the kitchen were preparing food for the wake that would begin later that night. The body was at Ferdy Frost's Funeral Home but would soon be brought to the home house on Crockett Street for the wake. The funeral would be tomorrow at the Burning Bush Baptist Church. Laura and Annie Mae, Mama Lucy's two married daughters from Cincinnati and Baltimore, had already arrived, as had Nish, one of the grandchildren Mama Lucy had taken to raise following the death of Rebecca Jane, her oldest daughter. Nish had become the man in the house after Papa Lucius had passed away fifteen years ago. He was now working his way through college at the famous colored school in Nashville, where he was one of a group of singers who traveled about to raise money for the institution.

And now everybody was proud that he had become somebody. Pushed by his aunts from Up North to show off his college training, Nish had attempted to take care of the funeral arrangements, at least until his Uncle Sweet Feet should arrive. But he reckoned without his Aunt Hester. Hester Collins was one of the children Omar Slater had left Mama Lucy to raise after his wife died and he took up preaching and managed to follow his call on away from Clayton. Hester was naturally bossy. She was the principal of the Clayton City Colored Elementary School, and as such she fully expected to demonstrate her place of leadership among the colored people of Clayton City. She had already built herself a house on The Avenue to match her aspirations. Now that Mama Lucy was gone, and since nobody else seemed to know what to do and Nish was only a college boy, Hester promptly took over the planning for the proper last rites and burial of her sister.

Early in the afternoon there was a mild commotion out front which could only mean one thing: Sweet Feet had come. Nish went to the front door and made his way to the front yard through the small crowd which had already gathered around the big car from Up North. There was a young woman with Sweet Feet whom he was busily introducing as his wife. That would be wife number three, Nish said to himself, as he gathered the suitcases out of the car and led the way into Mama Lucy's house. In the living room the mourners temporarily forgot the somberness of the occasion as they crowded around to hug Sweet Feet and to get a closer look at his new wife, Teresa. She was a very pretty girl, with large brown eyes and soft brown hair falling over her shoulders. Her skin was olive brown and very soft, and she looked to be less than half as old as Sweet Feet. Teresa certainly didn't look much like any girls in Clayton City, and Nish overheard one of his aunts say that she looked "mightly like one of them Eye-talians" she had seen Up North and that if she was, Sweet Feet was a bigger fool than she had thought he was for bringing her Down South and calling her his wife.

Whatever else Teresa was, you could tell right away that she wasn't accustomed to being in the middle of a lot of kinfolks gathered for a southern-style funeral. The women all introduced themselves as Cousin So-and-So, or A'nt So-and-So, with much kissing and hugging. Some of them seemed deeply disappointed when Teresa confessed with much embarrassment that she didn't know them or had not heard Sweet Feet speak of them. And she seemed very distressed in turn that people kept referring to her husband as "Sweet Feet" when she insisted that his name was William Clinton.

Hester rescued Teresa and had Nish put her and her bags in the back bedroom where Sweet Feet used to live. She needed rest, Hester said, after such a long trip. Then she ordered Sweet Feet to bed as well, assuring him that Teresa needed his company. "And take a bath," she added with some impatience. "You smell like a stale whiskey still." But the women in the kitchen were disappointed that Sweet Feet's wife went off to bed without eating anything, so they sent a platter of fried chicken and boiled pig feet around to her in case she might want to snack before lying down. When Nish knocked on the door with the food, Teresa was sitting on the bed, but Sweet Feet was nowhere to be seen.

Sweet Feet had no intentions of going to bed. Despite fifteen or sixteen hours under the wheel of his Buick, he didn't feel tired. He felt weary, perhaps, but not tired. And somehow he knew that all the sleep in the world could not relieve his weariness. He wandered aimlessly across the long back porch and into the kitchen, where some of the women of the neighborhood were frying chicken and making potato salad and cornbread for the wake. Somehow he felt an uncomfortable resentment that these strangers were in Mama Lucy's kitchen, using her things, and without her permission. But then, he also knew within himself that they were not strangers at all. He could call every one of them by name, and some of them had put diapers on him or rocked him to sleep many years ago.

He went out to the old barn and climbed up into the hayloft where he had played as a boy. The hay was gone. The old mule was gone. The cow. The hogs that used to wallow in the pen on the far side of the barn were all gone. The old one-horse wagon was gone. The plows. The harness. He remembered when the last piece of Papa Lucius's meager collection of farm equipment left. It was an old cotton planter, and the day Mama Lucy let it go, he learned one of the many lessons she had taught him over the years by her own deliberate behavior. Papa Lucius was on his deathbed, and hard times gripped the family. Nobody lived in the old house right then except Sweet Feet and Mama Lucy and Papa Lucius. Papa had been sick for almost a year, and Mama Lucy had sold off his farm stuff piece by piece in order to buy something to eat. First the mule, then the cow, then the wagon, and so on down to the last singletree. It was not that Papa Lucius had much to sell. He was just a part-time farmer with only the six acres around the home house. He never made any money, not even enough to live on. But working the land was what gave him his greatest satisfaction in life, and with one mule he planted cotton on his six acres with all the sense of accomplishment he would have had with a thousand-acre plantation.

Mama Lucy wouldn't sell the singletree because it was something Papa Lucius had made himself. He had whittled it out of a piece of seasoned hickory when the one he was using broke while he was plowing one day. It outlasted two or three others he had bought, and he was proud of it. Same way about the old barn. Sweet Feet recalled that once on a cold day in the dead of winter, when there was no food in the house and no wood for the fire, he had managed to pull a loose plank off the barn and was about to chop it up for firewood. When Mama Lucy discovered where he had gotten the plank, she made him return it to the barn and nail it back in place. That barn was something Lucius had built with his own hands. It wasn't much, but it was his own creation. Somehow Mama Lucy seemed to feel that if the old barn went, Papa Lucius would follow. She was like that. She had a real feeling for what she thought was important to other people.

Fortunately on that cold day in question it wasn't long before Sweet Feet could hear the cries of the woodman as he drove his team slowly down the street toward Mama Lucy's. The wagon stopped in front of the house, and the man got off and knocked on the front door. Sweet Feet ran to tell Mama Lucy that a white man was out front with a load of slabs. "Well, tell him to come around to the back," she said testily. "I'm in the kitchen."

"It's a *white* man," Sweet Feet had insisted, afraid they were going to lose a chance to have some heat in the house.

"I don't care if he's a purple man," Mama Lucy said firmly. "You jest tell him what I said. I'm in the kitchen!" She pointed her finger toward the front door, and Sweet Feet ambled out to do her bidding. In the meantime, Mama Lucy put on a fresh apron. When the white man rapped at the kitchen door, she opened it and spoke to him through the screen: "Yes, suh?"

"I got a load of firewood to sell," he told her. "Some pine slabs."

There was no money in the house, but they agreed on a

swap of the load of slabs for the cotton planter—worth five times as much. The man drove the wagon into the yard and unloaded the slabs, and Mama Lucy told him where to look inside the barn for the planter. After loading the planter on his wagon, he went back into the barn and came out with Papa Lucius's old hickory singletree and threw it into the wagon with the planter. Mama Lucy was watching from the kitchen door.

"You, suh!" she yelled at him, coming out of the kitchen in a hurry. "You, suh! Put that singletree right back where you got it from. It belongs to Lucius, and I ain't trading it to you. Put it right back!"

The man started to climb on his wagon as if he was going to ignore her. "Aw A'ntie," he said, " 'tain't nothing but an ol' homemade singletree. 'Tain't worth nothing."

Mama Lucy reacted with instant rage. Sweet Feet had never seen her so angry before. "Don't you come here to my house to tell me what I got ain't worth nothing!" she shouted. "That ain't for you to say!" And with that she picked up a pine slab and threw it at the white man, hitting him on the shoulder and causing him to leap from the wagon and retreat hastily into the street. "And don't you *never* call me no A'ntie," Mama Lucy yelled at him, advancing into the street with another stick of wood. I ain't *never* been no A'ntie to no trash, and I ain't never going to be. I'll go to my grave first." With that she let loose a second slab as the white man jumped aside in time and ran around the house and threw the singletree from his wagon. Mama Lucy snatched it up and took it back to the barn and returned it to the nail where it had hung since Lucius left it there when he took to his bed.

When the man was gone and Mama Lucy had had a chance to pray and calm down some, Sweet Feet finally mustered nerve enough to ask her why she got so mad at the woodman.

Her anger threatened to return at the mention of what had happened.

"Didn't you *hear* that po' white trash come here in my own yard and tell me your papa's work wasn't worth nothing?" she asked, her voice still quivering with rage. "Well, Lucius *made* that singletree. He *made* it! Didn't you hear him call me 'A'ntie' right to my face? *Well, you look at me. Do I look like his A'ntie to you?''* Well, do I?''

Sweet Feet was ready to let the matter drop, but he was still puzzled. Finally, he ventured: ''But, Mama Lucy, some of the white folks you work for downtown call you 'A'ntie.' ''

''They do,'' she said, ''and that's different! *He* ain't from downtown, and I don't *work* for him. And when I'm standing on my own property, my name is Lucy Lunceford to everybody unless I say different! I ain't never let no po' white trash A'ntie me, an' I ain't about to start with him.''

Now Lucy Lunceford, *Mama Lucy*, was dead and Sweet Feet was sitting there alone in the hayloft of the old barn he used to hide in when his doings got him into trouble. Papa Lucius had been dead almost fifteen years. Now Mama Lucy. Funny how the old barn was still there, and the old singletree Papa Lucius had whittled out of a piece of hickory still hung beside the door.

The funeral was scheduled to be held at Burning Bush Baptist Church at one-thirty in the afternoon. At about one o'clock Ferdy Frost came with the hearse and removed Mama Lucy's remains from the living room, where the wake had been held the night before. Cars began to line up behind the hearse for the funeral procession, and the street was soon crowded with people who had come to pay their last respects to Miss Lucy or to get a glimpse of the pageantry. The Sisters and Daughters of Zion were to turn out in her honor, and Burning Bush, where she had been a member all her life, was sure to be packed with people from all over the county.

All of the women in the house were busy dressing for the event except Teresa. She had been crying off and on since the night before, when Sweet Feet had not come home. The other women tried to comfort her since she was something of a stranger and since she was so young. But their assurances that Sweet Feet's staying out all night was nothing unusual to worry about made her cry more bitterly. Hester was disgusted and embarrassed, but she had taken charge of the details of getting Mama Lucy decently buried, so while she was sorry for Teresa, she had no time and no patience for

worrying about Sweet Feet and his various women, wives—
if any—included.

At twelve o'clock all of the family and relatives were
dressed and ready to be led out and seated in the cars provided by Ferdy Frost and his assistants. Two of the neighbor
women were in the kitchen, fixing dinner for the funeral
party, and another was looking after the children of the bereaved. Sweet Feet had been temporarily forgotten by everyone except Teresa, or it was simply assumed that he would
be unable to attend the funeral for reasons quite familiar to
the folks of Clayton City. But it was hazardous to reckon
about Sweet Feet. Just as the family was leaving the house,
the unmistakable rumble of his big Buick was heard down
the street, and a minute later Sweet Feet pulled into the yard,
bumped the car against the porch, and got out. The usual
grin on his puckish face was missing; his car was spattered
with mud, as, indeed, was Sweet Feet himself. And while it
was obvious that he had been drinking, it was equally obvious that he was cold sober. "Got stuck in a ditch out in the
county," he said matter-of-factly to no one in particular.
"But I'm here. I've come to bury my mama. Mama Lucy.
She's dead."

He climbed slowly up the porch steps and went into the
house, followed by Hester and Nish. Nish fought back tears
he couldn't explain, but Hester was almost incoherent with
rage. "Sweet Feet, how could you do this to Mama Lucy?"
she demanded. "There she is, your own mama, out there
lying in the hearse, and here you've been out drinking all
night with some no-good whore! Now you come staggering
in here nasty and drunk, talking about burying your mama!
You're not fit to bury anybody but yourself, and you're not
going to that church to embarrass Mama and the rest of us
on her last day on earth!" Hester never had thought Sweet
Feet's escapades were amusing, and now she thought he was
downright disgusting.

Much to the consternation of the men from the funeral
parlor, who wanted to get the procession on its way to the
church, the funeral party had started filing back into the house
to see what was wrong. Somebody began to whimper and

then to cry as the crowd milled around in the living room. Soon several women were crying and moaning, and Ferdy and his men were having a hard time trying to keep more people from coming in from the street. Suddenly Sweet Feet, who had slumped into a chair at the kitchen table, began to shake with sobs, the tears streaming down his face.

"Shut up, Sweet Feet!" Hester Collins snapped at him. "Nobody's got time for you to be putting on. We ought to be at the church right now." At a signal from Hester, two of Ferdy's men escorted Sweet Feet to the bedroom where Teresa was. Hester spoke a few hurried words with Teresa and ordered her to keep Sweet Feet in the house until they got back after the funeral. Calm was finally restored to the funeral party, the cars were loaded again, and the procession moved off toward the little Baptist church two blocks away.

The church was crowded. The Daughters of Zion, resplendent in white and gold uniforms, formed an honor guard and marched in at the head of the procession. The casket was then wheeled in and positioned in front of the pulpit, and the flowers were banked around it. The family of the deceased was escorted in by Ferdy's men and seated in the pews reserved for them at the front of the church. Ferdy had set aside the first four pews, then five, and finally six for the convenience of the weeping, strained-faced relatives, blood kin, and others bound to the dead woman by ties closer than blood who seemed to keep crowding in and who insisted on making their way down to the front of the little church to be seated near Mama Lucy for her final hour among them. Inevitably the spillover from the pews reserved for the family became too much for the ushers to handle, and some of those with family claims had to take seats wherever they could be found. The first two pews across the aisle had been reserved for the white folks who would most likely come to pay their respects to Mama Lucy. Both of these pews were filled all at once, for the white folks seemed to have come in a body. Misses Charity, Dovie, and Effie, Clayton's three old-time spinster sisters, sat straight and prim in the middle of the first pew. Mama Lucy had washed for them, keeping them in proper crinolines and ruffled blouses for years on end. The sisters were flanked on one side by Judge Carson and his wife, and on the other by Mr. Gilligan, whose face was flushed with sorrow and corn whiskey. Miss Molly Gilligan, for whose family Mama Lucy had cooked for nearly two generations, sat beside her husband, and Miss Flossie Reed and Littie, the colored women who doubled as her maid and personal nurse, sat beside the Gilligans. Miss Flossie had dropsy, and weighing nearly three hundred pounds, she needed Littie to help her to sit, or stand, or move 'round. Mama Lucy had worked for her family when Miss Flossie was a young belle fifty years before, and now Miss Flossie had come at some personal inconvenience to remember. Chief Cody Evans arrived after the services had gotten under way and eased himself down on the end of the back pew nearest the entrance, beside Dr. Walter Tait. The chief's corns were hurting, and he was sweating profusely, and when one of Ferdy's men standing behind him began to fan him vigorously with a pasteboard fan from the funeral home, he grinned broadly and bobbed his massive head up and down in approval and gratitude.

Some of the people from The Avenue had taken seats immediately behind the white folks from downtown. Most noticeable among them were Angus and Clara Sue McVey from the Upper End. Both of the McVeys were light-skinned, and both had deep roots in antebellum Clayton County. Neither of them had ever been in Burning Bush Baptist Church before. Indeed, the McVeys were Episcopalians, and proud of it. Like their parents before them on both sides of the color line, they still worshiped at St. Jude's Church downtown, sitting alone in a balcony built for slaves a hundred years before. But Angus farmed 640 acres down near The Forks of the River and kept black tenants just like his white counterparts. Beside the McVeys sat Sadie Sawyer, a county schoolteacher; Clara Binnewater, also from the Upper End of The Avenue; and Sam Witchard. Sam was caretaker at the city trash pile, and he didn't live on The Avenue; but he appeared to be oblivious of any difference that was supposed to make to anybody. He had come to say good-bye to a long-time friend, and he sat down as close to where she lay as he could manage. Just as the minister was entering the pulpit, Fess McClain, headmaster at the Academy, disdaining the efforts of Ferdy Frost to seat him with the other whites, slipped into a seat beside Nish in the first family pew. The bench was crowded with somber-faced relatives of the deceased, but room was quickly made for the professor despite the disapproving stares from across the aisle.

At a nod from the Reverend Ruffin Rusoe, who had seated himself in the high-backed red and gold chair reserved for the pastor, the choir began to sing softly, and a momentary hush pervaded the sanctuary. As the choir was concluding its offering, Deacon Teeter Sloss came forward from his seat in the Amen Corner and sank slowly to his knees beside the lectern to pray. The deacon was almost eighty years old, and his ancient bones creaked aloud as he positioned himself upon the floor, his eyes and his long, bony arms raised to heaven on behalf of Mama Lucy. Deacon Sloss prayed a long time, rocking back and forth in a stately cadence measured to his petition. "O Lawd God Jesus," he prayed, "I want to thank you that when I riz up this mornin', my bed was not my coolin' board, and my bedclothes was not my windin' sheet. An' though in your righteous wisdom, you have laid your tender hand on our beloved Sister Lucy, we stand ready to walk with her whenever our name is called, wherever your path may lead. Great God! Great God Almighty! You was heah befo' time was heah! You'll be heah when evermore has ceased to be. Your power is beyond the measurement of the universe, and your wisdom is like a ocean that never had no shore. Your lovin'-kindness is deep as the deepest deep, high as the highest high, wide as the widest wide, enduring beyond enternity. So, O Lawd, we's satisfied! Sister Lucy is in your hands. We's satisfied! You is the Ruler an' the Judge. We's satisfied! You is the Redeemer of us all. We's satisfied! You is our Buckler an' our Shield. We's satisfied! You is the Warden at the Gate. We's satisfied! I'm talkin' 'bout the *Pearly* Gate. We's satisfied! I'm talkin' 'bout the Heavenly Gate. We's satisfied!" Long before the deacon decided to say amen, the congregation had picked up his declaration of satisfaction and made his cadence their own. "We's satisfied," they chanted softly. "We's satisfied. We's satisfied."

When Deacon Sloss had finally finished his prayer, he grasped a corner of the lectern, pulled himself to his feet, and was helped back to his place in the Amen Corner. A quiet shuffling of feet and a chorus of amens marked the approval of his long conversation with God, and a few women waved their hands palm outward and fingers extended in signification of God's presence and approval. A tall brown girl named Mildred Peterson sang a solo, after which the condolences were read, and a poem called "Everybody's Mother" was recited by one of the women in the choir. Another solo preceded the obituaries, and then the Reverend Rusoe approached the pulpit to preach the sermon he had designed to honor the dead and comfort the bereaved who had gathered there to mark the final transition of Lucy Lunceford. But before the reverend could announce his text, one of Ferdy Frost's men hurried from the back of the church to whisper in the preacher's ear. Reverend Rusoe nodded his head and looked toward the rear of the sanctuary. Standing there in rumpled white duckings and a maroon shirt was Blind Bates, his steel guitar fixed across his chest with a leather thong. At Reverend Rusoe's signal two of Ferdy Frost's ushers led Bates down the aisle and sat him down in a folding chair from the funeral parlor just in front of Mama Lucy's coffin. "This brother," Reverend Rusoe explained, "has just heard of the passing of Mama Lucy. He says she was good to him, as indeed, she was good to so many of God's children, and he wants to say good-bye to her in his own way. God bless you, Brother Bates. Sit down and have your say."

Blind Bates began to caress the strings of his battered old guitar. Mostly he had played the blues on it for the twenty-five years or so he had owned it. Cakewalks and chitlin struts and Saturday night fish fries had always been his forte. This time it was different. This time he was playing for love. Love for a woman he had never seen, but whose love he had known not only through the meals she had fixed for him, or the shirts she had patched, but through the sharing of her time, her wisdom, and her compassion. Tears flowed from beneath the dark glasses covering his sightless eyes as he riffed the steel strings with the glass bottleneck on his little finger and launched into the song he had written in his mind for Mama Lucy. It was a sad, lonesome song.

> Train done gone
> Train done gone
> Lawd, I wonder if
> My soul got on.
> I say the train done gone
> O Lawd, the train done gone.
>
> Train done gone
> Heav'n bound
> Ain't nobody
> Can turn it 'round
> Because the train done gone
> O Lawd, the train done gone.
>
> Train done gone
> To the pearly gate
> If you ain't on board
> Well, you jest too late
> Because the train done gone
> O Lawd, the train done gone.
>
> Train done gone
> But I b'lieve I see
> Ol' Sister Lucy
> Wavin' back at me
> But now the train done gone
> O Lawd, the train done gone
> Train done gone-n-ne, Lawd.

Blind Bates strummed gently to a close, riffing the strings with glass on his little finger and causing the old guitar to moan and tremble with the agony of loneliness and death. Suddenly there was a scream from somewhere in the back of the church: "O Lord, the train done gone! Gone! Gone!"

Then spiritual bedlam broke loose as the shouting became general, and two or three women had fainted before calm could be restored and the funeral could go on. Two of Ferdy Frost's men were dispatched to protect the visibly shaken white visitors from the loosing of the spirit which now threatened to engulf the church. Two others led the weeping Blind Bates to the rear of the church so that he could cool off and compose himself. Finally, there was an authoritative announcement from the organ, and the Reverend Ruffin Rusoe arose and stationed himself in the pulpit and waited for the commotion to subside.

Reverend Rusoe was a lean, lanky man who always looked as if his clothes wanted to fall off his spare frame. Certainly he was not a dressy preacher, but he affected a string tie which accentuated his lankiness and made him seem stooped, even when he was standing erect. His coat sleeves were too short, and whenever he raised his arms toward heaven, his long, bony limbs seemed to pump out of his sleeves like pistons. Mr. Rusoe was also cockeyed, and while that did not seem to impair his preaching, it did add to the grotesqueness of his appearance. Now he opened the Bible, leaned on the lectern, and looked over his glasses at the grieving congregation. This was, he declared, a sad day. Sad because one much beloved of the church and the City of Clayton had laid down her burden and gone home. There was a scattering of "Amens!" But it was also a day for rejoicing, the preacher said, because she had gone to live in the City of Eternal Peace. A celestial city. A city where she wouldn't have to wash no more dirty overalls! Scrub no more kitchen floors! Where she wouldn't have to wonder how she was going to pay the groceryman every Saturday night. Where she wouldn't have to hide because she didn't have a dime to give the insurance man on Monday morning. "Her insurance is all paid up," he said reassuringly, "and Sister Lucy's gone home to collect her dividends." This time there was a strong chorus of "Amens!" and a rumbling of feet to let the preacher know his message was being heard with approval.

Warming to his subject, Reverend Rusoe removed his glasses and laid them on the Bible. "Sister Lucy is gone home to live with Jesus!'' he announced, his voice rising a little. "That's a beautiful thought! Don't you think so?"

"Amen! Amen!" the people responded.

"Even now," the reverend continued, "even *right* now I can see them sending out somebody to welcome her. Oh, yes! I can see them sending a messenger with wings on his heels and a white robe for her on his shoulder! They're tellin' him to go posthaste and tell the gatekeeper to get ready. Tellin' him to tell ol' a-Saint Peter that Sister Lucy is on her way! I can see them. I can *see* them! They're gettin' ready to receive Sister Lucy up there—'way up yonder in the heavenly city! I can see them!"

"Amen! Amen! Reverend. We see 'em, too! Yes, Lawd!"

"I can see ol' a-Saint Peter come down from the watch-tower—come down from the lofty fortress of the gatehouse. Oh, yes! He's tellin' them to let down the drawbridge across the moat of perdition! Let it down, Peter! Let down the bridge, Sister Lucy is here! Sister Lucy's done come home!"

"Amen! Amen! Preach! Preach! Preach right!"

"Don't you see him, children? Don't you see him let down the bridge an' rush on out? [Ah-ha!] Don't you see him with his arms stretched out and his robe, his robe a-billowing in the heavenly wind when he runs out to meet Sister Lucy? When he runs out to meet a sure 'nough child of God! Hallelujah! Come on home, Lucy! Come on home! Your troubles are all over. Your travail has done ceased. Your tribulation is all behind you. Come on home, a-Sister Lucy! Come on home!"

At this point several women began to shout, and Reverend Rusoe paused a moment to let the spirit have its way with them. Then he resumed his message with a more confidential tone. "They gonna take her before the High Commissioner," he said, looking far into the heavens to report what was happening there. "An' when she's been examined to His satisfaction, they're gonna write her name in the Book of Eternal Life. They gonna write it down!" Almost immediately someone in the congregation began to sing in a high, plaintive voice:

Oh well I want my na-ame
I want my name na-a-me
Oh yes I want my name na-a-ame
Written down
In the Book of Life!

The choir picked up the song, and then the whole church. There was more shouting, and once more the preacher had to wait before picking up his sermon again.

"Now some folks'll tell you that the preacher can *preach* you into heaven [Ah-ha!]," he told them. "They say the preacher can ferry you over to the *kingdom.* [Ah-ha!] Across the moat of perdition. [Well, ah-ha!] Around the rocks of retribution. That's what they say, ain't that right? Or they say the preacher can let the storms of justice and the shoals of tribulation claim their due. Ain't that what they say? You've heard 'em say that!"

"Yass! Preach! Preach on! That's what they say!"

"Now, I ask you, ain't that what they say?"

"Yass, Lord! That's what they say! Sho' they do!"

"Well, let me tell you one thing, brothers and sisters: The preacher cain't preach you *nowhere*! The preacher cain't *send* you nowhere! You got to go there for yourself! You got to stand the test for yourself!"

"Help me, Lord!" somebody screamed. "Help me!"

"Where you going when you quit this vale of tears, the preacher ain't got nothing to do with it. Ah'm tellin' you the truth now! The preacher can *review* your life [Ah-ha!], ah-but he cain't reprieve it. Your record is already on file [Ah-ha!], and you better believe it! On file! Yes, Lord! It's already on file. It's in the Registry of Deeds! *On file!* [Ah, well!] It's in the Book of the Judgment! *On file!* I'm a-tellin' you! And cain't *nobody* [Ah, well!] change one line! You can't add nothin' [No, Jesus!], an' you cain't take nothin' away! The preacher cain't change it! Ah, 'cause it's there to stay. It's on file! It's on file! It's on file! It's written down."

"Preach on, Reverend! It's on file! Preach it like it is! Preach!"

"The white folks cain't change it! (And I don't mean no

disrespect to nobody. No disrespect a'tall. God knows I don't.)''

''Help, Lord! Ain't no disrespect when you talkin' for the Lord!''

''The devil can't change it!''

''Preach! Preach!''

''It's your record. I say it's your record, an' you got to stand on it!''

''Yass, you do! Yass, you do! Stand on it 'cause you made it!''

''It's your record! An' it'll take you home to heaven!''

''Yass, Jesus!''

''Or it'll send your soul to hell!''

''Help! Help! Help, Lord! We's in your righteous hands!''

Several of the women began to moan and then to shout and rush about the church. They were restrained by Ferdy Frost's black-clad assistants, who roamed the aisles with cardboard fans, trying to anticipate where the next outbreak of the spirit would come. Reverend Rusoe walked around the pulpit to the edge of the platform and said: ''Stay with me, brothers and sisters, 'cause I'm near 'bout ready to preach now. The spirit done come down, and Sister Lucy is ready for to travel. Stay with me! Stay with me!

''Sister Lucy, she was a wonderful woman. Yes, she was. A member of this church for fifty-five years and four months and seventeen days. Glory be to God. Pillar of the community, she was—beloved by all who knew her name. God knows, if I *had* the power to preach anybody into the kingdom, I would do it for Sister Lucy!''

''Sho' you would! Sho' you would!'' a man shouted.

''But I don't have that power,'' Reverend Rusoe confided. ''And I don't need that power. Sister Lucy is standing on her record. An' her record is the best there is!''

Some of the women in the family pews began to sob and shake, and two ushers rushed over to fan them while Hester and Nish tried to comfort them as best they could. Nish was crying silently himself, in spite of his efforts to act like the man of the family, the man he knew Mama Lucy would want him to be.

"The Bible says that Jesus gave the keys to the kingdom to Peter and told him to bind and to loose," Reverend Rusoe continued. "Well, I believe that. I do believe the Bible. Don't you? I believe that's Peter's job, to say who comes in an' who stays out. I'm talking about the kingdom."

"Talkin' 'bout the kingdom!" someone echoed. "Talkin' 'bout the kingdom!"

"Yes, that's Saint Peter's responsibility, an' that's why he sits by the gate. To admit and to deny admission. That's what the Good Lord done ordered him to do. To sift out the unworthy an' cast 'em into hell, while the good folks pass on in to sit before the throne of grace. He got to separate the sheep from the goats, an' he got to turn in his report to the Master. That's what he's got to do!"

"Yass, Lord! Everybody talkin' 'bout heaven ain't goin' there! The *song* say that!"

"Well now, some folks'll tell you that Saint Peter done turned the keys over to the preacher. I'm talkin' about the keys to the kingdom! The keys to loose and to bind—the keys to put a soul in heaven or to send that soul to hell! Well, let me tell you something: That ain't nothin' but a lie!"

"Tell it! Tell it like it is!" the congregation responded, and the foot stomping from the Amen Corner shook the foundations of the little church.

"God ain't gon' give that kind of power to one mortal man to hold over another! An' I don't care what denomination he's in, God ain't give no mortal man that power!"

"That's right! That's right!"

"Ain't no mortal man got sense enough to know what to do with power like that!"

"Preach! Preach!"

"I don't care if he's black, I don't care if he's white (pardon the reference), ain't no mortal man got no business with that kind of power. It's a lie, I tell you. *Peter* got the keys! And Saint Peter better keep 'em up there with him where *he* can't stray too far from the throne!"

"That's right! That's right!"

The reverend ran his hand in his pocket and produced a ring of keys. "Now look at me, children," he said. "I got some keys. But they ain't keys to no kingdom! Ah, lookee here: This little key—well, that's the key to the automobile y'all gave me, God bless you! It's just a little bitty key, but when I turn it in the switch, it starts a mighty engine. Praise God! And I can get in my machine and travel anywhere I want to go. *On earth!* But it won't take me to heaven, 'cause it ain't the right key. It ain't the key to the kingdom. It's a convenience to my body, ah-but it ain't no good to my soul. So Ah'm gonna throw it away, because it's just a confusion!'' With that the preacher pulled the key off the ring and flung it away from him. There was a long spontaneous rumbling of approval.

"Now you see this key," Reverend Rusoe continued. "Ah, well, it's the key to my smokehouse."

"Yass, Lord."

"It's where I hang my little meat."

"Yass, Jesus."

"Well, you know a man gets hungry sometime, an' if he's saved a little something, well, he can eat a little bit.''

"Yass, Lord."

"But the Bible say don't lay up no treasures, 'cause men break in an' steal."

"It's the truth, Lord. Some folks is jest nachel roguish!''

"Ah, well, you know, if you try to have a little somethin', somebody always tryin' to figure out a way to take it away from you!''

"Preach! Preach! That's the livin' truth!''

"They'll steal your wife!''

"Oh, yass!''

"They'll steal your husband!''

"Yass, Lord!''

"They'll steal your good name!''

"Sho' they will!''

"They'll steal your job!''

"Oh, yass!''

"They'll steal your meat and bread!''

"Lord! Lord! Lord!''

"What good ah-is a smokehouse key? It don't stop no thieves. It ain't the *right* key. It's not the key to the kingdom!

Gonna throw it away. It ain't nothin' but confusion! It ain't nothin' but illusion! It makes you think you got what you might not have! It's the wrong key! Gonna throw it away, Lord! It ain't nothin' but a false security!''

"Yass, Lord! Throw it away!"

"Yass, Lord! Throw it away! I'm a-gonna git shed of it!"

The preacher took a second key from his ring and threw it on the floor near the front pew. Then he leaped nimbly over the rail and stomped it and ground it under his foot as if he was killing a snake. A large woman directly in front of him fainted, and the ushers carried her out to be revived. The shouting and rumbling became general now. The preacher strutted back and forth between the casket and the weeping, shouting congregation; then suddenly he whirled and leaped over the rail and was back in the pulpit again. "Hallelujah! Hallelujah!" he cried. "Stay with me, children. Ah'ma gonna preach to you *afterwhile*! Now look-a-here! Ah-do you see this key? Say do you see this key? Ah-well, it's my house key. It's the key to my residence. But I didn't say—ah-that it's the key to my *home*! I didn't say that!''

"Naw, you didn't. Naw, you didn't! Jest your residence!"

"That's right! It's the key to my house—ah-but not my *home*! That's cause my *home* is over Jordan! Wa-a-ay over yonder! Wa-a-ay over Jordan, Lord!''

"Yass, Lord! Yass! Yass! Yass! My Lord!"

"Ah-well, they tell me—they tell me, ah-that a man's home is where his heart is. That's what they tell me. An' ah-they tell me, that where the heart is—well, that's where the mind is. That's what they say. *Ain't that what they say?* Well, ah-amen! The heart is what you feel with—an' the mind is what you think with—an' *my* mind is set on Jesus! So that ol' house I live in, it can't be my home. *Be*cau-use! *Be*cau-u-use that ain't a-where my heart is!

"Naw! Naw, it ain't, Reverend! We know that!"

"That ain't where my mind is!"

"Naw! No siree!"

"My mind is set on Jesus!"

"Yass, Lord!"

"An' my home is over Jordan!"

"Oh yass! Preach on! Preach on! I hear you!"

"Then I don' need no *house* key!"

"Naw! Don't *need* no house key! Just don't need it! It ain't the right key!"

"It *can't* be the right key!"

"Naw! You know it ain't! You know it ain't!"

" 'Cause my *home* is over Jordan! My ho-o-m-me is in the Promised Land! My home is in the kingdom! An' this ol' key don't fit the door up there! It just don't fit!"

"Get rid of it, Reverend! Git shed of it!"

"I'm gonna throw this ol' key away. It ain't nothin' but *confusion*!"

"Hallelujah! Hallelujah!"

"Help me, Jesus!"

"It ain't nothin' but *illusion*!"

"Help! Help! Help!"

"It ain't nothin' but *delusion*!"

"Lord, have mercy!"

"There ain't but one key that's worth bothering about—and that's the key to eternal life! Everything else is a stumbling block!" Suddenly the preacher rushed to the window and flung the whole ring of keys outside to the ground. "I'll tell you, brothers an' sisters, if you ain't got the key to the kingdom," he shouted, "you might jest as well not have no key a'tall! You got to stand on your record—jest like Sister Lucy. You got to face the High Commissioner—jest like Sister Lucy. They got to give her a key 'fore she git into the kingdom. They got to give her the *right* key! But there ain't no need to worry. Saint Peter got the key ring, and he done already pulled one off for her an' put her 'nitials on it, most likely. *L L*, Lucy Lunceford! Don't that sound nice? Don't that sound right? I say Saint Peter—is got the keys to the kingdom! Saint Peter—is got the keys to the mansion. Saint Peter! Oh-o-o-o, Captain, listen to me! Sister Lucy is on her way! Peter! Oh-o-o-o, Peter! Sister Lucy's comin' home! Git you key ring ready!"

Suddenly someone in the congregation began singing in a soft tearful soprano:

> In bright mansions above
> In bright mansions above
> Lord, I want to live up yonder
> In bright mansions above.

"Hallelujah!" shouted Reverend Rusoe. "Hallelujah! In the name of Jesus! She's comin' home! Open up the mansion house! Give Sister Lucy her key to her celestial apartment. Ain't no three-room shacks in heaven. Ain't no railroad tracks running through the front yard. Every house they got up there is a mansion. *Jesus* said that. Every heavenly residence is on the celestial avenue. And the avenue is paved with gold."

The singing continued:

> I want to go to glory.
> I want to go there, too
> Lord I want to live up yonder
> In bright mansions above.

"Amen," the preacher declared when the song died away. "Amen! Bear with me, children. I'm gon' say this about Sister Lucy, an' I'll be through. I don't have to preach all day, because I know she's with the Master. I know she's done got over. Her reward is waiting, free and clear. She was a giant in the earth. God knows she was a giant. Ain't many left like she was. She was a noble woman. She was the eagle of her time and her community. Yes, she was! Did you ever stop to wonder how come the eagle is our national bird? How come the eagle stands guard over the White House and protects the president? Well, it's because he's noble. He got strength. He got principle. He keeps hisself clean an' stays away from no-'count, trash 'sociations. The eagle, ah-well, he can't stand to be with the varmints that create the cesspools of corruption. The eagle, well, he's in a class all to hisself! Ah-when the eagle screams out, you know the crows all run for cover, and the buzzards flap on out of the way! You hear me, Jesus? Ah-when the eagle screams, the hoot owl don't hoot no more! Hallelujah! When the eagle screams, ah-well, the coo-koo knocks off from his foolishness and rolls hisself up like a tumblebug! Don't want nobody to see 'im. Don't want nobody to even know where he's at! Ain't that the truth! Ain't it the living Gospel I'm agivin' you! Hallelujah, praise His name!''

"That's the Gospel! Preach on, Reverend! Preach! Preach!''

"All the jackrabbits and foxes and skunks and weasels of this world try to find a hole somewhere in the ground when the eagle is abroad! Yes, they do! Now listen to me, children, 'cause I ain't talkin' about no jaybird. I ain't talkin' about no snipe. I'm talkin' about that most majestical bird ever to fly the heavens. I'm talkin' about the eagle!''

"Tell the truth! Preach the word! Thank God we got some eagles!'' came the response.

Reverend Rusoe paused to wipe the perspiration from his face and to catch his breath. "Now it ain't every bird that's a eagle," he cautioned. "Jest 'cause you got a crooked beak on your face and feathers on your hind parts don't make you no eagle. An' it ain't every bird that you can call him noble. Take the coo-koo, for instance. He is a nothing bird. Jest nothing, that's what he is. An' some of us is just like the coo-koo! Let me tell you about that bird, jest what kind of creature he is.''

"Amen! Amen!'' There was a muffled tittering from the congregation; but before the preacher could get started on his coo-koo analogy, there was a slight commotion at the back of the church, and people began to twist in their seats to see what was going on. It was Sweet Feet, and clutching his arm was a frightened, tear-stained Teresa. The disheveled, troubled little man paused uncertainly and then started to walk down the center aisle toward the front of the church, where his sisters and other relatives were seated. At first he was restrained by the ushers, but at a signal from Ferdy Frost they escorted the pair to the family pew and made room for them between Hester Collins and Nish. The interruption was only momentary, and though there was still some straining and twisting to get a better look at Teresa, the preacher was soon able to continue his parable of the cuckoo. He fixed the new mourners with his more stable eye and waited until nothing could be heard except the dull, concerted whoosh-whoosh of the pasteboard fans as the women tried to stave off the heat a little until the long sermon was over.

"Some folks," he said slowly, "wonder why the coo-koo got such a bad reputation."

"Tell it. Reverend! Tell it!"

"Well, it's *be*cause the coo-koo is not a bird of principle. He ain't got no mother wit. No, sir! He's just a low-down opportunist—ah-waitin' to take advantage of somebody!"

"Yes, he will, Lawd. Yes, he will!"

"Well, now. You see, the coo-koo-oo-oo, well, he don't build no nest!"

"No, Jesus!"

"An' when you ain't lookin', a-why, he'll drop his eggs in *your* nest!"

"Have mercy, Jesus! Have mercy, Lord!"

"He wants *you* to carry *his* load! He wants *you* to hatch *his* eggs!"

"Yes, he do! Yes, he do!"

"He wants you to do the work while he goes 'round makin' a silly noise while he's out clownin'!"

"Yes, he do! Yes, he do! That's him, all right!"

"When everybody else is tryin' to sleep, he keeps everybody awake tryin' to sing. Oh, yes, the coo-koo-oo! Well, he's just a e-e-e-e-vil bird!"

At that point Sweet Feet, who had sat crying softly ever since he and Teresa had been seated with the family and who had not heard the eagle part of Reverend Rusoe's parable, rose unsteadily to his feet and in an anguished voice cried out: "Looka here, Reverend, *damn* the coo-koo! *What you gonna say 'bout Mama Lucy?* I come all the way down here to bury my mama, an' all you're talkin' is a lot of foolishness about some doggone coo-koo too dumb to hatch his own eggs!" With tears cascading down his face Sweet Feet began to sob and shake uncontrollably. Everybody in the church strained to see who it was who had disrupted the solemn service, and the ushers beckoned by Hester Collins ran to escort Sweet Feet out of the church. The choir struck up a gospel hymn to help restore attention to the pulpit. But none of that was necessary. Reverend Ruffin Rusoe was still in charge, and he proved more than equal to the occasion. He signaled the choir to be silent, and then he commanded the ushers: "Let him alone. Bring him forward. This is God's house. Turn no man away!"

"Amen! Amen!" came the response. As Rusoe leaned forward from the pulpit to meet Sweet Feet, suddenly the church grew dark and thunder began to rumble in the distance. The trees outside began to swish and bend as if they were being agitated by a mighty wind. The ushers rushed to close the windows in anticipation of a storm. Someone turned on the electric lights that Sweet Feet had installed in his mama's church years before, when he worked for Grigsby Gardner. And Sweet Feet, still wobbly from whatever experiences he had had the previous night, was escorted down the aisle and positioned before the preacher, Teresa still clutching his arm. Suddenly the trees stopped waving and the air grew still. The pasteboard fans were silent and forgotten. "This brother," said the preacher, placing his hand on Sweet Feet's shoulder, "has suffered a great loss. A *great* loss. It may be that his loss is too much for him to bear alone. That's why he's here. He didn't come here to disgrace us. He didn't come here to shame his Mama Lucy. He came here for our understanding and God's compassion. Judge not, that ye be not judged!"

"Amen! Amen!

"Let him who is without blame condemn him. Let him who is without blame turn him away. He came here to hear what we had to say about his mother, his Mama Lucy. That's all. Ain't that right?"

"That's right! That's right!"

"Well, Brother Lunceford, your Mama Lucy is gone. Brother Lunceford . . . she's up there in the kingdom! Someday, oh, someday, you'll see her again face-to-face. I know you will. Someday, if you can overcome the tricks of the devil, if you can break loose from ol' Satan's bonds an' set your mind on the high road to your salvation, well, you can one day shake her hand, right up there in the kingdom where she's gone. Someday, if you can clean yourself up again—

jest like she always ah-wanted you to be, jest like she started you out—well, one day you can see your Mama Lucy smile again! I know it's the truth! She'll be waitin' for you. If you'll jest straighten up a little bit, Mama Lucy's gonna be there to receive you in glory, ready to fall on your neck with lovin' arms, squeeze you to her breast, an' whisper in your ear, 'Well done, my son.' Well done! Well done! I know it's the truth. Mama Lucy loves you, ah-Sweet Feet. The church loves you. And God Almighty loves you. Straighten yourself up, my son, an' go your way in peace.''

Reverend Rusoe turned again to the congregation. "Now, brothers and sisters, I know the hour is late an' we still got work to do. It's God's work. The Devil is never idle, y'all know that. But we're on God's time. It's late, but it ain't *too* late. Praise Jesus, hallelujah! It ain't never too late if your business is with God on the bee-half of God's children, ain't that right? An' Sister Lucy is a sho' 'nuff child of God. Hallelujah!''

The reverend closed his eyes for a few seconds and then looked away into the heavens as if to find out the latest news about Mama Lucy. "Sister Lunceford's done had her interview,'' he reported. "Yes, suh! And yes, ma'am! Sister Lucy's done took her seat at the welcome table, smack-dab in the middle of the mansion, *that's* where she's at! I can see her! Glory to God, hallelujah! Sister Lucy's done got over. She's gone to live with God! Amen! Amen!''

With tears and perspiration streaming down his bony cheeks, Reverend Rusoe left the pulpit abruptly, mopping his face with a large blue handkerchief as he collapsed in the red and gold pastor's chair. Very softly the choir began to sing:

> In bright mansions above
> In bright mansions above
> Lord, I want to live up yonder
> In bright mansions above.

The shouting had subsided now, and Ferdy's men came forward to open the casket so that the congregation could view the last remains. The immediate family of the deceased was alerted to stand. As they did so, a subdued chorus of sobbing and moaning broke out and spread rapidly throughout the whole church. Ferdy Frost's men strove to organize the viewing procession in as orderly a manner as possible; but the screaming and fainting soon overwhelmed them, and for a few minutes the sorrow and misery of survival took over the pageantry of death. The ushers escorted the family forward, two of them grasping Sweet Feet firmly by either arm, placing him at the head of the viewing procession. But Sweet Feet shook off the ushers with a weary but resolute shrug and walked with firm and unwavering steps to where the body of Mama Lucy lay enshrouded in the simple gray casket. As he neared the coffin, there came a sharp clap of thunder which seemed to shake the foundations of the church. The lights went out, and there was a strange rush of cold air, as if someone had suddenly turned on a giant electric fan. But even before the thunder had rumbled on off into the distance, the sun was beaming in through the windows again. The stained window above the choir loft stood open, but nobody remembered opening it or seeing it open itself in the hushed silence that suddenly descended upon the little church.

Sweet Feet paused for a long moment before the open casket. Finally, he bent over and kissed the forehead of the woman who had been his mama.

"Good-bye, Mama Lucy," he said simply; then, taking Teresa by the hand, he walked out of the church. He was never seen in Clayton City again.

A few days later Fess McClain went with Nish to the colored cemetery to see the new headstone erected at Mama Lucy's grave. "I have to leave tomorrow to go back to school," Nish explained on their way to the gravesite. "I wrote a sort of elegy for Mama Lucy, and I wanted you to comment on it before I commit myself to leaving it. Nobody else has seen it yet. Sometimes, as you know, my poetic inclinations get carried away." They both laughed at that.

When they reached Mama Lucy's grave, Ferdy Frost's men were just finishing up the installation of the marker. It read:

LUCY LUNCEFORD
Born July 1, 1879

Mother to many
Friend to all
Gone to answer
Her Savior's call

"I think it's eloquent," the professor said, gripping the shoulder of his young friend. "Simple and eloquent. But you forgot to close the parentheses. You forgot to inscribe the date of her death."

"Death?" Nish echoed absently. "How could Mama Lucy be dead?"

The Final Appointment

DR. TAIT did not join the cortege of mourners formed outside Burning Bush Church to follow the hearse to the colored cemetery where Lucy Lunceford would be buried. The burying ground was hard by the city dump, an apposition the doctor thought too obvious to be happenstance and too vulgar to be overlooked. Such an explicit unconcern for the life and dignity of colored people was made even worse by the fact that it tolerated a health hazard and a constant danger to the people who went to the cemetery for burials or to visit the graves of their dead. Hordes of big gopher rats from the dump roamed boldly through the cemetery, burrowing into the graves and even attacking the mourners on occasion. He did not have to be a part of all that, he told himself. He did not have to go. He had been to the funeral, and that was enough.

But it was not just the rats and the dump, loathsome though they were, that kept Dr. Tait from the interment of Mama Lucy. Although he never accepted the enormity of it all, he had braved the stench and the ugliness of the dump and the horror of the gopher rats before. People die and they have to be buried, that is a fact of life, and the only other cemetery in town was barred to the colored citizens of Clayton. There was a more compelling reason that sent him scurrying out to his old De Soto and out of the churchyard the moment the benediction had been pronounced and before the crowd could spill out and block his exit. He was already late for an appointment, and he still had to stop by the drugstore downtown before heading back to his office on The Avenue. It was not that he really cared about being late, although as a man of precise habits he had no patience with tardiness. But this particular appointment was different. It was long-standing. Too long-standing. And today it would be final. It would be Cap Butler's final appointment, and perhaps it would be his own as well. At first he had allowed himself to forget about Lucy Lunceford's funeral because he preferred not to be a part of the embellishment of a myth. But the myth had its way, as myths will do, and he went. On the other hand, could it be that his last-minute decision to participate in the ceremony at Burning Bush was an unconscious effort to actually delay his arrival at the office—to keep Cap Butler waiting? If it was, he mused, then three cheers for his subconscious; it was making more sense than the conscious decisions he was trying to live by. His mind wandered back to the funeral. Even in death life was so inflexible. Lucy Lunceford was just about everything the preacher said she was: God-fearing, faithful, hardworking, self-giving, and all the rest. And yet that inevitable nemesis that seems to stalk all those destined to be the wretched of this world manages in the end to make of the most circumspect life a monstrous joke. Lucy Lunceford, "beloved of black and white," he mimicked, had lived by all the rules. Yet in her final hour she had no effective exemptions, and her tenuous hold on dignity on earth was battered and warped and violated before she could finally escape to the security of the grave. A grave in a rat-infested patch of nothingness down by the city dump.

How much better would it have been if she had never lived at all! Then she would not have had to run the gamut of obscenity that life is for every black individual who dares it in the Clayton Citys of America. In the final analysis Lucy Lunceford was a pawn, not a person; a set piece, just as he knew himself to be. And to mix a metaphor, he continued ruefully, if the canvas is rotten to begin with, no matter what you paint on it, the colors will run and the texture will blister. Lucy Lunceford was no more than a detail, a caricature in a gigantic mural larger than life itself. And so was he.

The funeral then, as far as Dr. Tait was concerned, had been a charade, like every other experience in Clayton City, even though it was a necessary happening in the dull and wanton existence of the poor blacks whose brightest prospects for living were the anticipation of dying. It was dying that was the sure occasion for pageantry and for pomp. It was occasion to strut with somber and becoming restraint, to pose and posture in the dubious finery of funeral fashion. It was an opportunity for the celebration of old relationships and the remembrance of those whom death had severed. But most of all, it was an occasion licensed by the whole community to break down—to scream and to shout, to moan and to weep, to engage the delirium of temporary relief from sadness, from fear, from hatred and frustration, from misery and the oppressiveness of nothingness. All in the name and in the presence of God. It was the one occasion on which black and white Clayton City ever sat down together, but it was no less an exercise in inanity for all that. A capitulation to fantasy. Nothing was changed, and tomorrow would be like yesterday and all the yesterdays before that.

Dr. Tait drove on into downtown Clayton, circled the square, and parked in front of Phillips's Drugstore. The store was empty except for the counter girl up front and the pharmacist in back behind the prescription counter. The girl was sitting on a stool at the soda fountain chewing gum and reading a confession magazine. She had stringy blond hair, and she wore a white smock with buttons down the front, white saddle shoes, and apparently little else. She saw Tait leave his car and casually unbuttoned the upper and lower buttons of her uniform. As he entered the store, she swiveled slowly around on the stool to face him.

"Well," she said, popping her chewing gum like a barrage of small-arms fire, "ain't you sure 'nuff dressed to kill this afternoon! Jest look at the crease in them pants! Is it real?" She reached out to touch the crease in his trousers as Tait sidestepped instinctively and backed away. The girl then swung her legs across the narrow aisle between the soda counter and a rack of school supplies. The smock which was already too tight popped another button as her legs strained against their confinement. The button dropped on the floor at Tait's feet and rolled near the counter on the other side of the white girl. "Darned ol' buttons!" The girl pouted. "Always a-popping off, and at the most embarrassing times!" She looked at the wayward button and waited for the doctor to reach under her legs and hand it to her, but he stood stockstill without seeming to know what was expected of him. The girl's thin, red lips were painted with cheap, sticky lipstick which reminded the doctor of a thin red welt on a ball of powdered wax. The staccato popping of her chewing gum reminded him of a firing squad in some far-off adventure he had yet to live. "Well, Doc," she was saying, "can I do something for you since it looks like you ain't about to do nothing for me?"

"I'm on my way to the prescription counter, Miss Judy," Tait said. "I don't need anything from your department today."

"*Pree*scription! *Pree*scription!" she mocked at him. "You always say that," she said, lowering her voice to a more confidential tone. "Really, Doc, I don't reckon you like me a'tall! I mean, maybe you want me to fix you a Coca-Cola or something?" She lowered her voice still more. "You don't have to take it out like the rest of 'em. After all, you're a real doctor, and ain't nobody here this time of day but me and Ol' Dr. Beasley in the prescription department, and he don't care if you stand right here at the counter and drink it, long as ain't nobody here."

"Thank you," Tait said without visible emotion. "But I do have to get a prescription filled." He tensed his body as if to move forward, and she turned slowly on the counter stool and swung her legs out of the way.

"Thank you," Tait said again. "I'll go get my prescription."

"*Pree*scription! *Pree*scription!" she mimicked again. "Everytime you come in here you just want a *pree*scription!"

Her voice was loud now. "You jest give Dr. Beasley all of your ol' business and you don't give me none a'tall! I think you ol' doctors are jest too proud to do business with ordinary folks like me. Dr. Beasley!" She turned toward the prescription counter. "Here comes your favorite colored doctor to do some business with you. He's all dressed up, and I can't sell him a thing today! All he wants is a *pree-scription*!"

Dr. Tait got the drugs he was after and placed the tiny bottle of capsules carefully in the pocket of his vest against the probable requirements of the evening. Then he drove back to his office. He tried to dismiss the white girl at the drugstore from his mind but could not. Cheap cup of cyanide, he said to himself. On the word of that silly, ignorant, gum-popping, overpainted, underwashed, stringy-haired tramp, they'd take my life without a second thought. Someday, he mused, some black boy is going to walk into that drugstore looking for a pack of gum and end up hanging from a tree. For nothing.

He thought about Hucky Brown, who had come very close to being a case in point. Hucky worked for Solomon Jaffe, who used to own a shoe store called Sol's Shoes a block off the square on East Washington Street. Mr. Jaffe was a dapper young Jewish merchant, soft-spoken, gentle, and doing a good business. Hucky, who started working for him as a janitor and stock boy, tried in every way to emulate his boss, whom he admired very much. He learned quickly, spoke softly, and dressed neatly in the suits and the ties and shirts Mr. Sol gave him whenever he grew tired of them. Sol Jaffe was as proud of Hucky as Hucky was of Mr. Sol, and soon Hucky was doing most of the fitting for the colored customers who came into the store. That's when the trouble started. Clayton City did not take well to the notion of a colored clerk in a white store, even though Hucky only served colored people. When the grumblings reached Sol Jaffe, he put a partition across the back of his store and required his colored trade to use a side entrance. This seemed to make the arrangement even less acceptable, for now Hucky was allowed to ring the cash register in the back of the store while Sol attended to his white customers up front. One Saturday afternoon a white woman named Marney Wilkes came into the store. When she was not immediately waited on by Mr. Jaffe, she picked up a pair of shoes from a display shelf and marched into the colored section in back of the store, sat down, took her shoes off, and demanded that Hucky fit her with the new ones. When Hucky said he'd get Mr. Sol, she said she didn't have time to wait for no Jew and began to scream and shout obscenities. All of the colored customers in the store sidled out of the side door and put as much distance between themselves and Sol Jaffe's as possible, and when Jaffe himself rushed to the back of his store to see what was going on, the Wilkes woman accused him of being "a stinking little Jew with a smart nigger who likes to put his hands all over white women's legs pretending to be trying on shoes!" Hucky's protests that he never touched her legs or anything else only made her scream louder, and Mr. Jaffe immediately recognized that he had a problem on his hands. He urged the screaming, cursing woman out of the side door, locked the store, and hustled Hucky into a shipping box in his delivery van. Then he offered two colored men loading appliances behind the hardware store two doors away fifteen dollars to drive Hucky across the state line, but the men ran into the hardware store and disappeared, so Sol had to do the driving himself. He outraced a freight train headed north as it slowed down for Bannersville twenty-six miles away, gave Hucky what money he had in his pocket, and saw him safely inside a boxcar. When he got back to Clayton City, his store had been wrecked and looted, and red paint had been splattered over the fixtures. There was a crudely lettered sign on what was left of the front window: WARNING. NO JEWS. NO UPPITY NIGGERS. NO CUMIST ALLOWED IN CLAYTON CITY. THIS MEANS YOU!

Sol Jaffe never did reopen his store but went on back to Cincinnati, some said, to work in his daddy's clothing store. The colored folks in Clayton City got the word that Hucky had got clean away and was back working with Mr. Sol in Cincinnati. But the white folks never said anything at all about Hucky or what happened to Sol Jaffe's business. Or why. Things just went on in Clayton City just as they had before.

When Dr. Tait reached his office on The Avenue, a green panel truck marked U.S. MAIL was parked in his garage. He parked the De Soto beside the garage, walked around to the front of the house, and let himself in. This was the day. It was five minutes to four o'clock, and Cap Butler was still in his house, waiting. Well, let him wait. The doctor was in no hurry; today he intended to be in charge. Complete charge.

Cap Butler was a damn nuisance. Cap Butler was his personal nemesis. He had fastened himself on Tait the first year he opened practice in Clayton, and over the years he had become increasingly annoying. Some said that Dr. Weems gave up his practice there because he refused to be bothered with Cap Butler, but Dr. Tait had initially accepted him as part of the price of doing business in Clayton City. After all, Cap Butler was a member of the most powerful family in the county. In fact, the Butlers and the Spencers ran Clayton County and the town of Clayton as well. Everybody knew it, and all but a few accepted it.

The colored people of Clayton County generally considered the Butlers the "good" white folks—i.e., they were never arbitrarily mean or hostile to Negroes. That was a tremendously important factor in the welfare and security of the colored element of Clayton. There were still large concentrations of Negroes on the Butler farms and plantations in the western part of the county, and the patrician-style benevolence of the old southern aristocracy was still a feature of white-black relationships. The Negroes who worked for the Butlers were duly looked after in times of trouble, and they were automatically insulated to an important degree from the hostility of the white rabble they occasionally had to contend with. If they were hungry, Cap Butler's family fed them. If they were in jail, the Butlers freed them. When they died, the Butlers went to their funerals and saw that they had a plot to be buried in beside the city trash pile where all colored citizens were buried. In return the Butlers had for generations been assured of a constant supply of cheap, reliable, grateful labor, and generations of young Butler hot-bloods enjoyed the privilege of distributing their wild oats throughout their farms and plantations with telling effect. In certain communities the Butler breed as a physiological type was easily recognized among the dozens of otherwise non-descript mulattoes who worked for the Butlers but did not bear the Butler stamp. Oddly enough, or perhaps it was not really odd at all, the Spencers did not share either the Butler patience with black men or their passion for black women. The Spencers treated the existence of Negroes solely as a necessary means to a desirable economic end. "We don't love 'em and we don't hate 'em," as Darby Spencer put it. "We just work 'em and let 'em alone.

Cap Butler was hooked on morphine. The story was that he took it to ease the pain of cancer. If that was true, he'd had cancer a long time, for Dr. Tait had been giving him a shot of morphine almost daily for almost twenty years, and he had the habit when Tait first came to Clayton. Every afternoon at two o'clock Buford Atkins drove the post office truck to Tait's office and Cap Butler got out and went into the house through the back door. Buford was the post office janitor and handyman, and he always waited in the truck until Cap Butler came out. As the white man's visits at the doctor's grew longer and longer over the years, Buford, perhaps out of some instinct for propriety, or perhaps to increase the chances of being able to nap undisturbed while he waited, had taken to pulling the mail truck into Tait's garage whenever the doctor's car was not there.

Dr. Tait went directly to his office at the front of the house. There was no one there. He set his bag on the floor and rummaged casually through the circulars that had come in the morning mail. Presently the old house began to creak under the stress of some weight being shifted from one joist to another, and Cap Butler lumbered into the office. His face was flushed, and he swept at a tousle of tawny gray hair dangling across his forehead with one hand, while he managed to clutch an ice-tea glass half full of bourbon in the other. His necktie was missing and his feet were bare except for a pair of blue silk socks.

"Well! 'S about time the goddamn doctor come back to

his office to see the sick, ain't it?'' He raised his glass to Tait. "Here's looking at you, Doc."

"Good afternoon, Mr. Butler," Tait said flatly. He hesitated a moment, and then he heard himself saying to the white man, "You're not sick. You're drunk."

"I'm drunk? Hell, I was drinking whiskey from a tit before I was drinking milk! Titty whiskey! Get that?'' He bellowed at his own joke. "Hell, I ain't never been drunk."

"You're drunk now, Mr. Butler," Tait insisted doggedly. All his life he had tried to walk the thin, wavering line between what it took to live in the white man's world and what it took to hold on to some semblance of self-respect, but he had never been so blunt with any white man before. Often, when his dignity was cornered, he had resorted to professional jargon to say what he would never say in plain speech, but never before had he had the temerity to look a white man—not just some poor cracker, but *The Man* himself—squarely in the eye and tell him precisely what he wanted him to know. It was a good feeling—a liberating feeling—and he felt no fear except the fear of not being afraid. Suddenly both men seemed to realize that something unusual was happening to their relationship, something that transcended both of them as individuals and threatened the larger relationship in which they were both immersed. Cap Butler began to sober rapidly. He pushed the ringlet of hair away from his eyes again and blinked several times to focus on the black doctor in the stiff white shirt and striped pants.

"Doc," he said slowly, "I think you tellin' me I'm drunk, while all the time I'm tellin' you I'm not. Is that correct?"

"That's right, Mr. Butler."

"And another thing, Doc. You keep on callin' me 'Mr. Butler' when everybody else in town, black and white, seems to be able to get along by calling me 'Cap' or 'Captain.' Now I never understood why you do that, and I think this here is a good time to ask you."

"I don't call anybody except children and personal friends by their first names," the doctor said. "I was taught that it wasn't polite, and some people consider it so offensive they fight you about it."

Butler took a long drag from his glass. "Doc," he said, "either you're pretty damn dumb for a doctor, even a colored one, or you don't belong in Clayton. Captain is not my name, as I believe you damn well know. My name is Hoyt—Hoyt Horacio Butler—and it's been that ever since you been in Clayton. Captain is a title all my friends use—from far and near, black and white. It don't mean nothing. They called my daddy Captain Butler—I got his name, H. H.—so that's what they call me. Everybody but you."

"Your daddy got his title in the war?" Tait asked innocently.

"Which war? My daddy got his title from workin' more colored people on his plantation than anybody else in the county."

"What you mean is more niggers," said Tait. "That made him a Captain?"

"I don't personally like to use the word, but if you want it that way—more niggers than anybody else in the county. Yes, that's where he got to be called Captain. But we don't call our hands 'niggers.' You know that. They're all like, in the family, and we call 'em 'colored people,' which by the wisdom of god-a-mighty is what they are."

"And I call you 'Mr. Butler,' " Tait said without passion, "because you aren't in the business of working niggers anymore. You're in the business of running the local post office, and since all the colored people are in your family, to call you 'Captain' would seem to be somehow inappropriate. Families don't usually recognize their members with military titles. Do they?"

Butler was startled by this impudence. "Doc," he said with slow and measured tones, "Doc, I don't exactly need you to tell me what my business is or what kind of title is appropriate for me. And don't you forget it either. And speaking of niggers: You may be a doctor, but you're still a nigger doctor, and that makes a great big difference anywhere you go in Clayton County; anywhere you go in the United States of America; anywhere else you go in the world except Africa, and I don't believe you want to go there. They'd eat you and make head rags out of your fancy britches before

THE AVENUE, CLAYTON CITY   263

you could get off the boat. Now let's get done with this fool-ishness and get our business over before somebody says something he can't take back." The white man was clearly angry now. His eyes flashed, and his hands began to tremble a little. He drained the last swallow of bourbon from the tumbler, but his intoxication had given way to a kind of un-easiness. He had gone from high to cold sober in the space of five minutes of this strange conversation with Dr. Tait. Nobody had ever spoken to him like that, and yet he knew that both he and the black doctor had said less than they felt, less than they would say if they kept talking. He wanted to get his shot and get out. He did not want either of them to say anything more. He didn't understand what had come over Tait. Tait wasn't drunk. Tait didn't drink. Yet he seemed to be acting like somebody out of his mind. Of course, Tait *was* a colored man, a nigger when you come right down to the nub of the matter, but he had never heard of him being mis-treated by anybody in Clayton. As a matter of fact, the But-lers wouldn't have stood for it. Clayton needed a colored doctor. He just couldn't understand what had come over Tait, but he was ready to forget that business about "Captain" Butler, and he wished Tait would forget it, too. What's past is past, and if the Butlers worked a lot of colored people, or niggers, or whatever, they never mistreated them, and they always looked after them when they got in trouble. Any nig-ger in Clayton would tell you that. Butler sighed heavily and sat down on the examining table and began rolling up his sleeve. "Come on, Doc," he said. "I've got to go back to the post office."

Dr. Tait sat down in the old swivel chair in front of his desk. "There'll be no shot today Mr. Butler," he said. "Or any other day. I'm not sure I can tell you why, after all these years, but I'll try. In the first place, you've been drinking. I've told you before that whiskey and morphine don't mix. For years and years I've dreaded the day that double dose would put you under before Buford could get you in that post office truck and back downtown. I've told you that. What do you think would happen to me if that happened to you?"

"Aw, ain't nothing like that gonna happen! It ain't gonna

happen a'tall," Butler argued. "And if it did, you know my family ain't gonna have no scandal here. You know that! Everything would be taken care of, proper like. But it ain't gonna happen. My body's done built up every kind of resistance to handle any little problem like that. Why, I been drinking too long. *Too long!* Why, you know that! Now come on like always and give me—"

"I'm sorry, Mr. Butler," Tait interrupted him. "I've given you my last shot. If you want me to, I'll call Buford and he can take you home." Tait rose as if to leave the room. He walked out and to the end of the narrow hall toward the back door just in time to see the shadowy figure of Ramona disappear into the bedroom. She had been drinking, of course, and she had been listening. Good for her, he said to himself. This meant the end of a lot of things, and she might as well know it first hand. Tait called to Buford from the back door, and the handyman scurried into the house, rubbing sleep from his eyes.

"Yes, suh. You call me, Doc?" he inquired. "Cap'n Butler, he ready to go?"

"He's in my office," Tait said. "He may not be ready, but I'm ready for you to take him."

Buford looked at Tait uncertainly. He didn't like Tait's tone of voice. Nobody, black or white, ever talked to him like that about his boss. He peered at Tait more closely, wondering if he had been drinking. "Cap'n Butler, he sick or something?" he asked.

"Cap'n Butler," Tait mimicked, "has been sick for a long time. And so have I," he added. "And so have you." He looked at the words "Buford—U.S. Post Office" embroidered on the khaki-green coveralls the handyman was wearing. "We're all sick," he said. "Now get your goddamn cap'n out of my house and don't bring him back here anymore!" Thoroughly frightened now, Buford skittered around the doctor and hurried into the office.

"Cap'n Butler, suh, you in there?"

"Yes, goddammit, Buford, I'm in here. But I don't want you in here. Can't a man take a crap without you tracking him like a goddamn coonhound?" Buford looked quickly from the white man sitting on the table to the black man standing in the doorway. Something was going on, something bad, and he didn't want any part of it. He just wanted to go on back to his job at the post office. At first he had been proud to be chauffeuring Cap'n Butler around in the mail truck, but then, when they never went anywhere but to the doctor's, the novelty wore off and he still had the same amount of sweeping to do when he got back. Besides, somebody was always trying to make something out of his hauling Cap'n Butler to Dr. Tait's house when Dr. Tait wasn't there—that's why he started pulling the truck in the garage. Now look what was about to happen, and he was going to be caught right in the middle of it. He had to protect himself. Tait, being black like himself, couldn't hurt him, he reasoned. Cap Butler was something else again.

"I sho' ain't aimin' to be trackin' you, Cap'n," he said hurriedly. "It's this here doctor. He's the one told me to come git you, an' I—"

"I don't give a goddamn what anybody told you," Butler scolded. "I told you to wait for me in the truck! Now I want you—Wait a minute. Come on back in here, Buford. How long you known me?"

"'Bout long as I know myself, I reckon," Buford said, hoping the white man had gotten over his anger at him.

"I ever mistreat you?"

"No, suh! No, suhree! Cap'n. You ain't never mistreat nobody, 'specially colored folks."

"Buford, how long you been bringing me out here for treatment?" Cap Butler asked.

Buford scratched his head and fidgeted with the keys to the truck. "Cap'n I ain't never counted it up, but it been a whole long time. Yass, suh! It sho' been a long time."

"I ever mistreated ol' Doc here?"

"No, suh!" Buford asserted emphatically. Dr. Tait looked at him with open disgust, and Buford realized that he might have been hasty in presuming to know what went on between the colored doctor and the white man he brought to his house every day.

"Leastwise," he added, "I ain't never heared the doctor

say you done ever mistreated him." He looked quickly at each man in turn to see if he had said the right thing.

"Well, goddammit," Butler yelled at him, "if I ain't never mistreated you, and I ain't never mistreated him, and I ain't mistreated no colored people nowhere, then you tell this doctor friend of yours to give me my treatment so you and me can get back to work! Tell him!"

Buford was so frightened by the white man's outburst that he almost tripped over Dr. Tait as he backed off toward the doorway. "Yass, suh!" he said. "Yas, suh! We sho' need to go back to work!"

"Tell him!" Butler screamed. "Tell this black bastard to give me my shot! Tell him!"

Buford looked at Tait with alarm and pleading written on his plain brown face. Perspiration had begun to collect on his forehead in large droplets. "Doctor," he mumbled, "he, Cap'n Butler, he need his treatment 'cause we got to go. He, Cap'n Butler, he *like* colored folks. See! He even come out here for you to doctor on him. He *like* colored folks! He sho' need his treatment, though, 'cause we got to go back an' close up. We sho' do!"

Tait looked at the helpless man slobbering and quaking in front of him. This was the product of the system he'd lived with until today. Today he would end all the compromises he had made with that system. "Get out of my office, Buford," he said without rancor. "I am the doctor here. I know who to treat and when to treat. Now you go on and get out." Buford ducked through the doorway, down the hall, and out through the back door. A second later the door of the mail truck slammed, and the motor cranked into action.

Cap Butler shook his finger at Tait. "Boy, you shore done tore your ass now. If Buford goes back to town without me, people are gonna wanna know why, and I expect somebody'll be out here to see how I am. You come on now, give me my shot and you can run me on down to the office in your car before Buford gets things stirred up. I can't be responsible—"

"Mr. Butler," Tait interrupted, "the only thing I hold you responsible for is leaving my office. You don't seem to understand," he said quietly, "our relationship, whatever that relationship was, is over. It took me a long time to get to this decision, but I knew this morning when I got out of bed that the decision time had come and that I would make a decision and stand by it. I know you don't care anything about my decisions. They don't even entertain your consideration. But they are important to me."

"Boy, you said one thing there that's right," Butler said, pulling himself up from the examining table. "Your decisions don't mean a shit to me. That's the trouble with you educated niggers, you want to make decisions. You want to run things. Well, let me tell you one thing, it ain't gonna be that way, *ever*!" He crossed the narrow room and stood looking down at Tait, shaking his finger. "The world would be a jungle, a cannibal camp if niggers like you had to run it. Why, the more education you give a nigger, the more he acts like a monkey." He paused and drew back as if to recover his composure. "Doc," he said finally, "ain't no sense in all this foolishness. I ain't responsible for you being black or me being white. God made us to be what he wanted us to be. Now I know that being an educated man, it might be hard on you sometime. But I can't change that. Nobody can change it. You gonna stay black, I'm gonna stay white, and the world's gonna stay like it is. Now you and me, we need to stop fussing and make the best of what the Good Lord's done for us." His face softened, and he sat down on the table again and waited for the doctor to follow his cue for reconciliation.

"The Lord giveth," Tait said dryly. "The Lord also taketh away."

"Don't preach to me," Butler said impatiently. "By now that boy is halfway downtown with that mail truck, and in a few minutes I expect the police will be out here to see what's happening to ol' Cap Butler. How you gonna explain that?"

"How'm I gonna explain what?" Tait asked. "I haven't done anything. I don't believe I've broken any law." Tait sat down at the desk again and waited.

By now the white man was thoroughly confused—and angry again. Never in all his life had he wanted anything from a nigger he didn't get; never in his life had any colored man sat down at a desk and bandied words with him. And never in his life had he seen any black man retain his composure when threatened with the police. Suddenly Butler rushed over to where Tait sat with the apparent intention of striking him, but stopped short and shook his fist in the black man's face instead. Tait instinctively shrank back in the chair, and the sinister presence of Cap Butler hovered over him, dwarfing him, diminishing him. Yet somehow he was not afraid. Only startled.

"Well, boy, you let me tell you one thing," Cap bellowed. "You *have* broke the law, and I know about it. You sleepin' with a nigger's wife over yonder on Blossom Street. Sleepin' with somebody else's wife! That's against the law. I know about it. You been sellin' narcotic drugs to the innocent and unsuspecting citizens of Clayton. That's against the law. That's against the *federal* law! I know about that, too, because you been sellin' 'em to me for nearly twenty years! When I think of all the money I paid you, it makes me sick. You been gittin' rich giving abortions to these hot-assed nigger women who go around gettin' themselves bigged every three months like rabbits in a pen. Doing away with a baby is murdering human life. I know about that. And *that's* against the law! And let me tell you one other thing, nigger doctor: You been going to bed with your own daughter, and you got her knocked up. I know about that, too, and that's called incest. *Incest is against the law*, whether or not you realize it! You goddamn niggers'll sleep with your mammies if you git half a chance. Now! How you gonna explain all that to the police, Doctor?"

Tait smiled slightly, but his face was drawn and ashen. He knew now that his day had come full circle and that whatever he said or did after the next few minutes would be anticlimactic. He had sensed this day would come. All his professional life he had expected and dreaded this very moment, yet he had lived for it. He looked up at the enraged white man hovering above him like some gigantic bird of prey. His eyes were bloodshot; his nostrils were flaring. His hands trembled as with the desire to throttle or to smash the little black devil who tormented him. Cap Butler's breathing was hard and loud. "You done broke the law all right. Now what you gonna tell the police when they git here?"

Tait had regained his composure. "Mr. Butler," he said, "I don't imagine it would make a lot of difference what I said to the police, if they should come here. Chief Evans is your cousin, I understand, and his deputy's daddy runs one of your plantations. But that's beside the point; color is thicker than justice anyway. So I'm not going to worry about the police. They will do what they've been hired to do. But before they get here, I do want to set the record straight in *our* relationship." He stood up slowly and faced the flushed and angry man.

"Hell! *We* ain't got no relationship," Butler spat at him. "I don't carry on no relationship with colored people. I tell 'em what to do and they do it. Your mammy did it. Your pappy did it. And you'll do it."

"Well all right, sir," Tait said. "I'm sure they did. You see, you've been playing the dozens with all of us a long time, myself included. But I'm not playing anymore, and I don't intend to pat my foot anymore while you play. My mammy and my pappy, as you put it, couldn't help themselves. I can. You put me in the dozens twenty years ago. Well, the game is over now and if you can't pat your foot, you can scratch your ass. I don't care one way or another."

"Boy, what in hell are you talkin' about?" Butler interrupted. "I don't know nothin' about no dozens, and I ain't got time to play no games. Doc, are you drunk or something? Yeah, goddammit, you *got* to be drunk! Ain't you, Doc?" he asked almost hopefully. Maybe the doctor was drunk after all. If the colored doctor was drunk, that would explain his impudence. When he sobered up, why, he'd just warn him and forgive him, and then things would go on as before. "Nothin' wrong with gittin' a little drunk now and then." He tried a conciliatory grin at the doctor. "I know you didn't know what you was saying about Ol'Cap scratching his ass, an all. I expect I git a little high myself every once in a while. Whole lot of people do."

"Well, I don't drink, Mr. Butler," Dr. Tait reminded him.

"So I'm not drunk. I've never been more sober. And if you don't understand the dozens, more's the pity. I haven't got time to explain it to you now, it's too late. But I'll say this: You may not know the name, but you were born to play the game. And that's the real reason they all call you 'Captain.' Your whole life is a put-down of people you loathe and despise."

"Well, if that's the real reason the other niggers call me 'Captain,' what's the real reason you don't? Tell me that while you runnin' down my pedigree," Butler challenged.

The doctor looked at him as if seeing him clearly for the first time and continued: "I'll tell you why, Captain Butler. Whatever it was that was supposed to distinguish you from all those colored hands you and your daddy worked that made you their 'Cap'n' must have gone down the drain long before I met you, because I've never been able to see what it was. And as for myself, whatever I thought I was, or hoped I could become, never recovered from the first needle I stuck in your arm. In short, Captain, for all your titles and for all your power, you know from introspection, and I know from observation, that you and fresh chicken droppings have a lot in common. I can't claim any more for myself, but at least I know the reality of the charade. The rationale, if there is one. What you and I are involved in is the official version of fun and games for this godforsaken town. But except for being more vulgar and more obscene, and more deadly because the people who are 'it' are real, it's the same game they play under the streetlight in front of the Blue Flame across the street. And for the same reasons: to avoid a reality that is simply too rotten to bear. You ought to hang around there sometime, you might learn a lot about yourself they never told you at home on the plantation. Or at the post office."

"Whatever it is you tryin' to tell me," Butler said peevishly, "I don't see what it has to do with you breakin' the law. You did all them things I said, and they're bound to take your license when I tell 'em about it. And I'm sho' as hell gon' blow the whistle on you, boy!"

"I don't think I'm reaching you, Mr. Butler. My license

to practice is the least of my concerns at this time. It was never much of a license, was it? And I'm sure I abused it on occasion. But that's all over now. It is as obvious to me as it is to you that this is my final appointment. And by *my* choice.''

''What you aimin' to do if you quit doctorin'?'' Cap Butler wanted to know. He didn't want to have to bother with finding somebody else to give him his treatments, and he still hoped that Tait would come to his senses, even though he had vexed him more than a little. Mighty few white folks and no niggers a'tall had ever talked to him the way Tait had, he mused half aloud. ''What you aimin' to do now?''

''First of all,'' the doctor said, sitting down again and swiveling his chair around to position himself directly before Mr. Butler, ''I want to set the record straight. You accuse me of adultery. Tell me, Captain Butler, where are your shoes?'' The white man blushed deep red and tried to steal a glance at his feet. ''Never mind, they aren't on your feet. They're in my bedroom,'' the doctor continued matter-of-factly. ''I won't ask you how they got there, or why. I will only say men have been killed for less.''

''You threatenin' me, boy?'' Butler snarled in outrage.

''No, sir, Captain Butler, I am not threatening you. I'm just reminding you. There is a difference. Next, you accuse me of selling narcotics. I'm guilty. Guilty as sin. I'm also sorry. But, Captain Butler, until that so-called emergency visit you paid to my office twenty years ago when I was trying to get that *license* you are now threatening to take away, I'd never used morphine in my practice. And I've never used it since, except for that continuing 'emergency.' Do you know of any instances to the contrary?''

''Hell, it ain't my business to keep track of who you stick in the arm,'' Butler retorted. ''But I know you're doin' it. If you do it for me, you'll do it for somebody else!''

''A not unreasonable assumption, but not necessarily a factual one,'' the doctor said. ''But since it doesn't really matter, we'll let it pass. You also accuse me of incest.''

''I shore'n hell did!'' Butler pointed his finger at Tait to drive home the accusation. ''Yeah, you been doin' it all right—with your own daughter. All you niggers do it. Just like a bunch of hawgs!''

"You mean Makeda?" the doctor asked without emotion.

"Hell, yes, I mean Makeda. That's your gal's name, ain't it? Well, that's who I'm talkin about. Makeda Tait."

"But Mr. Butler," Tait insisted, "I'm afraid you've got your facts a little confused. You see, whatever your allegations of incest, Captain, Makeda Tait is not my daughter."

"Well, that's a hell of a kettle of fish." Butler laughed harshly. "Now that's some kind of lie, even for a nigger. She's using your name. She's living in your house. She's born to your woman. And she's passing herself off as your daughter. Whose gal is she if she ain't yours?"

Tait cleared his throat quietly and collected himself before he spoke again. He wondered vaguely if what he was about to say had ever been said before. Certainly he never said it, and it felt heavy on his tongue. "Makeda passes as my daughter because she doesn't have much choice," he said quietly. "Her daddy hasn't seen fit to give her his name, or anything else. So she uses mine. Makeda is *your* daughter, Mr. Butler. She knows it. I know it. And you know it. Makeda is *your* daughter. Probably she is one out of many you have not chosen to recognize. You see, those abortions you complain about that are making me so rich were all performed on my own wife. There were two. I did them because I had hoped we'd not be completely overwhelmed with the Butler presence in my house. Perhaps it is clearer to you now what I mean about being 'it' in the fun and games of Clayton City. It's the dozens all right. Now you pat your foot and listen while I play! If Makeda is pregnant and I am responsible, that can't very well be incest, can it, Mr. Butler, since you are her daddy? But what does that make me to you?" There. It had finally been said, and there was a note of final triumph in Tait's voice that he had nurtured in his mind for twenty years.

Cap Butler sat down again on the examining table. The strength seemed to flow from him. He looked down at his blue silk socks, and then with both hands he pushed the tawny gray hair back from his face—a face now drawn and gray. He avoided looking at Tait.

"Not a goddamn thing," he muttered, finally. "Not a goddamn thing. *Not a god-damn thing*! You, nigger doctor, ain't a goddamn thing to me and as long as the heavens hang above the earth, you never will be!"

Off in the distance the ominous sound of the siren of the chief's car could be heard clearing The Avenue. The Clayton police were on their way. Headed west. Instinctively the doctor fingered the small bottle of capsules he had bought at the drugstore and tucked away in his vest pocket in anticipation of this moment.

Suddenly Ramona Tait materialized in the doorway like some spectral Lorelei summoned up by the deep and twisted emotions of the two men whose tortured lives had ensnared her own in their bitter, silent conflict of twenty years. It was easy to imagine that she had been a handsome woman. The dark eyes, the high cheekbones, the sensitive lips were still there. But now her eyes were wild and furtive, and her lips quivered with apprehension and from the nervousness that too much whiskey too long imbibed can produce. A perpetual frown knitted her thick black eyebrows as if she were in constant indecision, and the long black hair that in other years must have been a cascade of glory now wreathed her troubled face in a tangled mass of wild confusion before tumbling listlessly about her narrow shoulders and on down her back. She stood there in the doorway, momentarily framed against the gathering darkness that seemed to seep into the room from The Avenue. In her hands was a pair of patent leather gaiters, worn like herself into a kind of personal conformation for a convenience that had long since transcended their existence.

The wild eyes of the disheveled and wasted woman searched the room for some confirmation of her presence. There was none. Only silence. Only the tension of hatred. No eyes bothered to engage her own, to recognize her intrusion. Perhaps no eyes dared. She hesitated for a moment, looking from face to stony face for some cue. Finding none, she carefully set the shoes on the floor in front of Cap Butler and turned to leave the room. Suddenly she turned again, as if compelled by instinct or by some entrenched habit and knelt beside the examining table. Gently grasping Cap Butler's left foot, she tugged at the blue silk sock until it was straight and carefully guided his foot into the soft leather shoe she held in her left hand. At first the white man seemed oblivious to what she was doing, for with his preoccupation with the strange torment of the moment, he accepted her ministrations as part of a familiar ritual he had long since come to expect. It was the wail of the police siren—nearer now, and more ominous—that jolted him back to a new and unpleasant reality. Instinctively he kicked the gaiter from his foot, bowling over the bewildered and frightened Ramona in the process. His pale blue eyes blazing and throbbing with hatred and chagrin now that the last possible moment for reversal had passed with the latest blast from the chief's siren, he leveled a snarl at the defiant black devil who had caused him so much trouble and embarrassment: "Get your black-assed slut from under my feet, doctor man. I can put on my own damn shoes!"

Her already wasted countenance distorted with horror and rage, Ramona scrambled to her feet and with an anguished scream she fled from the room, leaving the two men in bitter tension as she had found them moments earlier. Dr. Tait remained at his desk, silent and immobile, as if in a daze. He, too, had heard the latest announcement from the police siren, and he knew that his final appointment was about over. But if he heard the white man's slur about Ramona or saw her distress when she lay spread-eagled under the white man's feet, he gave no sign. He sat motionless in the swivel chair and watched the evening shadows blot the dying sunlight from the room.

The siren wailed again and then died as the chief's car turned off The Avenue and pulled up at the back of the house. Almost in the same instant Ramona reappeared in the doorway, her wild eyes darting around the room as if in frantic search until they came to rest on Cap Butler, who still sat on the examining table with his back to the door. In her right hand was a butcher knife. For a long second she stared at the man who had kicked her away from him; then with a wild, sobbing scream she raised her arm high above her head and plunged the knife between his shoulders. Cap Butler shuddered for a moment; then with a long sigh he toppled from the doctor's table and fell in a heap on the floor. A small trickle of blood oozed up along the blade of the knife and splotched the pale blue shirt that matched the Captain's socks. Ramona whimpered a moment and pleadingly sought Tait's eyes. For a big moment their eyes met with the despair of understanding; then the doctor's gaze slipped past her and focused on the darkness that had closed in around him and his house. Once more the distraught woman screamed out her loneliness and agony. Then, like some tortured dervish, she whirled from the room and fled out into the deserted avenue and disappeared into the night.

A car door slammed, followed almost immediately by a timid, questioning knock at the back door of the doctor's residence, and the plaintive voice of Buford Atkins echoed through the silent house: "Cap'n Butler? Cap'n Butler . . . you in there, Cap'n Butler?" Buford pushed the door open a few inches and thrust his head inside, trying furtively to penetrate the gloom that separated him from the white man he worked for. "Cap'n Butler . . . you done got your treatment? Chief Evans, he out here in the car. We done come to take you home, Cap'n Butler. Cap'n Butler . . . ? Cap'n Butler . . . ? Please, suh, Cap'n Butler . . . we need to take you home. . . . Cap'n Butler . . . ? It's dark out here on The Avenue."

About the Author

C. ERIC LINCOLN, poet, novelist, essayist, and scholar has addressed significant audiences in America, Canada, Western Europe, Africa, and the Middle East where his work is well known in academic and literary circles.

Since 1976 he has been Professor of Religion and Culture at Duke University. He lives and writes at Kumasi Hill in historic Hillsborough, North Carolina.

CONTEMPORARY FICTION

FROM SOME OF THE FINEST CONTEMPORARY BLACK AUTHORS.